PENGUIN BOOKS

THIS SUMMER'S SECRETS

Books by Emily Barr

THE ONE MEMORY OF FLORA BANKS

THE TRUTH AND LIES OF ELLA BLACK

THE GIRL WHO CAME OUT OF THE WOODS

THINGS TO DO BEFORE THE END
OF THE WORLD

GHOSTED

THIS SUMMER'S SECRETS

EMILY BARR

PENGUIN BOOKS

PENGUIN BOOKS

UK | USA | Canada | Ireland | Australia
India | New Zealand | South Africa

Penguin Books is part of the Penguin Random House group of companies whose addresses can be found at global.penguinrandomhouse.com.

www.penguin.co.uk
www.puffin.co.uk
www.ladybird.co.uk

First published 2023

001

Set in 10.5/15.5pt Sabon LT Std
Typeset by Jouve (UK), Milton Keynes
Printed and bound in Great Britain by Clays Ltd, Elcograf S.p.A.

The authorized representative in the EEA is Penguin Random House Ireland, Morrison Chambers, 32 Nassau Street, Dublin D02 YH68

A CIP catalogue record for this book is available from the British Library

ISBN: 978–0–241–48190–5

All correspondence to:
Penguin Books
Penguin Random House Children's
One Embassy Gardens, 8 Viaduct Gardens, London SW11 7BW

www.greenpenguin.co.uk

For Gabe

Prologue

2008

The toddlers were playing on the grass, in the sun. Felicity sat back on the picnic blanket and watched. It had been a drizzly summer so far, and they were taking advantage of a rare day of sunshine.

'Can you believe we've got children?' she said to Jenna, leaning back on her hands. 'I mean, who decided it was OK for me to keep an actual kid alive?'

'Would you have done it,' said Jenna, 'if you'd known what it was like?'

They watched the two-year-olds, dressed only in nappies, both smothered in suncream. Little Senara was wearing a hat, but Clementine had ripped hers off so many times that Felicity had given up trying to put it back on. You had to choose your battles with Clem.

Felicity tried to work out how to answer. That was the thing with Jenna: she just came out and said things.

Clem yelled, 'Mummy! I want dink!' and Felicity ran into the house to fetch more juice for the girls, and another cup of tea for herself and Jenna. Or wine? Should they have wine? The mums in London had afternoon wine.

Here in Cornwall they probably didn't. She put the kettle on and tried not to show how shaken she was by Jenna's question.

Would she have had Clem if she'd known what it was going to be like?

No.

Having Clem had been a mistake, even though she'd been planned.

She put four drinks on a tray, added a pack of biscuits (she couldn't be bothered to bake these days) and carried it all outside.

Clementine was eight months older than Senara and was trying to start a game that involved running round in circles, laughing, but Senara wanted to walk along the edge of the grass. Every now and then, she stopped and picked something up, looking at it hard. Clementine was blonde and chubby, a smiling, strong-willed toddler with a bright orange aura. Senara was half her size and watchful, and the colours around her were blue and yellow. Their girls had pulled Felicity and Jenna back together, tentatively rekindling their shattered friendship.

Felicity had never managed to tell anyone about the way motherhood had ripped her life into pieces and thrown them up in the air. She'd felt obliged to pretend to her parents, her husband, her brother that everything was wonderful, that Clementine was the perfect baby, and that Felicity had *found herself*, in that way you were supposed to do. The reality, though, was chaotic. She'd lost the thread of herself, had seen it snap.

Having Clem had been a huge mistake because now Felicity had too much to lose. She loved Clementine too much. She wondered whether Jenna felt the same. It must be even worse for her.

She put the tray down on the blanket.

'There we go,' she said. She looked round. 'Where's Senara?'

When she saw her, the world turned black and white. Felicity jumped up and ran. She ran faster than the speed of light, to the camellia bed at the edge of the garden. Senara had picked up a little trowel from somewhere and was digging right there, in exactly the wrong place.

'No!' She heard the harshness of her voice and even as she was shouting she knew Jenna would never forgive her, but this couldn't happen. 'No! Senara! Naughty! Stop!'

Felicity never shouted. Senara turned, her face full of concern. Felicity wanted to be nice, she did, but she couldn't help herself. She couldn't do it. Her voice became a monstrous thing. She was scared of what Senara would find down there.

'No!' she bellowed.

The toddler's face crumpled, and her lip turned over. She took a deep breath and burst into sobs.

Jenna ran over and snatched her daughter up. She turned on Felicity.

'She's a *baby*,' she said, stroking Senara's hair. 'It's OK, darling,' she said. 'Don't worry. We're going home. We won't come here again.'

Then they were gone. Clem hadn't noticed. Felicity knew that she had exploded the friendship, again, and that Jenna would never speak to her after this.

In fact, they would speak again, but not until fourteen years had passed, when the girls were sixteen.

1

'Above us stands Cornwall's most haunted house.' Josie was using a gravelly voice, leaning into the camera. 'It is poised, empty and cursed, on the cliff.' She paused. 'Should I say on the *edge* of the cliff? It is poised, empty and cursed, on the cliff edge. No – the first one.' The wind blew her hair across her face, and she took an elastic off her wrist and tied it back. 'No one knows what lurks in its grounds . . . No one living, that is.'

Gareth joined in. I turned towards him, holding up the old camera. 'Even the people who own it – and remember these are people who literally call locals "peasanty scum" – stay away. Such is their fear of the evil that lurks within, no one has set foot in the grounds of this house for over three hundred years. And today, my friends, we are going to find out why.'

'Gareth!' Josie was exasperated. 'Why did you say three hundred? It's *three* years. And that's only a guess. It's probably less. Plus, you can't include any of this.'

He pulled her close to him and kissed her. 'Sorry, babe. I got carried away. Three hundred sounds better. We'll do a sensible one afterwards. This is the director's cut. The rogue version.'

'Go again,' I said. 'Just from where you come in, Gaz. Remember: *three*. And if you can keep it submittable, that would be great.'

This was Gareth's digital-media project, but it was turning out to be more than that. I wasn't appearing on camera; holding it was fine by me. That was how I was comfortable. I was never the star, and I didn't want to be. I wasn't even the star of my own life. My friends, my mother, even the dogs I walked had more presence than I had. Definitely, in fact, the dogs. I was the eternal sidekick, the one who stood back and watched.

The video camera was an old one that had belonged to Gareth's mum; he'd found it at home and added it to his box of tech when he discovered that it used a memory card that also fitted the drone. 'We can combine aerial footage with talking heads. We'll probably win a BAFTA,' he had said at the time, though we were still waiting. Meanwhile his GCSE coursework was overdue.

When we'd finished the intro, Gareth and Josie got to work setting up the drone, and I walked down the beach to keep warm. The bay was deserted because it was the middle of winter and freezing. Everyone who wasn't at work was at home watching TV. I stomped across the stony shore and looked out at the water, which was a sheet of corrugated metal. The sky was grey, and the water was grey, and I was pretty sure that if I stopped moving I would die of cold and turn grey too.

I turned back and looked up at the house on the cliff. You couldn't see much of it from here: just a row of upstairs windows in what was, clearly, a huge building. There was a girl of about our age who was part of the family who owned it and used to come down for the summer, though as Gareth had said they hadn't been for years. She was the one who, wanting to get past us on the path down to the beach a few years ago, had said, '*Jesus! Excuse me? Peasants.*' Gareth had added the 'scum' part for effect.

We would all have been about thirteen at that point. Children. And she had called us 'peasants'. None of us had ever forgotten it.

'Senara!' They were both calling to me.

The drone had been a cheap purchase off eBay, and we had no idea whether it was going to work, but Gareth, at least, was optimistic. His actual project was to make a film of the Cornish coastline, using aerial media, and that had led us to the local big house and all its mysteries. We were going to fly the drone up and over the gardens of Cliff House, filming whatever was in there, bring it straight back to us on the beach, and then we'd see what the garden was like and use the unobtrusive bits for Gareth's coursework. I was picturing overgrown lawns, and flower beds that would be ideal hiding places for imaginary monsters. The test flights had gone well.

I ran back up the stony beach.

Now Gareth was holding up the camera. When I was close enough, he said, 'Before we send her off on her mission, what's she going to find? Senara?'

'Zombies!' I shouted.

'I think it's ghosts,' called Josie. 'But hopefully ghosts that are visible to the camera.'

Gareth turned the lens on himself and said, 'Senara says zombies. Josie says ghosts. I say bodies. The family who live there murdered each other, and that lawn will be strewn with old corpses. The old lady did it. Last one standing.'

'The girl who hates us was the first to die,' said Josie.

'The vultures have taken the flesh,' I said, 'and all that remains is bones. The lawn is littered with the bones of the Roberts family. And that girl who went missing. Lucy's sister. You're not putting this bit in, are you?'

'Course not,' he said, and he put the memory card into the drone, laughed and flew it up and up and up, and then it was gone.

2

The next morning, we leaned our bikes against the fence and tried to work out how to sneak into the garden to retrieve the crashed drone before anyone else spotted it. We'd given up last night because it was getting dark, and today it was essential that we got it out of there. Specifically, we needed to find it before Mrs Roberts, the old lady Gareth had called a serial killer, did; not only would we be in all kinds of trouble if she caught us, but she'd probably kill us next. She had to be a hundred years old; she lived in a little cottage at the bottom of the Cliff House drive, and was famously salty.

We had no idea whether the place was full of zombies, ghosts or bodies. I didn't really think we'd find anything more than aggressive guard dogs, spiky traps that clamped your legs, and Mrs Roberts herself, who might not have been a mass murderer, but who was certainly mean.

'I didn't know the fence was this high,' said Josie. She put her cycle helmet in her bike basket and replaced it with a woolly hat, which she pulled down over her ears.

'We have to get it, though,' said Gareth. 'Can you imagine the shit if we don't? The family will come back at some point, and they'll find it. And watch it. And see the things we said about them.'

I felt Josie shudder. 'That must never happen.'

I looked up. 'There's barbed wire on top.'

'They really don't want visitors.' Gareth stepped back to inspect the top of the fence. He looked at me. 'You could do it, Senara. You should go first. Climb over, go and find it, come back.'

'Excuse me?' I was outraged. 'You were the one who called an old lady a murderer and then crashed the record of our suspicions into her garden.'

'But you're small. Agile.'

'I'm not *agile*,' I said. 'You're tallest. Longest legs. You should do it. You could practically step over in one stride.'

'All right. We'll all go,' he said. 'Yeah? All for one, one for all.'

'How, though? We can't tunnel in.' I looked at the ground. 'Can we?'

The wind was coming straight off the sea, chilling my face. Mum would go mad if I was caught doing this. She hated this house and always told me to stay away.

Josie opened her rucksack. As well as a water bottle and a sandwich, she had a long rope, coiled and ready to pounce, a harness, and some metal clip things.

'Borrowed these from Treve,' she said. 'I thought it might be tricky. I mean, if it was meant to be easy, it wouldn't be called trespassing.'

Our friend Treve worked as a climbing instructor, and Josie was a genius.

Some people said Mrs Roberts sat in her cottage over the other side of this fence like Miss Havisham, staring at herself in a mirror. Others said she was a witch, though Josie would have none of that. 'Witches are just everything the patriarchy fears in women, packaged up and othered,' she would say. 'She's not a witch. She's just a human being. But that doesn't mean she's nice.'

Whatever she was actually like up close, the only thing everyone agreed on was the fact that she would be furious to catch us in her garden, and that if she found the drone and worked out how to watch the footage we'd be in trouble. More than that, though, I'd feel terrible. She was a very old lady, living on her own, and we'd called her a serial killer on camera and then thrown it into her garden. She had people who came to look after her. All she had to do was spot the drone and ask one of them to go and pick it up, and we were buggered.

Josie started unpacking the climbing stuff. 'So we have one harness, but apparently it'll more or less fit us all.'

Josie had learned basic climbing from Treve over the years, and she gave us a quick tutorial. The two of them agreed that I was going first, and I didn't have much of a choice. Gareth claimed that the only CCTV in there was focused on the house and the gates, though he was probably bullshitting to make us feel better.

It was raining now, heavy drops soaking through my fleece as I climbed into the harness.

'This is worse than crashing a cheap drone. I mean, that was just stupid, but this is illegal.' I was scared. It was, as

Josie had said, trespassing. 'And even if she sends someone out to pick it up, she'll never work out how to get the memory card out and watch it. We should leave it in there.'

Mrs Roberts had once seen our friend Dan throwing fir cones over the electric gates to see if he could trigger the beam on the other side to make them open, and she told him to '*Fuck right off*' and then lots more in the same vein. He obeyed her: he said afterwards that he'd never run so fast.

'It'll be fine,' said Gareth. 'Seriously – we can't leave that thing in there. Remember, the family have kids. If they come back, they'll find it for sure, and they already think we're scum.' He paused. 'Also, I really need my drone back. Cheap, yeah, but also the most valuable thing I own.'

I climbed a metre or so, then attached a clip to the fence, and fixed myself to it, and carried on. It was easy. This road didn't really go anywhere and no one came along it, so there was hardly any danger of being spotted. All the same, I was trembling, looking back along the road constantly.

'That's it!' said Josie. 'Now climb a bit higher and put in another one.'

The fence was wire, with diamond-shaped holes, and it seemed strong enough to support my weight right next to the pole. It was easy enough once I got going, and soon I was stepping carefully over the barbed wire at the top, pulling my trousers away when they got caught, and letting the rope out to abseil down the other side.

I stood against a tree and looked around in case the drone was right here. It wasn't, so I closed my eyes and breathed the place in. Damp leaves, mulchy things, rain from the ocean. A different world. It was silent, the dark clouds and the shade of the trees making everything monochrome and strange.

I couldn't see the house because of the trees. Even from here, though, I could tell that we'd been wrong and the garden hadn't been deserted for years. I'd pictured a wilderness, nature reclaiming everything. I'd wondered how we would spot one drone in the tall grass, the nettles, bushes, creepers. In fact, I could see that every blade of grass on the lawn was the same length, and the trees were all neatly pruned. It was a perfectly manicured garden, and it was massive.

That meant gardeners came in. I hoped they weren't here now; hoped they hadn't been here early this morning, found a crashed drone and taken it away.

'Careful!' I called. 'It's . . . different.'

I wondered why the family did this when no one except the gardeners (and random intruders) would ever see it, when it would grow and be cut back, grow and be cut back, again and again and again, unseen. Why do that when you never came anywhere near the place? And why stay away for the past few years when everyone else had dashed down to Cornwall to hide out from the pandemic?

Or was that all wrong? Were they actually living here quietly? Were they in the house, watching us right now?

Gareth landed beside me, and then Josie, bringing the clips with her. We stood among the trees and looked at each other, eyes wide.

Gareth held up his phone and started filming. 'Here we have our brave gang of trespassers,' he said in a low voice. 'Making a daring raid to retrieve military hardware. Say hello, everyone.'

I waved.

'You are not uploading this,' said Josie.

'No, but I'm going to video as we walk around. Souvenir.'

'You twat. I want one photo. Not a stupid video. Smile!' Josie bunched us together for a selfie.

'Say *trespass*!' I said, my voice shaking.

'Trespass!'

Gareth promised us, again, that as long as we stayed away from the doors of the house we would be safe enough CCTV-wise.

As we set off, he started narrating in a David Attenborough voice. 'And our intrepid explorers navigate the forest,' he whispered. 'Unsure where their prey is located, they stay close together for safety.'

'Tell me you're not doing this the whole time,' I said.

'There is some discontent among the ranks,' Gareth continued. 'But the primate wielding the primitive recording device confirms that he will not, in fact, be doing this the whole time.'

Birds moved around out of sight, clacking the bare branches. The rotting smell stuck in my nose, and I started to think about the dead animals under the soil, decomposing into it, and my mind spiralled to all the creatures that had died here over the years, the centuries, the millennia.

'You OK?' Josie took my elbow.

I nodded. 'Yeah. This place is a bit freaky.'

Her face was glowing. 'I know! Don't worry, Senni. We'll find the drone and get out. No one's going to send us to prison, even if they did catch us, which they won't.'

I couldn't find the words to say that I hadn't been worrying about that, that I'd been thinking about things in the soil, about all the life and death that had happened on this planet since the first creatures climbed out of the ocean. I wanted to say that being up here on the cliffs above the beach was weird, that the whole place had an atmosphere that was doing something strange to me. It was so close to home, but a different universe, a wormhole into a new world.

I didn't say it, even though it was Josie and I could've done. I knew zombies weren't real, but if they could have climbed out of the soil and eaten our brains, this felt like the place where they'd do it.

We all stopped when the house came into view. It looked like a castle. It stood, blocky and stone, glaring at us. There was a car parked outside it, which was alarming. It was a green one, small and battered.

I had the strangest feeling. *I know this place. I've been here before.* I hadn't, though. I'd never been here. My brain was jumping around, being freaky.

'It's OK,' said Gareth after a moment. 'I bet it's there all the time.' It took me a moment to realize he was talking about the car.

'It'll be the *runaround*,' said Josie. 'The one they keep here.'

'But it looks crap.' I was confused.

'That's what posh people do.' Gareth sounded sure of himself. 'They don't care about things like that. That's the kind of car the Queen would have driven.'

I didn't believe him, but as long as no one was here I didn't care. We stood as close to the house as we dared, and looked up. I counted: there were twelve windows facing forward. Four on each of the three floors. All of them blank.

Twelve windows, and those were just the ones that faced this way. I counted up the rooms we had at home, which didn't take long: five. How many windows facing out the front? Three.

We skirted past the house, looking for something shiny. The garden was the size of the whole of the rest of the village, and it seemed to be organized into different zones, like the best-tended municipal park, but classier and without swings. There was the perfect lawn with the white stone driveway cutting it in half, and around it there was the woody part, the vegetable garden, and the flower beds with paths between them. It was all empty. Empty of people, and empty, so far, of the thing we needed.

We grew in confidence as no dogs or old ladies ran at us with bared teeth. Behind the house we found that there was a swimming pool. It should have been surprising, but it wasn't. It was an outdoor pool, with a pale-blue-and-white-striped shed next to it that I guessed was full of sunloungers and cushions and lilos. The pool was protected by a mossy blue cover, and I watched a beetle run across it.

'Bet it's heated.' Gareth pulled back a corner of the plastic and put his hand in. 'Freezing! I mean, it's not heated now. But there's no way they'd build an outdoor pool in Cornwall and then swim in cold water.'

'Yeah,' I said. 'If you're going to swim in cold water, you can ... you know.' I indicated the Atlantic Ocean, far below us, with a tilt of my head.

'But then you'd have to mix with regular people,' said Gareth. 'The hoi polloi.'

'It's not *the* hoi polloi,' said Josie. '*Hoi* means *the*. In Ancient Greek. So you can just say hoi polloi.'

'Yeah,' said Gareth. 'Or I can say "peasants".'

'"Scum",' I said.

'Yeah,' said Josie. 'Or that.'

I stared at the pool, imagining it in summer if the family ever came back. It would be bright blue, sparkling in the sunshine. I knew it would be, and I knew I'd never see it.

But I also knew that I *had* seen it. I'd been here.

The cottage was at the end of the drive, separate from all this but backing on to the garden, and it was too far from the house for Mrs Roberts to see us (I hoped). According to Gareth, her two living-room windows opened on to the bottom part of the lawn, and as long as we kept to the edges and the top half of the garden we'd be fine.

'There's no way the drone made it that far,' Gareth had said. He'd said it confidently, but he said everything confidently.

All the same, I hoped she wasn't at a window because, although I was no expert, I was pretty sure when I looked over towards her cottage that those windows gave a better view of the lower part of the garden than we'd thought.

We edged round the boundary, walking in single file.

Josie screamed.

Not a gasp, not a shout, but an actual terrified scream.

My heart went mad, pounding right through me, and my legs started to wobble.

'What?' I said.

'Jose?' said Gareth.

Her breathing was loud, but she started laughing through it.

'Oh shit,' she said. 'Oh God. Sorry. I just. I nearly stepped on this. Oh my God.'

We gathered round, keeping our distance until we saw what it was.

A dead fox was staring up at us with a glassy eye. It hadn't been dead for long. It almost seemed to be alive. Its eye wasn't blank; it still looked as if it was thinking. There was a shiny gash in its side, with a couple of flies buzzing round it. I turned away.

'Gross,' said Gareth.

'Right?' said Josie, still breathing fast.

I looked back at it. I thought its face moved, thought its mouth was trying to tell me something. But it wasn't. Of course it wasn't.

I knew it was going to take me a long time to calm down. There wasn't much we could do about the fox; we were hardly going to bury it, or do anything other than step over it. We carried on skirting the flower beds, but my heart didn't settle. I was jumpy, on edge, waiting for the bad thing to happen.

At the furthest point from the place where we'd come in, tucked out of sight of everywhere else, there was a strange patch of messy garden with two camellia bushes that were clearly never cut back, shielded by a crumbling wall on two sides. We sat down. I pushed aside the feeling of déjà vu, but it was there again. *You know this place.*

'Where's your drone, babe?' said Josie to Gareth. He kissed the top of her head and didn't answer.

'If *we* can't see it,' I said, 'does that mean they won't?'

I looked up at the camellias with their tissue-papery flowers. One bush had red flowers, the other pink. The leaves were shiny and could have been made from wax, and there were petals all over the soil, which was full of weeds. Unlike the rest of the garden, this corner had been left wild. The bushes had used the winter sun and constant rain to grow as tall and as ragged as they could. They were gorgeous.

'I love these.' I knelt down and pulled out a few weeds. 'If I had a garden, I'd fill it with stuff like this.'

'Yeah. Look at them, flowering to themselves.' Josie joined me in pulling up weeds. 'Isn't that weird? That these flowers bloom and die, and no one looks at them. I mean, these people have plants that flower in winter, and they're never here, so they must *never* see them.'

'Don't do that, you twats,' said Gareth, nodding to the pile of weeds we were making. 'They'll know someone's been here.'

'Phantom gardeners,' said Josie. 'Emergency! Call the police. Gaz, this is obviously the least of our problems.' She stood up and grabbed a handful of the uprooted plants, setting off to scatter them in the undergrowth. I stayed where I was.

There was something poking out from among the tangle of weeds. It was smooth and light-coloured. A shiny stone? I reached out for it. Even though it wasn't the drone, I touched it, tried to pick it up.

My fingers couldn't close round it because it was bigger than the part I could see. It wasn't cold like a stone. Its texture was different.

I leaned forward, dug the earth out around it. I reached in with my fingers. It went down and down. I pulled at the top, realizing what it was the moment I yanked it out of the earth.

'Ugh!' I dropped it and jumped up.

Josie looked round. 'What?'

I took a step back, and then another. 'A bone! I thought it was a stone. But it's a bone.'

Gareth knelt beside it. 'Remember that fox, Sen? It'll be something like that. An animal that's died here years ago. Just nature doing its thing. Cool.'

He picked it up. It was a smallish bone, thin. When I saw that it wasn't a human hand or a skull, my heart started to calm. Most of it was a brownish colour, stained by all the earth that had been round it.

'I hate it,' I said. 'Put it back.'

'Fuck that,' said Gareth. 'Josie, can you film me?'

I left them to it: I was getting out of here.

I knew, now, that we weren't going to retrieve the drone.

I hardly cared. There would always be the danger that the family would find it and discover the memory card and watch us speculating about them, but no one was going to send us to prison for that. Gareth couldn't finish his coursework, and we'd never be able to make that secret film about Cliff House, though Gareth seemed to be making a new one now anyway.

Josie was filming him on his phone, twatting about with the bone, but I wanted to go home. If I ran fast, I'd be back at the fence in a minute or so. I could cut across the grass. I set off, running as fast as I could across the squelchy lawn.

It was colder than ever and starting to rain again. The trees ahead of me stretched spiky fingers into the air. Seagulls were gliding across the sky. I slowed a bit, in spite of myself, to take it all in.

It was only because I slowed down that I saw it. A shiny white thing poking out of one of the bushes by the driveway. The drone. It was close to Mrs Roberts's cottage, but there was nothing I could do about that. I ran over as fast as I could and yanked it out. It had flown into a rhododendron bush, and it would definitely have been found the moment anyone came up the drive. I was about to set off with it under my arm, back to the fence and freedom, when I heard something.

A tapping sound, quiet, insistent. Like our boiler when it malfunctioned.

I looked round, drenched in dread, and saw a face at the window, a hand tapping on glass. The face was deathly pale, its hollow eyes fixed on me.

I stared. She stared back.

The old lady had seen me in her garden. She was banging on her window.

I could run away.

She'd call the police because I was trespassing.

I could go up to her and try to talk my way out of it. I wouldn't know what to say.

I stood, paralysed. Run away or go over?

I heard Josie calling my name.

Mrs Roberts wouldn't know there was a camera on the drone. If I could smooth things over, apologize and leave with the footage, we'd be OK, and as soon as we got home we could delete the bit where Gareth had accused her of murdering her family.

But if I ran she definitely wouldn't know about it.

I grabbed my phone and messaged the group chat.

Go now. I've got drone.

Mrs R saw me.

I shoved my phone in my back pocket. As I got closer, the old lady opened the window. She was wearing a white shirt, and her long white hair was loose. Was she actually a ghost? I paused for a second, not sure there was anyone there at all.

'Excuse me? What the fuck do you think you're doing?'

Not a ghost.

I took a deep breath. 'Sorry!'

I might never have been this scared in my life. My knees wobbled, and I had to make an effort not to wet myself.

'I'm really sorry, Mrs Roberts. I promise we didn't damage anything. We were flying this plane from the beach, and it crashed into your garden. We just –'

She cut me off. 'Were you vandalizing my garden?' Her voice was clipped.

'No. Really. I swear. We just came over to see if we could find this.' I held up the drone to show her, hating the way my voice sounded. Like a kid in primary school trying to get out of trouble.

'How did you get in? You certainly didn't come up the drive.'

I cringed. 'I'm really sorry.' She glared at me, waiting, so I muttered, 'Over the fence.'

She nodded, and half smiled. 'Promise you haven't smashed the house up?'

'Promise. Honestly, I swear. We didn't go near the house.'

'Who are the other members of your gang?'

'Two friends. We're not a gang.'

'Well, you don't seem like a thug. Just don't use that entry route in future.' She sighed. 'It makes a change to see life around here. You can't imagine how boring it is, looking at nothing happening. But no more remote-control thingies, please. Who are you?'

Fake name.

What was the point? This was a small village, and I would never get away with using an alias.

'Senara.' I'd try to get away without a surname, at least.

She looked at me closely. 'Senara. Do you live in the village?'

'Yes . . . Are you going to tell anyone we were here?'

I felt my phone vibrating. I hoped they were getting away. There was no point in all of us being caught.

'No, but I have one condition.'

I waited, squinting at her, hoping it wasn't anything awful.

'Climb in through this window and make me a cup of tea. Weak Earl Grey with lemon, not milk. And stay and talk for at least fifteen minutes. What do you say? I'll set a timer, and you can leave as soon as it goes off. Get Siri to send a text to your friends to go home without you.' She gave a half-smile. 'My grandson Alex set up Siri for me. It's a godsend.' She held up shaking hands to demonstrate how difficult texting would be, and winced. 'Hey, Siri! Set a fifteen-minute timer.'

Siri confirmed that the timer was set. I tucked the drone into my waistband and climbed in through the window. As I turned to close it, I saw Josie and Gareth running across the back of the garden, in the distance.

Mrs Roberts, it turned out, wasn't a terrifying old battleaxe, and she didn't seem like a murderer, either: she was brilliant. That was my first visit, but after that I went back every week. I learned to make weak Earl Grey the way she liked it, and she'd tell me stories from her life. She was funny and outrageous.

By the time spring came round, in an unlikely way we were friends.

3

Dear Uncle Andy,

How are you? I hope things are good in Thailand. Mum's doing OK right now. It's really cold, but it should be spring again soon. Do you remember Cliff House?

Josie put her pen down and went to check on her mother because she had written the words '*Mum's doing OK right now*' but she didn't actually know that. Not *right now*. She could hear the TV. She could hear the neighbour's dog barking outside. But she couldn't hear Mum.

She stood in the sitting-room doorway. Mum was on the sofa, staring at the television. The latest medication had done this, and Josie felt guilty because it was a relief.

'*Tracy Beaker*?' she said.

Mum nodded without looking round. On the screen, Tracy was shouting at Justine Littlewood. Mum's hair was tangled, but she *was* OK. She was wearing pyjamas and twiddling the corner of a fleecy blanket through her fingers. Josie's old teddy bear was on the sofa next to her. Josie had given it to her a couple of years ago, and she kept it with her all the time now.

'Drink?' Then, when Mum didn't reply, Josie raised her voice and said, 'Cup of tea?'

Mum gave a tiny nod, and Josie went to put the kettle on. She stood in the kitchen and messaged Gareth: Hey babe!

She knew he'd reply. They'd been together three months, but having a boyfriend was still a strange new feeling. She wanted to talk to him all the time, partly to make sure he was still there. She thought about the way he'd been acting around Maya, and told herself that it didn't matter.

It was nothing. It was fine.

The kitchen was cluttered, but everything was under control because Josie worked hard to keep it that way. She put water in the kettle and switched it on, got out two mugs, did a bit of washing-up, keeping an eye on her phone.

Senara, Gareth and everyone else could come home from school and say, 'What's for dinner?' They could open full cupboards and complain that there was no Nutella. They could make four pieces of toast they didn't really want without worrying about finding 60p for the next loaf of bread. Their bathrooms were clean, their clothes washed, and that was normal. Josie not only had to do all that for herself but she had to do it for Mum too, and buy food because Mum didn't leave the house or open the door to delivery drivers, and Josie had to appeal the PIP payments, and budget for their spiralling bills, and . . . and, the fact was, she couldn't do all that and study properly.

The house was always messy, and there were black patches of mould in the corners of the rooms. Josie looked up; it was creeping across the ceiling right now. She couldn't stand the smell of the bleach spray – it gave her a headache and stained her clothes, so she always let the mould get really bad before she'd climb on a chair and try to tackle it in one go. It was nearly time to do that again.

She made Mum a cup of normal tea and herself a peppermint one, and carried them through. Mum still seemed fine, so Josie took her own drink to her bedroom, checked her phone again and picked up her pen.

We went to Cliff House the other day. We had this drone, and . . .

She wrote on and on. She'd never met her uncle Andy, but she was writing to him relentlessly. Perhaps this would be the letter that did it. Sooner or later he would come home. He'd have to because, as far as she could tell, Mum's big brother was the only family they had. Josie believed that if she wrote the right words she would unlock something and persuade him to come back and take charge for her.

He would find them easily enough because they lived in the house he and Angie had grown up in: a pebble-dashed bungalow on the outskirts of Pentrellis, ten minutes' walk from the north coast of Cornwall, and a jolting twenty-minute bus ride from the centre of Penzance. When Josie was younger, Mum had been better at looking after her.

And Nan had helped, but Nan had died, and Grandad wasn't interested because he thought Mum should pull herself together and get on with it. So, from the age of thirteen, Josie had done it all herself. Sometimes she asked Lucy, who lived next door, for help, but that was a last resort because Lucy was busy and had her own stuff going on. Mainly, Josie managed.

She had been to the village primary school, and now she was about to take GCSEs at secondary school in Penzance. Then it would be sixth-form college and after that –

Well, that was why she was stepping up her letters to Andy. Her friends were making future plans, but Josie couldn't. She wanted to go to university, to move far from everything she had ever known. She wanted to explore new places, meet new people. She wanted a new life. She was itching to escape, longing for it, feeling ever more imprisoned by this place. She had recently decided that, if she got the chance, she'd go to Edinburgh. She'd never been there, but she loved the sound of it. A big city, a world away from Pentrellis, filled with history and culture and new things? Yes please.

Uncle Andy must have felt the same because he'd left Cornwall too, except he'd gone to Thailand. He sent a postcard once a year, and Josie now posted her letters every few weeks.

He probably didn't even receive them.

His postcards came from Bangkok with no return address, so whenever she could afford the postage she wrote a letter and sent it to him c/o the General Post Office,

2 Charoen Krung Rd, Khwaeng Bang Rak, Khet Bang Rak, Krung Thep Maha Nakhon 10500, Thailand. She always ended with a plea for him to come back, and the pleas were becoming more and more emotional, the letters longer and more detailed.

One day. One day he would read them all and book a flight. Josie pictured a stash of blue envelopes waiting in a distant pigeonhole. She imagined the long-haired man she'd seen in old photos walking into the post office (which was huge and marble in her head, echoing and grand), and someone rushing off to fetch his mail. She pictured him opening a letter, starting to read. Then he'd move to a marble bench and sit down and read everything she'd ever written. He'd send her a quick card before he even left the building. It would just say: *Josie. Don't worry. I'm on my way.*

She checked the post for it every day.

It was hard to talk about Mum's illness to anyone because they didn't understand. Andy would, though. He'd known Mum for her whole childhood. She didn't have cancer or motor neurone disease or any of the concrete things (and that was, of course, good). She had bipolar disorder and clinical depression.

Depression was a tiny word for a massive, heavy thing. It made Josie cry hot tears when people described themselves as 'depressed', because they meant they hadn't done their homework. She had lived in depression's shadow her whole life, and she envied her friends with a secret jealousy that sometimes veered into rage because she couldn't imagine how light their lives must feel. Sometimes she ran down to the beach and stood on the stony sand and looked out at the ocean that imprisoned her and yelled at it. She shouted everything she wanted to say into the wind, and then she felt strong enough to go home and carry on. She hated the sea, the thing everyone else loved, because it cut off all her escape routes.

From time to time she glimpsed a future. Everything would lift for a while, and when it did Mum would hug her and look after her, clean the house, cook, tell her that everything was going to be fine now. And then, just as Josie was starting to consider relaxing, she would come home and find her mother cowering in bed, and it would start all over again.

It wasn't Mum's fault. Josie knew it wasn't.

She was reaching for a second piece of paper when her phone lit up. Gareth was calling; she snatched it up.

'Hey!'

'Hey, baby,' he said.

Josie wished she didn't like Gareth so much. She suspected, for instance, that he called everyone *baby* or *babe* to stop himself saying the wrong name. He wasn't great boyfriend material really: he had a lively dating history. She'd always felt a pull towards him, but had never expected him to turn his attention to her – they'd been friends for years. And yet, somehow, here he was: her boyfriend. In spite of everything, she loved that.

She pushed the letter under her maths book, even though it wasn't a video call. Gareth didn't know about her letters, and she didn't want him to. He knew about Mum, but not about how bad it was. Josie hid that from everyone except Senara.

'You OK?' she said.

'Yeah. I was thinking about doing some revision, and then I got distracted, and I thought it'd be more fun to talk to you than to revise science. I mean . . .'

Gareth paused, cleared his throat to announce an incoming pun. Josie braced herself.

'OK. Hear this out because it took me ages. I thought of you, and I thought, why do chemistry when we *have chemistry*? And why focus on biology when we could *focus on biology*?'

Josie started to speak, but he carried on, desperate to finish.

'And why do physics when we could be *getting physical*?'

She laughed. 'Time well spent. Well done. Where are you?'

'Might head to the beach? It's not raining.'

Mum was fine right now. Josie would get her to eat something when she came back. She wasn't really revising yet, though one of the books on the syllabus was *Pride and Prejudice*, and she was reading all of Austen as a piece of semi-useful revision, if that counted. (It didn't really – not when she didn't understand what moles were in chemistry.)

'See you at the postbox?' he said.

The postbox was in the village, the midpoint, they had decided, between their two houses.

'See you there,' replied Josie.

She told Mum she was going out (no response) and then tied her hair up, checked her reflection and ran through the village. As she ran, she felt the place closing in on her. She was so bored of it all. The streets were always the same. The same gardens neat, the same ones wild with weeds, the same ones paved for parking. Nothing ever changed.

She ran to get there sooner, to make her blood pump faster, to make it less boring. The air was grey and opaque with rain that wasn't quite falling.

Josie had wondered about Gareth lately because she knew he was talking to Maya at school in a way a boy with a girlfriend probably shouldn't, but now when she saw him – in shorts and flip-flops, even though it was too cold for those things, his hair that was almost long enough for the ponytail he wanted, his face lighting up as he saw her – she knew it was all good.

He opened his arms, and Josie ran into them and turned up her face for a kiss. Their lips met. For someone who had never been able to depend on anyone she was surprised to find herself feeling like this. He picked her up and spun her round, even though she wasn't exactly tiny and featherweight like Senara. He made her feel different about everything. She'd always had to be responsible, and he made her happy.

They walked hand in hand towards the beach. There was a car outside Mrs Roberts's house. Senara's bike wasn't there so she mustn't be, though she often was these days. She checked in with Mrs Roberts all the time now, probably to make sure she kept quiet about the trespassing. Gareth had cobbled together enough coastline footage for his coursework. He'd made his secret film too, with the bone and the bit where they said Mrs Roberts had murdered everyone, including Lucy's missing sister, and it had circulated among a very small circle of their friends before Senara had made them delete it because she was friends with Mrs Roberts now.

Everything was fine.

One day, though, Gareth, Senara and all Josie's friends would leave. They'd go to college or uni, or if they didn't do that they'd leave Cornwall because there were no jobs here apart from minimum-wage service-economy ones. They would go, and, unless her uncle came back, Josie would stay. She could hardly take Mum to uni with her, though occasionally she thought about it until she started picturing the details of how it would work and it all fell apart.

Unless Uncle Andy came home, she was stuck. She'd finish that letter tonight and post it tomorrow.

She nuzzled into Gareth's side so he had to put an arm round her shoulders, and they walked towards the water. The waves were wild, and they crashed on to the stony shore, trapping her.

1940

Martha Driscoll stood in the village hall and stared at the lady. This one. She needed to go home with this lady, and no one else. The lady had kind eyes and a bright dress, and everyone else was frightening. Martha kept her eyes on her, trying not to cry. *Pick me pick me pick me.*

The room had a strange smell because everything was strange. It was the *village hall*, a big room with a scuffed wooden floor, and the smell was as if people sometimes cooked in here, but not today. She wanted to see what was outside the window, but she couldn't because it was dark. It was noisy in here, but outside it had been so quiet that it scared her.

She looked back at the lady and concentrated so hard that she could feel her face screwing up into a frown. If the lady didn't pick her, she would cry, scream and run away home to London. There were a couple of tears coming already, but Martha wiped her eyes on her sleeve, then wiped her nose on her other sleeve, and swallowed it all down. She stood up straight. Her mother had put her in her best brown coat, but it was too small. Her wrists stuck out, and it was tight across her shoulders. Like everyone else, she had a label in her buttonhole and a gas mask over her shoulder. Her suitcase was cardboard and only had a few things in it because she only owned a few things.

Her label said: *Driscoll Martha*. It said: *3 Ridley Street*. It said the name of her school and some numbers.

3 Ridley Street.

Home.

Martha was ten. Daphne was fifteen, and she wasn't being evacuated because she worked in a factory. It was just Martha who had been sent far, far, far, far, far away from Ridley Street – a whole day away on a train and then a bus ride. She imagined Daphne next to her, taking care of her. She looked at the space where Daphne wasn't.

They had all cried, but Martha and Mother had been brave at the station, even though Martha had wanted to scream and scream and cling on to her and refuse to get on that stupid train. Her father was already away, actually fighting in a war. That fact made her wake gasping in the night.

He'd picked her up before he went and whispered in her ear: 'I'm not brave, Martha. I have no choice. Same as you. Same as Mother and Daphne.'

She was sure that made him even braver: he was scared, but he had still gone away to fight. Daddy shouldn't be a soldier because he made books. He knew everything about books, and nothing about killing.

Mother and Daphne were brave too, staying in London and working in factories, even though it was dangerous.

All Martha had to do was come to this strange place and live here for a bit. But even if it wasn't safe for Martha to be in London, she still needed to be there. London was everything she knew. If it was too dangerous for her, then it was too dangerous for Mother and Daphne, and the war was definitely too dangerous for Daddy. It churned inside her the whole time. She wanted to turn and run, fought her legs every moment to stop them doing it.

Martha was standing apart from the other children because Pauline wasn't here, so she didn't have a friend. She tried to make herself smile, but the tears were just behind her eyes, and she knew she was making a funny face. She wished Daphne was there to laugh at her. 'Oh, your face!' she would say. 'Your face, Marth!'

She turned back to look at the lady with the kind eyes, who was wearing a green-and-yellow dress. She was different from the others, who all frowned and muttered and worried and sighed.

A woman with a red face said, 'I'll have two strong boys and a girl,' and took Tommy, Peter and Jane. Martha was glad it wasn't her.

She pulled her plaits over her shoulders and tried to look appealing, then scowled when an old man stood in front of her and looked her up and down. She glared at him and held her breath, only releasing it when he turned and walked off.

Then the lady was there, right in front of her, and Martha felt her smile becoming real, her tears receding. Their eyes met.

'Hello,' said the lady. 'Well, you're a pretty little thing. Who are you?'

She could have checked the label. Martha looked down at it. It had flipped over so you could only see the side that said PENTRELLIS, CORNWALL.

When Martha tried to speak, no voice came out. She managed to whisper it in the end.

'Martha Driscoll.'

'Hello, Martha Driscoll! I'm Violet Roberts. How would you like to live at my house? I'm supposed to be taking four, and I haven't managed to get even one so far. Such a strange thing, choosing children. Terrible.' She shuddered. 'Gracious me, I want to give all of you a home, you poor darlings. So how about it?'

Martha answered as fast as she could. 'Yes please.' She tried to imagine how you could have a house with enough space for four extra people. She supposed they would sleep on the floor. Maybe in the kitchen, under the table.

Violet Roberts might have been Mother's age. She probably already had children of her own. Would they hate her? Martha tried to push that worry away. At least Violet was taking four evacuees, so it wouldn't be just her against the Cornish children.

'You can be my first one. Tell me all about yourself. We'll write to your family straight away and tell them that you're all right.' She put an arm round Martha's shoulders and pulled her in close. 'Wonderful. I've got myself one Martha Driscoll. Now. Who else? Who do we need, Martha? I think we should have two girls and two boys. Do you have a special friend?'

Martha pointed at Betty; she had spent years wanting to be Betty's friend, and this was her chance. Betty's label was the right way round. Violet read it. '*Elizabeth Jones*. Would you like to come with us, darling Elizabeth?'

'It's Betty,' said Betty. 'Yes please, miss.'

Violet spotted little Michael, who was only six, and said, 'Well, we have to take you home, don't we, darling?' and took his hand, then looked around.

'Now I'm going to have to find a big strong boy,' she said. 'Everyone will be furious with me if I don't. One strong boy to help in the gardens and all that.'

'Everyone wanted a big strong boy, miss.' Betty wasn't shy. 'Our boys are all useless really, and I think the big ones have gone by now.' She surveyed the ones remaining, then pointed at Roy. 'He's not much good, but I reckon he's the best one left.'

Roy seemed unconvinced. He wasn't happy about the idea of living with Betty (loud), Martha (drippy) and Michael (a baby), but his friends, who were less skinny, taller, less ginger, had all been taken already.

'My brother's at home,' Violet told him. 'He specially asked me to bring back a wonderful boy like you.'

Roy looked round the room, shrugged, then nodded.

'S'pose,' he said. Violet grinned and shepherded them over to the lady with the clipboard who was writing down who was going where.

Martha's head was spinning. The train from London had taken such a long time. She'd eaten her sandwiches straight away (they all had), and then she'd just sat there and tried to look out of the window, though most of what she could see was grey sky. Pauline had been sent to live with her grandparents in Wales instead of coming to Cornwall. She'd gone two days earlier, and Martha had her address. If the lady would let her have stamps, she'd see if she was allowed to write to Pauline too.

Her mother had plaited her hair for her this morning, and now it was night-time, and she was so, so far away. Martha felt her legs wobbling again. She didn't want to take her plaits out because Mother had done them and, when her hair was loose, Mother wouldn't be able to plait it again for a long, long time. She'd never been away from Mother and Daphne, ever.

She wiped her eyes again, drew in a deep breath, and they all followed Violet Roberts out of the village hall in a row, like ducklings on a pond.

The air outside was cold on Martha's face. The smell was different. It was strange, and she didn't like it. It hurt her to breathe. They walked away from the village hall, and there was long grass under her feet, and then they were crunching along a stony path.

'We'll have to walk, I'm afraid,' Violet said. 'But it's not far. Let's take the coast road so you can see the ocean.'

Martha looked up and nearly fell over when she saw the stars. There were so many. She had to grab Betty's arm to keep herself upright. Betty laughed and took Martha's hand, and they stood together, looking at the sky. It was black, with pinpricks of light all over it. Neither of them had ever seen anything like it. The stars were twinkling, like the song. Martha hadn't known they actually did that. There were bigger ones and smaller ones, and a smear of light all the way across the sky.

Violet had to wait for them to catch up. 'Looking at the stars?' she said. 'Well, they're the same stars as the ones you see at home. Sometimes that can put things in perspective.'

'We don't see them looking like this at home,' said Martha, but it came out as a whisper and no one heard.

'Do you have any children, miss?' Betty asked, when they started walking again.

'I do not,' said Violet, smiling. 'It's just me and my brother, Aubrey, rattling around at home. We need some young people about the place.'

When they got away from the village, from the people coming and going with evacuees and the lady with the clipboard and the houses and a dog barking, everything was too quiet. The silence was like a monster, squeezing Martha from all sides. She longed for the sounds of London: the buses, the shouts, the distant roar of everything. Here there was just the crunching of their footsteps, and Martha missed the backdrop to her old life almost as much as she missed her family.

She wasn't at all excited about seeing the ocean. The children had crowded round the windows of the train to look at it, and it had just been a grey mass with a flat line where it met the grey sky, disappointing and dull. Now, though, as she walked faster to try to hear what Violet was saying, holding her suitcase with both hands, she turned the corner, and there was something completely different.

It wasn't a grey, flat thing here. It was alive. It jumped around, splashing and roaring.

Martha gasped and stopped. The noise it made. The way it shone in the moonlight. The constant rolling. Water all the way to the horizon. Water forever. As far as she could see, none of it was still for a moment. The ocean. Its movement. The strangeness of it all. It made Martha's head spin.

The others had stopped too, and she could tell that they felt the same. Little Michael had started crying.

Violet turned back. She crouched down to hug him.

'You'll get used to this,' she said gently. 'You're going to see it every day. Lots of the windows at home look straight out at it. The house is just a little further.'

They followed her up the hill, and along a road that led away from the sea, and round a corner next to a fence, and then through a gate.

There was a sign that said CLIFF HOUSE, and a house next to it. They all stopped. Violet, up ahead, turned to see what had happened to them.

'Oh no,' she said. 'That's the gardener's cottage. He's away fighting.' She came back and took Michael's hand. 'You're going to have your lessons in there, but the main house is this way. It's a bit more walking, but not much. Then I think we can make you all a cup of cocoa. Are you hungry?'

Martha was too tired to take anything in. She didn't really notice the gardens, the trees, the moonlit lawns that had been dug up and planted with cabbages and cauliflowers. She followed Violet and Michael, and then they went round the corner.

This wasn't a house. It was huge, like a castle, with so much garden surrounding it that it reminded Martha of the time Daphne had taken her to Hyde Park.

'Here we are!' said Violet. 'My darlings, you are part of the family now. Welcome to Cliff House. I hope you'll be happy here.'

The four children looked at each other, astonished. Then they walked faster and faster towards their new home.

4

Mum arrived back from work just as I was leaving. Her work shoes rang out in the dusk.

'Your footsteps sound like you're going to be murdered in a horror film,' I said by way of a greeting.

She nodded. 'Cheers. Where are you off to?'

'I've been revising.' I said it pre-emptively. It was *pretty much* true. I was so bored. 'So I'm going to see Martha for a break.'

'Why do you visit Mrs Roberts all the time . . . ?'

Mum was a bit freaked out by the fact that I liked Martha so much. She seemed to find it unsettling. I knew she didn't like the big house any more than anyone else in the village did, but Martha wasn't the one who left it sitting empty for years at a time and called us peasants. Martha actually lived there. And, sure, everyone called her a witch and Miss Havisham and a ghost, but she wasn't. She *was* salty, but fabulous.

'Will you be back for dinner?'

'Yeah, but I'm not hungry.'

'Toast and biscuits all day long perchance?'

I tapped the side of my head. 'Brain food.'

'Non-stop carbs is not brain food. I'll make something nutritious. See if you can be back for eight. And take your bike lights! And wear your helmet. And be careful.'

Martha was waiting for me. There was a cake out on the table, a small Victoria sponge. More brain food.

'That looks amazing. Did you make it?'

'I added it to my supermarket shop just for you,' she said. 'So I *made it* appear on this table, so I'm going to say yes.'

I stepped into her little kitchen and put the kettle on. It was always clean and tidy in here: she had carers who came in every day and a cleaner who visited once a week. The cottage had bright white walls with paintings on them, comfy sofas and chairs, a new downstairs bathroom and a stairlift. It always smelled of cleaning sprays in lovely flavours. I was so happy here; it felt like a haven.

Practised now, I made a pot of Earl Grey and poured hers out first, adding a slice of lemon. I cut us both a slice of cake.

'Bigger!' she said, so I cut new pieces. 'How's the revision been?'

'Fine.' I looked at the cake. 'Mum says I shouldn't have non-stop carbs . . .' Martha's face showed what she thought about that. 'So, are your family coming down?'

I asked this every time, fascinated by these people who never came to their big house. Martha had pictures of her London family all over the place, and I felt I knew them: her son Leon, who had died a couple of years earlier; her grandson Alex, who lived in Devon, and visited often, though I hadn't met him. Then there was her granddaughter Felicity, Felicity's husband Dylan and their little boy Jackson.

But the one who interested me the most was Felicity's daughter Clementine, because Clementine was the one who'd called us peasants, and until meeting Martha I'd known nothing about her. She was beautiful (a younger version of Martha) and was doing GCSEs this summer too. I'd stalked her social media ever since I'd subtly managed to get Martha to let slip her surname (Parker), and she seemed to live a life of riding lessons, ballet, Latin exams and nights out. I was totally obsessed with her life. I'd never dare speak to her, even if I got the chance, which I wouldn't, but I loved hearing about her.

Normally Martha shrugged at this question, but this time she gave half a smile. I knew she was upset that she'd barely seen the London branch of her family for years. Her son, Leon, had died at the beginning of the pandemic, and she hadn't been able to go to his funeral in London. She wouldn't talk about it, but there were photos of him everywhere, along with pictures of the others and a few childlike sketches of some other people. She wouldn't talk about them, either.

'I don't know why they stayed holed up in London all this time,' she said. 'I mean, it was hard not to take it personally. Even Joe Biden made it to Cornwall, yet they didn't. Thank goodness for Alex, but he comes for me, not the house. I hate seeing it so neglected.'

She looked at me with another little smile. 'But to answer your question, Senara: yes, they'll be visiting. I have a plan. And I'd love you to meet them. When do your exams finish?'

'June twenty-third,' I said.

'Will Clementine's too, do you think?' asked Martha.

'Probably. Unless she does really obscure subjects.'

'I have no idea what she does, Senara. I haven't seen her since she was fourteen. So I'm not going to tell you my plan in case you need plausible deniability, but I'll aim to bring them here shortly after you and Clem finish your exams.'

I took a bite of cake. 'You're very mysterious.'

'I know their weak spot. So. How's your mother?'

Mum and Martha didn't know each other, but Martha loved news from my world as much as I loved hearing about her life.

'She's fine. She broke up with Richard, thank goodness.'

'Oh, I'm so pleased! I thought he might end up moving in with you.' We looked at each other and shuddered.

'Me too. I think he just pushed it too far in the end. He told her she looked cheap because she was wearing hoop earrings, and she went to take them off, then realized that she could wear whatever earrings she wanted. She had one of those moments when you see everything differently, and she dumped him on the spot.'

'And he accepted it?' Martha sipped her tea and looked at me over the top of the cup.

'Well, no, but he doesn't get a choice. He sent a million flowers and apologies, but she'd had enough, so then he turned mean, and now she's blocked him on everything.'

'Good for her.'

I was so relieved about this. Mum had met Richard on Tinder, and he'd been so charming at first. Then he hadn't. I saw it long before she did. It strengthened my feeling that relationships really weren't for me. I only knew ones that had broken up.

'Yeah. Thank God,' I said. 'So she's back on the market.'

Martha took a strand of hair that had come loose and tucked it into her ponytail. She rarely wore her long hair in a bun; she said it made her feel 'like an old lady'.

'What about you, Senara? You don't have to tell me. I know I'm three hundred years old, but since Siri doesn't seem able to whisk me back through time to relive my youth, I have to take my intrigue where I can get it. It's you or *Below Deck Med*.'

I sighed, wishing I had anything to tell her. 'It's *Below Deck*, I'm afraid. I just don't have anything to say. I never meet anyone I like enough. It should be Mum staying at home and me out on all those dates, but it's not. I've never met anyone who's made me feel excited or, you know, fluttery and obsessed and all those things that happen to other people. I don't think I ever will.'

'What *does* make you feel fluttery and obsessed?' she said. 'Because something must.'

I hesitated. I wasn't sure anyone had ever asked me this before. I felt self-conscious.

'Oh, nothing,' I said. 'Nothing interesting.'

'It's interesting to me!'

I thought about it. 'This is going to sound weird.'

'My favourite!'

'Being outside. Sitting on the beach, looking at the ocean. Swimming in the sea. Walking on the cliff paths. The sunshine. Even sometimes the rain. I kind of feel it lifting me up. But then I see Josie so obsessed with Gareth, and, like, everyone else hooking up, and I wonder what's the matter with me.'

'You might find someone one day,' Martha said. 'Or you might not. And either way that's OK, my dear.'

I grinned. I felt that Martha was the only person I knew who thought that you could have a happy life without a partner.

'Tell me more about Barney and Violet.' I wanted to focus on Martha and her amazing life, not on myself.

She slapped the table with both hands. 'Sure thing, but we can go one better. I have props! Can you run upstairs for me, Senara? Go into the second bedroom. Not my room, but the door on the right. That's where I keep my old clothes. They all think I should have given everything to charity long ago, but what can I say? I didn't want to. I never kept a diary or had a camera, and those clothes document my life. Look at the rail of dresses to the right of the window. There's a blue one. Very old. Violet and I made it from a pattern, and it was quite the triumph. It's a cocktail gown, not quite floor-length, with a tiny waist. Grab that one. It'll bring the story to life.'

'Can I go up in the stairlift?'

'By all means!'

Within seconds I was gliding up very slowly, accompanied by a clunking mechanical hum.

I'd never been in the second bedroom before, and it took my breath away. There were rails of dresses along two walls, and two chests of drawers under the window. The bed was covered in colour-coded folded clothes. It smelled like the midpoint between New Look and Oxfam.

For a while I just walked around, staring at things. I stroked a dark red dress that looked as if it belonged in a museum, and felt the satin stiff under my fingers. I looked at what I thought must have been Martha's wedding dress: it had a long skirt with lots of layers, and a beaded bodice. I imagined her gliding up an aisle, marrying Barnaby, who I knew from her photos as a seventies-style man with funny facial hair and a big smile.

This could have been a fashion museum. You could see the decades changing. I followed them through from the forties to the full-skirted fifties, the funky sixties, and beyond. There was a blue-and-yellow-striped minidress that I adored. The label said BIBA: even I'd heard of that.

When I remembered that Martha was waiting downstairs with a story, I looked for the blue dress and quickly found it. It was brighter than I'd expected, and the seams on the inside were hand-stitched. I could imagine how it brought out the colour of Martha's eyes.

I didn't dare take it on the stairlift in case it got tangled in the machinery, so I carried it down carefully.

'That's the one! Perfect. So Violet and I needed a boost: Aubrey – Violet's brother, you remember – had just gone to Scotland, and there was a dance in Truro, so we decided to go. To be honest, Senara, I was ready to meet someone.

The war had been brutal. Utterly brutal. You can't imagine. I'd rather told myself that the next presentable man I met, I'd marry.' She gave me a wicked smile. 'Enter Barnaby Campion.'

'Was it love at first sight?'

'I saw him across the room, and he looked up and smiled, and that was that.'

I sat back and imagined myself at a dance in Truro in 1949. Wearing a bright blue dress, needing something good in my life. I wondered whether I would ever see someone across a room and smile and change my future. I wondered whether it really had been that straightforward for Martha.

'Maybe I should do that too,' I said. 'Not marry. But the next presentable person I meet? I think I should try something like that. Just to see if I can.'

'I'll drink to that,' said Martha, and I poured us both another cup of tea.

5

Exams were over, and we had left school.

I was walking across the beach, heading towards my friends who had made a fire and were sitting around, eating and drinking. We'd done it. We had all finished our exams two days ago.

I had a tote bag containing a bottle of red wine that Mum had let me take 'as long as you share it', a multipack of crisps, a packet of Maryland cookies and a net of clementines. Mum had stuffed them into my bag in the hope that we might get some vitamins, as part of her campaign to make me eat things that weren't carbs.

Josie had her guitar out, and as I got closer I could hear that she was playing 'American Pie', with everyone singing along badly. Josie had a busking book and generally went for crowd-pleasers. I knew she played in Penzance sometimes, guitar case open for coins, when she needed money for food or bills. Her home life was different from everyone else's, and it was easy to forget that because she didn't talk about it much. She'd asked me not to tell anyone what it was really like for her, but people kind of knew.

We all rallied round as much as we could, casually giving her things we 'didn't need any more', inviting her for tea, passing on bits of uniform, but I was the only one who had any idea how she felt about it, how scared she was about the future, how fixated on her uncle.

'Hey, Senni!' she said, breaking off from her song.

I looked at the flames, almost invisible in the sunlight, distorting everything behind them. I loved Josie and admired her for being here tonight: she and Gareth had broken up just before our exams, and here he was, sitting on a beach blanket with his arm slung round Maya's waist. As a response, Josie had cut off her long hair and bleached what was left. It suited her. Tonight she was wearing shorts and a vest and big clumpy boots, and she looked amazing. I sat beside her.

'Nice fire,' I said. 'I've got wine and a bit of food.'

Gareth reached out a hand. 'Give.'

I handed him the whole bag.

'What've you been up to?' said Josie.

'Walking dogs. Five today. My legs are killing me. You?'

'Work. Home. You know.'

I nodded. Josie looked after her mum, and she had a Saturday job in the bookshop in Penzance. She busked. She was always busy, always responsible.

She raised her voice a little and said, 'Treve took me climbing on Wednesday, though. Over at Bosigran. His brother drove us there. I went right up the cliff. Epic.'

I knew this already, and I also knew she wasn't saying it for my benefit.

Gareth had genuinely broken her heart when he'd ended it over text. I'd worried about her, had held her when she cried that her life was never going to amount to anything, and that everyone always left her. I'd told her she'd come through it and, seeing her now, I thought she had, with short bright blonde hair and a hard new shell.

'You're so cool,' I said, also using a loud-enough voice. 'No one's as cool as you are.'

'And she's an awesome climber!' called Treve, overhearing us. 'Such a natural. But you know that already.' He gave me a significant look, and I made an innocent face. Treve was still annoyed that he'd missed the famous Cliff House trespass.

It turned out that Gareth hadn't actually deleted the footage for ages. He'd made it into a little film first, and we'd shared it with a few of our friends. It showed us sending the drone up from the beach, and then climbing over the Cliff House fence to retrieve it. It was secret, and legendary. Now, though, it was deleted. I hoped so, anyway. I couldn't bear the idea of Martha ever hearing about it.

I noticed that Gareth had finally managed to get his hair into a man bun, that he was wearing a *Point Break* T-shirt and positioning himself, these days, as a surfer. I looked around at my friends and saw how they were all changing. Maya had put her hair up so she looked like a ballerina, and was wearing a little dress with a white shirt over it. It wasn't *her* fault, I reminded myself (though it was a bit). It was Gareth's.

Treve was dressed in a lumberjack shirt over a tight white T-shirt, and Amina was wearing a bikini top and tiny denim shorts and looked cold. Everyone was finding their style. Everyone except me.

I looked down. I was wearing a plain blue T-shirt that used to be Mum's, and a pair of regular, non-stylish shorts. I had no idea how people knew what looked good and what suited them. I didn't even know how they knew what they liked. When I started trying to work it out, I panicked and stayed in my pyjamas. I knew I liked pyjamas; they were comfy.

I decided that this summer I'd find myself a style. I would become interesting so that when I was old I could have a room like Martha's. I had no idea how, but I would start trying out new looks, and, by the time I went to sixth form, someone would have said to me, just once, 'You look nice!' or 'I like your . . .'

I like your *what*, though? Boots? Dress? Shaved head? Tuxedo? No idea.

I thought of Martha's blue dress. She'd still been in her teens when she met Barnaby. How did you become someone who rocked a party dress? These days Martha dressed in drapey, comfy clothes that suited her; she looked cooler than I did, and she was ninety-two.

I felt the little stones digging into my bum, and looked out at the sea. The waves were coming in perfect symmetry, smashing on to the shore every . . . I counted. Every twelve seconds. For twenty-four seconds they transfixed me – then Gareth handed me a tumbler of cider.

'Oh, posh,' I said. 'Glasses?'

'Plastics,' Treve confirmed.

'Have you got anything we can burn?' said Maya. 'We thought we had enough wood.'

She seemed unworried about Josie, her former friend, being there. She didn't seem to care that she'd broken her heart; she was happy with Gareth at the moment. It wouldn't last. It never did. He was terrible at relationships, and it made me like him a lot less.

'We started the fire too early.' Treve sounded glum. 'I knew we should have waited. It's not even getting dark, and we've burned through everything.'

I checked my pockets and chucked a receipt and an old dog-walking schedule on to the fire. They burned brightly and crumbled into ash. I looked around for something else. It was a warm evening, but the flames were magical. We burned the packaging from the food we'd all brought with us. Maya found some litter, and we burned that. Everyone added random bits of paper from pockets and bags. The flames danced and died, and my face was hot and then cold. I stared into the ashes. We had fire. A huge mass of churning water. The stones beneath us. The salty breeze.

Josie played that Green Day song, the one about the time of your life, and we sang along, slurring the in-between words that we didn't know, passing cider and wine between us.

It wasn't as if everything was ending. We were going on to college in September. But, still, we had known each other all our lives and now school had finished forever. We would drift away from one another, absorbed into the ocean of thousands upon thousands of students. We'd make new friends, turn in different directions, crash on to different shores. We all knew it.

'Senara!'

Someone was calling my name. I looked round and saw a girl walking across the beach in our direction. She was tall and slim with long blonde hair and expensive clothes, and she was carrying a bulging tote bag with *Shakespeare and Company* written on it, and swinging a net that was full of small pieces of wood.

I knew her immediately from her Insta, from her perfect life. Martha had said she was going to make them come down right about now, and it seemed she'd done it.

'Hey, guys!' said Clementine Parker.

She looked so much like Martha that I wondered, for longer than I should have done, whether younger Martha had found a way to time-travel.

'Hi!' said Gareth.

'Is that fire still going?' Clementine talked with a cut-glass voice, the way I imagined Kate Middleton might speak. 'I was coming over before, but then I saw you were struggling a bit so I went back up and got this from the house. It's mostly kindling. I brought some firelighters and matches too, just in case. Can I join you?'

'Whoever you are, you're an angel sent from heaven,' said Gareth, smiling up at her. She gave him a wicked smile back.

'I've got wine too,' she said, patting her tote, 'and I took a bunch of stuff from the kitchen.'

I saw her starting to sit next to Gareth, then changing her mind and walking round to squeeze on the end of Josie's towel, beside me, instead. She took out a cardboard box of wine, and a metal tin that turned out to be filled with cakes.

She turned to me with a big smile. 'Hi!'

'*You* can come again,' said Josie, putting her guitar down and taking a chocolate cupcake. 'This is amazing! Oh my God, I think I love you.' She clearly hadn't realized who it was.

'My mum's a baker. She brought loads of stuff down from work. I'm Clemmie. I live up there.' She pointed to the big house.

We all went quiet, and then everyone started welcoming her at once. Everyone apart from me; I was wondering how Martha had done this. How had she checked with me when Clementine's exams would finish, and then made her materialize in Cornwall two days later?

Everyone introduced themselves, but when it was my turn she said, 'Don't be silly, Senara! I know who you are. I came here specifically to meet you.' She smiled around. 'And you guys too, obviously. Hello. I'm down for the summer. I'm lonely, and I would like some friends, please. Gran speaks highly of you, Senara, and so I've come to see if I can be your friend too.'

When Josie was playing again and everyone was singing along to 'The Drugs Don't Work', Clementine leaned in towards me. I wondered what it would be like to have a fraction of her confidence.

'Everything OK?' I said. Honestly. *Everything OK?* That's what my mum would have said.

Her voice was low. 'Yeah, I mean, this is lovely, isn't it? Exactly like a Cornish summer should be. Can you come and see me tomorrow? We just want to talk to you about Gran.'

The 'we' sounded ominous. 'Oh God! Is she OK?' I felt it like a punch in the gut.

'She's not dead or anything. She's fine, and the thing is we need her to stay that way until we work out what she's up to because she's acting weird. Have you noticed anything? Like maybe . . . dementia?'

'Not at all,' I said, annoyed. 'She always seems really sharp.' I tried to think of anything unusual. 'She's more on the ball than anyone I know. I'm pretty sure she's less confused than I am.'

'When did you last see her?'

'A couple of days ago.' I cast my mind back. 'I didn't stay because she had another visitor already there. You know that Mr Mitchell guy? She said they were doing boring admin. She said it right in front of him. *Boring fucking admin, Senara*. Then she pretended to shoot herself in the head.' I demonstrated.

Clem knocked back her drink and motioned to Gareth to pass her the wine box.

'Mr twatting Mitchell,' she said, holding her cup between her knees and letting a stream of wine fill it almost to the brim. I held mine out, and she filled that too. 'The lawyer, right? I knew it. See, that's why we're here. We weren't going to come until the middle of July, but Gran messaged Mum and kind of implied that she was changing her will. Now! When she's ninety-two! So we had to rush down before it's too late and work out if she was serious.'

She gave me a look, and for a second I felt the force of her suspicion. Did she think I'd been enacting some nefarious plan to get hold of Martha's money?

And had Martha really done this? Had she pretended to be changing her will because she knew it was the one thing that would bring her family down early? Was that manipulative or tragic? I remembered what she'd said: '*I know their weak spot.*'

Then Clem's face changed. 'And we haven't been down for years because of the pandemic, so the house is covered in dust and full of mice, so that's nice. And the pool's freezing and full of algae.'

'Oh no!' I tried to sound sympathetic, though I wanted to laugh picturing the luxury of the house.

'Yeah, grim. My mum's frantic, sorting it all. So, has Martha said anything to you about any of that?'

'Clementine.' I felt a bit strange calling her by her name, as if I might not be allowed, but she didn't react. 'She hasn't said anything about her will.' How much should I say? Nothing probably.

Definitely nothing.

'But . . . ?' said Clem.

'Nothing. That's all.'

'It's not. You were about to say something else.'

I lasted about twenty seconds under her laser stare before I wilted.

'She asked me a while ago when GCSEs finished and said she would get you to visit after that. So I think she might have said it to make sure you were definitely coming down to see her as soon as possible. Because she's missed you.'

'Seriously?'

'Yep.'

'She said in her message that she was thinking about "giving the house back to the community".' Clementine made air quotes with her fingers. 'And then she wouldn't say anything else. Oh God – has she totally played us?'

I flinched. Clementine and her family had come racing down here because Martha had threatened to take away their inheritance. Martha had known that was her best weapon. The whole thing felt uncomfortable, and sad. Poor Martha, having to resort to that to get their attention.

'I'd guess so,' I said in the end.

Clem turned her head and, as the dusky light caught her face, I saw again that she and Martha looked exactly the same. They had the same silky hair and classical bone structure. They were different, though. So different.

She blew out, and a strand of hair flew up into the air. 'That would be quite funny. Respect, if so. But you saw Mitchell with her, and that is a bad sign, because he's literally the guy who did her will last time. Which wasn't long ago.'

'She changed it recently?'

Clementine leaned back on her hands and looked out at the flat horizon. 'Only because she had to. When my grandad died. You know, her son Leon?'

'Yeah. Sorry. That was awful.'

'It was shit, specially for Mum and Uncle Alex. And Martha. So she had to rewrite it because everything was originally going to Grandad. And she changed it to go to Mum and Alex, of course. I only found all this out yesterday. Alex hates the house for some reason, which is why he never stays, so basically it would have been ours, and everything would have carried on the same. I've missed our summers here. But Mum was so scared of Covid she wouldn't go anywhere. Even here.'

She gave me a sideways smile. 'I was thinking I could have parties once Gran was, you know. Maybe rent it out for weddings and stuff? Even have my wedding here, whenever that happens. I was making excellent plans. And then Gran shakes it all up.'

'I don't think she has, though.' I took a big gulp of warm white wine and felt it go straight to my head.

Clementine wasn't listening. 'I mean, giving it to the community? What's "the community" going to do? Put on plays? Fill it with drug addicts? No one would have the money for its upkeep and the whole place would fall apart.'

I put my cup down, building a ridge of stony sand round it, leaned back on my hands like Clem, and looked at the moon through a wispy cloud. I made a non-committal sound, but I was thinking of that house. Those huge grounds, everything in the garden perfectly maintained except that corner with the camellias. I was imagining it full of life, filled with people, trying to do good. Opened up.

I was also trying not to laugh at Clementine's idea of what *community* meant – amateur dramatics and drug addicts. Maybe that's what she thought happened outside London. This was, after all, the girl who had called us 'peasants'.

I decided not to think about that any more.

'So we have to keep her alive while we find out first of all if she really has left it to the drug addicts or whatever, and then, if she has, whether we can challenge it. Don't kill Grandma. That's the number-one rule of the summer. She can't die until it's fixed.'

'Sure.' I edged away a bit. We'd been right about her all along: she was horrible.

Gareth had shifted over to join us, and Clem grinned at him. She turned back to me and said, 'So, yeah – come up and see me tomorrow? Why don't you have a swim if the pool's sorted by then? Hang out a bit. We can talk some more. Come at one – have lunch.'

'Yes,' I said. 'Thanks. Are you sure?'

She didn't answer because she had turned to Gareth and they were talking about Eurovision.

It was after midnight when someone decided we needed to swim. The ocean was flat and the sky had cleared. The moonlight was reflected on the water, and it felt as if the wide sea existed just for us. The only towels we had were the ones we'd been sitting on, and they were sandy on one side and covered in crumbs and drink spills on the other, but no one cared. Clem stripped off completely and ran across the stones, screaming, and Josie followed.

I wished I could be that free, but swimming in my underwear was bad enough, so I charged straight into the cold water to hide myself from view. We splashed and swam and shrieked and laughed. The seawater was silky against my skin. I swam out a little way and flipped on to my back to look up at the sky, and everything was calm.

I was lying on my back in the Atlantic Ocean, staring up at the stars and planets. I wanted to hold the moment forever. The evening had been magical.

We stayed on the beach long after all Clem's wood had burned. We stayed after the food had gone, and the drink. We filled empty bottles from the tap by the closed kiosk and drank warm water because our mouths were dry. Clem went away and came back with her arms full of jumpers and fleeces, and we put them on. She brought more bottles of booze and we drank them all. It was just after midsummer, and the sky turned pink before five.

As the sun rose behind the headland, I saw that Treve and Amina were asleep. Maya was dozing with her head in Gareth's lap. Josie and Clem were deep in quiet conversation. I was cold and clammy in my clothes, covered in sand and salt, drunk, happy, tired. We didn't leave the beach until the guy came to open the little cafe at six o'clock.

1988

On the day her GCSEs finished, Felicity saw the man at the bus stop again. She tried to forget about him because she'd left school forever, and that was more interesting.

It had taken Felicity years to realize that school was different for her. Everyone else looked at a page and saw words. They didn't make a guess from the first few letters, or piece a word together from the context. They just looked at it and there it was: symbols that meant something solid, something that stayed the same and didn't jump around. It was easy for them. It wasn't that she was stupid, as she'd always thought; she was different.

Felicity found reading and writing weird and awful, but the rest of her world was (she had discovered) more interesting than theirs. When she was thirteen, she and Helena had chatted in Helena's bedroom about the things their brains did. She was staying over, and she was in a sleeping bag on a mattress on the floor.

'What colour's your name?' she'd said, sleepy and happy, in a bit of a sugar-trance.

'You *what*?'

'To me, Helena is green, and Felicity is a kind of orangey-yellow. Is it the same for you?'

Helena had laughed and rolled over to look at her.

'What on earth are you on about? You nutter.' Helena had, Felicity felt, laughed a bit too loudly, for too long, as if she had an audience, even though she hadn't.

When she calmed down, they established that Felicity saw things in colours, in shapes, often in smells, while Helena just accepted what was in front of her. The idea of seeing words in colours, associating them with shapes, picturing the days of the week running anticlockwise in a circle and the months of the year in a bigger circle, going clockwise, each a different colour – all that was alien to Helena and, it turned out, to everyone else Felicity knew.

She had recently discovered that there was a word for this: *synaesthesia* (obviously it would have to be a word that was impossible to spell). Alex had found it for her. Alex was her big brother, and he was the least dyslexic, the least synaesthetic person in the world. He had finished his A levels, and it didn't matter if he'd messed them up (though he hadn't) because he only had to get two Es to go to Oxford.

Felicity, on the other hand, was finally allowed to leave her academic private school and go to college. With Alex's help, she had persuaded their parents that she didn't have to fight through impossible A levels. Instead, she was all set to go to Penwith College with Jenna, and she was going to study cookery while Jenna did economics and business studies.

She walked out of that last exam and headed down the hill and into Truro with her friends. They bought chips and Diet Coke and sat in Victoria Gardens, and, while Helena and the others compared notes unendingly about the English literature paper, Felicity lay back and looked at the leaves above her, and the sunlight shining through them. She felt the grass pricking through her shirt, and she knew that this moment right here marked the beginning of the rest of her life. The air was silver and glittery. She would never forget it. From now on she'd be able to live according to her own rules.

Everyone else still had more exams because they did more subjects than her. They were taking ten, eleven or twelve while she had finished her seven. Felicity wished them good luck and walked back up the hill to school in time for the last school bus home ever.

When she got to the bus stop in Pentrellis, that man was there again. He was pretending to look in the window of the Spar. He'd been there when she got off the bus every day that week. She knew he was watching her reflection.

She half knew who he was, thought that he was called Andy. He had the worst aura she had ever seen. It had triangles in it, and it was grey like a bruise. She ran all the way home, knowing that he wouldn't be able to follow unless he ran too, and he probably wouldn't.

*

Jenna was waiting outside Grandma's cottage like she'd promised: as it was Thursday, Grandma was out at flamenco. They walked through the open gate, and Felicity closed it and put the chain on it. For a second she wished they had a high fence all round the house, with barbed wire on top and gates that you couldn't climb over.

'He was at the bus stop again,' she said as she tied the chain in a way that she hoped made it look locked.

'Oh shit,' said Jenna. 'Did he follow you?'

'I ran.'

'I thought he was going out with Rachel Thomas,' said Jenna.

'Rachel? Actually going out with *him*?' She had lost touch with Rachel lately. Maybe she'd call her and see if she was OK.

'Yeah. Anyway, what did you think about the English exam?'

They went straight to the tree at the bottom of the garden, and once they were settled Felicity tried to talk, to compare notes – again – about the exam, but instead she cried, and once she'd started she couldn't stop.

'Sorry,' she managed to say while Jen stroked her back. 'It's just –'

It was everything. School was over. Trying to fit in was over. The man who waited for her, but who hadn't, so far, tried to talk to her, was not over.

'You did it,' said Jenna, opening a bag of crisps, holding it out. 'Remember how much you thought you couldn't? And then you did.'

Felicity took a crisp. Jenna was so sweet. Her own exams weren't over yet, but she had still come to meet Felicity in a tree. She wiped her eyes and managed to say, 'How about you?'

They talked about the future, about how Felicity would set up a bakery and Jenna would come for cake after work every day.

Felicity wondered whether the man was in the road outside the house. She was glad she couldn't see because that meant he couldn't see them.

When she heard Alex shouting her name, she leaned down and waved.

'Hey,' he said, running over to her. 'Wow. You look horrible! I thought you'd be happy. Weirdo.'

'I am,' she said, rubbing her eyes. 'This is my happy face. Look, Jenna's here too.'

Jenna leaned down. 'Hi, Alex!' she said.

Felicity watched Alex blushing a deep red. Alex had the biggest crush on Jenna and never managed to say much to her.

'Hi,' he muttered.

The girls jumped down, and Jenna said she had to go home and gave Felicity a huge hug. Felicity watched Alex staring at her as she walked off. He forced his gaze back to his sister.

'You're in *luuurrve*,' Felicity said, to make him blush more.

'I came to say it's dinner time, but you'd better go up the back stairs and wash your face first.'

He covered for her, and she ran up the smaller stairs – the servants' stairs, Dad liked to call them, though there had been no servants here since the sixties – and into her room.

When she looked in the mirror, she saw what Alex meant. She was like a girl from a horror film. Her face was purple and swollen, her eyes barely there. Her hair was tangled as if she'd been dragged through a hedge backwards, which she almost had: she'd taken herself through a tree, forward.

Normally Felicity was neat and tidy. She had to be, to keep her head in the right place. Her bedroom was always ordered because she was scared that if she allowed chaos into her life it would never leave.

She forced a brush through her hair and laid out clothes to change into. The school uniform she didn't need to wear any more was disgusting: brown and cream, with a tie, and it was made of itchy material with horrible seams. Why would you make hundreds of girls wear that? If it was up to her, there would be no uniform at all, and if you had to have one it would be made from soft material, a friendly colour, comfortable.

She stepped out of the brown skirt for the last time and pulled on a soft grey dress with pink edging, and her slippers, and went to wash her face.

'Kind of you to grace us with your presence,' said her father.

'Leon!' Mum told him off.

'You're welcome,' said Felicity. 'Sorry. It was my last day of exams. I was . . .' She flicked her eyes to Alex. 'Celebrating.'

'Oh my goodness,' said Mum. 'So it was! Your last day. How did it go? What subject was it again?'

Other people's parents were more involved in their school lives than this, but Felicity was quite happy with the way things worked at her house. Her parents operated on the basis that if you told them about a problem they'd help with it, but beyond that it was up to you. Alex was the cleverest boy in the world, and the parents were mildly proud of him. Felicity wasn't at all brilliant, and she was no less loved.

'English lit,' she said now. 'I probably passed.'

'Well done,' said Mum, handing her a plate of spaghetti with puttanesca sauce. 'Alex, pass your sister the cheese.'

'Thanks. No more school. No more anything.'

Alex grinned at her. 'Same here. Summer of freedom.'

'You'll be OK when we're in Paris?' Mum asked.

'Of course they will,' said Dad.

Felicity and Alex lived in the big house on the cliff and had grown up roaming the beaches below, the countryside, the village, with no supervision at all. On a sunny day in the holidays, Mum would kick them out with swimming things and a picnic and tell them to be back by six.

That was how Felicity had revived her old friendship with Jenna. They'd been friends at primary school, but stopped seeing each other when they went to different secondaries. A couple of years ago Felicity had discovered that when Jenna's parents were working she went to the beach with a book. They'd met there and started talking, and now they were inseparable. Jenna was little and fierce. She took no crap at all, and Felicity adored that.

'Who else has had their last exam?' said Dad. 'Is it just you, Flick?'

'Yeah.' She spun her spaghetti round her fork. 'Just me. But Jenna finishes tomorrow. And we'll be fine when you're in Paris. We'll be lazing around here, doing nothing. Can Jen come to stay?'

'Of course she can,' said Mum. 'She's always welcome. You know that.'

6

I woke at midday, my head pounding, my mouth dry and my whole body feeling weird. The sun was filtered through my curtains, and I could hear cars going past. Pentrellis village was on one of the routes into Penzance, and in July traffic was often at a standstill all the way down the road all day. Right now, since it was still June, the cars shot by every few seconds, often at considerably more than thirty miles an hour.

I sat up in bed.

Clementine Parker had asked me to come for lunch and a swim. She'd said to come at one. It was nearly twelve.

But she'd said that relatively early in the evening. I was sure she'd meant it at the time, but would she remember? What if I turned up at lunchtime with my swimming things, and no one was expecting me?

But if she was expecting me, and I didn't turn up, that would be bad too. I wanted to message and check, but I didn't have Clem's number. I couldn't message her on Instagram because we didn't follow each other, so it would go into a requests folder, and she'd see it sometime in the future when she checked.

I stumbled downstairs and poured out a bowl of cereal, but one spoonful made me feel sick. I drank two pints of water and felt it sloshing in my stomach. I dressed in an old T-shirt and a pair of joggers, but those were the wrong clothes for Cliff House.

Mum had gone to work. I normally loved these parts of the day, when I had the house to myself. I switched on the TV and let *Homes Under the Hammer* play out to itself. I thought of Josie's mum, watching CBBC all the time.

I texted Mum.

Hey Mum. I'm up. Heading out soon.

Fifteen minutes later, she replied.

Good morning, young lady!! Did I hear you coming in just before I got up??

Mum was a big fan of the multiple punctuation mark. She never punctuated anything singly.

Yep. Came in about 6.15. We were on the beach. Clem from

cliff house was out with us. She thinks Martha's changed her will btw. Leaving the house to the community? They're not happy. I reckon Martha's messing with them.

I saw her starting to type and stopping, starting and stopping again. The three dots came and went. In the end, though, she wrote:

What was she like??
Clem.

Then there was another one.

What does 'the community' mean??

Clem was nice I think. A bit scary. She's invited me there for a swim. I'm not sure whether to go or not. Community-wise, no idea.

Mum didn't reply after that. I wasn't offended: she was an office manager for an insurance company in Penzance, and unlike me she didn't actually get to sit around texting all day.

At ten to one I got on my bike and set off back towards the beach. I'd taken paracetamol and ibuprofen, and had a shower and brushed my teeth for a very long time, but I still felt like shit. Those pints of water were heavy inside me. I could sense a vein going all the way through my brain, from the top right to the bottom left, pulsating with a sharp pain as I rode. I'd only drunk a bit of wine, so this didn't feel fair, until I remembered Clem going home in the early hours and coming back with bottles of spirits. I remembered us passing them around, drinking them neat until they were all gone. My delicate state made more sense.

I'd never met Felicity, but I'd seen her in Penzance during the summer when I was younger. Mum had pulled me out of the way, and we'd watched her from across the road, swinging a basket, wearing a smart dress, shopping in the delis and the boutiques, the shops I never even saw when I was there. My brain just filtered them out. I wondered whether Felicity's brain did the opposite and filtered out Sports Direct and Poundland, and I was sure it did. Penzance could be two different places, superimposed on each other.

The sun was warm on my face, and the air smelled of flowers and leaves, but I had to stop my bike and vomit into a gorse bush. Two pints of water, plus assorted extras, came straight back up.

That made me feel loads better. I freewheeled down the hill and across the wooden bridge over the stream, and then pushed my bike up the last bit.

The electric gates loomed. Martha's house, close to them, was the only part of the place that looked welcoming: bright white with a tiled roof and its own front garden and driveway.

There was a yellow car outside, and I knew it belonged to a carer I'd met a few times. That meant I couldn't disturb her because she'd be having what she called 'unspeakably undignified' things done. I couldn't go to her for help.

The gates were a little way down the drive. I pushed my bike over to them, my feet crunching on white stones, and stopped. There was a video entryphone, and I couldn't press the button.

I stood still for ages, hardly breathing. I thought I was going to be sick again, but it passed, and then I realized that my breath must smell of vomit and wished I had some mints. The gates were maybe twice my height. They had spiky tops so it would have been difficult to climb over them, but I could have done it with Josie's ropes.

Why would I climb over the gates? I'd been invited.

I jabbed the button quickly, not allowing myself to think about it. Then I did an awkward smile towards the camera that was angled down from the top of the gatepost, and waited.

Nothing happened. I stood still and kept the stupid smile on my face, regretting getting out of bed, wishing I hadn't come. My face was probably on a screen somewhere far away, inside the high fence, inside the castle.

I counted to thirty and exhaled.

I was off the hook; I would go and find Clem on social media and message her to explain. I was turning my handlebars round when a voice crackled.

'Hello?' It was a suspicious hello, not a welcoming one. I drew in a deep breath and turned back.

'Hi,' I said, looking up at the camera.

'Can I help?' said the voice, but her tone said 'fuck off'.

I cringed and said, 'Sorry. It's Senara, from the village. I was with Clementine last night on the beach, and she asked me to come by at one.' I didn't say *for lunch and a swim*. 'I wasn't sure if she meant it. So I thought I'd just stop by and check. Sorry for disturbing you.'

Silence oozed out of the speaker for ages, and then she said, 'Senara Jenkin?'

How did she know my name?

'Yes?' My voice came out so small I could hardly hear it.

'Right.' More silence. 'Come in, Senara. I'll wake her.'

'Oh no, don't –'

It was too late: the gates clicked and creaked and opened slowly, and the drive stretched ahead, cutting through the lawn and turning round a corner. The stones were whiter than normal gravel, and the bushes on either side had pink flowers all over them. The grass beyond the bushes was bright green. Everything was intense, much more so than it had been on that dull January day. It was like cycling into a painting. A Hockney. I passed the bush that had hosted the crashed drone without looking at it.

I had that feeling again, the weird sense that I already knew this place. The light was different this time, the colours. The fact that I was here legitimately. And yet it was every bit as familiar as it had been last time.

I rode slowly and looked around as I went. I was pretty sure even the air on my face was more refined here than it was outside.

The garden stretched out on either side. It went on and on. When I turned the corner, I stopped and put a foot on the ground and stared at the house.

I had definitely been here before. I knew it from long ago. I was certain of it. I hadn't been past Martha's gatehouse since January, but I'd seen this house in the sunshine before.

The windows were open. All the window frames were bright white, and the front door, which I'd barely dared to look at before, was wooden and carved like the door of a medieval castle. There were two cars outside: a massive white one, which was one of those cars that's much taller than me, the ones that drive down the middle of the road around the lanes all summer, and the little green one that we'd seen last time.

I sent a text to our group chat, which was currently called 'TA', short for 'Trespassers Anonymous'.

Guess where I am!

I took a photo and added it, then pushed the phone back into my pocket.

I thought of the house I'd lived in all my life. We had a square of concrete at the back and a patch of grass at the front. This house was in the middle of its own park. I made a note that, however friendly I got with Clem, I would never invite her back to mine. I smiled at the thought and found that actually I wanted to take her home with me, to shock her. She'd look at the house and think we must be 'drug addicts'.

I cycled up to the house, but the door stayed closed. I got off my bike and pushed its stand down with my foot because I didn't dare lean it on the house in case that wasn't allowed. It was like VR; I had stepped from the regular world into a new one, but in a game that I'd played before. Last time I'd half expected zombies to pull themselves out of the ground and chase me, had thought a dead fox was trying to speak. This time it was more like a backdrop for a virtual treasure hunt. The pixellated diamonds would be here somewhere.

Apart from gulls shrieking high overhead, everything was silent.

Footsteps crunched on the gravel from the side of the house, and then Felicity was standing in front of me, wearing a flowery dress and silver sandals, carrying a pair of secateurs. Her hair was dark blonde streaked with grey, and it was held back from her face by a pair of massive sunglasses on her head.

She was the midpoint between Martha and Clementine.

'Oh, that was quick,' she said. 'Ah. You cycled. Senara – how are you?' She held out her hand. 'Nice to see you again.'

Again? I'd never met her. Maybe that was a posh-people thing to cover the bases.

'You too,' I said, through a fixed grin. I shook her hand, blushing, the most awkward girl in the world.

'You don't remember. How could you? You and Clemmie were only tiny. And now look at you!' She set off round the side of the house, motioning for me to follow. 'We don't use the front door. It's a bit grand for us. So, since Clem invited you, I've done my best to haul her out of bed, but I fear it might take a while. I was up early, and I met her on her way in, looking like something the cat dragged in, and then I discovered that she'd helped herself to booze, cakes, firewood, you name it . . .'

She turned and gave me a warm smile. 'I'm glad you had a good night. Sitting on the beach until dawn? It's good for Clemmie to do things like that. She was very taken with the idea of local friends. To be honest, I think she had a rather . . . inaccurate idea of what local people might be like.'

She paused, and I silently begged her to change the subject, which she did. 'How's your mother?'

'Fine.'

I had so many questions, but I couldn't find the words. The thrust of it, though, was: *Why are you asking about my mother when you don't know her?*

She had known my surname, though. And she'd just said she knew me when I was tiny.

I followed her into a little courtyard. It was tucked away, with the house on three sides and a view of the sea on the fourth. There were bright flowers in pots, and what I thought might be a jasmine creeper growing up one wall.

The swimming pool was a little way away. It was sparkling and bright blue, just as I'd imagined.

'Have a seat.' She waved at a courtyard table with a mosaic top. I sat on a heavy metal chair. There was more of the white gravel underfoot, but it had flat stepping stones across it. I put my bag at my feet and looked around.

'This is lovely.' That sounded lame. 'I mean, really, really gorgeous.' I tried to think of a polite question. 'How old is the house?' That sounded like the kind of thing people said.

I felt sick again. *Must. Not. Vomit.*

'Victorian, largely.' Felicity looked to her right and pointed. 'Some of this part is older. There was originally a chapel here. St Petroc's. And an old burial ground, which we try not to think about too much.' I felt my breath hitch inside me, and pushed my hands under my thighs so she wouldn't see me shaking.

I remembered that thin bone we'd found here in January.

An old burial ground.

That bone we'd found could have been human.

She was still talking: '. . . all moved down to the village church, and the main house was built in 1881.' She reeled it off like a tour guide, then said, 'Now, what can I get you? I suppose you were up until dawn too?' I nodded. 'Then you'll need sustenance. Coffee? Tea? Water? I'm sure she'll be down in a minute. Do you eat bacon?'

'Would it be OK to have coffee *and* water?' I said. 'And I'm veggie but thank you.'

'Eggs?'

'Yes!'

'Fried-egg roll?'

I actually heard my stomach growl at those words. If she heard it, she didn't show it.

'That would be so wonderful!' I said, trying to use the politest words I could find. 'If you're sure? Thank you so much.'

While I sat looking out to sea, I took my phone out of the side pocket of my bag and checked the group chat. Josie had replied to my photo with ????? and Gareth was undoubtedly unconscious and snoring.

I wrote:

Clem asked me to come but she's still asleep. Awkward!!! But her mum's lovely.

She replied straight away.

OMG I can't even get up. Can't believe you're there. Take photos. Are you swimming? Loved last night. How are you feeling?

Shit. You? Clem's mum's making me breakfast. Not currently swimming. So glad I don't have to try to retrieve a drone by stealth.

Same. Get her to invite us for a pool party? Clem, not her mum. And stay

away from that place
where the bodies are
buried.

I put my phone down as Felicity came over with a tray that held a huge crusty roll, a massive cup of coffee, a little jug of milk, a sugar bowl, a pint of fizzy water and squeezy bottles of ketchup and mayonnaise.

My self-consciousness faded as every mouthful made me feel better. The coffee, the water and most of all the food. Felicity sat with her own coffee and talked about trivial things that weren't Martha's will or bones in the garden.

'Dylan and Jackson have gone over to St Ives,' she said, and I tried to pretend I didn't already know everything about them.

I was pleased they weren't here as I didn't want to have to try to be the right level of polite to anyone else. She asked about my exams, my plans for September. I wondered whether Martha had seen me coming past, even though her carer was there.

'You know,' she said, 'I see colours round people. It's a strange thing my brain does. Synaesthesia. I hope this won't sound too weird, but your colours are lovely, Senara. They always were.'

She instantly had my full attention. 'Wow. What colours?'

'It's a kind of yellow and blue stripes. It sounds odd but it's peaceful. The sun and the sea maybe.'

'Um. Thanks.'

This was bizarre. I loved it.

'What colour's yours?' I said.

'Oh God. I can't see myself because I'm in the middle of it. It changes every time I look in a mirror. But I get a sense of a person before I've even spoken to them because I see everyone in a swirling mass of colours, and sometimes shapes.'

'Shapes?'

She shrugged. 'Generally pointy means beware and curves mean lovely. Mostly it's colours, though.'

I wanted to ask her: *How do you know me? And Mum? Why do I feel that I've been here before?* But I didn't.

By the time I finished eating, Clementine still hadn't appeared. Felicity's voice changed, and she leaned forward.

'She's doing OK, is she then? Your mother? She always had lovely colours. A lot like yours.'

I nodded. 'I didn't know you knew her.' My voice was as casual as I could make it.

'Well. As I said, we haven't seen each other for years.' She was also too casual.

'She's fine,' I said. 'She works at an insurance company in Penzance. I mean, it's probably not the most exciting job.' I felt defensive because Clem had told us about Felicity's baking business, and that was clearly much more fun.

'Is she single?'

'She just broke up with someone. I was glad. He was bad for her. It's always just been me and her really.'

'He was bad? Good riddance then.' She grinned at me, a real, happy smile. 'My brother always had the most enormous crush on Jenna, you know. Have you met Alex?'

I laughed at the idea of anyone having a crush on my mum. 'No,' I said, 'but Martha's talked about him a lot.'

'Yes, she would,' said Felicity, and, just as I thought we were about to segue into Martha, Clem burst out of the house and ran over, throwing herself into a chair and drinking all the rest of my water in one go.

'Senni!' she said. 'Oh my God, you actually came. I would have slept all day if Mum hadn't literally thrown a glass of water on me.'

'I did not,' said Felicity. She turned to me. 'I didn't throw water on her. I threatened to.'

Clem continued: 'I'm glad you remembered because I didn't.'

I was so relieved that I started talking too fast. 'You said to come at one. Otherwise I'd definitely still be asleep too. I don't have your number or I'd have messaged to check. Or just to tell you we could do it later in the day if you wanted or whatever.'

'Nah, I'm glad you're here,' said Clem. 'Hey, *Muuum*?' She looked at my empty plate and raised her eyebrows meaningfully.

'Oh, fine,' said Felicity, standing up. 'Fine. Waitress service for you, but only because I remember what it was like to be hung-over after a night on the beach. Bacon or egg?'

'Duh! Both.'

Clem leaned back. She looked as if she'd thrown on the first clothes that came to hand (an oversized T-shirt, a pair of black sparkly harem pants), but she still looked stylish. She was like someone in one of those paparazzi shots of celebrities walking dogs in LA with a coffee in one hand.

I glanced down at myself. I looked like nothing, again. I was wearing denim shorts that were too long to be stylish and a red T-shirt I'd had for years. Maybe, I thought, I could try Clem's oversized thing. Penzance was full of charity shops.

'So, will you talk to Martha?' she said, trying to drink my coffee, but finding there was only a drop left. She yelled over her shoulder. 'And a coffee! And another one for Senni! You're the best!' She turned back to me. 'I mean, will you check that she just said what she did to make us come down early?'

'Yeah. Of course.' I paused. 'I mean, surely your mum would be better placed to do that?'

'Gran plays mind games with Mum, though. She'd probably tell you the truth.'

She grinned, and I tried to smile back. 'How do you feel this morning?'

'I've been better. You?'

'Yeah.'

I felt better, though, as the afternoon went on. We had more water, more coffee, and big slices of lemon cake. Clem was easy to talk to, and funny, and in spite of everything she was magnetic, and it was hard not to like her. When she said, 'Mum, will you make us some brownies?' I laughed. I'd never met anyone this spoiled.

'I don't do brownies.' Felicity's voice was clipped. 'You know that, Clementine. If you want one, you can make them yourself.'

'Mum hates brownies. She doesn't even do them at work. I just thought I'd try because you're here. Sometimes she's different when friends are round.'

Friends. The word lodged in my brain.

We changed into swimming things and jumped into the pool, which was, as Gareth had predicted back in January, warm.

'Is this pool heated?' I said when I came up.

'Yeah,' said Clem. 'Otherwise it's just too cold.' She paused. 'I know. It's not the best use of the world's resources. We should get a geothermal one. But we do only heat it when we're here, and that's not often, so that's something. It's only just warmed up. I'm glad it's clean.'

I turned and swam across the pool. The water was sparkling and clear. I realized I was feeling absolutely fine. My hangover, the jet lag from staying up all night: it had all melted away in the face of a blast of Cliff House.

Later we were wandering round the garden.

'Did our mothers use to be friends?' I wasn't nervous talking to Clem any more. She was treating me like a sidekick, and that was fine. 'I had no idea. I don't know why Mum didn't tell me.'

'They were, like, BFFs,' said Clem. 'They went to primary school together. Mum knows loads of people around the village because she grew up here. She doesn't really talk to anyone any more, though. She says she drifted away from them when she went to private school. But I'm not sure. Alex went to posh school too, and he still goes to the pub and catches up with everyone when he's down. Mum's just a bit of an oddball.'

'She said I had a nice aura.'

'*Voilà*.'

We walked across the lawn. I looked at the spot where that dead fox had been. There was no trace of it now. I supposed the gardeners must have taken it away, back in the winter. It had probably only been there for a few days.

I remembered the bone. Thought about the old burial ground.

'So we met when we were babies? They must have stayed friends long after private-school fallouts or whatever, for that to happen. You know, I do feel like I've been here before, and so it makes sense. It's strange, though. Mum never said anything.'

I'd always thought Mum was totally transparent about everything. It was weird to discover that she had secrets, and that they involved me. She'd lied to me, or at least hidden things from me. I decided to ask her tonight. It was better to do that face to face rather than by text.

'Yeah. They were best mates. I guess they drifted apart. I don't know.'

'Felicity said her brother had a crush on my mum. Mum's never mentioned him, either.'

'Alex is such a twat! He should have played it better and married her. Then he'd be your dad, and we'd be cousins.'

I tried to imagine a version of me that was half carved from Clem's family. My dad was the most regular person imaginable. If Clem's uncle Alex was my dad, I'd be tall and beautiful like the rest of them. I pushed that thought away, feeling too disloyal to my father.

We were close to Martha's cottage now, and I saw her at her living-room window, waving. Her hair was tied into a high ponytail, and she was wearing something green and silky.

Clem ran over. 'Gran!' she said, too effusive. 'How are you? Do you want to come up to the house? Look, Senara's here! She's my friend too now.'

'Hi, Martha,' I said. She winked at me when Clem wasn't looking.

'Hello, girls,' said Martha. 'How lovely to see you both. I'm afraid I need to have a little rest, but perhaps Dylan will drive down and collect me later.'

'Are you coming to dinner?'

Martha nodded and closed the window, and Clem and I walked on. When we reached the wild bit of the garden, I had to stop myself exclaiming about its transformation. The camellias had been cut back, and there was a pile of cuttings on the grass next to them. Lots of weeds had been pulled up, and they were in a different pile. The flower bed was tidy and manicured like the rest of the garden. There was no sign of that bone.

An old burial ground.

'This bit is Mum's favourite,' Clem said.

'It's creepy,' I said without thinking.

The garden was huge and beautiful, but there was something different about this spot. It was tucked away, set apart from the rest of it, and it felt dark and scary. Maybe it was just because I'd pulled a bone out of the ground here, and now I thought it might have been a human one.

'Right? I mean, duh, the best bit is the pool. But Mum loves the camellias. The gardeners aren't allowed to touch them. Only Mum.'

I checked the time, and because it was half past four the spell was broken. I longed to stay, but . . .

'I need to go,' I said. 'I have to walk a dog.'

Clem laughed. 'What, any old dog?'

'It's my job. I'm a dog-walker. I have to pick one up before five. Shit. Sorry.'

'Hey,' she said. 'Come back soon, yeah? Come and hang out. Bring the others. I thought Cornish people would be all, like, "Ooh-arr, have a pasty." But they were really nice.' We set off back towards the house. 'So how does that work? Walking dogs professionally?'

I couldn't believe she'd just said the pasty thing out loud, but decided to let it go. 'I get paid basically minimum wage,' I said. 'A bit more, but not much. I work for a company: West Cornwall Doggie Care. Most jobs here are seasonal, but mine isn't. I get to be out and about all year round. It's better than, like, working in Subway or something.'

Clem looked thoughtful as we crossed the lawn. 'Does everyone have a job? Everyone we were with last night?'

'Of course. You have to have a summer job. There are loads of them around this year.'

'Where does Gareth work?'

'He takes money at a car park.'

'Josie?'

'Bookshop.'

'Maya?'

'Cafe.'

'Treve?'

'Climbing instructor.'

'Amina?'

'Ice-cream shop.'

'Wow. Oh my God. And you walk dogs. You really do all work. None of my friends have summer jobs, though I guess some have internships, and that's kind of the same thing?'

I side-eyed her. 'I don't think it is, Clem. Everyone here works because they need the money.'

I thought about Josie, and how unfair it all was, but didn't say anything. That wasn't Clem's business.

Clem gave me a curious look. 'Well, yeah.' She looked thoughtful. 'Yeah, I guess internships are more of a career thing.'

I tried not to laugh, but I was finding that – in spite of everything – I liked her.

Before I left, Felicity handed me a rectangle of card.

'Can you give this to your mother, Senara?' she said. 'No pressure. Just it would be nice to catch up with her.

It's been a while, and we were so close when we were younger.'

She had given me a pale pink business card. It said *Felicity's Fancies* on it, and it had a line drawing of a cake, a phone number, an email address and various social-media handles. She had written something on the back, but I made a show of not reading it.

I put it in my pocket and said, 'That's a nice card. I'll give it to her.'

I read it as soon as I was away from the house.

1940

It took Martha a long time to remember where she was. When she stretched out in bed, Daphne wasn't there. She thought, half asleep, that Daffy must have gone to work, to the factory.

Then it flashed through her head, a series of pictures. Train. Coach. Village hall. Lady. MarthaBettyMichaelRoy. Stars. Ocean.

Castle.

Martha didn't know where Daffy was because she was a long, long, long, long way from home. She had been evacuated to Cornwall. She was waking up in a castle owned by a lady called Violet. And that meant that –

She opened her eyes. Betty was in the other bed, facing her, still asleep. Martha looked at Betty and smiled. She had a bed, and warm blankets, and there was Betty. If she was with Betty, this would be all right. They would become best friends. The war would end. Daddy would come home, and she and all her classmates would go back to their old lives; and in the meantime she got to live with Violet and Betty and the boys.

She sat up and looked around. The walls in here were yellow. The room had two windows, and one faced out towards the sea. Her bed was next to the sea window, and she knelt up and pulled the curtain back.

It was raining outside, raining into the sea. Miss Ward, their teacher who had come with them from London, had told them it wasn't 'the sea': it was the Atlantic Ocean. Peter had said, 'It's not the Atlantic, miss! My dad says it's the Pacific,' and Miss Ward had laughed and said they would look at it in the atlas when they arrived.

Martha hadn't known what to expect; she couldn't imagine that the ocean would be bigger than the Thames, even though she'd known it was, really. Last night it had shone in the moonlight and gone on forever, and now there it was, disappearing into the mist. Birds swooped around. She stared and stared and stared. There were waves crashing, sending white spray into the air. She could see down to the very edge of the beach. An actual beach! Her mouth hung open as she gazed and gazed at everything. There was a strange feeling inside her.

Fingers grabbed her from behind, and she screamed. Betty roared with laughter.

'Oh, Martha!' she said. 'I just had to tickle you. Sorry!'

Martha looked round, a bit cross, but then she saw Betty's face, and she was so pleased that she was there with her that she started laughing too.

'Look,' she said in the end. 'Look, Betty. Right outside our window! The Atlantic Ocean.'

'That's not the Atlantic,' said Betty. 'It's the Pacific.'

Martha knew she was wrong, but didn't say so.

They were almost dressed when the door opened and a girl came in. She was about Daffy's age. When she started talking, Martha liked her voice. It was so different. It was different from theirs, and different from Violet's. Violet sounded like the wireless. The girl sounded like nothing Martha had ever heard before. Her words were soft and shifting, and when she said 'girls' it sounded like '*girrrrrrrrls*'.

'Hello, maids,' she said. 'On with you then, girls. Miss Violet's waiting at the breakfast table. And Mr Aubrey, Miss Violet's brother. Don't go getting used to it; she's giving you a treat because it's your first day. Oh, look at you.' This was directed at Betty, who had left her corkscrew curls loose, so they were bouncing round her face. 'Aren't you a love? So, which is which?'

'I'm Betty,' said Betty, 'and this is Martha. Who are you?'

The girl laughed. 'Not shy then? I'm May. I'm the housemaid. There used to be twenty people working in the house and gardens, you know, and now there's only three of us. There's me, and then Mrs Lamb. She's the cook. And Mr Downing, the butler.'

Martha and Betty looked at one another, their eyes wide.

'*Butler?*' said Betty.

'Oh, don't you worry. He's not as grand as he sounds, and he mainly looks after Mr Aubrey.' She paused. 'You'll meet Mr Aubrey. As I said, he's having breakfast with you. Some days he stays in his room, and when he does, you're to leave him alone. Never speak to him unless he speaks to you first. And you can go anywhere in the house apart from his room, and Miss Violet's room. You girls are going to be helping me once you're settled in, and Miss Violet's setting up a little school in the cottage as there's no space in the village school for another class. Your teacher from London's going to do your lessons there. You can help in the gardens too. Ever done that before?'

'I have,' said Betty.

Martha dropped behind as they went down the stairs. She looked at everything. The stairs were stone, and she could feel the cold coming up through the soles of her feet. This huge house smelled old, like the museum they'd been to with school, like the corners of their house when it rained. The walls were covered in flowered wallpaper, which was peeling off where the sheets of paper met. There were paintings on the walls, pictures of long-ago people looking angry. She stopped to stare at a man with a wig on, certain that he was glaring at her, imagining his voice saying: 'What are you doing in my house, little girl?'

'Marth!' Betty was calling up to her. 'Come on, Martha! Breakfast!'

'What are you doing?' said May. 'Aren't you hungry?'

'Martha's always daydreaming,' said Betty.

May sighed. 'Just like Miss Violet. You two'll get along like a house on fire.'

There was a man sitting at the breakfast table with Violet, Roy and Michael. He had a pink-and-grey face, and he was wearing old-fashioned clothes that were a bit too small. Martha could see that he was older than Daddy.

The table was in a room with a big window and a faded red carpet. The walls were dark red, with darker rectangles where there used to be paintings.

'Hello!' the man shouted when he saw them. He jumped to his feet. He was smiling. 'It's the girls!' he said. 'Welcome, welcome.'

'Hello,' said Betty.

She sat down in the chair next to him, and Martha sat next to her and looked across the table at Violet. Michael was sitting beside Violet, holding her hand, and Roy was on the other side of the man, who Martha knew had to be Aubrey.

'Martha and Betty.' Aubrey stood up to shake their hands, so they had to stand up too, shuffling their chairs. 'I'm glad you're with us. I hope you have a wonderful stay at Cliff House.'

'Thank you,' said Betty, and she chatted away to him.

Aubrey was funny. He told them about the people in the village, doing funny voices and making silly faces. Violet told him to stop, though she laughed too; Martha thought she didn't really want him to stop at all.

'And the postman?' He stood up and did a bow-legged walk round the room. '*I did have a parcel for you, Mr Aubrey, but it was a bit heavy so you'll need to pick it up at the shop!*'

He put on such a funny voice that Martha couldn't stop laughing.

'Aubrey!' said Violet. 'For goodness' sake!'

'What about the schoolteacher?' said Roy, and Aubrey became stiff-backed and shouty. Martha was glad they were having their lessons with Miss Ward, who they knew, and not this angry person.

When May came back in, Aubrey made a puppet from a napkin and had it ask her for some more eggs for everyone. May rolled her eyes, but she looked pleased.

'You tell Mr Aubrey,' she said, playing along and leaning over to talk to the napkin puppet, 'that if everyone is agreeable to the idea, we'll be making a big cake to welcome our new friends this afternoon.'

The puppet looked at everyone in turn, then turned back to May. 'Everyone is agreeable,' it said. 'Thank you.'

'Can I help with the cake?' said Betty.

Michael's voice was tiny. 'And me?'

Martha and Betty looked at each other. This was better than anything they had ever dared to imagine.

7

One Thursday morning, in the middle of a heatwave, everything changed.

My phone rang as I was sitting on Josie's doorstep. We were laughing at her neighbour's dog, Molly, trying to jump up and catch flies out of the warm air. Molly was a small brown dog with a face like a teddy bear's, and curly fur to match, who was consumed by curiosity about everything. I walked her three times a week, and it was both my best and my worst job.

'Are you a brilliant girl? Yes, you are,' said Josie as I checked my phone. 'You must be so hot in your fur coat! Shall we take you to the beach?'

I looked at the screen. It was Clem, so I answered it.

'Senni!' she said. 'What are you doing? Can you come here right now?'

I turned to Molly. I was pretty sure she wasn't sophisticated enough for Cliff House. Her owner was a hospital doctor, Lucy, who lived next to Josie and Angie in an impeccably clean bungalow.

'I'm walking Josie's neighbour's dog,' I said. 'Molly. We

were going to take her to the cove for a swim. I could come and see you after that?'

'No, come now. Bring the dog. We can give it some water or whatever. I have to see you straight away.'

'I'm with Josie.'

'Yeah, bring her too.'

Josie, though, was shaking her head and making *no way* gestures with her hands. She had taken against Clem over the past few weeks.

'Does it have to be now?'

'Yeah. It's an emergency. Just come and Mum will explain.'

My heart contracted. I felt my hands starting to shake.

'It's not Martha, is it?'

'What? Oh God, no, nothing to do with her.'

I exhaled. 'See you in about half an hour then.'

Josie was subdued as I said goodbye, and I felt dirty with guilt. We'd been about to take Molly to the end of the cove that allowed dogs in summer, to let her go wild in the waves. Now I was dropping it all for Clem. Clem had an unspecified emergency, but everything in Clem's world was an 'emergency'.

'You sure you don't want to come?' I said to Josie. She nodded.

'I should check Mum's OK anyway. You go. Go on! It's fine. See what her *emergency* is this time.'

I could see from her eyes that it wasn't fine really. I vowed to prioritize Josie in future, just as soon as I'd found out what this was about.

I'd seen Clem almost every day for the past two weeks

because Clem wanted to see me, and I liked her company, and I knew she'd been spending time with Gareth too, when I was there and when I wasn't. Both Mum and Josie disapproved of our new friendship, but Martha seemed to like it.

Felicity's overtures to Mum hadn't gone well. I'd remembered the card a couple of days after she gave it to me, and left it propped against the kettle late one night so she'd find it in the morning. On the back, Felicity had written:

> *Jenna – I'd love to see you. It's been long enough, truely. Let's talk. F xx*

I thought it was weird that she'd spelled 'truly' wrong, but I thought Mum might laugh at the fact that it said ***Felicity's Fancies*** on the front of the card. I thought she might agree that it had been long enough, and that they might as well make up now. I thought she might tell me why they'd stopped being friends.

Not so much, it turned out.

Mum had got up early to go for a run before work (she did it every day, even when the rain was so hard that you couldn't see the end of the street) and seen the card and actually screamed. I heard her, though I went back to sleep, and only pieced it together later, when I woke up to a barrage of texts saying:

> Senara!! Did you put that next to the kettle?? It was

a bit of a shock. I don't
want to see her. Don't
pass on any more
messages!!

I'd apologized, and when she got back from work she had refused to talk about it. She'd been a bit weird ever since. When I checked the bin for Felicity's card, it wasn't there. I snuck into her room while she was at work and found it beside her bed, and there was a piece of paper torn from a notepad that said: *Dear Felicity, I don't think* – and then it stopped.

'Senara!' said Felicity when I reached the house. She was wearing a summer dress and trainers, and she had a purposeful air. 'Thanks for coming. Oh, who's this? Hello! Are you a lovely doggie? Yes, you are! Yes, you are!' She crouched down to pet Molly. 'Is the dog on holiday?'

'No. She's my most regular regular. She belongs to Lucy – Josie's neighbour. This is Molly. She's more agent of chaos than lovely doggie, but I'll keep her on the lead. Clem asked me to come over – is everything OK?'

Felicity paused for a second. 'Lucy Thomas?'

'Yeah. Do you know her?'

Felicity shook her head. 'Not really. I – well, I used to know her . . . family.'

Lucy's sister, Rachel, was a local legend. She had disappeared years and years ago and, in spite of a huge search and a big poster campaign, she'd never been found. Everyone knew about her: there were all kinds of stories at the village school about her haunting the corridors. Felicity had been about to say *I used to know her sister*. I was sure she had.

I watched her pull herself back into the moment.

'Anyway. Senara, we need your help.'

I followed her. 'Um, sure? If I can.'

She picked up a huge bag of clothes and handed it to me. 'Oh, see if there's anything you want in there, by the way. I was going to drop it off at a charity shop, but events have rather overtaken us. There's a couple of things that I think could be gorgeous on you.'

The bag appeared to be full of expensive women's clothes. Cast-offs, I guessed, of Felicity's and possibly even Clem's. Maybe this bag contained my stylish future.

'Thank you,' I said.

We walked round the house and into the courtyard. Clem was swimming, and Martha was sitting at the courtyard table, a mug in front of her. She patted the empty seat beside her. I put the bag of clothes under the table and joined her. Dylan, Clem's stepdad, came out with Jackson, Clem's eight-year-old half-brother. Jackson scowled at Clem, who waved from the pool, swam to the side and climbed gracefully out. She was wearing a tiny silver bikini, but pulled on a kaftan thing and came over to sit at the table. Water dripped from her hair and soaked through the material.

I thought for a moment of the missing Rachel. She'd been a teenager when she vanished. Our age.

'Are you OK, Gran?' Clem said, speaking loudly. She patted Martha's shoulder. 'Need anything? More coffee?'

'I'm fine,' said Martha. 'Look, Senara's got Molly. Molly often comes to play in my garden. She's a twat, but a cute one!' Molly sniffed her hand and allowed Martha to pet her.

Felicity handed me a mug of filter coffee and visibly bit back a comment about her grandmother's language.

'So, an emergency has come up,' she said to me. She sat down, stood up again, sat down and stood up.

'My father died,' said Dylan from somewhere behind me. His voice was flat. 'Out of the blue. Heart attack. That's what Felicity is trying to say.'

'Oh my God,' I said. 'I'm so sorry.' Was that what you said? Was I meant to say 'Sorry for your loss'? I was too self-conscious to try it.

He nodded and looked away. 'Thanks.'

'Dreadful,' murmured Martha. She stretched out a hand, and Dylan stopped pacing to allow her to pat his arm. 'Always so awful when it's a shock like that. Poor Dylan. And so far away.'

'So we have to go to Hong Kong,' said Felicity. 'Dylan and Jackson and I. We're leaving today. Flying from Newquay in –' she checked her watch – 'four hours. Newquay to London. Then overnight to Hong Kong. Clementine has expressed a . . .' She hesitated, gave a tiny eyeroll. 'A *strong preference* for staying here, and since she's not related to the Hong Kong side of the family and only met Dylan's parents at our wedding I feel there's no point taking her halfway across the world. So she's going to stay here, with Martha.'

I glanced sideways at Clem, and saw that she was having to make an effort not to smile. I looked at Martha, who was petting Molly and making no eye contact with anybody.

'At Martha's house?' I thought of the spare bedroom filled with vintage clothes.

'Course not. Here, and we need you to move in with me.' Clem turned to me, her eyes big. 'Move in and be the responsible one for me and Gran. Otherwise they're going to make me go back to London and stay with my dad, and I'm all settled here now.'

'Felicity trusts neither me nor Clem, Senara,' said Martha. 'Can you imagine?'

'I'd just feel better if there was one more person around,' said Felicity. 'Someone sensible and grounded. Someone who knows the area.'

'I've lived in the area for an awfully long time,' said Martha. Felicity ignored her.

'So, would you?' she said. 'When my brother said no, Martha suggested asking you. We'd compensate you for your time, so you don't need to walk these dogs while you're here, unless you're committed to it. Molly and co. are also welcome, of course. I just feel it wouldn't be wise to leave Clemmie by herself.'

'Even though I'm nearly seventeen.'

'And despite the fact that I appear to have survived the past few years without you coming down at all,' said Martha.

'In spite of all that,' Felicity agreed. 'I'd be so much happier.' She lowered her voice to a stage whisper. 'You're the only person they both like, to be honest. Would you see if your mother agrees?'

Before I could reply, Felicity and the others dashed off to carry on packing. Clem got back into the pool. Molly tugged at her lead, and Martha told me to let her off.

'She might do anything, though,' I said, pulling Molly back.

'Exactly! I hope she jumps into the pool.'

I grinned at Martha and did it. I, of all people, knew how secure the boundaries were around Cliff House.

'Do you want me to make you another drink?' I was aware that this was not my kitchen, but I'd made Martha many cups of tea over the past six months.

'Yes, please, dear. Felicity always gives me coffee but, as you know, I don't really drink it any more.' She smiled. 'She's quite evangelical about her coffee so she tends to forget.'

I walked into the kitchen, which was enormous, with a massive wooden table and every kind of gadget you could imagine on heavy wooden surfaces. It smelled of something garlicky and rich, something that would take ages to cook and be lovely. I pushed the big metal doorstop with my foot, to keep the door to the courtyard open.

It was like a restaurant kitchen, big and scary with pans hanging down and massive chopping boards. Still, it had a kettle, and I saw an open packet of biscuits on the side.

I popped my head back outside. 'Biscuit?'

'You know it,' said Martha.

I found a lemon in an overflowing fruit bowl and cut a slice of it, hoping I was allowed. Then I put the drink and four Hobnobs on a plate in front of her.

'So my job is to look after you?' I said quietly with a little grin. 'I didn't see this coming.'

She raised her eyebrows. 'You know what they say: "don't kill Grandma".'

I bit back a smile. 'I don't think you're meant to know they say that.' I paused. 'Josie says it's one of those phrases where a comma changes the meaning. I can't remember what it's called. Like "don't eat, Grandad".'

'"Don't kill, Grandma"?' She laughed. 'Dark. I like it. Bring Josie to meet me, will you? I like the sound of her.'

'Of course. If you like.'

'They're all being very nice to me. They can't have me dying on them until they know for sure what's in the will.' She flashed me a wicked grin.

'You're an evil genius.'

'I'm using the tools at my disposal,' she said. 'And, when you get to my age, you'll find you don't have that many left.' She sipped her tea. 'Thank you, dear. You're the only person who gets this right.'

'You're welcome.'

'Felicity's putting you in the yellow room. Best room in the house, in my opinion. It's got the view on two sides.' She gestured, indicating the sea and then the coastal path. 'It was my first bedroom here. She's already made up the bed. That's how much we hoped you'd say yes.'

'I've never even been upstairs,' I said. 'All I know of this house is the kitchen, the garden and the pool. And the downstairs loo. And that's a lot more than I thought I'd ever see.'

She gave me a look. 'Don't forget about the garden in winter.' She put a finger to her lips.

I forced myself not to think about the bone under the camellias. I tried to mirror Martha's wicked smile.

They left a while later in a flurry of taxis, suitcases and rules. Jackson was furious, but he didn't say anything. He frowned at Clem and got into the back of the cab. If he'd been in a cartoon, there would have been spiky waves of anger coming off him. I wondered whether Felicity was looking at his colours, and if so what they were.

Dylan looked sad and closed off. Felicity kept dashing back into the house to get more things, checking how hot it was in Hong Kong in July, and saying things like, 'Bother! Can we use the cashpoints out there, Dyl?'

Martha climbed in for a lift back down the drive, and I promised to call in on my way home.

Felicity jumped out of the car one last time and made us walk out of earshot of Martha before saying: 'Three big rules, girls.' She counted on her fingers. 'One: don't kill Grandma. She has to be alive when we come back or there'll be hell to pay. Two: have Senara's friends over if you want, but no more than three or so at a time, and no one but you two overnight. Three: absolutely no parties. Understood? Oh and, Senara, these are for you.' She pressed something cold into my hand. 'The big one's for the gate, and the Yale one is for the courtyard door. So you don't have to get Clem to buzz you in and out. You can come and go as you please. And there's this.' She took an envelope out of her pocket and closed my other hand round it.

I put the keys in my shorts pocket. 'Thank you.' I didn't know what to do with the envelope so I just kept hold of it and didn't even look down.

She jumped back into the car and finally they left.

Molly was tearing round the garden, and I knew I'd been out with her longer than usual, but I couldn't quite bear to leave, not now. Clem dived straight back into the pool. As soon as her back was turned, I checked the envelope: Felicity was paying me £300 in cash to live here.

'Come and swim with me, Senni!'

'I need to take Molly home before she destroys your garden. I'll be back, though. And then I'm diving straight into that pool.'

She pouted. 'You're leaving me on my own! I thought you were my *companion*!'

'You're welcome to come.'

She lay on her back and stared up at the sky. 'You're all right, actually.' Then she sat up straight. 'If I came with you, could I meet your mum?'

I checked the time. 'She's at work.'

'Nah, then.'

I picked up the lead and looked for Molly, but she had run out of sight, and in the end I found her in the distant corner of the garden, scrabbling at the loose earth in the camellia bed. She was like a dog in a cartoon, with earth flying up behind her. I ran over and pulled her away, realizing with horror what she might be going to find in there, but her head was right down in the surprisingly deep hole she'd made. She looked as if she was going to end up in it, nose first.

I knew there were bones there. We'd found one before. I had to get her away.

'Come *on*!' I tugged her collar, but she pulled back. 'Molly! Stop it! Molly!'

Molly finally emerged from the hole with a long stick in her mouth.

I knew, though, that it wasn't a stick.

It wasn't the bone I'd found before because she was digging in a different patch of earth. This bone was longer and thicker and looked less ambiguous.

She pulled it out by its end, then dropped it on the grass and looked at me, delighted with herself.

I stepped forward, my hand shaking to take it. I could just put it back, cover it up, like Josie had with the other one.

My legs went strange, and I had to sit on the grass.

Molly snatched it up in her mouth and trotted across the garden.

I ran after her.

8

Josie had an afternoon off work, and she'd been looking forward to taking Lucy's dog to the beach with Senara. But Senara had gone, and now she didn't really know what to do. She decided to sit on the doorstep with a book.

When she went in to get it, though, she found her mum sitting at the kitchen table, staring at her phone. Josie was instantly alert.

'Are you OK?'

'Yes,' said Mum.

The silence hung there for a while. Josie noticed that the room smelled a bit weird and thought she'd better go through the fridge and cupboards later. She opened the window, which took a shove as she hadn't thought to do that for maybe a year.

'Tea?'

Mum shook her head, but then she nodded.

Josie popped tea bags into a couple of mugs and grabbed the just-boiled kettle. She was about to say, 'Has something happened?' when Mum started speaking.

'I had a message,' she said, and stopped. Josie's mind jumped around all over the place. Something medical? Grandad?

Uncle Andy was coming back? *Please, please, please, please be that.*

She held her breath.

'You probably don't remember.' Mum's voice was quiet, creaky. She didn't use it often these days. 'But I have a brother. He went away a long time ago. You've never met him.'

The kettle shook so much that Josie had to put it down.

This was it.

It was actually happening.

Uncle Andy had got her letters. He was coming back so Josie could go to university.

Something inside her shifted; it was like the first rays of sunrise. Life was changing.

She worked hard on using a normal voice.

'I do remember.' She kept her voice steady. 'I mean, I remember you talking about him. He sends postcards from Bangkok every Christmas. I like them.'

'Yes, of course. Well, I had a message from a man in Thailand. On my Facebook account. A very kind message. Saying he was Andy's friend and, well, letting me know that Andy had been ill, and then he died. Some months ago, it seems. But this gentleman, he's Australian he says, and he remembered that Andy talked about having a sister. So . . .' Her voice trailed off.

'No!'

Josie's voice rang round the kitchen. She hit the worktop so hard that everything on it clattered. Mum didn't notice. She was wrapped up in her own thoughts.

Oh God! Mum. How would this affect her? That was more important right now, than how Josie felt.

'It makes no difference really. He left a long time ago, and I knew he wasn't coming back. I never expected more than those cards. I was surprised really that he even did that.'

Josie looked at her. She was nodding, over and over again, lost in an internal monologue.

No. Nonononononono.

'Mum, he can't be dead. He can't be. Not Uncle Andy.'

The sun set. Winter arrived. Everything turned to dust and crumbled. Mum's face crinkled. She was confused.

'Josie, darling. It's OK. It doesn't make any difference to anything whatsoever. We'll carry on exactly the same.'

Josie wiped her eyes with her sleeve. Mum didn't get it at all.

She managed to make them each a cup of tea and then had to stop pretending she wasn't crying because she couldn't hide it. Even when Gareth dumped her, she'd managed to shield Mum, but this time she couldn't.

For the rest of her life she'd be filling in impossible Universal Credit and PIP forms and appealing when the payments were taken away. She'd be working multiple jobs and busking (not so far removed, really, from begging) for enough cash to buy a tin of soup and a loaf of bread. If she was going to work properly for A levels, she would have to go back to the food bank.

As Mum had said, everything would carry on exactly the same. The doors slammed, one after the other. No university. No new place. No new people. Pentrellis all her life, hemmed in by thousands of miles of ocean and one small escape route to the east that was blocked to her. Being a carer all her life. Working as many jobs as she could just to scrape the money together, forever. Her friends would leave and start their new, real lives, and she'd be here, not through choice but because there was no one else.

She sat next to Mum and let the tears drip down her face. Then she took a heaving breath, put her head on her arms on the table, and let it all out, sobbing and gasping. It was the first time since she was about eleven that she'd let Mum see her struggling.

'Josie! Darling. Oh, it's OK.'

Josie shook her head, unable to speak. It wasn't OK. Mum moved her chair closer and patted her back. It never happened this way round, and it felt wrong. Josie cried for a while and then wiped her eyes. Mum handed her a tea towel. That was, it turned out, one of the sources of the smell. It was disgusting, but she used it anyway and threw it at the washing machine.

'Can I see the message about Uncle Andy?' Josie managed to say.

'If you want to. But, darling? I don't think I understand why this means so much to you.'

She shook her head and took Mum's phone when she handed it to her.

It was a Facebook message from someone called Mike Clark. Mum had a Facebook account, like everyone her age, but she rarely used it.

Dear Angie,

I'm not sure if this is the right person. Please accept my apologies if not.

My name's Mike and I'm an Australian expat in Thailand. I was friends with Andy Teague for the last few years. He always said he had a sister in Cornwall and as far as I can see this might be you. Forgive me if not.

I'm writing because I think you probably don't know the sad news that Andy died a few months ago. He had cancer. He found out not long before it took him. His friends out here held a service for him, but I knew he didn't have much contact with his family back home, just sending a card at Xmas, and I realized you might not know so thought I'd try to track you down.

I'm sorry to be the bearer of bad tidings. Again, apologies if I have the wrong person and also if you already know.

My sympathies. Andy was a great friend to many of us over here.

Mike

Josie read it over and over again. She looked at Mike Clark's profile, but it was pretty much locked. She checked through Mum's profile, but she hadn't posted on it for five years, and even then it had just been a repost of a charity thing. Andy didn't have an account, but Mum's was in the name Angela Mary Teague, and it said 'Pentrellis, Cornwall' under her name, so she'd clearly been easy to find.

Should they get a death certificate? Could she ask the British Embassy or something? Those things cost money, though, and what was the point? Why did they need one?

When Gareth dumped her, it had been bad. This was a million times worse. Josie felt the world crumbling around her. She was a dinosaur, and the meteor had hit. It was over. All her dreams, all her plans.

'Josie?' Mum was clearly baffled.

Josie pulled her head up and looked at her. Mum was wearing jogging bottoms and an old T-shirt that had once been white and was now pinkish-grey because Josie wasn't very good at separating the washing. Her hair was pulled back into a ponytail. She looked both younger and much older than fifty-one.

Josie was going to have to say something. Could she do it? Could she explain?

'I always thought,' she said, her voice husky, 'that he might come back one day.' She didn't say the rest.

Mum was silent. Josie went to her room.

There was, as always, a partly written letter on her desk, and she tore it in half and then into pieces, and carried on ripping until it was confetti, and threw it all over the room. She'd hoover it up one day. She sat on her bed and stared at her phone, wishing she could talk to Senara. If anyone would say the right thing, it would be her best friend. She needed her. The need overwhelmed her, and she sent a message without stopping to think.

Are you free?

She waited, imagining Senara splashing in that pool with Clementine Parker, seduced by Cliff House. There was no way she could let this be shared with Clem, who she didn't trust an inch. She had no idea why Senara couldn't see that she was being played. She wasn't sure what Clem's motivation was, but it was something. She hadn't actually suddenly decided she wanted to be friends with Senara. It must be lovely for Senara to think that, but it wasn't true. Josie had tried to tell her that, but Senara didn't want to hear it, and it just ended with Josie feeling mean.

Josie remembered, even if Senara didn't, the way she'd felt when Clem had scoffed at them and called them peasants.

When the reply came, it was worse than she'd expected.

Not right now sorry.
Felicity asked me to stay
at cliff house with Clem
bc they have to go to HK
urgently. I'll be here for a
week or so 😌 come visit?

It took Josie ages to work out what 'HK' even meant. She actually had to google it. So Clem's parents had gone to

Hong Kong, and Senara had moved in. Senara, Josie's best friend, was lost to Clementine for the rest of this summer, at least. Uncle Andy was dead, and Clem had won.

Josie tried to imagine having the freedom to go and live somewhere else for a while on a whim. Then she tried to stop imagining it.

She switched her phone off. There was no one to turn to. Gareth might have got it, but he was with Maya. Or was he with Clem now? Josie wasn't sure, and either way it didn't matter.

Of course her best friend would find the rich girl with the huge house and swimming pool more fun than Josie. In the same way that her boyfriend had found the graceful ballerina more interesting. In the same way that her dad, whoever he was, had found every single thing in the whole of the rest of the world more appealing than his daughter.

In the way that her uncle Andy had found Thailand more interesting than his ill sister and struggling niece and had stayed there until he died.

She threw her phone on the floor, then hoped it was all right and picked it up to check. It was a second-hand iPhone with her old sim in it. She didn't get much data, but that was OK; as long as there was Wi-Fi, she was the same as everyone else. However, this was actually Maya's old phone, and that meant Josie didn't want it any more.

She remembered Maya giving it to her. She had done it so sweetly, back in the middle of Year Ten. She'd known Josie had the worst phone because she'd never been able to find the money to pay for decent phones for herself and her mum. She remembered Maya taking her aside as they walked to the bus stop and saying, in a fake-casual voice, 'Oh, Josie? I don't suppose you'd want my old handset? You'd be doing me a favour. It's just an iPhone 8. Save me the bother of working out what I'm meant to do with it when I don't need it any more.'

Their eyes had met. At the time Josie had been more grateful than she could possibly say. A year later Maya had stolen her boyfriend. Josie was still using her phone, and she knew she had to keep it really. Mum used one that Jenna had given her. They were both charity cases.

Josie spent a full hour picturing what it might be like to die in a Thai hospital, and trying not to imagine her own future. One day Mum would die too, and then Josie would probably be old, with no money and no qualifications. What would she do then?

It had been so much fun when they'd climbed that fence to find the drone. They'd been together, united by curiosity and by the fact that they hated feeling like the village peasants while the big house was empty. Those people treated their palace as a playground, and they not only left it locked up, but they also put barbed wire along the top of the fence and cameras all over the place and spikes on top of their gates. They were awful people, the worst.

All that Josie and her friends had wanted to do was to take some footage and see what was in there.

Josie had been burning with rage when she saw the garden up close. She'd felt brilliant about trespassing. How dare these people think that they owned the trees, the flowers, the grass, the dead fox? How dare they shut everyone out, even though they weren't using it?

Senara had taken the rap when the old lady caught her, and Gareth hadn't really been interested in going back, but Josie had been loads more times after that. She'd taken sandwiches and eaten them beside the pool. She'd walked round all the parts of the garden that were out of sight of the cottage, imagining herself a Du Maurier heroine. She had been working on a plan to disable the cameras and alarm systems and break into the actual house when the reality of GCSE year kicked in, and she'd come to her senses. She'd never told anyone, not even Senara.

And now Senara had switched sides. Clem was fun – even Josie had to admit that. But that didn't mean Senara had to move in with her. Josie pictured her cycling up the drive. Walking in through that front door.

She had to get out of here. She had to. She needed to get away from this village, from West Cornwall, from everything. It was the one thing she wanted, the thing she couldn't have.

Could she and Mum move somewhere else? What would that change, though?

There was a tap on the door. Mum hadn't been into Josie's room for years.

'Darling?' Her voice was shaky.

'It's OK, Mum.' Josie stood up. 'Let's watch some TV, yeah?'

'No, no. I'm trying to work out why you're upset about Andy. It's me, isn't it? You thought one day he might help you by looking after me. Is it that?' She waited for an answer, but Josie couldn't give it. 'Oh, darling. I'm so sorry. I'm so, so sorry. I don't know how to . . . you do so much.'

Mum was distraught, and there was only one thing to do when that happened.

Josie pulled herself together. She put on her best face.

'I just liked the idea of having family.' She put everything she had into acting this because she had a horrible feeling about what kind of solution Mum might alight on in a dark moment if she thought she was a burden. 'I hoped he'd come back and tell us all about Thailand one day. I always thought about him. I wanted to meet him because we don't really have any family now, do we? I was curious. But that's OK. I mean, I never met him, and I never will. I got upset about nothing.'

Mum nodded and turned to go to the living room. Josie followed, but Mum stopped abruptly in the hallway, and Josie nearly walked into her back.

'He wasn't a nice person,' Mum said without looking round. 'Don't wonder about him, darling. Don't. He's not worth it. I'm not sad he's dead. I'm – well, I always thought . . .'

'You always thought what?'

'Oh,' said Mum. 'Nothing.' She paused. Josie waited. 'I know everyone has heard about Lucy's sister. Rachel.'

Josie nodded. Rachel's ghost was part of village folklore. 'Of course.'

'They all think she came to some terrible end, but I've never been so sure. Andy was spending time with her before he went to Thailand. I heard them talking, saw them together. Rachel was different from Lucy. She was kind of a rebel, and their parents were so proper. Their dad was the vicar. I don't think things were good for her at home. And she disappeared at the same time that Andy went to Thailand.' She took a deep breath in. 'I always wondered if she went with him. If that's where she's been all this time.'

This was a swerve. 'Mum – she can't have done. Didn't they have a huge search? If she'd caught a plane, they'd have found her details. Did you tell the police you thought she'd gone with him?'

Mum shook her head. 'Honestly, darling? I was relieved that he'd gone away. I didn't want to stir things up. I thought that if Rachel had gone too, she'd be back at some point. Oh, let's not even think about it. Andy wasn't a good guy. That's all. He would never have come to our rescue, and if he had turned up I wouldn't have wanted him in the house.'

Josie followed her into the living room and sat next to her. The foundations of her world were shifting. She could tell Mum hadn't finished talking, so she waited. Minutes ticked by.

'He preyed on girls. My friends. Rachel was a small part of it. It was awful. Mention Andy Teague to anyone who was around back then and look at their face. He was a creep, and I was glad to see him go. So don't be sad. Be happy. I hated to think of him in Thailand, what he might have been doing out there. If Rachel did go with him, I hope they parted ways quickly.'

Josie shuddered. She thought of the letters she'd written. She wanted to curl up and die.

'Thanks for telling me,' she said, and her voice sounded tight and strange. 'I wish you'd told me before. All this time I've been building him up in my head.'

Mum smiled. She actually smiled.

'I'm glad he's dead,' she said. Her smile was genuine. 'Isn't that awful? But I am. I'm glad.'

'It's not awful.'

The walls were closing in, but Josie didn't think about it. Mum was happy. She was genuinely happy. Maybe Uncle Andy, the fucking bastard, would save her after all.

She took her cue from Mum. Mum's reaction was ten per cent sad because he had still been her brother, and ten per cent guilt at the fact that she was eighty per cent delighted. Josie watched the change in her, and wondered what that man had done.

It was better not to know.

She was going to have to find another plan.

9

Molly was running across the garden with the bone in her mouth. I followed her, as fast as I could, shouting. The afternoon sun was hot on my head.

'Clem – the dog dug up a bone.'

Clem swam to the side of the pool. She was like a mermaid.

'Like a dog in a cartoon! Cool. Where did she find it?'

'By the camellias.'

It's not cool, I wanted to say. *Stop making everything into a joke.* I didn't say it because I could never stand up to Clem.

She pulled herself out of the water and squinted into the sun, over at the dog. 'Looks like a stick.'

'It's a bone. Look!' I caught up with Molly and clipped the lead in place, then waited for Clem to come over.

'Wow!' Clementine yanked it out of the dog's mouth and held it up in the sunshine. It was smooth, cracked along the side, long and thick. 'Maybe it's from the plague pits.'

'Plague pits?' I had no idea whether or not she was joking.

'Mum once said there were plague pits up here. I didn't know if she was serious, though. Sometimes she says things because she has a *feeling*, rather than because they're literally facts.'

'It's probably from an animal,' I said. 'Don't you think?' We looked at each other and then back at it. 'Though she did also say there was an old burial ground.'

'It's an animal for sure.' Clem dropped it on the grass and rubbed her wet hair with a towel. 'Mum and Uncle Alex would *so* have had big dogs, or ponies or whatever, and buried them in the garden when they died. They'd *so* have made a pet graveyard.'

'And planted camellia bushes on top.'

Clemmie pointed at me. 'Exactly! Mum would have given her pets names like, I don't know . . . Mr Smiffles. Uncle Alex would have called his . . . Albert Einstein.'

I hoped it was that. 'Shall we just put it back in the ground?'

'I can't be arsed right now. Here – wrap it in this towel and you can stick it in the pool house, and we'll sort it out in the morning, yeah?'

'Yeah,' I said. 'OK.'

I took the towel from Clem and wrapped it round the bone. I wondered, briefly, about a life in which you could sacrifice a fluffy beach towel without thinking about it. I put it on a pile of cushions in the musty pool house, which was actually a shed.

'I'm going to get Molly out of your garden before she does something worse. And then grab my stuff from home, and come straight back.'

*

'Absolutely no way, Senara.' Mum was just back from work, still in her sensible suit. She put her work bag down on the table and kicked off her shoes. 'I don't like you spending all your time there as it is. I can't have you *staying* there. Just – no. Trust me. You can't go and live up there. Hanging out in that kitchen . . .'

I'd had a feeling she'd be like this. '*Why*, though? I know you hate the house, and you hate the family, but you've never told me *why*. How am I meant to understand?'

'I don't hate Martha.'

This was the first time I'd heard Mum call her that.

'So you just hate Felicity? What did she do to you?'

'I am not getting into it, Senara.'

I was trying to keep calm. The fact was I was going to stay up there anyway, no matter what she said. I made an effort to sound reasonable.

'I'm sixteen. All I want to do is spend a few days swimming in the pool and hanging out with my friend, and you can't stop me. It's all arranged, and Felicity's already left, and she's paid me to look after Martha, so I have to anyway.'

Mum looked at me for a long time. Her face was impossible to read.

'Fine,' she said in the end. 'You're right. I can't stop you. I can just tell you I wish you'd listen to me and stay away. Be careful, and don't –' She stopped.

'Don't what?'

'I don't know,' she said. 'Just be careful. That's all. Take care. Check in with me every day. Bloody Felicity.'

I shoved the things I thought I'd need into three bags, and left quickly. Mum gave me a tight smile and looked as if she was going to cry. I turned back at the end of the street, and went to hug her. I had no idea what this was about, but I was feeling guilty about upsetting her now that I'd won.

I soon got over it. My bedroom, 'the yellow room', was on the corner of Cliff House, filled with light that made the pale yellow walls shine. Here I had a double bed with a yellow-and-white flower-patterned duvet cover. The floor was polished floorboards and rugs. There was a tiny bathroom attached; I literally had my own en suite. I put my bathroom stuff away, my clothes in the chest of drawers. I opened both windows, and a blast of sunshine fell across my bed, warming the duvet.

Plague pits, burial grounds, bones poking out of the earth.

I pushed them all out of my head.

Mum was being so weird.

I pushed that out too.

I stepped into a dress, an old one of Clem's from the bag that Felicity had given me earlier. It went down to my knees (so it would have been much shorter on Clem), and was patterned in pink and brown flowers, with a halter-neck. I'd never worn dresses, and I wondered whether to fight my instinct to rip this one off and change into something safe.

I looked in the full-length mirror and saw someone new looking back. My hair just touched my shoulders and I could barely manage to tie it back, but I attempted a tiny ponytail. It looked stupid, so I gave up and let it hang there.

Dresses didn't suit me. I'd always worn trousers to school and shorts all summer. I reached up to undo it.

Then I forced myself not to. I would keep it on for a bit and see how it felt. One day I would stumble upon 'my style'. Until then I had to give everything a chance.

I sat on the bed and took a moment to contemplate this new world. Hanging out with Clem was proving to be a learning curve for both of us. A few days ago she'd looked up from her phone and said, 'Senni, do you ride?'

And I said, 'Yeah, you know that. I always come over on my bike.'

'Not your bike! I mean horses.'

'Of course I don't ride *horses*!'

At that point she'd shown me a load of photos of herself in Hyde Park in London, wearing a tweed jacket and jodhpurs, sitting on a massive horse. I'd had to pretend I hadn't seen most of them already when I was stalking her Insta. She went to a school that cost over twenty-five thousand pounds a year; Mum's job as office manager paid twenty-three.

The fact that Clem's education was apparently worth more than my mother's job made me feel sick. I'd known there was a gulf between us, but this was obscene. Clem was from her world, and I was from mine, and those things were accidents of birth.

I made a point of never letting her assume I'd been to ballet, or that I'd done Latin, or fencing. I never pretended that my options for buying clothes extended further than Shein, Primark in Truro and the charity shops of Penzance.

Clem was wearing a tiny playsuit, and was stretched out on a sunlounger looking like someone from a magazine. I felt her world pulling me in. It was magical. Nothing seemed to matter up here.

'Hey,' I said. Clem propped herself up on her elbows.

'Oh, you look cute!' she said. 'Like a little doll.'

I did not look like a *little doll*: what she meant was that I was short.

'I look dorky.'

'No – adorable. Adorkable. So you have to help me plan this party. We'll need your friends, Senni – Josie and Gareth and the rest, plus everyone else you can rustle up. Do you know anyone who's eighteen?'

It took me a moment to catch up.

'Clem! We're not allowed to have a party. It's rule three.'

'Oh, Senni! She'll be, like, forty thousand miles away and she'll never know. We've got house, pool, heatwave, and no adults except Gran. Hello? So my friends managed to get train tickets to come straight down, and they'll be here tomorrow. Main event on Saturday? That gives us a couple of days to prepare and time to clear up afterwards.'

Her friends.

I felt as if she'd kicked me in the stomach.

'I guess it's all going to be party time really, but Saturday's the big night. Can you find someone to buy booze, though? We can just drink Mum and Dyl's stash until then.'

I looked down the drive, to the point where it went round the corner. Clem's friends were arriving the next day. I felt my new life slipping through my fingers.

I remembered my envelope of cash, and the rules.

'We really can't have a party,' I said. 'Your mum trusts me.'

She swept my objection away.

'What are you going to do about Martha?'

Clem gave me a little smile. 'Don't worry about Gran. I've invited her down here for an *apéro*.' My face must have betrayed me. 'Aperitif. A glass of champagne. I got some snacks from that place in the village.' I smiled: *that place in the village* was the Spar. 'So she'll be happy with us, no matter what we do.'

I nodded. I was pretty sure Martha wouldn't stop a party.

'So, I've added you to the group chat and made you an admin. Can you add Josie and, literally, everyone else you know who's cool? Anyone who's not going to trash the place. More the merrier. They might need to bring some drinks, though. And swimming things! Put that.'

I sat on a lounger and looked at my phone: Clem had, indeed, added me and Gareth to a chat that was called 'PARTY BY THE SEA ☀🌊🥳'.

Her friends were arriving tomorrow. That was the worst bit. I didn't want to be the only local person in a house full of Londoners. I wouldn't know how to be. I'd have to go home if that happened, and Mum would be pleased, but I couldn't because Felicity had given me all that money to stay here and be the responsible one.

I lay back and closed my eyes. I was here now, and that was what mattered. I tried to breathe deeply, to focus on the moment.

I thought about that bone, imagining a big dog rotting away underground. I pictured its eyes rotting, its ears, its tail . . . everything, until all that was left were bones. And a dog was the best-case scenario . . .

When I tuned back in, Clem was on the phone.

'Yeah,' she was saying. 'She's asleep, but Gran's coming in a minute. We can have our first party meeting after that.'

When she finished the call, which I surmised was to Gareth, I said, 'Are your friends staying all week?' I kept my voice as casual as I could. I supposed if they were travelling tomorrow then at least they'd arrive late in the day.

'They'll go home when Mum calls to say she's at Hong Kong airport,' Clem said. She stood up, and I followed her into the kitchen. 'So, do you know what time the sleeper train gets in?'

'Sleeper train?' I knew it existed, but I didn't know anything about it. 'Morning, I guess?'

'Yeah. I told them to get a cab from Penzance.'

I hardly dared ask, but I knew I had to.

'How many?' I was imagining ten people rocking up. Twenty. A convoy of taxis. Me, edged right out, slinking back to my bedroom at home, returning Felicity's cash.

Clementine started getting glasses out of a cupboard. 'Two. Rik and Meg. They come as a pair. They're gorgeous, and you'll love them. Honestly, they're inseparable. Adorable. Finish each other's sentences kind of thing. The cutest. Don't tell your mum they're coming. Can you put these on a tray?'

I looked around for one.

'Even if I did tell her,' I said, 'she'd never tell Felicity.'

'Yeah. I need to meet Jenna. Can I?'

I winced, certain that Mum would hate to meet Clem.

'Where are the trays?' I said instead of answering.

1988

Felicity and Alex waved their parents off and sat on the stone doorstep waiting for them to come back for things they'd forgotten, which they did twice. When an hour had gone by and they hadn't returned, they looked at each other and grinned.

'Could this be . . . ?' said Felicity in a quiet voice.

'Looks like,' said Alex.

'Why does it feel different?' she said. 'They've always let us do what we like. It shouldn't make any difference.'

'Because we know they're going to be abroad. It's just us.'

'And Grandma,' she said, but Alex shook his head.

'Not Grandma. She's meeting Betty in Exeter. They're going to a show and staying all weekend. So, right now at least, it's just us. Is Jenna coming over?'

Felicity nodded and suppressed a smile.

'Grandma's so cool,' she said. 'I hope I'm like her when I'm old. You'd never know she's nearly sixty.' She paused. 'I heard Dad say she never stays still because she can't bear to be alone with her thoughts.'

Alex stood up. 'Dad talks a lot of shit, Flicky. I think

Grandma's incredibly happy with her thoughts. Anyway, she's not here, and we're in charge. Music?'

Soon they had the ghetto blaster outside, and it was blasting out 'Faith' as loudly as it would go, and the sun was shining and everything was amazing. Alex poured them each half a tumbler of gin, without tonic water, so it would burn their throats as it went down and make them feel warm and daring, though he only had a couple of sips of his because he was going to drive to the shops later.

Felicity wanted to stretch out and listen to music and swim and relax for three days. She wanted to bake brownies and eat them in the sun. Jenna would come. Alex's friends could come, if they wanted. Rachel could too. Mainly, though, this was a weekend for her to hang out with her brother and her best friend, and she didn't care how low-level that was. The air was twinkling at her.

Felicity and Alex had always been close. Alex was everything she wasn't, and she was everything he wasn't. She thought that was why they got on better than other siblings. Together they made a complete unit.

The sun was shining, even though it wasn't hot. The house was full of food. They had a freezing-cold swimming pool. There was nothing they needed to do except exist.

'Swim?' said Felicity.

Later they set off for Tesco in Penzance to buy alcohol and chocolate. Felicity half wanted to stay by the pool, lazing around on her own, but the idea of being alone – without her parents, without Alex, without Grandma in her cottage – made her feel uneasy. It was more fun to be in the passenger seat, to choose the snacks together. They bought more junk food and drink than they could possibly consume, and headed back.

'Who's that?' said Felicity as they approached the end of the drive. There was a man there looking at the gates. She was glad they'd closed them as they'd left.

'A discombobulated walker?' said Alex. 'Bet it's one of those people who think the coastal path should go through our garden.'

As they got closer, though, the man changed into someone horribly familiar.

The creepy man from the bus stop. Andy. She recognized him first by his colours, his greyish aura that looked like a bruise, the little triangles. She shrank back in her seat. Triangles were bad.

Jenna had said he was going out with Rachel. Felicity hoped he wasn't. That man was at least twenty-five. Rachel was seventeen. Andy had straggly long hair, and when he looked at Felicity his eyes were sharp and spiky.

Alex stopped for her to do the gates, but she didn't open her door. She leaned into the car, away from the man.

'What?' said Alex. He looked at her, and then at the stranger. 'Oh right. Sure. I'll do it.' He paused. 'That's your bus-stop guy?' She gave a tiny nod.

He left the engine running. Felicity watched through his open door as he said, 'Hi – you OK?' to the man.

Then she held her breath as Andy said, 'Yes. Sorry. I was

just walking this way. And I wasn't sure which was the path to the beach.'

'It's that way along the road, round the corner, and there's a track that takes you all the way down,' said Alex with practised ease.

'Thanks.' He didn't leave, though. 'You're the kids who live here.'

'Yeah.'

'Brother and sister?'

Alex gave a nod and got back in the car. He drove it a few metres forward, then stopped, got out again and closed the gate behind him. He put the chain through and locked it with the padlock. The man was still standing there, looking at them. Felicity watched in her wing mirror until they went round the bend in the drive, and out of sight.

That man lived in the village. He knew the way to the beach.

10

Josie had worked at the bookshop in the morning, and ever since she got home she'd been online.

It was hard to find missing-person reports from the eighties because they hadn't had the internet, but she was beginning to piece it together. She only had her phone, so she sat on her bed and went as deeply into vintage internet as she could.

There had been a huge campaign in West Cornwall called 'FIND RACHEL'. Rachel Thomas had been the vicar's daughter, and so the community had been shocked by her disappearance back in the summer of 1988. Josie had found a PDF of a front-page local newspaper appeal by her parents, who looked sweet and sad and out of their depth, calling her their 'precious girl' and saying 'someone out there knows where she is'. Even though she'd been seventeen, everyone had spoken about the case as if she'd been a snatched toddler.

Josie had to enlarge the text to read it. At the end of the article was a quote from 'Rachel's best mate, Felicity Campion-Roberts', which said, 'We're all shocked about what's happened, and, Rachel, if you're out there, we hope you're safe.'

Felicity Campion-Roberts.

Clem's mum. Rachel's best friend?

As far as Josie could tell, Rachel Thomas had never got in touch, and no trace of her had ever been found. She certainly hadn't come home, and so, over the decades, the disappearing vicar's daughter had morphed into a village legend. Poor Lucy must have been about fourteen at the time. Josie couldn't imagine what the whole thing had been like for her. What it was still like now. Never knowing.

Clem's mum had been her best friend. Rachel had been hanging around with Josie's uncle. Did that mean Felicity had known Uncle Andy too?

There was no trace of Andy Teague online. It would have been so much easier if they'd had the internet back then. Josie carried on searching. She looked for their three names together, scrolled through pages and pages of useless results.

Mum knocked on the door, and Josie shoved her phone under the duvet as she appeared in the doorway.

'I'm going to make an appointment to see the doctor, Jose. Ask if there's more we can do. I feel . . . I don't know. I feel that it might be time to try something different.'

Josie stood up and made herself smile. They'd been here before; there was no way she was getting excited.

Rachel Thomas and Andy Teague. Felicity Campion-Roberts. Mum. It was swirling round her head.

Her obsession with Uncle Andy had been refocused on

to this. She needed time to clear her mind. She needed to offload.

She said, 'Is it OK if I go out to see Senara? I'll come back and make dinner.'

'Of course! I can make dinner, darling.'

'Don't worry. It's only soup and bread. I won't be long. I just want to –'

'Have a nice time with your friends! You need to do more of that. I'm fine. I really am.'

There *was* a slightly different energy to Mum since the news about Andy. It was bizarre to see her genuinely happy that her only brother was dead.

She kissed Mum's cheek, realizing she hadn't done that for a while. Mum pulled her in for a hug. 'Have a lovely time,' she said.

Josie stood at the gates of Cliff House and tried to get Rachel Thomas out of her head. Just how creepy had her uncle been? She looked at the gates and nothing happened because she didn't press the buzzer.

It wasn't the big house with its swimming pool that put her off. It wasn't the weirdness of walking through the gates when she had climbed the fence so many times. It wasn't the fact that Senara wasn't expecting her. It was Clem Parker.

Josie didn't trust Clem an inch. For one thing, Clem had marched across the beach and stolen her best friend. Senara had been seduced by the pool and the ease of it all – and had gone willingly. Josie couldn't just walk in there and tell

Senara that Andy was dead, because now that she'd seen this other life Senara might not care.

And Clem might laugh.

In fact, Josie was pretty sure that Clem *would* laugh if she discovered that Josie was devastated by the death of someone she'd never met, thousands of miles away; someone who she now knew had been a creep anyway, someone who, according to Mum, had fled the country at the exact same time as the village's famous missing girl had disappeared.

At the bottom of the drive leading up to Cliff House her legs stopped working, and she sat down. Uncle Andy would never have saved her, and now he was dead. Josie had grabbed on to him as a lifebelt years ago. Now, not only did she have nothing, but she'd never had anything. It had been a mirage in the first place, a lifebelt made of paper, of string, of sugar.

'It's Josie, isn't it?'

She looked up, and saw Mrs Roberts leaning on a walking frame, peering over the fence.

'Sorry!' She jumped up and stared into the lined face, alarmed. 'Sorry. I'll go. I didn't mean to disturb you, or trespass or whatever.'

'You look terrible.'

Josie stepped away. 'Thanks!'

'Well, you do. Come in, and you can tell me what's up.'

'Seriously?'

'Yes, seriously! I can't have waifs and strays despairing outside my home. If there are waifs and strays, they belong inside the house. Come on! In!'

Josie couldn't think of a way to say no, so she followed Mrs Roberts into her cottage.

'The thing with Clementine,' said Mrs Roberts. Martha: that was what Josie was supposed to call her now. 'The thing is, she's spoiled. It's not her fault. I'm sure she has her own insecurities and worries, not that she'd ever let me see them. But she expects everything to be handed to her, and so far it always has been. One day it won't be, but she can't imagine that. She's beautiful, and rich, and realistically she's never going to have to worry about where the next meal's coming from, is she?'

Josie leaned back. This sofa was insanely comfortable. She'd never been in here before, and the inside of the cottage was surprising. She liked the abstract art on the walls, the photos everywhere, the childish line drawings of people. She liked the smell of Earl Grey and cleaning spray.

'Lucky her,' she said. She knew she couldn't say anything too bad about Clem because she was Martha's family; she was getting as close as she dared.

Martha seemed to be looking into her soul. 'Do *you*, Josie? Worry about where the food's coming from?'

Martha was so direct. Her gaze pierced Josie's defences.

'Yeah,' said Josie. 'I've got better at working it out, but sometimes we have to use the food bank. Mum can't work, and I'm at school. We have no income.' She explained the complexities of their financial situation, and Martha listened.

'Shocking,' she said when Josie had finished. 'Those absolute bastards in government. You know, we were running out of money when I met Barney. My life could have been – should have been . . .' She drifted off and didn't finish her sentence.

Josie did feel better, having explained it. When she said it all out loud, she could see that, in spite of everything, she managed.

Martha visibly pulled herself together. 'Josie, my dear, I'm so sorry you have this burden on you. It shouldn't be that way. People shouldn't slip through the cracks like this. Do you like pizza? Does your mother?'

'. . . Yes?'

'Hey, Siri!' Martha placed a Domino's order for that evening, surprisingly efficiently, checking with Josie what she and her mum liked best. 'At least you don't need to worry for tonight. Let me know when I can do that again. I could make it a repeat order once a week. Maybe some supermarket shopping too?'

Josie blinked hard. 'That's the nicest thing anyone's ever done for me,' she said.

She wanted to say more, to tell Martha Roberts everything. She wanted to stay here, to live with her. She had worked so hard to build herself a shell, and now she felt it cracking. She turned away, looked at the drawings on the wall, wondered whether to ask about them. Her mouth trembled.

'It's nothing. As I say, we'll do it regularly. Now, I think I'm expected up at the big house in a moment because my great-granddaughter wants to butter me up, probably so she can have a party. Do you know about a party?'

Josie smiled. This woman didn't miss anything. 'I did get added to a group chat, yeah.'

She wondered, for a moment, whether to ask about Rachel, about Felicity, but before she could work out how to phrase it Martha spoke.

'Will you give me a hand? It's terribly undignified, but I need to get myself on to this God-awful scooter thing. It's outside in the shed.'

Josie reversed the scooter out of the shed, which was fun, helped Martha on to it, and watched her setting off up the drive. This had been surprising.

11

It was nearly seven on Thursday evening, and the light was golden. I was arranging bowls of olives on the table, half listening to Clem talking crap to Gareth.

'Yeah, but it's not just you that get tourists,' she said. 'I mean, hello – London? London's literally one of the tourism hotspots of the whole world. There are *loads* more there than in Cornwall, so you don't need to complain. We don't.'

'But in London you have millions of people,' he pointed out. 'I bet in London you don't notice the tourism as much. Here, right now, it's our entire economy.'

'Oh God, we do notice them, though! They get everywhere. My friend Benjy? Some tourists stopped him and asked him the way to Big Ben, and he told them he actually *was* Big Ben, and showed them his ID. They all had their photos taken with him.'

I'd had enough of listening to this.

'Hey, Clemmie? It's seven. Do we need to fetch Martha?'

'Oh shit,' said Clem. 'Yeah. Right. Senni, can you go and see if Gran needs a hand with her mobility scooter thing? Gaz, can you make it all look nice?'

The air was warm, the pool was sparkling, and there was a table out on the lawn in the shade, covered in lovely food.

'It already looks nice,' Gareth and I said together.

I looked around and saw that the bone wasn't in the pool house any more. It was on the mosaic-topped table.

'But you need to put that out of the way!' I said. 'What's it doing here?'

'Yeah,' said Clem. 'Sorry. I was showing Gaz. Gazzy, can you shove it in a cupboard or something?'

Gazzy.

'Bones in cupboards,' he said. 'Got it.'

Then I said, 'Martha has a mobility scooter?'

'Yep – she keeps it in the shed. She could go down to the village on it if she wanted, but she says it makes her look like an old lady. But she'll ride it up here, and we can feed her champagne and be the most lovely people ever. If she wants to see some life in this place, she can have it.'

'So you want to invite her to the party?' I asked uncertainly.

'God, no! But she'll be able to sit at her window and see everyone arriving, and hear the music, and she'll know that the house is alive, just like she wants it to be, and that I'll keep it that way, so she can change her will back and give it to me after all.'

I hated the way that, as long as Martha's will was sorted, Clem was transparently looking forward to her dying.

I met Martha on her way up the drive. When she saw me approaching, she stuck her legs out on either side of her scooter thing and shouted 'Yee-ha!' like a cowgirl.

I turned and fell into step beside her. 'Nice wheels.'

'I don't use it in public. So undignified.' She sighed and accelerated, so I had to trot to keep up. 'Ridiculous really,' she said. 'It gives me much more agency. I should just do it, shouldn't I? This is better than hobbling round my cottage.'

'How did you manage to get it on the road?'

'An angel helped me.'

I nodded. I supposed she'd had a carer over.

I sat next to Martha under the tree: my job was to 'look after' her because Clem wanted to be the one to present the champagne. Clem didn't understand that Martha would have preferred Clem's wholehearted attention to any amount of Veuve Clicquot.

Martha's skin was papery and a bit see-through. Her hair was perfectly white, and I could see her scalp through it.

'. . . and that Olivia,' she was saying, 'well. She's a piece of work. Who would have seen that coming?'

'Do you think she was hiding her true self for the first part?'

Married at First Sight Australia was our current shared pleasure. We were watching it on catch-up, at approximately the same pace.

'Must have been. She was trying to be like Jules and Cam, and I have to say even I was taken in for a while.'

I wondered whether I would ever be as old as Martha. It was impossible to know, and that was dizzying. Would I be ninety-two, fighting to stay independent, refusing to move into a home or even a flat with a warden? Or would I die before then? I might die when I was sixty, or forty, or twenty, or even . . . sixteen. I shuddered.

Clem came out of the house and popped the cork from a bottle of champagne. It flew away across the garden, landing out of sight in an unnerving echo of our drone.

'How marvellous!' said Martha. 'Gracious me.' She accepted a glass from Clem. 'I know when I'm being buttered up, people. When's the party? Thanks for the champagne. My favourite.'

Gareth hadn't met Martha before, and I could tell he was impressed. We smiled at each other.

Clem laughed out loud and said, 'That's why we love you, Gran.'

'So?'

'Well,' said Clem, looking coquettish, 'we have to make the most of the hot weather, right? We're so lucky to have the pool, and the sea right on our doorstep. It would be a shame not to share it. I actually turned the pool heating off.'

She passed me a glass. I sipped it, and the bubbles prickled my tongue. I'd never had champagne before. I liked it.

'Thank you, Clementine.' Martha held up her glass. 'Chin-chin. Well, you can't have a party without my knowing because your mother has security like Fort Knox around this place. All your guests will have to file past my window.' She gave Gareth and me a quick look. 'Unless they manage to scale the fence. I may be old, but I'm not stupid. I still, praise the Lord, have my marbles.'

Clem gave her a half-smile. 'You sure do. Though no one would get over this fence. It's literally got barbed wire like a prison camp.'

'Definitely, literally impossible,' said Gareth.

I saw Martha half smiling. Clem was instantly alert, wondering what she was missing.

'I don't mind a jot what you do as long as you don't destroy the house,' continued Martha. 'I'd think less of you if you didn't make the most of it, to be honest. Felicity, Alex and –' she flashed a quick look at me – 'their friends certainly would have done, back in the day. So would Leon.'

She had been about to say *Jenna*. I knew she had. I immediately wanted to quiz her, but this wasn't the moment.

'What about you, Mrs Roberts?' said Gareth. 'Would you?'

Martha smiled. 'Gareth, call me Martha. It was different in my day, but, yes: Barney and I would have done. I loved my party frocks, as Senara well knows.' I nodded. 'We entertained here whenever we could manage it. Life is fleeting, and we need to take our pleasures where we can. So, when is it to be?'

Clem narrowed her eyes. 'Is this a trick?'

'It is not.'

'You won't tell Mum?'

Martha mimed zipping her lips. 'All I ask is one thing,' she said, speaking through one corner of her zipped mouth.

I hadn't seen her this happy for ages.

'What?' said Clem.

'You let me come. I want to sit beside the swimming pool and observe. I want to dress up and drink champagne and eat strawberries. I want to watch young people misbehaving, to see them swimming, to listen to the music, even if I don't understand it. To feel like a part of it all. That's what I want. And then I'd like someone to stick me in a wheelbarrow and take me home by ten, and I'll put my earplugs in and go to sleep.'

Clem held out a bowl of crisps. 'We're not putting you in a wheelbarrow, Gran.'

Martha took a crisp. 'Fine. I'll ride the stupid scooter thing.'

'So if we did that,' said Clem, 'do you think you might, you know, keep the house in the family?'

I froze. As far as I knew, they hadn't discussed this openly before. Martha didn't react. She picked up an olive. The silence stretched out.

'The party's on Saturday,' I said, to break the silence. 'Day after tomorrow.'

'And who are you planning to invite? The lovely Gareth, I assume?'

'You're making me blush, Mrs Roberts,' said Gareth. 'Sorry. I mean Martha. Yes, I'll be here. So will Maya, and Josie, and some of mine and Senni's other friends from school.'

'A couple of my friends are coming down tonight,' said Clem. 'On the sleeper train.'

'Oh, how fabulous. I used to love that,' said Martha. 'Now, how are you buying your alcohol? If you drink your way through Felicity and Dylan's supplies, they'll notice, and the last thing poor Dylan's going to need is no wine when he gets home.'

She looked thoughtful. 'None of you are eighteen yet – is that right?' We all shook our heads. 'So I could probably get a supermarket slot for Saturday morning. It might raise some eyebrows, my getting crates of alcohol delivered to the cottage, but who cares? Not me, and they're not going to ask *me* for ID. In fact, there are some bottles from various ancient holidays in the cottage somewhere too. The kind of things that never seem so appealing when you get them home.'

'Gran,' said Clem. 'Oh my God. You're amazing. I had no idea you were this cool.'

'I might be five hundred years old,' said Martha, draining her glass, 'but I still feel eighteen. They never tell you that part.'

'I'll get the laptop – let's see what delivery slot we can get,' Clem said. 'We'll give you the money. Would that be OK? We could just order all the party stuff at once, and we wouldn't need to go to the shops. Gran? You're the actual best.'

But Martha's face had changed. 'What the hell is that?'

Her voice was low, her expression different. She looked angry; I'd never seen that before.

We all turned to follow her gaze. Then Clem and I looked at Gareth.

'Oh God, sorry!' He leaped up, took the bone from the edge of the grass and put it away in the pool house. 'It was nothing. I was supposed to tidy it away before. I got distracted.'

'I told you!' yelled Clem.

'Sorry, Clemmie! I totally meant to do it.' He turned to Martha. 'It was just a thing the dog found.'

'Where?'

'In one of the flower beds,' said Clem. 'I know. Spooky, right? Is there a pet graveyard?'

Martha looked at me. 'Senara – you mustn't bring your dogs in here. This can never happen again. You can't mess around with these things. Put it back where it came from.' Her voice was shaking.

'Sorry,' I said. 'It won't happen again, I promise.'

'Put it back, or I'll do it myself.'

The silence hummed in the air for a few moments. A bee flew past. I wondered why she'd been so shocked. A bone was a weird thing to see on the grass – but was it *that* weird?

'I'll put it back right now,' said Gareth. He stood up.

'There's an old burial ground here,' said Martha. 'You can't treat these things as a big joke. You know that.'

And then she leaned back in her chair, and her chin sank down.

For a moment I thought she'd fallen asleep, and then I thought she had died. Gareth, Clem and I exchanged glances.

'Gran . . . ?' said Clem.

And Martha jerked back to consciousness, blinked at us and reached for her glass, holding it out for a top-up.

12

The next morning, I woke, confused, to the sound of something buzzing. It stopped and started, urgent and annoying. It wasn't a wasp. It was further away, mechanical. Lawnmower?

My head was fuzzy and pounding. What happened last night? Martha had been angry about the bone. Gareth had reburied it. I'd taken Martha home, and then gone back to the pool, where we'd drunk wine. Clem and Gareth had kissed all evening, some of it in the pool. I'd texted Josie, at Clem's insistence, and asked her to come over, but she hadn't replied.

Josie always replied. I hoped she was all right. I hoped her mum was OK.

I was glad, though, that she hadn't come over. I'd drunkenly thought she'd be pleased to witness Gareth cheating on Maya, but actually it would have been awful for her. I was a crap friend.

How did people fall so easily into relationships? I had never got close to one. I'd kissed two people, just to get it done, and regretted it both times. I'd never met anyone I wanted to go out with. There was something wrong with me. There had to be. Mum was delighted I was 'a slow developer' since it gave her less to worry about, and that hadn't made me feel any better.

When I opened my door and blinked out on to the landing, I realized the sound was coming from downstairs. It was buzzing over and over again.

I checked the time: nine thirty.

I stumbled down the stairs, starting to understand that this was the buzzer from the gate, and that it meant Clem's friends had arrived in their taxi from the station. Meg and Rik: an inseparable couple who did everything together. They sounded nauseating.

I checked my phone. Martha had called me twice but had only texted a dry: I think your Londoners have arrived.

I could just see one person on the video screen, a boy with black hair who looked like Keanu Reeves in *The Matrix* apart from his frowny, sulky face. I inhaled deeply as the buzzer sounded yet again, and pressed the button.

'Hi,' I said. I watched his face change. He smiled at the camera.

'Oh my God, Clemmie! We've been here hours! We had to let the cabbie go and hoped we were in the right place. Let us in already!'

'It's not Clem,' I said, 'but come in.' I pressed the button and ran upstairs.

When I hammered on her bedroom door, Gareth's voice said, 'Hey!' I pushed it open and saw that he was sitting on the bed, wearing just his pants, his hair lustrous over his shoulders, and that Clem was fast asleep, curled up on her side like a little child.

Clem's room was stunning. The walls were pale blue, and everything was blue and white. There was a huge mirror on one wall, a corkboard filled with photos of her London life, clothes all over the floor. Her curtains were blowing in the breeze. It smelled of perfume and sleep.

Gareth reached for his T-shirt and pulled it on.

'That them?' he said.

'Yes. Clem!' I rapped on the open door and raised my voice. 'Clem, your friends are here. You have to get up. I don't want to deal with them on my own. I don't know them.'

Gareth reached over and patted her shoulder. 'Clemmie. Wake up.'

She sat up in bed, clearly naked, and yawned. 'Jesus! I was asleep.'

I sighed. 'Make her get up,' I told Gareth. 'They're your friends, Clem! Not mine, not Gareth's. We've never met them. Yours! And they're here. So you need to put some clothes on.'

I'd never spoken to Clem like this before, but there was no way I was handling the new people on my own.

Josie would know how to talk to the London couple. What would she do? She wouldn't go and talk to them while wearing a huge T-shirt and a pair of knickers, for a start. I went into my room and changed into the first thing that came to hand from the charity bag, a knee-length dress, and ran my fingers through my hair and managed to scrape it back into a ponytail to stop it looking so crap.

I opened the front door, even though no one else ever seemed to do that. It was heavy, and it creaked, and I liked it. As I watched the visitors approaching, I enjoyed the illusion of being the lady of the manor, though it was quickly overshadowed by intense self-consciousness. They were walking slowly, dragging wheely suitcases loudly across the stones. That boy and a girl. Rik and Meg. He was tall. She was small.

They looked so rich.

I found myself hoping they weren't going to despise me. I willed them not to be the sort of people who did comedy Cornish accents and called people 'yokels'. 'Peasants'.

'Hi there!' called the girl when they got closer. She had long tangled hair and perfect make-up, and she was wearing a perfume that even I could tell was expensive. 'We're Clemmie's friends – I'm Megan and this is Rik. Thanks for letting us in. I think we might have scared Clem's great-grandma back there.'

At least she wasn't being horrible.

'Come in,' I said, forcing a smile. 'You can leave your bags in the hall if you want. Clem's on her way down. And it would take a lot to scare Martha. She texted to tell me you were here actually.'

The two of them looked at each other.

'You see! Old people do use phones for things other than calls,' said Rik. He looked at me. 'Sorry. Ongoing discussion. So, where do we go?'

They both spoke like Radio 4.

I led them through the house, checking for a reaction at

how beautiful it was, but there was nothing. Clearly, a big house was no big deal.

I texted Clem again.

We're in the kitchen!!!! Come down.

Rik, too, smelled amazing. I looked at him and felt a twinge of something I didn't usually feel. There was something about him. Something I couldn't name. An electricity that crackled from him. I had the impression that if I touched him I'd get a shock, that it would pulse through me, and my hair would stand up on end.

He was probably a millionaire, and I was no one. I was Clem's sidekick. Still, it was a nice feeling: more like admiring a movie star than anything real.

What would happen, I wondered, if I did touch him? Just brushed him in passing? Would there be electricity?

Megan was running her fingers through her hair. She had long eyelashes and very white teeth, and she seemed more Instagram image than real person.

'Do you want to sit in the courtyard?' I was winging it, channelling Felicity who was my role model for this scenario. 'What can I get you? Coffee?'

I went inside to put the kettle on. I started loading last night's dirty stuff into the dishwasher. There was a surprising amount of it. Champagne glasses, other glasses, plates, bowls.

Every now and then, I looked out. Rik and Megan were the most together couple I'd ever seen, and I had no business having electric feelings for someone else's boyfriend. I would have to admire him from a distance and remember not to make a fool of myself.

Clem shrieked and ran past me wearing pink shortie pyjamas with an unnecessary fluffy blanket wrapped round her shoulders. I gave her a hard look that she didn't see.

'Oh my God!' she shouted. 'I can't believe you're here! Why's it so fucking early?'

'Babes,' said Rik, 'we've literally been travelling all night.' He stood up and held out his arms for a hug.

I sensed Gareth behind me and turned. Our eyes met, and we both half smiled. He shook his head and walked backwards out of the kitchen like Homer Simpson disappearing into a hedge; I knew that Clem's world of Londoners was too much for him. Me too, but I'd offered coffee, so I felt obliged to make it for them before I, too, could vanish backwards. I remembered Felicity sitting at the table with me, between bringing food and drinks, so I went and sat down next to Megan.

'Welcome to Cornwall,' I said. '*Kernow a'gas dynergh*. I'm Senara.' Why did I say that? So stupid. Was I showing off?

'Cool name. What was that other thing you said?'

I repeated it. '*Kernow a'gas dynergh*. It's "Welcome to Cornwall" in Cornish.' I cringed.

'Oh my God, you speak Cornish! I love that. Can you teach me some?'

'Yeah. The first word you need to know is *splann*. The only one really. It just means *great*. You can say it about anything. Would you like some breakfast?'

She held eye contact and nodded. 'That would be *splann*. Right?'

I nodded. 'Correct.'

Megan came with me, back into the kitchen, exclaiming about the lovely view of the ocean. I put the kettle back on and dumped the stuff that hadn't fitted into the dishwasher into the sink and put the empty packaging into the bin and recycling. Then I looked for some way of making coffee, while she sat at the table. I had no idea. I'd only made tea in this kitchen so far.

'Oh my God, the night train is amazing, isn't it?' Megan said. 'I didn't even know there was one. I love the way you wake up and look out of the window and it's, like, oh hello, you must be Cornwall. Travelling in bed? It's like an overnight flight, but so much greener.'

What would it be like to have this much confidence? To chat randomly and charmingly to strangers?

'I've never been on it,' I said, 'but, yeah, it does sound good.'

I found a big cafetière thing, and a tin of brown stuff that smelled like coffee, so I spooned it in. I turned the oven on too, and poured boiling water on to what I hoped was the coffee.

I reminded myself not to let Megan assume I came from her world. I wasn't going to be embarrassed about anything.

Who was I kidding?

'I've only been to London once,' I said, working hard on keeping it real, 'and that was on a school trip.'

'Oh right!' Megan said, looking out of the French windows at the sunshine on the swimming pool. 'Yeah, if I lived here, I'd never leave either. It's so beautiful. I can't wait to get in that pool. What's the beach like?' She went to stand in the doorway without waiting for an answer. 'Hey! When's the party, Clemmie?'

'Tomoz!' said Clem. She came over, standing on the stepping stones. 'So, there's *us*, and loads of, like, really awesome local people too. You'll love them. We meet down the beach, and have fires and swim in the sea.'

I stifled a gasping laugh at that: Clem had done it once. Once. Now she was selling it as her Cornish lifestyle.

'And my gran – my great-gran – is *fine* with it. I mean, I was going to try to pitch it to her as a "gathering of friends" rather than a party, but she basically said we have to have the biggest party we possibly can, and she wants to be there too, until ten.'

I stepped into the courtyard beside her. It was already hot, the sky a deep cloudless blue, the sun bright. That would be because (I checked the time) it was quarter to ten. Clem was standing on the smooth stone, so the surrounding gravel was spiky under my bare feet.

'There's coffee brewing,' I said. 'Who wants a croissant?'

I knew there were croissants in the freezer because Felicity had shown me. Mum and I had them once a year, on Christmas Day. Last year we hadn't, though. Mum had made a fry-up for horrible Richard, her boyfriend at the time, and I'd had a bowl of cereal because I was pissed off.

'Oh my God!' said Rik. 'Yes, please. Yours'll be better than the train one.'

I went in and started to take mugs out of the cupboard.

'Hey there.' I looked round; he had followed me inside this time.

He was very tall. Like incredibly tall. And well mannered. He made me feel flustered and odd. *Breathe, Senara.* I shivered a bit, without wanting to.

He was with his girlfriend.

'Can I do anything to help?'

'All under control, I think.' I pushed the plunger down on the coffee and poured it into five cups. 'Thanks, though. Croissants will be another –' I checked the display – 'twelve minutes.'

'Great. Well, I'll keep an eye on them if you like.'

He looked at me with velvety dark eyes. I took half a step back, but kept staring at him.

This was new. I never felt like this. It really did feel as if some alien had stepped into my world. I was transfixed.

Seconds ticked by.

I pulled myself away before he noticed me ogling him, and put a jug of milk and the sugar bowl on the tray, copying the way Felicity had done it.

'Thanks,' I said. 'That would be great.'

Rik put three cups on to the tray and said, 'And let me take this for you. Save you coming out.'

I frowned. 'Why?'

'Oh sorry. I just assumed you'd be . . .' He gestured round at the kitchen, which was, despite my efforts, still messy.

I tried to work out what he meant.

And then I did.

'The coffee's made. The breakfast is in the oven. You assumed I'd rather carry on tidying the kitchen than . . .' I kept my voice as level as I could. 'Actually, yeah. You're probably right.'

'Oh God, sorry!' He stepped back, half smiling. 'I didn't mean to be rude. I apologize.'

I couldn't believe I'd thought, even for one second, that he was good-looking. I hoped his stupid electricity fried him from the inside. I put milk into my cup and Gareth's, then gave us each a spoonful of sugar because we needed it. I picked them both up, then left the room, shaking. I took the stairs as fast as I could without spilling anything, wanting nothing but the sanctuary of my room. The room I really wanted was my bedroom at home, my real room in a world that was mine, but this yellow one would have to do for now. I kicked the door open, gasped and jumped, sloshing coffee over the tops of both cups.

'Sorry, Senni.' Gareth was sitting on my bed. 'Didn't mean to be creepy. Lurking in your room. I couldn't think where to go where they definitely wouldn't find me. I know they're together, but do you think he's Clem's ex?'

I handed him his coffee, and he gulped it back.

'Who cares? She was nice, but he's a wanker.'

I told him about Rik offering to keep an eye on the breakfast and take the tray out so I could tidy up the kitchen.

'He probably thinks I'm unpacking their cases or something. Did Clem even make up a bedroom for them? I bet she didn't.' I put my head in my hands. 'Does he think I'm a maid? Oh God, he does. He does, doesn't he?'

'I thought Clem and I were getting on,' Gareth said. 'We were having an amazing time. Why do her friends have to ruin everything?'

I gulped my coffee. 'No idea. Glad you're here.'

'Glad you are. Have to say, I won't be sticking around for long.'

We shared a little smile, an acknowledgement that we had somehow stepped into the wrong world. I thought of Josie and decided to go straight to her and check in. Josie was real.

There was a shout from outside: it was unmistakably Clem. The window was open so Gareth put a finger to his lips and stuck his head out. I joined him. We couldn't see them, but we could hear them. I held my breath.

'Shut *up*, Rik!' Clem's voice was loud and she was laughing. 'Oh, you absolute twat. She let you in and made coffee because she's *nice*. She lives in the village, but she's not *staff*! My mum and hers used to be best friends. Mum would go *insane* if she heard you! And so would Gran, and she's actually here, so you need to watch yourself.'

'Oh shit. But – she's wearing uniform. Like Holly does at home.'

It took me a moment to process that.

Clem carried on talking. 'Don't worry. She's cool. Just explain that it was a misunderstanding. Nothing could offend Senni. So, tell me about the night train? Next time I'm going to catch it and make them all drive my stuff down without me.'

I glanced at Gareth and closed the window. I looked down at myself, and he looked at me. I moved to the mirror. Our eyes met in the reflection, and I saw him trying not to laugh.

It *was* funny. Almost.

The dress I'd grabbed from the bag this morning was black, made from T-shirt material. It was a shift, knee-length on me, and plain. I'd scraped my hair back.

'Oh my God,' I said. 'Did I accidentally wear uniform?' I could barely finish the sentence because I started laughing (it was that or cry).

Gareth was laughing so hard I thought he was going to hurt himself.

'You look like *Holly at home*,' he said, mimicking Rik. 'Oh my fucking God! He literally thought you were a maid! In uniform! Because they have one at home! That's more normal for him, than for you to be a friend wearing a black dress.'

I laughed until I cried, and he did too, but underneath it there was something hard and spiky.

'I'm done,' I said when I could speak, and I felt my laughter turning to tears, and tried to hold it all back.

'Senni.' Gareth stopped laughing abruptly. 'Oh God, you poor thing. It's shit. Look, you're doing nothing else for the three of them, OK? You're not being *Holly*. No making up beds or anything. No more coffee and croissants. You're here to keep an eye on Clem and Martha. Those two, Meg and what's-his-name, are not allowed to be here at all.' He took me by the shoulders and looked into my eyes. 'Fuck. Them. OK?'

I nodded and put my cheek on his chest. 'No more Holly,' I said.

'Wish she'd come down instead, whoever she is. Right, you'd better get changed, and then let's get out of here.'

I took some of my normal clothes into the bathroom, showered and dressed as myself.

'I'm going to obsess about this if I'm on my own,' I said when I came out. 'Can I hang out with you?'

'Course. Let's head down to the beach. It's too sunny to stay in.' He gave me a mock-confused look. 'But why are you going to obsess? I thought that *nothing could offend Senni*?'

That made us laugh again, but I didn't like this. I didn't like it at all.

Josie refused to meet us at the beach, even though we knew she wasn't at work. She was offhand and distant. We spoke to her in turn, passing the phone between us, trying to coax her, but she wouldn't engage. In the end, it took the Holly story to bring her out.

'I *knew* this would happen,' she said. 'OK, fine. You've worn me down. I'll be there in twenty.'

She arrived fifteen minutes later. There was a cloud of fury around her, and I didn't think it was just because we'd spent the night at Clem's. There was something else, but she wouldn't talk about it.

'Seriously, guys,' she said, 'what did you expect? Your little love-in with Clem Parker was never going to work out. She's always going to treat you like servants.' She side-eyed Gareth. 'Or the sexy gamekeeper, or whatever. I can't believe you stayed over.'

He nodded and looked down.

'You need to tell Maya,' I said, even though my policy was to stay out of his chaotic relationships.

'I know.' He held up his phone. 'Totally gonna.'

'You're going to tell her you spent the night with Clem Parker?' Josie's voice dripped with scepticism. 'Yeah, right, you are.'

'Shh!' Gareth covered his phone with his hand, as if it would convey this fact to Maya through the ether. He wasn't going to tell her; we all knew that.

Josie rolled over and looked at the sky. I did the same. The beach was lumpy under my back, and the sky was deep blue. 'Why do you do it, though, Gaz?' she said. 'Why are you such a shit? I'm way over it, but why? Why do you literally love-bomb any girl you fancy until she agrees to go out with you, wait until she's really into you, and then dump her for the next one? What's it about? Some deep-seated inadequacy?'

'I don't do that!' We both raised our heads to stare at him. 'I don't know. It just happens.'

'Are you always looking for The One?' I said. 'Is it a search for the perfect girl? Because, mate . . .' I pointed to Josie.

'That ship has sailed,' she said at once.

He shook his head. 'It's not that.'

'Thrill of the chase,' said Josie. 'Right, G? The bit you like is the pursuit. The excitement. The moment it settles into a relationship, you get bored and look for the next one.'

'I mean, I'm sixteen,' he said, defensive. 'I'm not exactly . . . I don't know. Who do I mean?'

'Henry the Eighth,' we both said.

'Or Donald Trump,' added Josie, to annoy him.

'Yeah. You make it sound like I've had a hundred girlfriends. I've actually had . . .' Josie and I looked at each other while he counted on his fingers. She gave a little eyeroll, and I mirrored it. 'Six,' he said. 'And that's if you count Clem, who is obviously not my girlfriend.'

'You see!' Josie was triumphant. 'Henry the Eighth. Which am I?'

He looked down. 'You know that. Fourth.'

'Anne of Cleves. She got the best deal. I'll take that.'

'OK,' he said. 'I'll stop asking people to be my girlfriend. I'll keep it light in future. Because I do know that this is shit. Better?'

We both nodded. Gareth looked around, clearly hunting for a new subject. He landed on something and turned to Josie.

'Remember that bone Senara found in the garden, in the winter? Your neighbour's dog dug up another one. Mrs

Roberts saw it because I forgot to hide it, and she went mad.'

'You *what*?'

I filled her in, thinking again about how angry Martha had been, how quickly that had happened. Josie was picking up little handfuls of stones and letting them slip through her fingers.

'That's kind of creepy,' she said when I'd finished. Her voice was distant, strange. 'Do you think there really is a plague pit? Or a burial ground?' I watched a range of emotions pass across her face, things that she wasn't saying.

'Clem says it's a pet graveyard.'

Josie stood up. 'We have to go and see. I don't give a shit what Clem says. You know that she just comes out with anything that makes her life easier. If we dig down a bit more, we'll find out if it's a dog or a plague pit. Or –' I watched her face change, wondered what was going on with her – 'something else.'

'I'm not going back to Cliff House,' I said. 'No way.' I thought about Rik thinking I was his servant. I hated him. I didn't want to see him ever again.

'Same,' said Gareth. 'No way am I going to dig in that garden with my bare hands. Plus, what else could it be, Jose?'

I didn't understand. 'Why, Josie? Why do you care about some old bones?'

I watched her hesitate, could see that she was trying to decide what to say to us. In the end, she shrugged. 'I've been thinking about death,' she said. 'A lot. And I don't know, but the idea of a plague pit puts everything in perspective. You know, imagining the people who lived here hundreds of years ago, who got ill and died. It's kind of comforting. And it means that everything at Cliff House isn't perfect, and I like that too.'

'You'll come to Cliff House?' I said. 'Because of the plague pit?'

It wasn't that. It was something else, but she wasn't saying.

'I'll go for the dead people, but not for the live ones. You've got a key for the gates, yeah?'

I patted my backpack. 'Yeah.'

She stood up. 'If anyone treats you as staff, Senni, I'm going to punch them in the face.'

1940

Martha settled into her new life in Cornwall. She wrote to Mother and Daphne often, and received replies whenever they had time and a stamp. Her letters were longer than theirs because she had lots of time. She imagined Mother sitting at the scratched table in Ridley Street, the table Martha had known all her life, licking the tip of her pencil, writing a few sentences.

> *All is well with us. We miss you. Tell us about Cornwall. Say thank you to Mr and Miss Roberts for looking after you.*

She didn't know whether Mother was just saying *all is well* to stop her worrying. They didn't tell her anything that actually happened, and she wished they would. She knew about air-raid shelters and bombs, and she wanted them to tell her what it felt like. Did they have to sit underground for hours and wonder whether their house would still be there when they came out?

She wrote long, long letters in her rounded handwriting,

all about the sea and the cliffs, about the cows and the sheep, the deer she would sometimes see in the woods. She told them that she lived in a big house, and drew a picture of it, with the cliff dropping down below it and the waves and the beach (Mother's reply: *See that you stay away from that cliff*). She described Violet and how kind she was and how pretty her clothes were. She said that Aubrey was sometimes funny and sometimes tired.

> *He puts on the best puppet shows. He's so funny.*
> *But then other times he's too tired to talk.*

She didn't say anything more about Aubrey. She didn't tell Mother how, after three days of being funny at the breakfast table, he had scared them when she and Betty and Michael had seen him in the upstairs corridor. They'd said hello, and he'd turned and shouted at them. His face went purple, and he yelled: 'Get out of my house! Go on! Get out!' Then he'd called them a very bad word as they turned and fled. Michael and Martha both cried, and Violet had explained that Aubrey was still upset by the last war, and that sometimes he had a bad day because of it, where he 'wasn't himself'.

Martha didn't tell Mother and Daffy that. She didn't say how much it made her worry for Daddy. She had thought, before, that when a war ended everyone would be happy.

When she imagined them reading her letters, she knew that Mother would be pleased with Martha's new life, but Daphne wouldn't believe anything she said. Daffy would think Martha was really in some horrible place being treated badly, inventing a fairy-tale world in which she lived in a castle on a clifftop. Her sister would be worrying about what was really happening, just like Martha worried about them.

At home in London they lived in three rooms; Martha and Daphne had shared a bed all Martha's life. She'd thought that was normal. Here Violet had two rooms all to herself: one was her bedroom and the other was her 'dressing room'. Aubrey mainly stayed in his bedroom, which had a bathroom next to it, and there was another bathroom too. The boys shared the green bedroom, and Martha and Betty shared their yellow one; they could have moved into separate rooms, but they didn't want to. The girls lay in bed at night and whispered to each other. Betty was her best friend now. Pauline hadn't replied to any of Martha's letters.

Some nights they would hear Aubrey yelling. He would scream and shout as if someone was attacking him, and Martha couldn't bear it. Not even Betty dared to leave the room when that happened. They would reach out and try to hold hands over the gap between their beds.

One morning, after he'd shouted all night, Violet told Martha and Betty that Aubrey had something called 'shell shock', which meant that his mind took him back to the last war that he'd fought when he was only a boy, and that it had been so awful he couldn't get over it.

'He has his good days,' she said. 'You know that. But he's never recovered. I can't believe they're doing it all over again. Truly, girls. I just can't believe it.'

Martha relied on Betty to help her be brave, and Betty leaned on Martha when it came to reading and arithmetic. Martha didn't know what would happen when they went home and Pauline was back from Wales, but she was lost now when Betty wasn't with her. The other evacuees walked up from the village, and Martha, Betty, Roy and Michael walked down the drive to do their lessons with Miss Ward in the cottage.

All the children missed home. Some didn't come to school: they worked on farms and in fields, or helped at houses or were trained as maids, even though they'd be going back to London when the war was over. Some cried the whole time – but most of them stretched out into the Cornish landscape, and ran in the fields, threw stones into the ocean, paddled in the bits of beach where it was allowed. Many, like Martha, found that they were pulled in by the rocks and the water and the fields, and felt that this was a magic place, a place that looked after them when they couldn't be with the people they loved.

Violet called Martha 'my special friend'. She let her pick flowers from the garden, and one time they packaged them up with damp cotton wool and sent them to Mother and Daphne in London, which Mother said made her cry: *the most lovely surprise*. They read books together: Violet reading to Martha and then, shyly, Martha reading to Violet. They read a copy of *Little Women*, and Martha adored it. There were so many books at Cliff House. There was a whole library.

*

One morning in the spring, Martha was walking along an upstairs corridor when she saw Aubrey at the other end of it. She froze; she had never come across him on her own before. He was walking towards her, and she didn't know whether to keep going or not.

She took a deep breath and carried on along the corridor. When she got close, Aubrey turned red, gasped and ran at her, shouting. He wasn't shouting words, just a huge sound that didn't stop. Martha turned and fled, but he was faster, so she ducked into the nearest room and banged the door behind her.

It was an unused bedroom. The furniture was covered in dust sheets, and Martha slid herself quickly under the bed. She lay there, on the dusty floor, so scared when Aubrey opened the door that she thought she was going to die of fright. Under the bed was a stupid hiding place. She saw his feet; he was wearing big black boots, even though he never went outside. She held her breath, hoped against hope that the dust wasn't going to make her sneeze.

'Where is he?' he shouted. She heard his footsteps walking round the room. After a thousand years, he knelt on the floor and looked under the bed. She screwed her eyes closed, but when his voice came it was friendly.

'Hello, Martha! Playing hide-and-seek?'

She opened her eyes and nodded.

'You haven't seen a . . .' He stopped. 'No. Of course you haven't. None here. At Cliff House. No.' He stood up and said, 'I won't tell anyone I found you.'

*

Martha was still shaken that afternoon when Betty took her by the hand.

'Shh,' Betty said, eyes wide.

Martha let herself be led across the hallway and up the main stairs. She followed Betty past their own bedroom door, down the corridor, all the way to Violet's room. They both knew that Violet was out in the village. And they both knew that they weren't allowed in her room unless they were invited. It was one of the rules May had told them on their first day.

'We can't go in there!' said Martha.

Betty ignored her, clicked the door open, and crept into Violet's grand bedroom (she had a four-poster bed!) and through a door on the opposite side.

Martha's heart was beating fast and hard. She had no idea what Betty had discovered, but she was curious too, and she was close behind when Betty walked through that other door.

It was strange to imagine having a room for your clothes to live in (however much they tried to explain, Violet could never quite understand what it was like to grow up in the East End), but it wasn't nearly as strange as the other things in this house. Martha looked at the dresses. They were the most beautiful things she had ever seen. There were long dresses, shiny ones, beaded ones. Ballgowns. They were Cinderella going to the ball; they were princesses and grand weddings and coronations. They were the Queen, and they were Princess Elizabeth and Princess Margaret.

Martha stood in front of the dresses and touched them. Some were silky. Some were stiff satin. She stroked a deep red one. She turned to Betty, but Betty wasn't looking at the dresses. She was sitting on the floor next to a cardboard box, a piece of paper in her hand.

'Look,' she said. 'These are letters. They're to Miss Violet, from her sweetheart. She has a *sweetheart*! Listen to this! He's called –'

'*Girls!* What are you doing?' came a voice from behind them.

Violet looked angry. Violet was never angry.

'Sorry, Miss Violet!' said Betty, and she shoved the letter back in the box.

'You know you're not allowed in here on your own,' Violet said. 'Betty, were you reading my letters?'

'We were looking at your dresses,' said Martha.

She couldn't meet Violet's eyes. If Violet had a sweetheart, where was he? Why did she never talk about him?

'Yes, we're sorry,' said Betty. 'Only we thought you were in the village. I didn't mean to read them.'

'Those are very private, and very personal. Never come in here again. I'm absolutely serious. Do you understand?'

They both nodded, and scurried away, feeling rotten.

That was the only time Martha saw Violet being cross. Life at Cliff House was, considering everything, extremely good. She and Betty worked with May around the house, and they helped Mrs Lamb in the kitchen, and they ran around in the gardens and planted things and cut lettuces and stayed away from Violet's room. They only spoke to Aubrey if he spoke first, in order to tell what sort of day it was for him. Martha felt that, since there was a war and she couldn't be at home, she was in the best place in the world.

And then the letter arrived.

13

Josie didn't think for one moment that there was a plague pit. Of course there wasn't. She didn't give a shit about that.

She cared about the fact that her uncle had disappeared at the same time as Rachel Thomas, who was widely assumed to be dead. She cared about the burden that had lifted from her mother when she heard the news about Andy. The very things she'd been working so hard not to think about – the fact that a girl had vanished without trace; that there were bones in the garden; that Rachel, as Felicity's friend, must have visited Cliff House – were coming together to create a picture that Josie didn't like, and finding out about the second bone had tipped her over.

She needed to investigate, to prove herself wrong. She wanted to pull out a cat skull or something, macabre as that was, and then she'd be able to stop worrying.

She missed the days when she could have said anything to Senara and Gareth. Now she was swirling with thoughts she didn't want to put into words. Senara still thought

Josie had everything pinned on Andy, and she didn't know that he was dead. Josie didn't want to tell her yet.

They walked in through the gates, which felt wrong after all the times Josie had arrived over the fence. None of them wanted to see Clementine and her horrible friends, so they skirted round, past Martha's windows (no sign of her watching; Josie wanted to thank her for the pizza, but not in front of the others) and went straight to the camellia bed.

It was impossible not to think back to the first time they'd been here. Josie could feel the January air in her lungs, could see the shadow of her breath puffing round her, even though the heat was so heavy today. The tension of trespassing, the terror of their drone being found with its footage. The ease of being with her boyfriend, and her best friend. The unifying fact that they had all disliked Clementine Parker, even though they hadn't known her name.

Josie pulled herself back into the moment. This wasn't the place for nostalgia, and anyway she had no idea why she'd been so into Gareth. She didn't like him any more, let alone fancy him, though she was working on seeing him as a friend. It didn't come easily, and if she'd had a wider pool of potential friends she'd never have spoken to him again. She really hadn't wanted to come and meet them today, but she missed Senara so much – and it had turned out to be better than not meeting them. At least she had something to do now, a mission to uncover what she hoped would turn out to be a pet cemetery.

She knelt by the camellia bed and looked down. Molly had dug a hole that was bigger than she was, which was fully on-brand for that dog. The soil was stony, but here it looked dark and rich. Josie shuddered, realizing that it was nourished by whatever had rotted away underground. The earth scratched her bare knees.

'That dog really went for it,' she said.

'Yeah.' Senara knelt beside her. 'You know Molly.'

Gareth was already wandering off.

Senara leaned down, reached in. 'What the fuck?'

Josie's heart pounded as Senara pulled something out of the bottom of the hole and held it up. It wasn't a bone; it was dull metal, and when she brushed the soil away it unfolded and became an old watch.

It doesn't mean anything.

People dropped things in their gardens all the time.

Senara was staring at it, rubbing it with her finger as if a genie might appear.

Three wishes. *One: Mum gets better. Two: pet graveyard. Three: Mum gets better.*

'It's got an engraving on the back,' Senara said, holding it closer and peering at it. '*With love on your twenty-first birthday*'.

That meant it had nothing to do with Rachel Thomas. She had been seventeen, and this was clearly not a teenager's watch from the eighties. It was heavy, old, masculine. Josie felt her feeling of dread starting to lift.

'That's it?' she said. '*With love on your twenty-first birthday*? No name?'

'No.' Senara brushed the face. 'It's got hands, stopped at five to two. Do you think they dumped it in the garden? Why would you do that?'

Gareth was back. He took the watch from Senara.

'Nice,' he said. 'Surprising, though. I guess it's Clem's technically.'

They all looked up the garden, then exchanged glances. Josie could hear voices drifting down on the still air; the rich people were playing in their pool. Of course they were – why wouldn't they be? She was scared by the way this made her feel. It made her hot and furious and powerless. It wasn't fair.

Senara and Gareth were hanging back too. Josie grinned at them. She had her friends with her again.

'I really don't want to see them,' Senara said.

Josie nodded. 'Head back to the beach?'

'Yeah.'

'Yeah,' said Gareth.

They turned and headed towards the gate, but stopped when Clementine appeared, pelting down the garden to intercept them. She threw her arms round Gareth's neck, shouting, 'Where have you been?' and 'Come and meet my friends!' and then she instructed Senara and Josie to come too.

Josie found herself trailing up the yellowing grass towards the things that made her rage. Even *she* didn't seem to be able to say no to Clem Parker. She walked as slowly as she could, wondering whether she'd be able to get out through the gates if she turned and bolted. At least she felt better about Rachel. That watch had kind of proved her theory wrong.

There were glasses and plates round the pool. A tall guy, who must have been the horrible Rik, was doing a stupid showy dive, and a girl was sitting on the side, legs in the water, her eyes closed and her face turned up to the sun.

Josie looked at her. She was beautiful.

'Look who I found in the garden!' shouted Clementine, who, Josie thought, did everything at top volume because she'd always been told that what she said mattered to everyone in the world. That she had the right to take up space, to be heard.

Rik surfaced, saw them and leaped out of the pool in one bound.

The girl, whose name Josie didn't remember, turned to them, and a huge smile spread across her face. Josie found herself smiling back, in spite of everything.

She stared at the girl. The sun shone off her hair. They were a couple, she and this boy: she remembered Senara saying so. They looked good together.

Rik was at their side in seconds. He was a ball of energy. Josie stepped away from him. Senara took two steps away. Three.

'Hello, Senara!' he said. 'Oh my God, I have to apologize one billion trillion times. I'm such a twat.'

He glanced from Senara to Josie and Gareth and then back to Senara again. Josie wondered what they looked like through his eyes. A baldish girl with muddy hands.

A long-haired Cornish boy who hadn't put his shirt back on. A cast of oddball extras. *Locals*.

'It's just . . .' he went on. 'I don't know how to say this without it sounding worse.'

None of them said anything. Josie checked Senara's reaction. Her face was blank. She wasn't being won over.

Rik smiled nervously. 'Oh shit. Are you going to make me try?'

Senara still didn't answer, so Josie said, 'Yeah, we are.'

She watched him. He was awkward. Kind of gawky, and embarrassed, but at least he seemed properly mortified.

'So,' he said, 'at home we always have help. You know, housekeepers, maids, whatever. I know, it's messed up. I just assumed Clem did too, because I'm an idiot. And you were wearing black, and at home . . . Well, I'm going to stop there. Can I get you a drink? Anything at all. Put in an order and let me wait on you.' Josie looked at Senara, ready to follow her reaction.

Senara made a 'rewind' gesture, twirling a finger. 'At home you have staff in uniform?'

Awesome. She wasn't capitulating.

Rik winced and gave a tiny nod.

The silence stretched out. Josie waited to see what Senara said next. She would back her up either way. The sun was warm on the top of her head, and Josie found that she hoped that Senara was going to forgive him because, now she was here, she wanted to swim in this pool.

Was she being reeled in by Clem and Cliff House?

Yes, she was, but it was only for a day. She looked at the girl again. Something flickered between them. They held eye contact.

'Fine,' said Senara eventually. 'Do you know how to make iced coffee?'

The girl said, 'Excellent choice. Me too, Rikky.' She spoke without moving her eyes from Josie, a small smile on her lips.

'And me,' said Gareth.

Josie was the first to drop her gaze. She said, 'I'll just have water, thanks.' It was too lame. 'Actually, no. Can I have water and a coffee, but a real coffee, not a cold one? No milk, one sugar?'

Rik nodded. 'I'll give it a damn good go. Three double-shot iced coffees coming up, plus one hot coffee, and cold water all round.'

Josie and Senara exchanged glances, and Senara told her wordlessly that it wasn't over yet, that she was going to make him work for forgiveness if he really wanted it. Josie's eyes flicked back to the girl, who was laughing at Rik. She caught Josie looking and patted the spot next to her.

She really was the most beautiful person Josie had ever seen.

'Hi,' Josie said as she sat down. 'I'm Josie.' She leaned over and rinsed her muddy hands in the pool water.

'Nice to meet you. I'm Meg.'

She knew Gareth was handing the watch over to Clem, but she wasn't interested in that any more.

She knew it was temporary, but Josie found that, at last,

she could stop caring. She checked in with Mum by text, and, when Mum answered uncharacteristically quickly and cheerfully, left her phone on the courtyard table. The sun shone. Clem morphed into a brilliant hostess, and everyone relaxed. It was, of course, easy to relax into luxury: that was what made it luxury.

She stayed close to Meg. They seemed to have skipped all the early stages of friendship.

Josie could see Gareth was watching Clem and Rik, clearly trying to work out whether they had ever hooked up, whether Rik was a threat, even though he was with his girlfriend. Clem was flirty with Rik, but she seemed to flirt indiscriminately with everyone, so it was hard to tell. Josie enjoyed seeing Gareth uncomfortable.

She felt Meg's eyes on her, and turned to her.

'We were together for three months,' Josie said by way of explanation, inclining her head towards Gareth. 'Earlier this year. He said he loved me and then dumped me by text. It fucking destroyed me.'

'The bastard!' Meg said it loudly, and everyone looked round. Then she smiled and pointed at Gareth. 'Yes – you, mate.' He looked stunned for a second, then shrugged and gave a tight smile. She lowered her voice. 'The bastard, though! I can't believe you still talk to him.'

'I have to,' Josie said. 'It's a small village.'

Meg had long glossy hair and long eyelashes. Her eyes were so light brown they were almost yellow. She was like an entrancing creature from a different world. Josie found herself explaining Gareth's subsequent history, with Maya and now Clem.

'Well, Clem and Rik have never hooked up,' Meg said, 'but let's not tell him that. He's met his match with Clemmie. This is going to be good.'

Josie had brought her swimsuit with her when she met Senara and Gareth at the beach, and changed into it now in a white-tiled downstairs loo with a sturdy wooden seat. She drifted around on the water on a flamingo-shaped lilo, her face tipped up towards the sun. She borrowed some coconut-scented sunscreen and lived in the moment, still intensely aware of Meg. It was like meditating, but better.

When Senara produced warm baguettes and cheese and salad for lunch, Gareth said, 'Cheers, Holly,' and there was a sense of tension before Senara broke it by curtseying and telling him he was welcome.

Josie felt it taking hold of her. Cliff House, Clem, Martha – the whole world of money and possibility. She knew it was wrong, knew that it was against all her principles, but now, just right now, she wanted to stay here and feel like a part of it, because she knew that soon it would be gone.

Most of all, although it was hopeless, she wanted to be with Meg.

1988

Alex walked down to the village to meet Jenna and walk her to Cliff House. It was, Felicity felt, a bit strange of him since Jenna was sixteen and walked round the village all the time, but she didn't seem to mind him chaperoning her.

Felicity was going to be brave and remain at home on her own while he was out. Alex promised to lock the gate behind him, and she wanted to stay here so she could cook pasties and brownies. She'd already made the pastry. She wasn't going to freak out.

The man had waited for her, looked at her, probably followed her. He had turned up at the bottom of the drive. He hadn't ever come on to their land, and Alex was only going to be out for half an hour. She was safe at home. It would be fine.

She could hear the whispers of the sea across the stones and the distant screeching of seagulls. Other than that, it was silent. This was, Felicity thought, the first time she had been home entirely on her own for years. Maybe ever. She felt self-conscious as she walked back to the house, even though no one was watching. She imagined his eyes on her.

Her flip-flops made too much noise. She thought about the layer of rubber sole between her feet and the stones, and then the soil beneath that, and the Earth's crust, and the magma and everything below it, all spinning. It made her dizzy.

She stopped and looked up at the house. Even that felt freaky. She had never told anyone that the house sometimes had an aura too, but it did, and today it was a murky green. She told herself that it was her own projection, that the house didn't have its own shifting personality. She didn't actually know that, though; maybe it did. It might have had a soul.

She walked through the carved front door, closing it behind her and making sure the lock clicked back into place, then made her way through the house and into the kitchen. This was her favourite room: it was chaotic and full of stuff, but it was where she had first begun to suspect she might be good at something. Just one thing. That was all she'd ever wanted, and she was good. She could cook.

She put the oven on and got to work. She'd get the pasties done first, and then whip up the brownies while they were in the oven. It was unusually warm so she opened the door to the courtyard and propped it with the big metal doorstop and, with their parents' radio reset from Radio 4 to 1, she lost herself in making the filling for her pasties to the backdrop of loud music.

She was singing loudly to 'Always On My Mind' by the Pet Shop Boys when she realized there was another voice in the mix.

Someone was humming along. Someone who wasn't her. There was someone else in the room.

She had bolted the front door but left the courtyard open. Even with the gate locked that was stupid. She whipped round, noticing that there was a knife on the worktop, covered in meat juice and garlic, wondering whether to pick it up.

She realized, though, that it was a woman's voice, and when she looked she saw that, although she'd changed since they last met, it was Rachel. She was sitting at the table.

'Oh my God!' said Felicity. 'Rachel! Oh my God!' She put a hand to her chest, felt her breathing calming.

Rachel had been crying. Her face was puffy, and her eyes were red. Her colours were different, darker, pulsating. 'Sorry! I didn't mean to scare you.'

Felicity sat next to her. 'Rach! What's wrong?'

Rachel was her only other friend in the village; her dad was the vicar, and somehow, because of the way village life worked, that meant their two families were friends. Mum went to church every week. Dad went when Mum told him he had to, but Felicity had managed to attach herself to Alex's logic-driven rebellion a couple of years ago and stop going.

'I don't believe in God,' Alex had said to Mum. 'And that's my prerogative, yes? But you seem to think I should go, once a week, to a building devoted to the worship of an entity I don't believe in, to actually kneel down before it, and sing songs about how brilliant it is. If we're going to do that, Mother, I'd prefer to worship the sun god. At least the sun gets results.'

'Alexander!' Mum had known she was beaten. 'Fine. You're old enough to make your own decisions, I suppose. It's about kindness, though. Forgiveness. Things like that. Not just worship.'

'Not the way the Reverend Arsehole tells it.'

'Alexander!'

Dad had looked up. 'Where are you building your temple to Helios?'

'Down by the camellia bushes?'

'I'm joining Alex's religion!' Felicity had said, and that had been it. They'd negotiated a tiny bit and agreed to go for Mum's sake at Christmas and Easter, but other than that they were off the hook.

That had been several years ago, and it meant she didn't see Rachel as much (she had no idea whether Rachel still went to church), but whenever their paths crossed they were friends. And, according to Jenna, Rachel was going out with creepy Andy.

What if he was here too? Felicity looked around, but he wasn't.

She felt her heart rate slowing so noticeably that she could feel the blood ebbing to a crawl inside her. Was that how it worked?

'Are you alone?' she said quietly.

Rachel was staring up at the ceiling. 'Yeah.' And then: 'It's my parents.' She sniffed and wiped her nose on the back of her hand until Felicity handed her the kitchen roll.

'Shit! Sorry. I was trying to be brave. It's just –' She swallowed hard. 'We had a fight. I didn't know where to go. My legs kind of walked me here. Is that OK?'

'Of course it is! I'm glad you came here. Stay as long as you want. Stay forever!' She took Rachel in properly. 'And may I say – you look amazing.'

Rachel gave a self-conscious wince and wiped under a heavily made-up eye. 'Thanks.'

She'd had her hair cut and coloured since Felicity had last seen her, and now it was parted way over to one side with a curtain across her face. It had once been dark brown, but now it was peroxide blonde, and where it had been straight it now curled. Rachel was wearing mismatched luminous socks and short dungarees and trainers, and Boy George-style make-up. She'd always had a shimmering blue aura, but now it was purple, and kind of moving.

'Really,' said Felicity. 'Look at you!'

'Lissy,' said Rachel, using her old primary-school name. 'I really am sorry to scare you like that. You were terrified, weren't you?'

'You're lucky I didn't stab you.' They both looked at the knife. 'Have you run away, like, permanently?'

Rachel deflated, and her blue shimmer was back. 'I wish. I don't know. I climbed over your gate. Your grandma's car wasn't there so I thought I'd probably get away with it.'

Felicity shuddered at the idea of the gate being barely any impediment at all, that everyone could see at a glance that Grandma wasn't home. She wished Grandma hadn't gone to Exeter.

'Do you want a drink?'

She poured Rachel a glass of juice.

'I hate them both,' Rachel said, staring straight ahead. 'It feels weird to say it, but it's true. I hate my parents. I can't live there any more, and I don't know what to do. I don't think I can go back, Lissy. This is weird, but it feels too dangerous to stay at home. Like, my dad was trying to hit me.'

She froze for a few seconds, took a deep breath, then pulled her hair back from her face and showed Felicity a bruise.

'Fuck it. He *did* hit me. I'm done protecting him. He goes at us with his fists, and no one would believe me because he's the vicar. He's great at choosing places that aren't visible.'

'He –' Felicity didn't know what to say. She'd always disliked the vicar, but had never imagined this. She felt sick. She fetched some frozen peas and handed them to Rachel, because that was what people did. Rachel gave her a little smile and held them to her forehead.

'Does he do it to Lucy too?'

'Rarely. Lucy keeps her head down.'

'What are you going to do? Why don't you come and live with us? There's enough space. I'm sure it'll be fine.' She knew she couldn't let Rachel go home.

Rachel didn't answer for ages.

'I want to go away,' she said eventually. 'I want to go so far from here, and never come back. Never, never, never come back.'

'You've got one more year of college,' said Felicity. 'Stay here, with us, and do your A levels. Then you can leave forever if you want.'

'I do want,' said Rachel. 'I have so many plans, and none of them are going to involve seeing my parents ever again.'

'Rach,' said Felicity. 'Sorry to ask, but you're not seeing that Andy guy, are you?'

Rachel put the bag of peas on the table. They were starting to drip.

'Who told you that?' she said.

14

We messed around as if we were all eleven, and the late afternoon passed by in a haze of sunlight and clear water. It was a separate world up here. You could live in your own universe, and I forgot about bones and watches and everything but the moment.

Clem sent Rik inside for more drinks. 'Something fun,' she commanded, and he rose to the challenge, coming back with six Coke floats with sprinkles on the ice cream, and six glasses of wine. We sat round the courtyard table and tackled the floats with straws and teaspoons, before drinking the wine.

I stayed away from Rik, in spite of his million apologies. At some point in the afternoon I found myself sitting next to Megan (or Meg as she told us to call her now that we were friends), who was watching Josie diving into the pool. I said the first thing that came into my head.

'Have you been to Cornwall before?' *Inspired, Senara.*

'Yes, but not by train,' said Meg. She stretched out, getting as much sun on her legs as she could. Her voice was low and husky. She was so cool, like a movie star. 'We came on holiday last year – you know, because hardly anybody was going abroad. We stayed at St Mawes. Oh. My. God! It was so, so beautiful over there. That hotel there, you know the one? Where you go for afternoon tea? I adored it. How far are we from St Mawes actually? Could we get a cab over there? Me and Rik loved it.'

I'd never been to St Mawes, but I knew where it was.

'Quite far.' I pointed inland, vaguely towards the south coast. 'It's over there. I've always lived here, on the north coast. St Mawes is on the south coast. Opposite Falmouth.'

'Yes!' Meg grinned. 'I loved that ferry from Falmouth. It was epic. So this is the north coast? Honestly, my geography is, like, so bad.'

I liked Meg. I loved how easy she was to talk to. I wondered how I could be more like that.

'It's calmer there, and wilder up here.' Then I remembered that I had to keep it real. I made an effort not to be embarrassed by my life and said, 'Honestly, Meg? Someone like me would never go to a place like St Mawes. I bet if you tried to get a coffee it would be, like, seven pounds fifty. It's all about second homes and Airbnbs. I've lived in the same house here my whole life, and it's almost always just been my mum and me.'

'Almost?'

I sighed. 'Twice Mum's boyfriends lived with us. One was nice, one wasn't, but either way I was glad when they left. I didn't even leave Cornwall until I was eight, and that was only because my dad moved to Plymouth.'

'Right,' said Meg. I was sure she, like Clem, went to a

school that cost over twenty-five grand a year, and I knew Rik did because he had uniformed servants. 'Tell me more about it here. It's so interesting to hear what it's really like.'

I took a deep breath. She'd asked, so I would tell her.

'My mum grew up in the village,' I said, 'but she didn't inherit her parents' house because she had to sell it to pay for their care. And even though we're not a pretty village – except up here and down by the beach – and it's not popular with tourists except to drive through, the house where she grew up is an Airbnb now. And that means it's empty lots of the time. And then in the summer upcountry people arrive with cars full of supermarket shopping and wine so they don't even need to visit the local shops, and walk around trying to find the path to the beach – and saying stuff like it's not very picturesque, and this isn't what they thought Cornwall was going to be like, and "Can you believe there's no Deliveroo?" Then when it rains they all go to the art galleries in Penzance and complain that it's too busy.'

I was pretty much parroting things Mum said, but she was right.

Meg made a face. 'That sounds grim.' She paused. 'Not sure I necessarily want to know, but what are *upcountry people*?'

'Oh sorry. It's just shorthand for "not Cornwall". It means anything from Devon onwards.'

'I like it. It's a *splann* word.'

I nodded in appreciation. Meg was cool. I liked her a lot more than her boyfriend, even though he was trying so hard.

'Tourists are fine,' I said. 'It's the . . .'

I stopped short before I went too far. You can't diss second homes while your feet are literally in the swimming pool of one. Rik, who had taken another drinks order, came out with a tray.

'Iced coffee for the ladies,' he said, putting them in front of us.

'Hey,' said Megan. She pointed at him. 'You're from upcountry.'

Rik took a step back, baffled. He shrugged and carried the tray over to the pool and put two Coke floats down on the edge. 'Clem – yours has the pink stirrer. Gareth, yours is blue.'

That irritated me into responding. 'Sexist!'

'There's vodka in Clem's, and brandy in Gareth's. As requested. Pardon me for accidentally pandering to gender stereotypes though.'

We glared at each other for a moment, and then Rik went back into the kitchen. I tried to breathe deeply and live in the moment and absolutely not at all think about why it was that I disliked him so much.

15

Josie couldn't stop looking at Megan. She had a few sips of wine and found herself gazing at her swishy hair and her shining tiger eyes.

She had wondered this about herself before, but had never found the person who would unlock it. And now, perhaps, she had. Perhaps that person was in front of her.

With her boyfriend.

Still, she could look. And she did. She looked. She stopped caring how obvious it was because this was a moment out of time, a world away from her normal life.

The sun shone brighter around Megan. The grass was greener under her feet. The water was warmer, the air clearer. Even her voice was sweeter than everyone else's.

She manoeuvred herself next to her again. Meg was wearing a silver bikini. Josie was highly aware of it.

'Do you live in the village too?' Megan said, leaning back on her hands. 'Like Senara?'

'Yeah, I do. I've always lived here. Just me and my mum, but it's . . . well, it's complicated.'

And just like that she was spilling it all out in a way she'd never done with anyone before. She told Meg about Mum, and how life was now, but she didn't touch on the future.

Meg said the right things (not too sympathetic – just right). She asked the right things, and took it seriously, made Josie feel more normal with a story of a friend's brother with schizophrenia. After a while, Josie told her that her uncle had just died, and that even though she'd never met him she was gutted.

'It made my world shrink,' she said. 'And it was small to start with.' (She didn't tell Meg that it sounded like he used to prey on younger girls. She didn't mention any of her internet research.)

'Oh, Josie. That sucks. How's your mum dealing with it?'

'Fine. Weirdly fine. I never knew this, but it turns out she didn't even like him. He wasn't the person I was imagining at all. I wish she'd told me that before.'

They lay back and talked about anything and everything. When Meg spoke about her exes, she sometimes said *he* and sometimes *she*. It didn't feel complicated with her. Josie had only known her for a couple of hours, but Meg was filling her mind, her nerve endings, her entire soul. Just lying next to her kept Josie's body on high alert.

She kept having to remind herself: *Meg is with her boyfriend*. Some of her exes were women, but her current boyfriend was quite clearly a guy. And he was here. Meg wasn't available, except as a friend.

When the conversation paused, Josie sat up and eased herself into the pool, hoping that Meg would follow, but she didn't.

The water was warm now, heated by the sun, and Josie swam up and down a few times and floated on her back to appreciate another moment, and to digest these feelings. They were new. She'd thought she'd had them for Gareth, but she knew, now, that she hadn't. She'd never felt anything like this before. It had been instant.

She supposed she had better stop hating Clem now that she was swimming in her pool, talking to her friends, eating her food and drinking her coffee, water, wine, juice. She looked at Senara and found herself grinning. They were in this together: it was next-level trespassing.

Meg was sitting up. Josie worked hard not to look at her in her bikini. She made an effort, instead, to mess around with Gareth and, particularly, with Clem, but her eyes kept being drawn to Meg. She swam, drifted, swam and floated. She tried not to look at Meg with Rik. She hated him more than Senara did, even though he was, objectively, being nice. She hated him because he had Meg. The two of them finished each other's sentences, laughed at in-jokes, were incredibly close. Josie didn't want to know how long they'd been together, didn't want to know anything at all about them.

She had met someone amazing. Just looking at Meg made her feel like a different person. It stopped her caring about anything else. It made her see that there were things about herself that she'd never even realized before.

And she was sure Meg felt it too. Maybe she and Rik had an open relationship. Maybe there were possibilities there. Josie tried to convince herself (Rik was trying so hard after all to make Senara like him), but she knew they were the faintest of possibilities. The universe was twisting the knife. Just when she'd discovered that her future held nothing, that she was trapped in the same place forever like a mosquito dying in amber, she met someone magical from far away who was entirely unavailable.

1940

Martha lay awake at night, in Violet's bed, trying to cry quietly.

Her father was dead. Her lovely, funny daddy: the man who'd loved books, who had never wanted to be a soldier at all. Someone had shot him with a bullet, and now he was dead. They had murdered him.

Sometimes she was so angry that she didn't know what to do with herself. She was angry with the people who had made him go to war, but she didn't know who they were, so instead she focused her anger on Hitler. Everyone hated Hitler, but Martha felt she hated him more than anyone.

She cried at night while Aubrey yelled and screamed, and Violet whispered about the horror of it all. Daddy would never have to shout in the night now, but that was no comfort.

He was thirty-five years old, and he was dead. So he wasn't thirty-five. He was nothing. There was no Daddy any more.

She couldn't get it to make sense. He had had to go away and fight because they told him to, not because he wanted to, and then he'd died. That shouldn't have happened.

Violet had brought her in to sleep with her. They huddled together in her grand bed, the four-poster with a canopy on top.

Violet had been cuddling Martha ever since the news arrived three days ago. She looked after her. She stroked her hair and called her 'poor little mite' and 'poor scrap'.

Martha knew that this had happened to other people, other children at school. Their fathers had been killed in the war, and everyone was sad for them and said that they were heroes who had died for their country. Now that it had happened to her, she didn't find the 'hero' thing made it any better. It made her feel worse because she knew Daddy would have said he wasn't a hero, and that made it all seem like lies.

She could hear his voice in her head. '*I'm not brave, Martha. I have no choice.*'

She had known this might happen. She wasn't stupid. But she hadn't thought it would feel like this. She couldn't help it; another gasping sob burst out of her.

'Oh, Martha.' Violet's voice was sleepy. She sat up in bed and put her arms round her. 'That's OK. You can cry, dear thing. You can cry.'

Martha cried in the darkness, into the silence, until she felt a bit better.

It was so quiet here. The quiet was still the thing she found the strangest. At home you could hear buses and voices all the time. Here it was silent. If you listened very hard, you could sometimes hear the sea, but that was it. The quiet was a big blanket over everything.

'I didn't like the quiet, but now I do,' she said once she'd managed to gather herself.

'Is it so different from London?'

'*So* different.'

'Martha. I've had an idea. A big thing. A thing for us to talk about. Hang on, though. We need sustenance. I'll be back in a mo.'

Martha nodded and stayed in bed, blowing her nose loudly and messily on the handkerchief Violet had given her. Violet took a torch down with her to avoid waking anyone else, and came back with two cups, two apples and the torch on a tray.

'I'm afraid I couldn't manage much of a midnight feast,' she said. 'But maybe this'll do. It's not real coffee, just the chicory stuff.'

Martha smiled through her tears. 'You're so nice,' she said.

'Do you want to look at the dresses?'

'Am I allowed?' She knew it hadn't been Martha looking at the dresses that had made Violet angry last time; it had been Betty reading her letters. All the same, she was scared to go back into the dressing room.

Violet took Martha to wash her hands, and then led her to the dresses and let her touch them. She let her stroke them all she liked.

'If you weren't such a scrap of a thing,' she said, 'you could have tried them on.'

Martha wanted to say she was actually quite tall for her age, but she didn't. The dresses were much too big for her.

'Which is your favourite?' she asked Violet instead.

The dresses were just as magical now she saw them for the second time. They were stiff and rustly, or smooth and silky. Violet said they were from before the war, some of them even from before the other war, when her family had had lots of money. They were beautiful colours, and they had wide sleeves, long flowing skirts. Some were so silky that touching them was like touching water.

Violet and Aubrey used to go to parties all the time, she said, before he went away to fight in 1916. She had been fourteen, Aubrey sixteen, when the first war began, and she'd had all these clothes. Between the wars, Violet had loved dressing up and going out. She didn't any more.

'This one. This is my favourite.' Violet picked out the dark red one Martha had noticed last time.

'Mine too!' Martha was pleased. The dress was long and beautiful, with wide sleeves and a tiny waist.

Violet stroked it with her fingertips. 'Last time I wore this, a man proposed to me. Can you imagine? Asked me to marry him. I've always thought of this dress as my lucky charm.'

Martha's eyes were wide. 'Oh! What happened?' She remembered the letters and decided not to mention them.

'I said yes.' Violet breathed quickly in and out.

'So why –?' Martha stopped when she realized what the reason might be. Tears sprang to her eyes again.

Violet nodded. 'All our stories are sad, I'm afraid, darling. I'm sorry. Including this one. Still want to hear it?' Martha nodded. 'Let's get back into bed. We'll freeze out here.'

When they were tucked under the blankets, Violet said, 'I was quite old to get married and had almost given up hope, and there he was. This lovely man who loved me back. I wore my dresses, and we had wonderful times. We were so happy. I loved him so very much. But it wasn't to be. He died too, not so long ago. In this war. Like your daddy.' She drew in a deep breath. 'You might already know this, Marth. I know Betty was reading my letters. They're so precious. That's why I was angry. They're all I've got left of him.'

They were both quiet for a long time, and then Martha said, 'I didn't know. She just said you had a sweetheart. What was his name?'

'Edward. You'd have liked him, Marth.' She shook herself. 'Oh, the dresses were supposed to cheer us up! Sorry, my darling. One day you'll wear lovely clothes and go to parties. You might not feel like it now, but you're going to be a grown-up lady, invited to soirées, meet interesting people and wear beautiful dresses. You'll proposed to by exciting men.'

Martha wouldn't do those things. She would work in a factory. She knew that Violet didn't understand what life was like at home. It was hard to remember, even for Martha, from here. She could see that she had changed. Even her voice was changing; she didn't talk in the same way she had at home. She didn't talk like the local children, either, although she loved their voices. But she could tell she was starting to talk more like Violet, like the voices on the wireless.

'You said you had an idea,' said Martha, putting her cold feet against Violet, who gasped, and smiled, then reached down and rubbed them.

'I do. All right,' said Violet. 'Marth, how would you like me to take you to London? To see your mother and Daphne? We'd travel by train. You can't make that journey on your own, and I know you need to see them, so I've decided we should go together, have an adventure. May can look after the other children here. I'd like to meet your mother and tell her what a darling girl you've been and how brave. Perhaps we could stay in London for a few days? Then we can come back together afterwards because you really can't be there for long. It's too dangerous.'

Martha stared at her, though she was really just a shape in the dark bedroom. She couldn't believe Violet had been making a plan to take her home. To see Mother and Daphne. To hug them, to talk about Daddy. Violet knew what she needed. Martha loved Violet so much.

'*Really?*'

'Really.'

She tried to work out how to say it. 'Our house in London . . . well, it's small. I sleep in the same bed as Daphne, like this, but it's because there's not enough space, not because I'm sad.' She thought about it. 'And the bed's a small one,' she added.

She could hear the smile in Violet's voice. 'Darling, I'm not inviting myself to your house. Don't worry. I've got places to go and stay in London. I'll drop you off and then come back for you three days later, do you think? Would that be all right? I know you absolutely have to see them, and they must be longing to see you too. It's brutal that at a time like this you can't hug your mother and sister. I've been thinking and thinking of the best way to get you there.'

Martha thought about Mother and Daphne. She pictured them at home without Daddy and without herself, and she needed to run to them. Cornwall was a strange other world, and she loved it, but London was home. Violet and Betty weren't the same as Mother and Daphne.

The worst thing about going home would be having to leave it again.

'Yes,' she said, and she felt the tears coming again. 'Oh yes, please, Violet.'

'There,' said Violet. 'Think about that. You're going to go home for a few days. We'll arrange it all tomorrow, or rather today. Now, see if you can sleep.'

Daddy had been thirty-five. Mother was thirty-three. Just as Martha was drifting into sleep, she wondered whether Violet was the same age, and how old Edward had been.

'How old are you?' she muttered.

She could hear the laugh in Violet's voice.

'Me? Forty-one,' she said. Martha felt surprise. She was about to say so when she froze.

Aubrey was screaming. He was shouting very bad words loudly. She pulled the blanket over her head and tried to block it out.

16

'I'm going down to check in on Martha.' I remembered that Felicity was paying me to keep an eye on her, and I felt bad about the six of us having fun so close to her, while ignoring her. Particularly after she'd been so brilliant about the party.

I felt Rik's eyes on me as I got up, put on a big shirt I'd found in my new bag of clothes, pulled on my shorts and set off down the drive. I wished he'd stop looking at me. I threw him a stony look, and he shifted over to sit with Meg, as he should have done. I saw him reaching over to touch her arm, taking her attention away from Josie.

It was late in the afternoon, and the shadows were so long, the light so golden, that I felt I was living in a film. Everything was honey-coloured.

I remembered what it was really like here. Most of the time the sky was grey, the wind wild. It was cold. It rained. From time to time there was random hail. It wasn't usually like this; there wasn't often a fairy-tale blast of summer.

But that didn't matter. I loved it like that too. I loved it all. The low winter skies, the rain that made the landscape bright green. This was my place. I knew Josie was itching to get away, but I wasn't. I didn't think I'd ever stray far from West Cornwall. I ran down the driveway, the white stones crunching under my feet.

I knocked, then let myself in; Martha had reached the top of the stairs when I called up to her. She glided down, looking regal in a fluffy dressing gown, and I helped her to her armchair.

'Sorry to disturb you.' I realized I didn't quite know what time it was; when I checked her oven clock, it was nearly five. 'You weren't asleep, were you? Tell me if I woke you up, and I'll go away.'

'Me? No, Senara darling. I was looking out of the window and thinking. Just drifting really. I was three-quarters in the past, to be honest. I find it hard to ground myself sometimes. I drift off, like a balloon. It scares me.'

It scared me too: I didn't want Martha drifting off like a balloon. I needed her to stay the same, always here, always wise and funny and present.

I walked into the kitchen and held up the kettle. She nodded, and I started making tea. Weak Earl Grey with lemon felt like just the thing after an afternoon of sunshine and random dehydrating drinks, so I made one for myself too.

'Which bit of the past were you in?'

She gave a little smile. 'Never mind.'

Then she looked at me with something like panic in her pale blue eyes and spoke quickly. 'Tell me things, Senara. Tell me about now. About you. You kids. What's going on?

I saw those Londoners this morning. Are they as agitated as they seemed?'

I didn't want to go into the Holly thing again, but Martha clearly needed entertaining so I told her anyway. She was, of course, horrified.

'What a so-and-so!' she said. 'I hope Clemmie put him right.'

'She did actually. And he was, like, so, so, so embarrassed. It blew over, kind of, and we've had a brilliant afternoon.' I paused. 'And guess what, Martha – here's some distraction. You know how I never meet anyone I like? Well, there's something even worse than that. It turns out that in spite of everything I just said I do actually like Rik. I felt it the moment I saw him.' I remembered his face filling the screen of the entryphone. 'Maybe not the *first* moment, but as soon as he was near me. Then I hated him, and now I still hate him.'

I took a deep breath and wondered whether to go on. Because it was Martha, I did.

'But there's something about him. I never thought I'd be drawn to someone like that, and he's with Meg, so it's impossible anyway. I hate myself for feeling attracted to him because his girlfriend is right there, and I don't even like him.'

She leaned forward. Her eyes were different now. She was sharp, focused.

'How long have they been together? Is it very serious?'

'I guess so. I mean, I have no idea. But they're on holiday together, and they went to St Mawes together last year, and Clem treats them as a unit.'

'Does he give you all the smouldering eye contact behind her back?' She demonstrated, and I burst out laughing, even though underneath it didn't make me happy.

'Tries to,' I said. 'Yeah.'

'Sorry, my dear, but the boy's a wanker.'

It was nice to laugh, and I couldn't argue with her logic.

'Yes. It's classic, isn't it? I meet someone, and I hate him, and then it turns out he's a Martha-certified wanker.' I remembered her talking about Barney. 'What would you have done if Barney had been one? It's quite a risk deciding you'll marry the next presentable person you meet, and then doing it. I was going to give it a go with the next half-interesting person I met because you inspired me. But now I can't because it's Rik.'

'If Barney hadn't been up to scratch, I wouldn't have given him the time of day. I mean, I probably ignored other contenders along the way.' Martha's expression softened. 'But he was, Senara. He very much was.'

She sighed, and I could see that she was drifting away again. 'I think of the other people in my life all the time. I just sit here and think about them. My parents, my darling sister Daphne. Violet. Her brother . . . Well, Aubrey left us a few years after the war ended. And then came Barney, and I was widowed at fifty. That probably sounds ancient to you, but it's not. It's half my lifetime ago. Then Leon, my baby. My actual baby. I can't help feeling that I'm doomed to carry on alone forever while they all die around me. It's like a fairy-tale curse. Destined to sit here for the rest of my days, useless, outliving all the people I love.'

She took a deep breath and her tone changed. 'That's why I'm looking forward to your party. It's why I need life in the old house. Youth. Future. Possibility. I'm not going to outlive you lot, and that's a fact.'

'Oh, Martha.'

She had such a capable manner, and she was so funny; I'd never realized how much she missed everyone, even though, of course, she must. Her husband and her only child had died, and I'd never given it more than a moment's thought.

I sat next to her and patted her arm, feeling useless, and tried to say the right things. 'You've been through so much. You're not cursed. You're really strong and healthy, I guess.'

I looked down at my hands. Hands were strange things. They were just there, tools on the ends of your arms, flexible and easy to command, with opposable thumbs. I flexed my fingers and crunched them into fists. They were incredible things to have, and I took them for granted all the time.

If I lived long enough, my hands would become like Martha's. They would shake, seize up, grow liver spots. They would stop working properly. I wouldn't be able to pick up a kettle of boiling water; I'd have to rely on other people to make my tea, and they'd probably do it wrong. I wondered whether I would have children, grandchildren, great-grandchildren like Martha, or no one at all.

I asked her the first question that came into my head, something I'd always wondered.

'Why do you call your mum Violet? Why don't you call her Mum?'

Martha was gazing out of the window. She didn't look at me. 'For a very good reason,' she said. 'She wasn't my mother.'

'Oh sorry! I didn't realize.' I thought of what she'd just said: *My parents, my darling sister Daphne*. 'Was she your . . . aunt?'

'A kind of adopted aunt, I suppose. Really just the greatest friend I could ever have had.' She turned to me, her eyes unreadable. 'Haven't I told you this before, Senara? I came here when I was ten. As an evacuee.'

'An evacuee? Were you from London?'

She didn't answer for a long time.

'The crack in my life was too much for me to deal with, and I was scared of what would happen to me if I let it in, so I shut it out. But, yes, I spent the first ten years of my life as a Londoner. We had no money . . . I can barely remember it, you know, but when the memories come I hang on to them and go back in there. That's what happens when I drift off sometimes. I'm going back to Ridley Street. The older I get, the more I find myself able to do it. It's like going home.'

I looked into her face and saw that even now she was only half focused.

'I came down here with my whole school,' she said. 'I thought I would go home, but I never did. I was both extraordinarily lucky and so unlucky that I've never been able to look at it straight on. Honestly, darling – it's like the sun. It's always there in the corner of my vision, but I'm grateful that I seem to have made it through the rest of my life without ever quite looking directly at it. These days you'd have had counselling and all that, but back then you just got on with things because you had to . . .'

I felt she needed me to ask a concrete, trivial question, so I said, 'Did you have a label and a gas mask?'

I watched her pull her focus back with a smile.

'Both. Arriving here is one of the strongest memories of my life. You don't often get a day like that, when you wake up in one life and go to sleep in another. We came down on the train. It's a long journey even now, but in those days a train full of confused London kids who had no idea at all where we were going – can you imagine? I was terrified when I saw a cow.'

'That must have freaked you right out,' I said.

I tried to imagine it, to reframe Martha as a confused young Londoner, rather than the local landowner I'd always imagined her to be. A bewildered child arriving with a gas mask as protection against biological weapons. For the first time I realized that giving children gas masks wasn't cute. It was a sign of a barbaric, brutal world.

'We were put on different buses. My first piece of luck was being assigned to the Pentrellis bus. Being picked out by Violet was the luckiest thing that ever happened in my whole life. I knew it too. As soon as I saw her, I felt it: I had to go home with her. Her brother Aubrey was unpredictable – poor man – but when he was good there was no one better. And Violet managed to be everything we all needed.'

'Why was he troubled?'

'Shell shock from the Great War. When he was on form, he'd be so funny. He did little puppet shows and put on silly voices. But most of the time he stayed in his room, and he'd scream. Blood-curdling. To this day I've never known anything like it. Poor Aubrey.' She nodded a few times. 'So, yes. Although it wasn't his fault, I did learn that it's difficult living with an unpredictable man. An unpredictable person. Man or woman. Before I married Barney, I made sure he was gentle and steady above all else. And he was.'

'Shell shock,' I said. 'That's PTSD?'

'Oh, they're always changing the names of things.' She took a deep breath. 'Everyone forgets I was an evacuee. It might be because I forget to tell them. I spend most of my life believing that Martha Roberts is a real person. Isn't that funny? When she shouldn't have existed at all.'

17

Everyone was gathering things up at the pool when I got back. They looked purposeful. They were packing towels into bags rather than just taking stuff inside.

'I didn't know Martha was from London originally,' I said as I approached.

'Oh yeah,' said Clem. 'Her evacuee thing. It's cute, isn't it? Coming here with her little suitcase and taking the family name. She's not really one of us at all.'

'Clem,' I said, 'she's your ancestor. You're descended from her. Of course she's one of you. You're part of her.'

'Gareth, grab that. Yeah, but we're the real Robertses. The Campion-Robertses. We've been here forever. Tin-mining money, and then Gran married well because the tin mining stopped, so without Barney she would have been poor. You can look it up. The Roberts family go back for generations.'

'All families go back for generations,' said Josie. 'I mean, where do you think the rest of us came from? We didn't just jump down from a tree. We literally all go back to the moment life crawled out of the ocean.'

'You know what I mean.'

'Not really,' said Josie, and there was a moment of tension, which Rik broke.

'We're going to the beach,' he said. 'I mean, me and Meg are so far beyond the point of needing to sleep after our crap sleep on the train, and we've been looking over the fence, and it's literally the ocean.'

'So it feels a bit lame to stay here in the pool all day, like we just did, and ignore the fact that there's a beach right there and an ocean that goes all the way to America,' said Meg.

'Lame?' Clem was obviously feeling combative this afternoon – maybe Gareth hadn't been paying her enough attention. 'Well, *excuse me*. Sorry that you find my house and garden *lame*. Jeez.'

'Not your house, you twat. It's the least lame house ever. Not your garden. Not your pool. Us.'

Clem looked out towards the ocean. This was my favourite time of day, with intense honey-tinted light, and the water was entirely flat. She looked as if she was going to say something, but for once she didn't. I watched her face as she changed her mind.

'When this is mine,' she said instead, 'I'm going to put a zip wire in. So we can go to the beach from here without having to walk miles in the wrong direction, all the way down the drive, first, and then all the way back.'

I prepared myself for Gareth to start bullshitting, and, sure enough, there he was, looking around and talking crap, pretending he knew anything about zip wires.

'You'd need to build a little tower up here,' he said. 'A platform, to set off from. It would be too steep to just drop down. So I reckon you'd have to make it kind of a slalom in the sky over the beach, with a few supports along the way. You'd be like this.' He demonstrated with a hand, swooshing first one way and then the other.

'Cool. We'll do it.'

I could sense Josie rolling her eyes, but she couldn't help joining in.

'The beach is pretty small at high tide,' she said. 'You'd land in the sea half the time.'

'Perfect!' Clem swung her bag on to her shoulder. 'So, until I've built it, we'd better head, like, five miles down the drive in a massive detour. So annoying.'

I wondered what it was actually like in Clem's head. From what I could tell from the outside, she was so insulated by money and confidence that nothing in the world bothered her, as Martha had said. The only thing that had rattled her was the panic about Martha's will.

We stood knee-deep in the ocean and looked out at the horizon. There were a few other people on the beach, sitting round barbecues, drinking from cans. The people with the kids slathered in sunscreen and UV bodysuits had left, and evening people were arriving. The beach smelled of burning sausages.

Clem ran through the water, shrieking, and I sensed people looking at her. I felt the undercurrents that she didn't notice at all, the strangeness of finding myself on the other side of this divide, of being *the people from the big house*.

Gareth ran after her. Josie and Meg had disappeared into the shadows, and somehow there was just me, standing in the water with bloody Rik. Great.

I took a step away, and another. I fixated on Martha's words – '*Sorry, my dear, but the boy's a wanker*' – and looked out to the horizon.

'Senara,' he said after a moment, 'it's the only thing I can think of. My faux pas. It's going to haunt me for the rest of my life. In fifty years, if someone asks for my most embarrassing moment, I won't even have to think about it.'

I stared at the sea. The flat surface was shining as if it was solid. I leaned down and touched it to check it wasn't, even though I could feel it lapping against my legs.

'Don't worry. It's fine.' I kept my voice chilly.

'It's not, though.'

I shrugged. 'We come from different worlds – and Clem's from your world, so you made assumptions.' I relived the scene in my head. 'I just grabbed the first thing I could find because I was asleep when you arrived. I didn't mean to be wearing a maid's dress. I didn't know it was one. I mean, it wasn't. It was a black dress.'

He turned his head and smiled down at me, and I felt my stomach doing something strange, in spite of myself.

'You know – your world looks OK to me.'

A Martha-certified wanker, I reminded myself. And he's with Meg.

'That's because it's a heatwave, and it's July. It's not quite the school holidays so it's not too busy. You're seeing it at an exceptional time. I mean, yeah, my life is fine, and I do love it here. If I had kids, I'd want them to grow up here. But the other thing is, you're looking at Cornwall from Clem's house, which is not what life is actually like. Come back in January when it's been raining for weeks, when it's cold, and everywhere you'd want to go to is shut, and Clem and her family are living it up in . . .' I tried to think of somewhere that might be warm in January. 'Barbados?'

'Maybe I will.'

We stood in silence for a bit. I hated him. I had to keep hold of that fact because inside I was on fire. I wanted to touch him, but I couldn't even look at him. I felt the electricity, little flames leaping through the air between us. I felt myself unfurling inside, warmth going through me as if I'd swallowed poison.

Good poison.

No. Bad poison. Bad, bad poison.

I took a deep breath. 'How long have you and Meg been together?' I tried to be as casual as I could.

The silence was unbearable. It was broken only by Clem yelling 'You bastard!' somewhere out of sight and a wave of annoyance from the other people on the beach. Then we were back to silence. Seagulls. More silence.

'Um,' he said in the end. 'OK. Weird question. All our lives?'

'All your . . .' It shouldn't have taken me as long as it did to piece together. The cogs and wheels shifted in my head, and everything resettled. It wasn't possible. Was it?

'You mean . . . ?'

'I mean, you know we're brother and sister, right? Twins.'

I replayed the afternoon. They had been close, yes, but had I seen them even touching each other?

Just that once, and he had just touched her arm to get her attention. They were close because . . .

'Oh my God.'

He gave me a hard look. 'Seriously?'

'I had no idea. None of us did. Clem said –' I tried to remember what, exactly, Clem had said. I darted a quick look at him. Did I hate him now?

It all seemed to be melting away in the sunshine, dissolving into the ocean.

'What did Clem say? Because Clem might not be great with details, but this is pretty big.'

My mind was racing, recalibrating everything. What were the exact words she'd used?

'She said you were inseparable and adorable, and that you come as a pair, or something like that. She one hundred per cent implied you were together. I mean, Gareth and Josie and me, we totally thought that. You arrived together, you kind of finish each other's sentences and all that.'

'Ew.' He half gasped. 'Right. That's super weird and icky. Meg's my very slightly older sister, so, yeah, it's a bit grim to find out that the three of you have been thinking that all day.'

Everything was different. The sparks jumping between us were ten times as bright. I didn't care about the Holly thing any more. The sun shone brighter; the sea was gentle on my legs. I felt the electricity coming off him. I felt it inside myself, in places I wasn't usually aware of.

There was one thing I had to ask, and I felt the universe pause while I did it. The ocean stopped moving. The seagulls were still in the sky.

I tried to keep my voice steady. 'Do you have a partner at home?'

'No,' he said.

The birds started gliding again. The waves lapped at my legs. The earth turned.

His word, those two letters, opened things up. *No.*

Could we have a holiday romance? Maybe I could have a week of not being a sidekick.

'Does Meg?'

'She was with someone for two years, but they broke up about a month ago. She's been cut up about it. It's going to do her a lot of good being down here.' He smiled, a little private smile. 'A *lot* of good.'

'She's really lovely.'

'Yeah. She's always been the good twin. The one people warm to. I'm the one who says stupid things to girls he likes. I guess I'm the evil twin.'

Girls he likes.

He was talking about me. Wasn't he? Should I say something back? What could I say? What if he was just talking generally? He probably meant he liked me as a friend. I couldn't even look at him in case I blurted out something stupid. *I like you too.* That kind of thing. Cringe.

'Clem is the worst hostess,' he was saying. 'The actual worst. I mean, how hard would it have been? All she had to do was say, "*This is Senara, my friend. This is Meg and Rik – they're brother and sister.*" A few words. That would have been all it took. She did go through a phase of calling us "twinnies". It drove us crazy, but now I kind of wish she still did it.'

I nodded. We looked at each other. I looked up at his dark eyes, his cheekbones, his black hair. I looked at the hairs on his arms, his broad chest. I longed for him and wondered whether he could see it in my face. I tried to force him, through the power of my mind, to step towards me and touch me. Just a hand on my arm. My shoulder. I longed for contact, but I couldn't do it myself.

He was going to do it. I felt it, felt him moving towards me.

'Senni! Rik!'

It was Clem, shouting so loudly that people must have heard her all over Cornwall. The others were perched on the big rocks at the side of the bay. I looked up at the cliff and flashed back to Josie, Gareth and me standing down here in January, freezing cold, filming with that old video camera.

When Rik and I reached them, I climbed on the rock next to Josie and tried to calm myself down. What had just been about to happen? I wanted to tell Josie everything, but not now, when everyone was here. I needed to talk about something else to stop myself accidentally babbling on about Rik, and so I whispered the first thing that came to mind.

'Remember the drone?'

We looked up. The cliff rose above us, grey and blank.

Josie answered in a low voice. 'If we hadn't done that, you'd never have become friends with Martha, would you? So I guess it worked out for the best in the end. Martha's so cool.'

I was about to ask when Josie had ever actually spoken to her, but Clem's voice cut through the quiet.

'*What* made you become friends with Martha?'

How had she heard that? Josie had been talking so quietly.

'Oh, nothing.' She managed to make it sound casual.

Clem shuffled over. 'No, tell me.'

I looked at her face, bright in the last of the day's light. Clem was strange. Most of the time she appeared to live for fun, on the surface, though for some of this afternoon she'd been jumpy and difficult. I wished, for a second, that we could swap places. I wanted to inhabit Clem, to find out what really went on. Also, if I could inhabit Clem, I'd know what it felt like to understand Latin, to be good at ballet and street dance, to be able to ride horses and buy anything I wanted. If I could inhabit Clem, I would know exactly what to say and do to make Rik like me. I'd be confident and experienced. I wished I could take those skills from Clem, and then jump back into my own body.

I pulled myself back to the moment. Rik was on the next rock, and I was pretty sure he was telling Meg about our confusion.

'I want to know how you did actually become friends with Martha, Senni.' Clem was looking into my face, holding my gaze with her blue eyes. 'You never said. Neither did she. One minute I'd never heard of you, and the next Mum was telling me that Gran was banging on about you on the phone all the time. How Senara makes the Earl Grey just right. Senara was so helpful. Working so hard for her little exams. All that. What happened?'

Little exams. Clem's exams, the exact same ones, hadn't been *little* in her world.

I took a deep breath and tried to choose my words carefully.

'She saw me walking past her window,' I said. 'And she tapped on it and asked me to come in and make her a cup of tea.'

That was true. I'd run with that.

'Seriously? You were literally walking down the street, and Gran banged on the window? Was she OK?'

I was getting ready to style it out when Gareth jumped across from another rock and sat behind her. He put his legs on either side of her, and she leaned back into him.

'Senara was just telling me how she met Gran,' she said lazily. 'Apparently Gran tapped on her window and made Senni come in?'

Josie and I started talking at the same time, but Gareth

was closer to Clem, speaking right next to her ear, so nothing we said could drown him out.

'They told you?' he said, looking furiously at us, oblivious to our reactions. 'Shit. OK. Yeah, it wasn't our finest moment. Sorry about that. We wouldn't have done any of it if we'd known how cool you were.'

Josie and I tried to signal to him to stop. I waved. She shook her head. We both tried to talk over him, but he'd spoken, and Clem had heard, and the silence lasted a thousand years. I felt the ocean warming, the cliff crumbling, the coarse sand becoming fine and white.

Then Clem said, her voice bright: 'What wouldn't you have done?'

Josie and I exchanged panicked glances.

'It was Gareth's school project,' she said loudly. 'That's all. He was filming different parts of the Cornish coastline, and we were helping him get some footage of the cliff.' She pointed to it.

I thought this was sounding OK, considering, so I joined in. 'He just needed some shots of this bit here.'

None of that counted for anything, though, because Gareth was answering her question too, and both of them ignored us.

'Well, your house had been empty for so long,' he said. 'I really wanted to include it in my coursework, just the outside of it, because it was so amazing and deserted, and that was kind of atmospheric. That's why we sent the drone up to see if we could have a look.'

'You sent what?' Clem was laughing. 'Shut up! What?'

And I stopped trying at that point, because Gareth was telling her the whole story and nothing Josie or I could say was going to make any difference. Clem seemed to find it hilariously amusing, and that was almost reassuring.

Almost.

'You went over the fence? With ropes and a harness? To get your crashed drone? Oh my God, you guys are *total* trespassers! And Gran knows about this?'

Gareth finally realized he'd confessed unnecessarily. 'I mean, I thought that was what you guys were talking about?' He flashed his eyes over to me and Josie. Josie drew a finger across her throat while I shook my head. I saw his face change. 'She only caught Senara, but she knows it was the three of us. We needed to get the memory card back because . . .'

I watched his face fall as his mind finally caught up with his mouth.

'Because what?'

I remembered Gareth calling Martha a serial killer. '*Last one standing.*' That was what he'd said.

Josie had said, '*The girl who hates us was the first to die.*'

And I'd said, '*The lawn is littered with the bones of the Roberts family.*' Then I'd said, '*And that girl who went missing.*' Why? Why had I done that?

We'd shown that footage to a few of our friends, and then Gareth had taken what he needed for his coursework, then destroyed the memory card. He'd promised us that.

I remembered him promising that he would do it. I couldn't remember him confirming that it had been done.

'Because we were twats,' he said now.

Clem met my eye. We looked at each other for what must have been a few seconds, but it felt as if another ice age came and went. She was unreadable.

'You're hilarious,' she said. She smiled and her eyes lit up and everything clicked back into place. 'Is my house in your coursework then?'

He shook his head. 'Nah. It felt wrong to use it after all that.'

'Well, you don't need to climb the fence any more. Senni has her keys, and she's taking care of us. And I kind of forgot that there was a time when we didn't even know each other. I'd have done the same thing if I were you.' She stood up. 'Shall we go home?'

1988

Rachel asked Felicity not to tell Alex and Jenna about her dad, so when they came back they'd swum in the freezing pool and talked about nothing in particular. It started raining, and they couldn't get warm, so as soon as they'd done a few frenzied lengths they ran back into the house and wrapped themselves in big towels. They sat in the sitting room, wearing jeans and big jumpers, with their hair in towel turbans and mugs of hot chocolate in their hands, and half watched a video of *Crocodile Dundee*. Felicity kept meaning to go and bake her brownies, but Rachel's revelations had shaken her, and she wanted to be next to her all the time, to make sure she was OK. Alex produced a pile of blankets from the airing cupboard, and they snuggled up.

The film was funny, but she didn't really watch it. Her head was full of Rachel. She had so many questions for her.

How long had her dad been violent? Did he hit her mother too? Why didn't her mum protect her? It was overflowing, and all she could do was grab Rachel's hand and squeeze.

'Rach is staying here tonight,' she said when she couldn't stay quiet any longer.

'Me too,' said Jenna.

'Great,' said Alex, but he was mainly talking to Jenna. When Felicity got up to go to the loo, Rachel followed her out of the room.

'I'm scared,' she said, her words falling over each other. She took Felicity's sleeve and led her into the kitchen and outside. 'About staying here. My dad's going to be looking for me. He'll be panicking that I'm telling people. Showing them what he did to my face. He's going to want to drag me home. I don't want to bring him into your lovely home, Lissy. You don't understand what he's like.'

'No way. You stay here. We'll look after you. We'll call the police if we have to. Can I tell Alex?'

Rachel blew out so her hair flew up in front of her face.

'I guess you have to. Just the outline, in case Dad turns up. Not the police, though. No way. Promise?'

'We'll tell Alex and Jenna, and we'll all be alert. If he comes, you can hide upstairs, and we'll say we haven't seen you.' She thought about the attic. 'There's a bedroom up there with a bolt on the inside.'

Rachel shook her head. 'If he found me here, he'd go berserk. I need to go much further afield. Seriously, he'd push me over that cliff if he caught me up here. Drown me in your pool. Bury me in your garden. I'm bringing shame upon the family.'

They stood outside, in the courtyard.

'I'll need to go thousands of miles away,' said Rachel. 'India. Thailand. Maybe Peru or something.' She paused. 'So you know Andy Teague?'

Felicity nodded. 'I didn't know his surname, but yes. Bad idea, Rach.'

It turned out that Rachel had met Andy Teague when he approached her at the bus stop (clearly his best hunting ground), and they were making fanciful plans to run away to Thailand together.

'I'm not sure if he means it,' said Rachel, 'but I hope he does.' She looked at Felicity's face. 'It's not like that! It's not a romantic thing. It's just a getting-away-from-here thing.'

'But, Rach!' Felicity felt helpless. 'He's a creep! You can't run away with him.'

Rachel started to say something, but stopped herself. 'Anyway,' she said instead, 'we'd better go back to the film.'

When *Crocodile Dundee* finished, Felicity put a mix tape on, and Jenna and Alex got up and started dancing. It was adorable. They were dancing to 'Wake Me Up Before You Go-Go', holding each other's hands and mirroring each other's steps, laughing. They looked good together: Alex so tall and serious, Jenna tiny and doll-like, but tough as anything. Felicity hoped they *would* get together, then hoped they wouldn't, because Alex was going to university so they'd have to break up, and it would be awkward for her, stuck in the middle.

She was distracting herself from Rachel. Rachel, and her parents, and the fact that Rachel's life was in such a state that Andy Teague felt like a saviour. Felicity knew that she couldn't let Rachel leave with him, but she didn't know how to stop her.

'Thanks for letting me hide out,' said Rachel, shifting up closer to her. 'You're so lucky living up here. And your parents just leave you to it.'

'I wish yours were . . .' Felicity didn't know how to end the sentence.

'I don't think mine have ever liked me,' said Rachel. 'I mean, you know my dad.' Felicity nodded at that. 'He wanted boys, but since we were girls he wanted perfect little girls in matching pinafores. Doing the flowers for church. Making cups of tea for the people who come to the house. The vicar's daughters. Probably one of us would marry well, and the other would stay a spinster to look after him and Mum in their old age. He thinks I'm an "abomination".'

Felicity gasped, and Rachel nodded. 'That's actually what he said. My hair. My clothes. The fact that I refuse to go to church. I told him I was an atheist. I wish I could just knuckle down and live his way like Lucy does. But I can't.' She sighed and rubbed her bruised forehead.

Felicity thought about Lucy, Rachel's angelic little sister.

'Does Lucy take the heat off you at all?'

'Poor Luce. The golden girl. Not as much as you'd think. He's always playing us off against each other, and I feel bad for her having to keep it up. I mean, I'm seventeen! Surely old enough to get the fuck out of here. I feel bad leaving her, though.' She was breathing fast now. 'Anyway, tell me about you. Distract me. Are you going to leave Cornwall when you've finished your course?'

Felicity apologized mentally to her dad for ever having considered him annoying. He was so gentle, so devoted, and both her parents had always let their children be whoever they wanted. She realized, again, how lucky she and Alex were.

'I don't know,' she said. 'I suppose that in a few years I'll be qualified to cook for a living, and I guess then I can go wherever I want. Maybe I'll go and live in Italy or something.' She lowered her voice. 'Doesn't your mum stop him?'

Rachel's voice was almost a whisper. 'She does it too.' She spoke louder. 'I can totally see you being the chef in a little taverna in Umbria or something. A restaurant in Paris. A private boat. You're going to have the world at your feet.'

Felicity wondered whether Rachel might be right. Clattery Parisian restaurants were far too scary, but a little taverna? A boat? Maybe.

Felicity had forgotten how much she liked Rachel. She couldn't let her go home, and she couldn't let her leave with Andy.

'Can I tell my grandma?' she said. 'Please?'

She felt her eyes filling with tears. Grandma would know what to do. Grandma already hated the vicar. She had called him a 'patriarchal arsehole – a patriarsehole'.

Rachel was wavering. 'Not until I've gone.'

'Please? She's brilliant.'

The other two were swaying now, Jenna's head resting on Alex's chest. The music was the song from *Dirty Dancing*.

Rachel was blinking fast. 'I'll think about it, OK? Can we talk about something else? Do you want children one day? If you could plan your own family, who would you have in it?'

The colours in Felicity's head cleared, in spite of everything. A picture appeared. A figure, surrounded by orange.

'A little girl,' she said at once. 'She'd be everything I'm not. Good at reading, and not afraid to talk to people. She'd have an easy life, and she'd always be happy.'

'What's her name?'

Felicity thought again about the orange colour around this imaginary daughter.

'Clementine.' She smiled at the vision of the perfect little girl in her head. In real life, she would never be able to manage a relationship with a boy well enough to get to the point of having a baby, but it was soothing to imagine it. 'What about you?'

'I don't want children. But, if I had to, I'd have a boy and a girl, and they'd be able to be whoever they wanted, and my parents would never get to meet them, not even once. They wouldn't even know they existed.'

Jenna and Alex left the room. Rachel took the remote control and put the TV back on. They sat and watched whatever was on.

18

Clem went inside and came back with a box of chocolates that looked as if it was an expensive present that definitely wasn't available for casual eating.

'Are you sure?' I said as she held it out to me. I was sitting next to Rik. We'd both made sure that happened. I wanted to lean on him, but I didn't quite dare. He was drawing me towards him like a magnet.

She shook the box at me. It was green and gold, and I thought I saw the words FORTNUM & MASON on the side, but it was hard to tell because her hand was partly covering it.

'Stop being so sensible! Of course I'm sure.'

I took a caramel. It was the best chocolate I'd ever had, by a million miles. The box went round once, twice, three times. I hoped this wasn't going to get us into trouble with Felicity.

Could I be a rebel? A bad girl? Could I not care about what Felicity thought?

No. I might be in search of a persona, but it wasn't going to be that one.

Clem was looking from me to Gareth to Josie, all of us with chocolates in our mouths. 'Look at you three,' she said. 'You've gone from breaking and entering to lounging on our lawn, eating our expensive chocolates.'

I felt the mango cream turning to dust in my mouth. I wasn't sure what to say, and I didn't think I liked her expression. I felt Rik leaning up against me, and I relaxed on to him. I could feel every point at which our bodies were touching. The things going on inside me were the best distraction in the world from Clem.

'That's harsh, babe,' said Gareth.

'Didn't mean it to be,' she said. 'I love you guys! I wouldn't know what to do with myself if you weren't here. Can we be friends forever? Can we do this every summer?' She kissed him on the lips.

I looked at Josie, who motioned with her head, and I tore myself away from Rik and walked down the garden a bit.

'Why did he have to tell her?' I said as soon as we were out of earshot.

I wanted to be back with Rik. I wanted him to follow us. Apart from the overwhelming longing that filled every single cell of my body, I also wanted his perspective on Clem. 'She's being weird. I don't know whether she means it, but I feel really bad about being here now. Awkward. I want to give back the money and uncancel my dog walks.'

Josie shook her head. 'I don't give a shit,' she said. 'Honestly, Senni, there are things to care about, and Clem Parker isn't one of them. She's nicer and more fun than I expected. We're here. Meg's amazing. And so's Rik. But they'll all be gone soon, and we'll be at college, and you know it'll be raining next week. If Clem finds it uncomfortable that we climbed her fence – well, I find it uncomfortable that she called us peasants, so go figure.'

We carried on walking.

'Oh God!' I said. 'Did you know that Rik and Meg are brother and sister? Twins?'

She stared at me. 'I did not! I did think they weren't a very tactile couple. Why did Clem tell you they were together?'

'She didn't. She said they were "inseparable" or something.'

'Are they single?'

'Apparently so.'

Josie's face lit up, and she looked the way I felt. My stomach lurched. Did she like Rik too?

We had reached the camellia bed, and we sat down beside the hole Molly had dug. It seemed to pull me back, every time.

'They do actually look alike,' she said. Then she took a deep breath and said, 'You like him, don't you? I can see it. He's the one. He's broken through your defences.'

I smiled. I had no idea I was that transparent.

'Do you like him too?' My voice came out tiny.

She laughed. 'Me? No! Absolutely no way. Anyway, I should get home.'

'How's your mum?'

Josie looked away. 'Different. I'll tell you everything next week.' She reached into the excavation and pulled out a stone.

'You know,' she said, looking at it, 'I came back loads of

times after that first trespass. I climbed the fence, and I just wandered round the garden whenever I had an hour or so. Don't tell Clem. Or Gareth, because apparently he tells her everything.'

'How did you get in on your own?'

'I figured out that I could get over the fence without the rope, and then grab the branch of a tree that had grown over a bit and pull myself from there. It was my secret garden. It didn't feel like it was Clem's back then.'

She flipped over on to her front and looked down into the hole. 'There are loads of stones down here.' She reached in and started scrabbling around. I sat and watched, and after a while she pulled out something shiny. 'Not a stone,' she said. It was clearly a fork.

'What the fuck?' We both looked at it for a while and burst out laughing.

We lay side by side and peered down.

Josie reached in again and took out what was clearly another bone. It was small, curved at one end. Too small to be anything but an animal bone probably. She put it carefully on the grass.

I edged forward. I was certain that this flower bed held secrets. I stared into the hole as she put her hand in once more. I knew we shouldn't have been doing this. I tried not to, but it hooked me. The whole day was surreal, and at least pulling forks out of the earth kept me away from Clem and her spikiness. There were times when you just wanted your best friend, and this was one of them.

'There's something else.' Josie was lying on her stomach,

searching in the hole with both hands. 'It's smooth. It might be Clem's family jewels. She'll like us again if we bring her some plundered African diamonds, right?'

When she pulled it out, I felt the world tipping from side to side. I grabbed a camellia branch to steady myself. I looked away.

I looked back. This answered one of the questions anyway.

Josie held it in her hands. I thought I was going to be sick. The colours were too bright. The evening sunlight was nauseating. I closed my eyes. I already knew that the ground beneath me was made of dead things. The world was built on death. Even petrol was made from dead creatures. Compost. Soil. The land, the sea. I thought of Martha, close to the end of her own life. I felt myself take a shuddering breath.

I opened my eyes. It was still there.

Josie was holding a skull. She had it in both hands like Hamlet, but it was real. We were both frozen. Time passed.

Josie placed it on the grass next to the little bone that was clearly half of its missing jawbone. Someone's brain had been in there, and it had rotted away. This had contained everything that made a human into the person they were, and now it was a shell. It had big blank eye sockets.

I heard a distant shout. 'Guys! Hey! Where are you? Did they leave?'

Gareth.

Josie and I looked at each other. We looked back at the skull. There was a moment when I thought we were both contemplating putting it back in the ground and covering it over, but the moment passed.

We snapped back to reality.

'Over here!' said Josie. Her voice was too quiet, and then she shouted it.

Clem and Gareth were walking towards us. I tried to tell myself that this had to be an old skeleton from the ancient burial site, maybe a plague victim. (Would it still have the plague? Should we be wearing gloves and masks?)

It had been buried with a watch and a fork. And old bodies would have been further down. Six feet under. That was a thing, wasn't it? The bodies in the old burial ground that Felicity had talked about would have been in coffins. Wouldn't they? Did coffins rot away? We waited for Clem and Gareth, as if either of them might have had a clue what we should do.

The skull was light brown, like the other bone. It had housed a brain. That was all I could think about.

Clem saw it and screamed. Rik and Meg came running down the garden.

'Human remains,' said Rik. 'You call someone if you find human remains. You have to. It's the law.' He reached out and touched the skull with a fingertip, then pulled his hand back.

We were sitting in a circle round it.

'We have to wait for my mum,' said Clem. 'Let's put it back in the ground and cover it over. We can deal with it after the party. Mum will sort it out when she gets back.

And that other one too, I guess. Probably belonged with this one. Not Mr Smiffles after all.'

'Clem – we can't do that,' I said. 'We can't just shove it back in the flower bed.'

'You still want to have the party?' said Meg.

'Of course I do!' said Clem. 'I mean, this guy's not going to mind. He's not exactly going to *tell* anyone. It's been a while. So he's probably jumped out of the plague pit.' She took out her phone and waggled it in the air. 'Hey, plague guy! We call this an *iPhone*.'

'It's not a plague pit, Clem,' said Josie. She indicated the fork with her head. 'And the watch. They were together. This isn't an old body. Well, not *old* old. Not plague-old.'

'Yeah,' said Clem. 'I mean, sure. Whatever. And we'll tell someone.' She reached over and ruffled Gareth's hair. 'Your mum, for instance, babes. There we go! Gareth's mum is the perfect person. But nothing we do now will bring this guy back, whether they're from fifty years ago or a thousand. And the stuff that was down there with the bones – well, let's just put it all back in and leave it. We'll get the police to come and look at it on Sunday. And I'll message my mum, I promise. On Sunday.'

Rik cut in. 'Gareth, why don't you call your mum now? See what she says.'

'No!' Clem insisted. 'Look, it makes no difference. We've got a party tomorrow. And on Sunday we're going to deal with all this, I promise. Guys! I promise. OK? Sunday. Two days makes no difference to anything at all.'

19

Josie was discovering that there was something about holding someone's dead head in your hands that made you appreciate every single thing about being alive. The only thing to do with her own fleeting life was to live it because one day her skull would be empty too, and she'd be that way for a long time.

Meg and Rik were twins.

She was amazed that Senara hadn't noticed the joy that had coursed through her at those words. Actually Senara had seen it, but she'd thought it meant she fancied Rik too. Josie wanted to laugh at the very idea. Rik! FFS. It was Meg. *Megmegmegmegmeg*.

She was transfixed by Meg. From the moment she'd seen her. She believed, now, in love at first sight.

Love?

It wasn't *not* love. It was *something* at first sight, something big, and the world had fractured. Meg didn't have a boyfriend after all. She had a brother.

This was the most real thing Josie had ever felt.

She didn't want to think about Meg going home. She pushed away all thoughts of Mum, of the future, of her uncle, and even of Rachel Thomas and the skull in the ground. She made an effort to seize this happiness.

'I'll come with you,' said Meg when Josie said she had to go home. 'I won't come in. I'll just walk back with you, if that's OK. I don't want to intrude. I'd like to have a walk through the village.'

'Brilliant,' said Josie, grinning at Meg, who held the eye contact. She ran her hand over her short hair and wondered what Meg thought of it. She'd been out of her mind when she did it, but now she was used to it she thought she might keep it short.

They set off down the drive. The two of them, walking together. Josie was taller. Meg took more steps than she did, to keep up, and Josie slowed her pace to accommodate her. 'I can't believe you spent the night on a train last night,' she said. 'You must be knackered.'

Meg turned her eyes on her. 'I kind of am? But also not. The whole day has felt trippy. I mean, did all that really just happen? All this.'

The skull and its implications were trying to push the exciting things away, but it wasn't working. The exciting bits pushed back because here she was, walking down the drive with Megan. She swung between the two states. Horror; excitement. Bad thing; good thing. Thing that had definitely happened; thing that might happen.

The skull could be there for a legitimate reason. It

didn't have to be sinister. It didn't necessarily mean that someone had been murdered. Old burial ground. That could be real.

Josie took her phone out of her pocket and looked at it. But then she pushed it back in. Like Clem had said, this wasn't exactly urgent. Human remains would trigger a serious, urgent response. She'd watched enough TV to know that much. It would probably be easier for them to come on Monday anyway.

'That skull,' she said. She hadn't meant to say it.

'I know.'

'I've been – well, the village has this story about a girl who vanished. And I'm just wondering if . . .'

'Tell me the story.'

'I mean, it won't be her, right? The watch wouldn't have been hers. But she was friends with Clem's mum, and she was – well, it's a long story, but it involves an uncle I never met.'

'Go on.'

It took about fifteen minutes to walk from the end of the drive at Cliff House to the centre of the village, and, by the time they got there, Josie had told Meg the whole story. She wanted Meg to say that the skull definitely couldn't have anything to do with the missing girl, but of course she couldn't say that.

The police would come on Sunday, and they'd find out.

By the time they reached Josie's house, they were holding hands. Josie had tried it, and Meg hadn't pulled away.

Holding Megan's hand made the world shine and glow and promise her things.

They turned into the cul-de-sac. She looked for Lucy, for Molly, but the house next door was quiet.

'That's Lucy's house,' she said.

'Oh God, poor her!'

Josie remembered the way the bone had felt under her fingertips, the way her stomach had lurched when she'd realized what it was that she was digging up.

'And this is us.' She worked hard on not being embarrassed.

Meg grinned. 'Cool.' They looked at each other. Meg knew about Josie's mum, knew that she didn't handle visitors, so she said, 'Shall we just sit here for a moment?'

It was starting to get dark. They sat on the doorstep. Josie filled her in on the story of the drone. 'I have a feeling that Clem's not as relaxed about it as she wants us to think.'

'Oh God,' said Meg, 'I've known Clem forever. Yeah, she'll have been offended for a bit, but by now she'll have forgotten about it. Specially after everything that just happened in the garden.' Their eyes met.

'Right,' said Josie, putting Clem out of her mind. 'Sure. I guess that's OK then.'

'It is,' said Meg. 'It's all going to be *splann*.'

Their little fingers touched. It was electric. It was everything Josie had ever wanted. It opened pathways inside her. New things flooded her.

She turned her face towards Meg. Could they kiss?

They'd only met today, but they had no time. No time at all. She started to lean forward.

The door opened behind them.

'Josie!' Mum was standing there. 'Oh, thank goodness. I didn't know who was on our doorstep. What are you doing out there? Come in. Hello.' This last bit was to Megan.

Meg stood up and smiled at her. Mum was wearing an actual dress, and Josie's heart broke for her. She was trying so hard, because of Uncle Andy, because of Josie. Her hair was tied back. There were bags under her eyes, but her eyes themselves were engaged in a way Josie hadn't seen for such a long time. She felt the surge of hope again in her chest and this time didn't squash it down quite as far as before.

'Hello,' said Meg. 'Nice to meet you. I'm Meg.'

'Angie,' Mum replied. 'And please, girls – come in! You don't need to sit out there.'

They looked at each other. Josie raised her eyebrows. Meg nodded.

Mum had clearly been up a ladder, cleaning cobwebs out of the corner of the ceiling. Once she'd said a few more polite things to Meg, she went back to it.

'I've been looking at these for weeks,' she said. 'Never quite had the energy to get up here and do it.'

'Where did you get the ladder?' asked Josie.

'Borrowed it from Lucy. I'm going to do all the corners before I give it back. I feel bad for the spiders, though. Look at me, bulldozing their homes.'

'If you were looking at them,' said Josie, 'you should have said. I'd have done it.'

She felt a tiny bit affronted; she couldn't help it. Mum was feeling better, and she was doing the housework properly. Not the way Josie did it. The whole place smelled of polish and cleaning spray and bleach.

'You're not killing them, though,' said Meg. 'And they'll just run off and make new homes. That's what they do. They'll be fine.'

Mum nodded lots of times. She really was trying so hard. Josie had never known her willingly invite a stranger into the house.

'Drink?' she said to Megan. Remembering the array of concoctions Rik had produced from Clem's kitchen, she clarified the options. 'We have tea, instant coffee and water.'

'Perfect,' said Meg. 'I'd love a cup of tea.'

They took their drinks into Josie's room and closed the door. There were little bits of torn paper all over the floor, but Megan didn't ask, and Josie decided she would tell her later.

They sat next to each other on the bed, and this time Josie didn't second-guess herself. She and Meg leaned in for the kiss together. Their lips met, and kissing a girl was different. Meg's lips were soft. Her mouth was small.

Josie's hands were on Meg's waist. Meg's hands were under Josie's T-shirt. They moved up. Josie gasped and leaned back. Meg pulled her own T-shirt over her head, and then Josie's. She looked at the door.

'It's OK,' whispered Josie. 'She won't come in. Don't stop.'

She didn't.

1940

Martha never made that trip to London.

She didn't go there again until the summer of 1953, when Violet took her to see the Coronation crowds, and they didn't go anywhere near the East End. London wasn't her home any more.

They were ready to set off on their three-day visit: everything was planned and the train tickets were bought. Martha had packed her bag. Violet had arranged to stay with friends, and Miss Ward was going to come and stay at Cliff House to help May make sure Betty, Michael and Roy were all right. Violet refused to leave them with Aubrey because his days were hardly ever good any more, and there was no way he could look after children.

Two days before they were due to leave, the second telegram arrived.

The clipboard lady came to the house, and she and Violet shut themselves away in one of the sitting rooms for a long time.

When they came out, the lady patted Martha's head and said, 'Don't worry, darling – we'll take care of you.'

Violet led Martha outside because it was nearly summer now, and they looked down from the cliff at the Atlantic Ocean, and Martha remembered Mother telling her to stay away from the edge because, she realized now, she had forgotten to draw the fence in her picture.

She couldn't bear the feeling of being alone in the world. She was so scared about what would become of her when she had to go back to London, because there was no Mother, no Daddy, no Daphne, no 3 Ridley Street. No other family. Martha didn't know where she'd sleep.

Violet interrupted her thoughts: 'Would you like to stay here, Marth? And live at Cliff House with me forever? I know it's not home, but we'd love to have you.'

'Yes.' Her voice came out as a whisper. It came from the places deep inside her where the bad things lived. 'Yes, please.'

'Then that's what we'll do. We'll be each other's family, you and me.' She held Martha so tightly that she couldn't move, and the wind blew their hair around as the ocean crashed on to the stony beach below. Martha didn't care about much any more, but she was glad she had Violet.

She couldn't think about Mother and Daphne. She knew the words. *Direct hit*. Her mind swerved away from them whenever they approached.

She knew they hadn't had time to get to the air-raid shelter, that it had happened in the middle of the night, that they might not even have woken up. The houses on either side had been destroyed too. Seven people gone all at once.

She looked around. Things like that didn't happen here.

In September, Aubrey found Martha sitting at the table, drawing. She wasn't thinking about what she was doing, but when he sat next to her they both looked down at the piece of paper, and she saw that she had been drawing her lost family. Daddy, Mother and Daphne. The pictures were terrible and looked nothing like them.

It wasn't fair! She didn't want to forget their faces, but she couldn't draw.

She glanced up at him, and away. 'This isn't at all what they were like,' she said. 'It's all wrong.' She stabbed the paper with her pencil, over and over again.

'Do you have a photograph?'

Martha shook her head.

'Oh, you poor thing. Keep drawing. Sooner or later you'll capture them.'

And so she did. Aubrey would sit beside her, and they'd talk while she drew. Aubrey concentrated on her, and he seemed better like that than he did when he was in his own world.

He asked her about her parents and made her remember exactly what they looked like. Daddy, with his round glasses and his sandy hair. Mother, dark-haired and smiling. Daphne, who looked like an older version of Martha, but with a wider mouth and different eyes. The more Martha did it, the closer she got; or maybe her memories were changing to fit in with what she could draw.

She found that while she was drawing she could tell Aubrey anything she wanted, and he understood. As the months went by, she would look down at her paper and pencil, and, without looking at him, tell him everything. She shared every memory she had of Mother, of Daphne, of Daddy. She told him about their home that had been destroyed, that would never exist again. He let her talk and talk and talk, and then he would squeeze her non-drawing hand and whisper, 'Stay here with me and Vi, little Martha. We'll keep you safe.'

She squeezed back. He never told his own stories, and she knew they were worse than hers, and so she didn't ask. She understood, now, how you could wake up screaming every single night. She understood that sometimes you could think you were happy for a few hours, and then it would all come crashing back, breaking over you in a wave like the sea.

Violet got her a black dress, and she wore it every day. When it became too small, she asked if it could be let out, and Violet cut up one of her own dresses to make a bigger one.

Some days she found she had to be looking at Violet all the time, to keep her safe. Other days she just wanted Aubrey next to her. Betty was sorry for her, but after a while, when Martha didn't go back to normal, she started playing with Roy and Michael, and with the other girls at school instead. Martha didn't care.

In time, she came to feel that Cliff House really was her home. London faded and, even though she never forgot it, it began to feel strange to her that she had lived so far away for the first ten years of her life. She couldn't imagine a time when she hadn't known Violet. She remembered seeing cows from the train window and finding them shocking and scary. Now she saw them every day. She even knew how to milk them.

Nothing bad happened for the rest of the war because all the bad things had happened at the start. That, Martha thought, was almost comforting.

20

I woke up at ten, taking a moment to orientate myself. The yellow room with two windows. The big house. Rik was a twin. Clem knew about the drone.

The skull.

It was Saturday.

Party day.

Clem was up, wearing a white shirt undone over a bra top, and the smallest pair of towelling shorts I'd ever seen.

'Senni,' she said, 'I was about to wake you. So you and Rik are going to Penzance to fetch party supplies. He's passed his driving test, so he's taking the green car. I know Martha's ordered all the food and drink, so you guys just need to get everything else. Fill the car with stuff.'

I put the kettle on. 'What's everything else?'

She rolled her eyes. 'Party stuff! Like I said. Get, like, helium balloons. Those lanterns people release.'

I interrupted. 'I'm not getting them. They're terrible for birds and animals, and a fire hazard, and they end up in the sea.'

I stopped and marvelled at myself standing up to her like that. It was because of Rik. I was more confident. I felt different.

'Fine, eco ones or whatever. Get decorations. I want to put lights all the way up the drive. Some fairy lights in trees maybe? Tealights. Candles and shit.'

'Candles and shit.' Rik was standing behind me, in the doorway, pretending to write it down. 'Fine. We'll get you some candles and some shit.'

I took half a step backwards so I was standing almost up against him.

'Oh, shut up,' said Clem. 'Where's Meggy? I need her to do that thing she does at home where she puts all the expensive things away. She can use the small sitting room because we can lock that. Can someone wake her and get her to do it?'

'What are *we* doing? You and me?' Gareth was in the courtyard doorway, his hair wet. Fair enough: I wanted to use the pool as much as possible too.

'You and me, baby? First of all, we're going to your house.'

I saw him tense up. 'Why?'

'I want to look at your clothes so we can coordinate outfits.'

That was so bizarre that I turned to leave them to it, forgetting for a fraction of a second that Rik was millimetres away from me. I walked straight into him. My body pressed completely against his. He steadied me with his hands on my shoulders. We stood there for a few beats.

He smelled amazing.

'Sorry!' I looked into his eyes. He looked back.

'Don't be,' he said, his voice soft. 'So – what's it like in Penzance? Is there parking?'

'Loads. Which room is Meg in? Shall we wake her before Clem does?'

Meg was supposed to be in a room called the green room, which made it sound as if she was preparing to be on telly. We located it, and I knocked on the door, but she didn't answer. Rik grinned.

'Step aside,' he said. 'Right, just so you know, I do this at home. She's used to it. I'm not like this with anyone else, OK? It's a sibling thing.'

I nodded. He pounded on the door five times, then flung it open and jumped into the room, shouting: 'FBI! This is a raid!'

He yelled it at the top of his voice, then stopped.

'Oh,' he said, and his voice was normal now. 'Shit. She's not here. Hasn't been here at all, by the look of it.'

'You must be *such* an annoying brother.' I was smiling at this new aspect of him, but then my brain caught up. 'She must have just got up and made the bed?'

I stepped into the room. The walls were minty green, the floorboards varnished like the ones in the room I was in. The window overlooked the drive, and the light was pale and soft. The bed was made up with a pale green duvet cover and pillow case.

Meg's bag was on the end of it, open with a few clothes spilling out. The duvet was perfectly straight.

'Got up, made the bed, put her bag back on it with everything exactly as she left it yesterday?' His phone was already in his hand. 'Nah. She hasn't been here. She went off with Josie last night. I thought she'd come back after I crashed out because that was early. Did you see her?'

I thought back to the end of the evening, and I realized that I hadn't seen Meg. I'd been disappointed when Rik fell asleep, knackered after a night on the sleeper train and a sunny afternoon with alcohol, and I'd gone to bed myself to think about him and replay all our conversations. I hadn't even thought about Megan. Only Rik.

'No,' I said. 'I went to bed early too. I'm really sorry! I should totally have checked that Meg was back first.'

'Shit! No, I should.' He put his phone down. 'She's not answering.' He was alert now, giving off a new energy. 'Is there anywhere she could have been in danger between here and Josie's house?'

I knew there wasn't, but I walked through it in my mind. 'No. There are two ways down to the village. You can take the coast road, or the footpath. The footpath is quicker. There's nothing dangerous.'

'What about the cliffs, on the coast road?'

'Not really. It's all fenced.'

I tried to think about this logically. The longer I spent mulling it over, the weirder it was that Meg wasn't here.

'She'd have to have gone past the house and further along the cliffs to get to an unfenced bit, and she just wouldn't, would she? Oh shit! She didn't have a key to the gates! We might not have heard the buzzer. The garden's a fortress. We should ask Martha.' I started to calm down. 'Actually I bet she's at Martha's cottage.'

'But I'd have a load of missed calls from her. And we'd have heard the buzzer because we woke you up with it yesterday, didn't we? Maybe she came back late and didn't want to disturb us. Can you go down and check with Martha, while I look in every other room in this house?'

The Sainsbury's van was outside Martha's place, so I had to ask her about Meg at the same time as helping with the delivery of a huge amount of alcohol and party food.

'No, dear.' She raised her voice. 'Can you stack it all just inside the front door? Thank you. Yes, I'm having a little gathering. All my friends. No, I haven't seen Megan. I'm not sure I'd know her if I did, but I didn't see anyone trying to get through the gates. Not at all. What's happened?'

I tried Josie again. She didn't answer.

'She was walking back on her own through the village, but we've only just realized that she never arrived.'

Rik pulled up in the green car. I decided not to ask about insurance.

'Go and find her.' Martha patted my arm. 'And for goodness' sake message me the moment you do. Promise?'

I was trying not to imagine Megan at the foot of the cliffs. Megan attacked and left beside the path. Megan lost, wandering in the dark all night long.

'Promise. And you'll call me if she turns up here?'

'You know it.'

I gave directions from the passenger seat, and Rik drove straight to Josie's house. Five minutes later he was pulling up on the street, and while he parked I ran up to the front door and pounded on it, like Rik doing his FBI raid except serious. I waited, and then he was at my side. I could feel the waves of tension coming from him, and reached out to squeeze his hand. He clung on to me.

Nothing happened. I knocked again, and still nothing happened. We looked at each other. He was so close to me that I could feel the edges of his arm hairs touching mine. Our fingers were interlinked. When he leaned down, I could feel his breath in my hair.

'She must have taken that country path. Fucking hell. Can you run along it and call me if –'

The door opened slowly, and there was Josie's mum. She looked nervous and then relieved.

'Oh, Senara,' she said, and then she looked at Rik and took a step back. This was massive: I knew she never opened the door to strangers.

'Hi, Angie,' I said. 'I'm so, so sorry to disturb you. Is Josie here? We're actually looking for Rik's sister Meg. Did you see her last night?'

Angie smiled quickly, then took three more steps backwards. She was wearing a shapeless knee-length dress. It was unusual for her not to be in pyjamas.

'Yes,' she said. 'Yes, I did. Do you want to come in?'

I wanted to shout at her to explain, but I knew I couldn't. We stepped into the narrow hallway.

'Do you know where she might be?' said Rik, clenching his teeth. 'I'm her brother, and we've just realized she didn't come home last night.'

Angie nodded, put a finger to her lips, and pointed to Josie's bedroom door. I opened it as quietly as possible, pushed it and peered in.

And then everything inside me relaxed. All the breath came out of me, and I motioned to Rik to come over. I felt him beside me, looking over my shoulder.

Josie and Meg were squeezed up in Josie's single bed. Meg's hair was all over the pillow, and they were curled into each other, covered by a sheet. They were both fast asleep.

I stepped back and closed the door.

Rik exhaled, long and loud, and leaned back against the wall.

'Oh my God,' he said. 'I have so much to say to that girl when she wakes up. I really thought the worst had happened. Really, really believed it.'

He held up a hand to show me that it was shaking. I patted his arm and wondered whether this would be a good moment to hug him.

Angie walked us back to the front door. 'I found them talking outside on the doorstep,' she said. 'Told them to come in. They carried on talking. Chattering away, they were. They had some tea, and leftover pizza from the other night, and they went to Josie's room. I only found out your sister had stayed over when I looked in this morning, same as you just did. Do you want to wake them?'

'No need,' I said quickly. 'Rik and I are going into Penzance for some shopping. Can you tell them that when they're up?'

'Course I can,' said Angie, and she looked happier than I'd seen her for ages.

'And please could you tell Megan to look at her phone?' said Rik. 'Jesus Christ.'

I texted Martha and told her everything was fine. She replied immediately with the 👍 emoji. I messaged Clem and Gareth, who didn't reply. We stopped at the big Sainsbury's on the way into Penzance and bought fairy lights and tealights and an approximation of Clem's shopping list. Rik paid for it on a credit card, and I tried to imagine what it must feel like to be able to do that. To spend a hundred pounds without stressing at all.

I remembered the envelope of cash that Felicity had given me, and wondered whether I should be using that to pay for things. I'd been planning to save it, but maybe I should be contributing to the party costs.

'Can I give you half the money?' I said.

'Absolutely no way,' said Rik.

We parked in the harbour car park and looked out to sea. The wind blew into our faces. I savoured the smell of the ocean mixed with exhaust fumes and harbour things. I loved that about Penzance: it was real.

It was real, and I was here with Rik. It was almost a date.

'Penzance!' said Rik. 'So. What do I need to see?'

I led him around, pointing things out as we went, and everything looked different because I was here with him. The Isles of Scilly ferry was bigger. The ice-cream shop was better (he had Jaffa Cake flavour; I had Twix). We took the outdoor escalator and went up to the main street, and I showed him the bookshop where Josie worked and hoped she wasn't meant to be working today because, if she was, I should definitely have woken her up.

'Cute shop,' he said.

The pavements were busy with people, all wearing as few clothes as they could get away with, so there was plenty of sunburnt flesh on display. There were pushchairs with babies shaded from the sun. We stepped into the road to let a mobility scooter pass, and I thought of Martha and her absolute refusal to use hers. I looked into the windows of the charity shops, alert for my elusive style, but there was nothing that appealed. We passed Tesco, Co-op, the old post office, and more, more, more charity shops. I felt the sweat on my scalp, under my arms, down my back. The sky was clouding over, the air crackling with electricity. I longed to throw myself into the ocean.

Penzance had been a focal point my whole life. I had come here every schoolday for the past five years. It was a cool town. A complicated one. It was arty and bookish, with a huge homeless population, massive poverty and immense drug and mental-health problems. Right now it was at peak tourism, so it was also a base for people going to Land's End and Sennen and the Scillies.

Although I knew that you couldn't say it was because of Clem's second home that there were so many people here with no shelter, no food, no hope, I also knew that you could, and I knew that Rik knew it too. Second homes and homelessness were what Mum, after a glass of wine, would call 'two cheeks of the same arse'. Life was unfair: some people had too much, and others had nothing, and I wanted there to be a way for everyone to have the right amount.

I decided not to say any of this. We walked in silence past a woman with a double pushchair, and I checked that it was babies rather than dogs. I couldn't believe how often it was dogs.

The storm was hanging in the air. Heatwaves lasted a week at most; everyone knew that the mizzle and the mist would soon be back. That was why the beaches were full of locals as well as tourists, why people were swimming in the sea at every opportunity, and why so many people walking around the town were bright red and peeling.

'It honestly usually rains,' I said. 'And I think you're about to experience that. I hope it holds off for the party, though.'

'It rained last time we were here,' said Rik. 'When we went to St Mawes. Absolutely pissed it down the whole time.'

'The trip that Meg was talking about?'

'She's rewritten it in her head so it was perfect.'

'She was telling me about some afternoon-tea place. That did sound nice, to be fair.'

'Yeah.' We waited to cross the road. 'A hotel. Everyone says you have to go for afternoon tea there if you're in St Mawes. I mean – *have to*?'

'I wouldn't have a clue.'

'We went because our parents saw it on a list of must-do things for Cornwall. Or something.'

There was a gap in the traffic. I set off after him, running to catch up.

'What are your parents like?'

He shrugged. 'Fine. I kind of hesitate to go there, but you won't be surprised to hear that we grew up with nannies. Our dad works away. Mum's a banker. They're nice but super busy. Like this week we just messaged them to say we'd be in Cornwall with Clem, and they were both, like: *Fine, have fun*. The real person we had to tell was –' He stopped.

I didn't finish the sentence, even though I could have done. They had to tell Holly. They had to tell their housekeeper.

'I'm not going to say we're poor little rich kids because . . .' We both looked at a group of homeless people across the road. 'So, yeah. I'll shut up.'

I took a deep breath and tried to think of something else to say. I didn't want the fact that Rik was so rich to make things feel awkward between us. It hadn't been feeling like that, and now it did.

I changed the subject. 'Are you hungry?'

'Shit! Yes, I am. We didn't have breakfast, did we?'

And just like that everything was fine again.

'Fancy getting some chips and taking them down to the beach? This time I'm paying.'

'Fish and chips?' said Rik. 'Oh my God! That's the best idea I've ever heard.'

I tried not to smile too broadly. This was definitely feeling like a date.

*

We sat on the stones with our food, and I warned him about the seagulls, who loved to snatch food right out of unsuspecting people's hands. The white wall of the Jubilee Pool jutted out into the ocean on our left. Newlyn and beyond were off to the right, and the ocean stretched out ahead of us. The sky was clouding over. The stones on the beach were heavy and smooth, the esplanade above us. We ate with our fingers.

'Penzance,' he said, leaning back on the wall, picking up his biggest chip. 'Yes. I like it.'

The chips were covered in salt and vinegar. They were thick and perfect. I watched the clouds reflected in the surface of the sea.

'Me too.'

'I was so scared this morning. I thought something really bad had happened to Meg. That skull last night, and then my sister missing this morning. I was freaking out.'

It was so easy to talk to him now. I was glad he was confiding in me.

'I could see you were. It was awful. But she's fine.'

'Yeah. She is. More than fine, I'd say.'

We exchanged a glance, and the lightning bolt shot through me again.

'You think that Josie and Meg . . . ?'

'Er – it certainly looked like it.'

I felt so naive. I had read that scene as two girls sharing a bed because they'd been talking and then fallen asleep. Josie had had two boyfriends, and she'd never mentioned girls. I recalibrated it all and felt stupid. I told him. He laughed.

'Meg's bi,' he said, 'and, judging by the way the two of them were looking at each other yesterday, I'd say Josie was receptive. You didn't see that? Not at all?'

We didn't speak for a while. Was this exciting tension? Or was it me not being able to think of anything to say? How were you supposed to know the difference?

I had to say something. We were on the beach, on a date. I opened my mouth to be brave.

I planned it in my head. I was going to say: *What about you, Rik? Relationships-wise?* I was going to hope that it would lead on seamlessly from Megan and Josie. I was going to see where that took us. My heart was pounding.

I tried it out in my head again. *What about you, Rik? Relationships-wise?* Would that do? Should I say: *What do you feel about holiday romances?* That would be more direct. Was that OK? The waves lapped at the shore. The gulls shrieked. The air was almost sparkling with future-storm. I could hear the cars going past above us. My lips were stinging with salt and vinegar. Should I say something even clearer? Maybe I should say: *What about you and me?* Was that too risky?

If anything was going to happen between us, it had to happen now.

I opened my mouth to do it. *What about you and me?*

I was about to speak when Rik said, 'I never fancy anyone.'

I waited. I waited for him to add 'except you', but he didn't. That, it seemed, was his full statement.

'Really?' My voice sounded wavery and stupid. I felt tears springing to my eyes and looked away, down the beach, so he wouldn't see them. I had been ready for this, ready to kiss him right here right now.

'Yeah. I call it being super-selective, but Meg despairs of me. If you can imagine someone the exact opposite of Clem and Gareth? The opposite, apparently, of Meg and Josie? Well, that's me. I just hardly ever meet anyone who I find even remotely interesting.'

I felt myself deflating, humiliated. This must be what it was like to have a regular, unrequited crush. I'd thought we were in this together, but we weren't. It was just me.

I replayed the moments. Standing in the sea. Sitting on the grass. He'd gone to bed early; that should have given me a hint. I'd taken his hand, and he'd held mine tightly – when he'd been scared his sister was dead. We had barely brushed against each other since he'd found out that she was fine.

I saw it all in the cold light of reality.

The whole thing had only existed in my head. He was probably laughing at me.

I talked, saying anything to fill the void. I kept my head turned away from him.

'Me too,' I said. I didn't want him to know how I'd been feeling, so I decided to join his team. 'My friends say I'm like one of those women in the olden days, saving myself for marriage, but I'm not. I just haven't met anyone I want to bother with yet. I bet there's a name for it. Not asexual, I don't think. Just picky.'

'You get it,' he said. I slumped back against the wall.

'Yeah,' I said. 'I get it.'

I didn't want to be here, on the beach with our chips, for a moment longer. I threw my last few to the birds, who went mad for them, and stood up.

'We should get back.'

We walked to the car in silence. He tried to start a few conversations on the way back, but I shut them all off. I directed him back to Cliff House and, when we got there, I went to my room and had a shower so I could cry without anyone knowing.

21

I tried to keep my distance from Rik after that. Everyone took a break from party prep by the pool, and I made sure I sat with Megan and Josie. I wanted to know what was going on with them, desperate to hear Josie's story, but as soon as I realized that Rik was completely right, that they were sparkling with lust and joy, I started to look for somewhere else to go.

Josie and Meg.

Clem and Gareth.

Me.

And Rik.

Separately.

Clem and Gareth were back from their trip to his house, which I suspected had been a poor-people safari on her part. They were busy kissing. Meg and Josie were kissing constantly.

The air was scorching hot, and the storm hadn't broken yet.

I'd imagined something where there'd been nothing. I'd been blinded by the fact that Rik was rich and handsome.

I'd filled in an entire love story, in a day, where there had been nothing. He'd gone out of his way to tell me that he didn't fancy me.

All I could do was avoid him. I was just glad he'd stopped me in time.

'Is your house like this?' I said to Meg, not caring that I was interrupting the smooching.

She was wearing a bright blue bikini with metal bits on it today. I was in my normal one-piece suit. Maybe I needed to get a nice bikini. Why, though? What was the point? No one would ever look at me.

She turned to me, and I leaned forward before she could answer. 'Your eyes are so pretty,' I said.

Josie's head snapped round. 'Aren't they beautiful?' she said, stroking Meg's hand.

Meg smiled. 'Thank you. Both. I believe that, officially, they're hazel.' She batted me back a compliment straight away: 'Your freckles are so cute. I wish I had them. They're adorable.'

She turned to Rik on the other side of her. 'Aren't Senara's freckles adorable?' she said.

I screamed internally. I cringed. I looked away.

'Yeah,' he said at once. 'They really are, actually. Super cute.' I felt every muscle in my body clenching.

'Um, our house?' said Meg. 'It's not like this, no. We live near Clem's dad. Our parents are friends with him. We've never met her mum, even though we seem to have taken up residence in her house.'

'We're drinking her wine and eating all her food,' said Rik.

'Even her Fortnum's chocolates,' said Meg.

'Oh right.' I hadn't given Clem's dad any thought. Once a month or so, I went over to Plymouth to see my own dad. I stayed in his flat and watched telly. He lived in a shared apartment, and it was always messy, and the bathroom was horrible, but it was usually fun. I smiled as I imagined how different Clem's '*dad* experience' must be from that.

'We live in Chelsea,' said Meg. 'In a townhouse. There's a garden, but it's, like, the size of Clem's pool. It's near the river, though.'

'And,' said Rik, 'the river is nothing like that.'

He waved his arm at the ocean, then stood up and dived into the pool. I caught myself watching, then remembered and snapped my eyes back to Meg.

'That sounds nice,' I said. I wondered what Martha's London home had been like. Nothing like Meg and Rik's.

'Oh shit – Martha. I should check on her. She's had all the party food and drink piled up in her house for hours, and I've done nothing about it.'

I jumped up, delighted with the excuse to leave.

I looked at my phone and saw a text. It said:

> Hey hey siri. Is it
> working? Text Senara.
> Can some of you collect
> these party things?

'Look at this message!' I held the phone out.

'Gorgeous!' said Meg. 'Shall we go and get it?'

I was so grateful that I wanted to hug her, though Josie would have pulled me away if I'd tried.

I messaged back.

On our way!

I turned to Meg. 'Thanks. We might need a wheelbarrow or something.'

Josie jumped up. 'I'll come too. I want to see Martha.'

This was the second time she'd implied she knew Martha. I wondered whether I'd missed something.

I waited to see if Rik was going to say the same thing. He didn't. Thank God.

'Why don't I drive the car down?' said Meg, and I nodded.

Josie set off on foot, and I went with Meg to find the car keys. I thought I felt a drop of rain on my arm as we walked to the house. I willed it to hold off until tomorrow.

By the time Meg had worked out the car, turned it round and driven slowly down the drive, Josie and Martha were sitting at her table, deep in conversation.

'This week is such a treat,' Martha said. 'I'm seeing you several times a day, Senara! And, Megan, I'm glad you're safe. We were quite panic-stricken earlier.'

'Oh God! I'm so sorry. I just fell asleep.'

Martha looked from one to the other, giving them a crooked smile. 'So I heard. I'm really glad you brought the car. You're going to need it. I have some questions, Senara. Questions about this evening's plans.'

I sat with her while Meg and Josie started putting crates into the boot.

'Go on then,' I said. 'Ask me anything!'

I actually wanted to ask her if Josie had told her about her romance with Meg, but I decided not to. It was none of my business. Somewhere along the way, Josie and Martha had clearly formed a relationship.

'Question one,' she said, 'how many people are arriving, and at what time, and is Clementine planning to leave the gates open?'

'Do you mind if I get a glass of water?' She gestured to the kitchen, and I poured one for me and two for the girls. 'So that was three questions,' I said. 'First: there won't be that many people. If it was in London, I'm sure Clem would be able to invite, like, a thousand friends or whatever. But even if everyone I know comes, and even if they bring their friends, it's not going to be massive.'

'Good.'

'I think Clem's told them to arrive at six, so we get the sunshine and the pool and all that.'

'Swimming pool and alcohol?'

I nodded. 'We won't let anything bad happen. What was the other one?'

'Gates.'

I hesitated. 'I guess we'll have to leave them open? You'll be up at the house with us, and we can't really post a sentry, because who'd want to do that? Is that OK?'

Martha sighed. I thought she was regretting the whole thing, but instead she said, 'Do you have any *idea* how happy that makes me? We never used to close the gates in Violet's day, nor in mine. Felicity's obsessed with security, and I sympathize with her more than you can ever realize, but I hate everything those stupid gates, and the prison-camp fence, represent. Leon wanted to put the fence round my house and enclose me too, but I wasn't having it.'

She looked out of the window, but I could see that she was miles away again. 'Honestly, Senara, it went on for weeks. He thought he could insist. "*It's for your own security, Mum. The world's changed. You're not safe.*" I ended up telling him to fuck off or be disinherited. It's my house. I wasn't going to stop him getting his fence and gates to keep Felicity happy, but having the cottage on the outside, and without a fence running along my back windows, was non-negotiable. That was the compromise.' She shook herself. 'And then the silly bugger went and died first anyway. Right. Final question: will you help me choose an outfit?'

She looked down at herself. She was wearing a blue-and-white-striped dress.

'You look lovely,' I said. 'You're always stylish.'

'I'm not wearing this old thing. How about you, darling? Do you have a costume planned?'

Meg and Josie came back into the room, holding hands. I tried not to be jealous, but I was. They looked so happy together, and I'd been brutally rejected.

'Look at you two,' I said. I tried to inject loveliness into my voice, but it sounded weird. They were amazing together. I was wild with envy of what they had.

'Yes, look at you,' said Martha. 'You gorgeous girls. Wonderful.'

They blushed, and time stood still for a moment.

'So, we'll take this up to the house,' said Josie. 'I think it's everything, but let us know if you want us to come back for anything.'

'Senara and I will be examining my wardrobe and picking out our party frocks,' said Martha imperiously, and she sat on her stairlift, pressed a button and made a slow exit.

'Oh my God, I love her,' whispered Meg.

'Me too,' said Josie.

Tomorrow I would ask her how come she and Martha were suddenly friends.

Martha's bedroom door was closed, as ever. She was private about that, though I supposed her carers had to go in regularly. We went into the second bedroom, and Martha sat on the edge of the bed.

'It's like a fashion museum,' I said.

'The museum of my life,' she said. 'Yes. I wish I had the little brown coat I was wearing when I arrived. With the label.'

I thought about Clem, about the way she had half disowned Martha from the family because of her background. The stupid, nonsensical snobbery of it.

'It's like the best vintage shop ever,' I said.

'Can you pass me that red one?' said Martha.

She directed me to it, and I took it out of the wardrobe and held it up. It was the deep red, floor-length gown that I'd admired before. It was silky and slinky, with wide sleeves, a plunging neckline, and fabric that would definitely cling. I laid it on the bed beside her: she touched it with her fingertips, and her eyes filled with tears.

'Yes,' she said quietly. 'I shall wear this if I can squeeze myself into it. It's a lucky charm.' Martha stared at it for a long time before pulling herself back to the present and looking up at me. 'So?' she said. 'How about you, Senara? Pick one. Anything you like.'

'Me?'

'They might not be a perfect fit. In fact, they won't be. But that doesn't matter. Let's make you dazzle that boy.'

'I don't need to dazzle him, Martha. He's made that really clear.'

'I wouldn't be so sure.'

It was a knife to the stomach. I wished I had a shred of hope to cling to, but I didn't.

I looked through the dresses with a new eye now that I was choosing one for myself. I didn't have the confidence or height for a full-length gown, and anyway this was a pool party.

'Over there – on the far left of the rail,' she said, and I followed her directions and pulled out a minidress on a hanger. It was yellow and blue striped, with buttons up the front and a collar. It was the Biba dress: I'd noticed this one before too, but I'd never imagined myself wearing it.

I held it up against myself, and Martha clapped her hands.

'Perfect!' she said. 'It's from the sixties. Very Twiggy. Pop into my room now and try it on.'

I remembered, weeks ago, Felicity telling me that my aura was yellow and blue stripes. I looked down at the dress. I was pretty much going to be wearing my own aura. That seemed like my very own lucky charm, and I was going to need one to get through this evening.

I stepped into Martha's room. It was the only part of the house I'd never seen before. The walls were white with abstract paintings on them. Her high double bed was in one corner, and she had an old-style dressing table against a wall, with make-up and cosmetics carefully arranged. I realized that she could sit up in bed and look out at the garden.

I went to the window to check out the view.

It was mainly just trees, but they were spaced far apart. You could see through the branches.

You could see through the branches straight down to the camellia bushes, the earth on the grass next to them, the hole that, we knew, had human bones in it. The place that was currently hiding a skull, some bones, a watch and a fork until after the party.

We'd thought that patch wasn't overlooked, but it was. Martha spent a lot of time up here. How many times had I texted her to say I was arriving, and seen her descending the stairs when I arrived? A lot.

We'd pulled a skull out of her garden, and Martha might have been up here, watching.

Did she know?

22

By half past six, the house and garden were full of people. They were in the pool, on the grass, in almost every bit of the downstairs of the house. More people had come than I'd expected, and everyone had brought alcohol. Clem was taking the spirits and half the wine and pouring everything into a bowl, adding orange juice and calling it 'punch'. I was pretty sure she'd tipped Martha's random old holiday bottles in too; I made a note to stay away from it and had a glass of wine.

The music was loud and relentless, and people were dancing, drinking, swimming, laughing. It was, I thought, shaping up to be an excellent night. The storm was just about holding off, though it was heavy in the air and the whole sky was threatening and overcast. I knew how easily it could have rained, and thanked the weather gods that the heatwave was holding.

Amina came past, her hands full of flowers she'd picked from the garden. She was walking towards the house and stopped and grinned when she saw me.

'Hey, Senara! I can't believe we're actually here.'

'Me neither.'

Martha was sitting on a chair by the pool. She had a little table next to her, with a glass of champagne and a bowl of cashew nuts on it, and she was wearing her dark red dress that shimmered in the sun and looked spectacular. People were going up to her all the time and commenting on it.

'It's the oldest thing I own,' I had heard her say to Maya. 'Older than me. It was at Cliff House before I was. Isn't that funny?'

Martha looked other-worldly, almost angelic. She had brushed her hair out so it was loose, long and white down her back, and she had put on more make-up than usual, including a dark red lipstick that matched the dress.

'You're the belle of the ball,' I said, sitting down next to her.

'Miss Havisham, more like,' she said. 'It's OK. I know they say that about me in the village. But thank you. In fact, you're the belle, my dear.'

I was self-conscious, but I was trying to style it out. The dress did fit me pretty well; I was sure it was quite a lot longer on me than it would have been on her, but I was pleased about that. The dress made me feel like someone else. It was the first thing I'd ever worn that made me confident the moment I pulled it over my head.

It had taken me a while, though, before I'd been able to try it on. I'd stared out of Martha's window and wondered when we should tell her about the skull. She might have seen us digging it up, but if she hadn't it would be a huge shock when she found out that there were human remains so close to her home. It would freak me right out if I was her.

'What about my feet, though?' I said, wondering whether I should do it now. No. Not during the party. I'd go down in the morning and talk to her.

None of my shoes worked with this dress, so I was barefoot. My toenails looked nude and stupid; if I'd thought of it, I would have borrowed some nail varnish from Clem, but I hadn't.

'Your feet are perfect. So delicate. What size are they?'

'Four.'

'See? Clem and I are cursed with great clodhopping sevens.'

I leaned back in my seat. Even though these were my friends, I felt a bit strange. I was straddling both worlds right now, but I was only visiting Clem's enchanted life. I was a tourist here, but moneyed life was heady and addictive, and, in spite of everything, I wanted more.

It was definitely the luxury that I wanted. Not Rik. I pushed his name from my mind and watched Josie coming towards us, looking brilliant in a silver dress with rips down the front and a huge pair of boots. Martha beamed at Josie.

'Look at this, Josie! This is all I ever wanted. To see this house full of people again. To have those gates open. To be sitting in this garden with a glass of fizz. I can't tell you how boring it is being old and alone, girls. I really can't. I've longed for an evening like this. I've been living for it. Now I can die happy.'

'Mrs Roberts,' said Josie, 'you look amazing, may I say?'

'You may, of course. But you know you're supposed to call me Martha.'

'Sorry, Martha. You look so beautiful.'

'Thank you, my dear. So do you. And where's Megan?'

Josie pointed her out, talking to a group I half knew from school.

'I'm so pleased for you both. Glad that things are easier now than they were in my day.'

'Thank you,' said Josie. I thought she looked as if she wanted to cry. 'Didn't Clem want to wear one of your dresses tonight?' she said. 'I mean, what an amazing opportunity.'

'And they'd fit her,' I said.

Martha shook her head. 'I've given up offering Clem my clothes. She's not a fan.'

We all looked across the pool to where Clem was holding court, wearing a tiny chiffon dress, her hair twisted over her shoulder, her feet also bare and decorated with toe rings and bright polish. She was holding Gareth's hand. Clem saw Martha looking and rushed over to her side, Gareth in tow.

'Gran,' she said, 'you are so fabulous. Gazzy, take a photo of me with Gran? Take loads.'

I looked for Maya, but couldn't see her. If I was her, I thought I'd be heading home. Gareth really was a shit.

'Excuse me a second,' I said, but no one was listening, so I walked away, and Josie followed. We went all the way to the fence on top of the cliff, and we looked out at the dark ocean. I couldn't believe how quiet it was here, out of range of the speakers.

'Senni,' she said quietly. Our heads were close together. 'This is weird, isn't it? Us being here. When we know it's going to be all closed up again for the whole winter. And we'll be locked out. And when we kind of know the police are going to come and dig up the garden.'

'We know a way in.'

'We know two. Over the fence, and through the front gate.'

I looked at her. I could see that she wanted to say something important.

'What is it?' I said. 'What, Josie?'

23

Josie was the happiest she'd ever been, and the most afraid. Even though Meg was making her feel wild and alive and open and ready for adventure, the other thing was tugging on her sleeve and forcing her to look at it.

The storm was gathering overhead. The clouds had been growing all day, and now she could feel that the rain was imminent. The prickly heat, the electric air: everything was gearing up. And, despite the fact that it sounded like a crap metaphor even in her head, she felt it mirroring the other things. The skull.

She had to tell someone because she knew it was obsessing her, and she couldn't bear for it to be Megan again. She didn't want Meg to have to listen because this was too grim and real, and Meg was everything light and happy. Instead she drew Senara away, over to the edge of the cliff. They stood in the dark, out of sight of everyone, the music just a thumping bass, and Josie started talking.

'It's that skull,' she said. 'I can't get it out of my head. As it were.'

She inhaled deeply and explained the theory that she

really didn't want to have, but that she couldn't shake off. She started with her dead uncle, and her discovery that he had never been a knight in shining armour. She moved on to the fact that he'd been hanging out with Rachel Thomas before she vanished without trace, and that Rachel's best friend had been Felicity.

'Felicity!'

When Josie finished, Senara nodded slowly.

'I guess it would make sense in a way,' she said. 'If that's all true.'

Josie felt crushed for a moment. She hadn't realized how much she'd wanted Senara to say the opposite. *It doesn't make sense. It's definitely wrong.*

She pulled herself together and nodded. She felt her shoulders slumping.

'It makes way too much sense,' said Josie. 'I can't stop thinking about it. These are the things we know.' She counted them out on her fingers. 'One: Uncle Andy preyed on young girls. Not necessarily an objective fact, but something my mother, his own sister, told me. Two: before he bolted to Thailand, he was in some way hooking up with Lucy's sister Rachel, who's famous in the area for vanishing without a trace. Three: Rachel hasn't been seen since. Four: everyone knows this house, and Rachel used to be friends with Felicity, so she would definitely have come here sometimes. Five: there's a body buried in the garden, and it could easily have been there for thirty-four years. I checked how long it would take to decompose in soil, and it all stacks up.'

Josie wanted Senara to laugh and say she was being ridiculous. She wanted that so much.

'Have you spoken to Lucy?' was her reply.

'No! I'm hardly going to say, *Oh, Luce, I have this theory about your famously dead sister. Want to hear it?*

They started walking round the edge of the garden, away from the party.

Senara spoke suddenly. 'I don't buy it, Jose,' she said. 'I mean, all those things are just rumours and hearsay. You're extrapolating millions of things there. There are so many other explanations. We don't know anything about any of these people, apart from Felicity, and if you're saying she was involved – well, you can only say that because you haven't met her. She's the least murderous person in the world.'

Josie felt herself beginning to relax. 'Really? I mean, I wasn't really saying Felicity was involved. It was just a link to this house.'

'Yeah. Look – Rachel Thomas could have died in an accident, or maybe she just ran away, but we'll probably never know. I think you're fixated on this because . . . well, I know how much the idea of your uncle meant to you, and the thought that he's dead has really knocked you, and I'm really sorry. But your mum saying he was a bit of a creep with teenage girls? It's a huge reach to say that means he killed someone and somehow buried her in the garden of a house where he didn't live. Why would you even do that? Why wouldn't you drop a body in the ocean? It's literally right there.'

Josie wanted to die of happiness.

'Yes! You're right. Thank you.'

'Also – it's not up to us,' Senara added. 'You know the police will do DNA stuff, and if it matches Rachel, they'll find out. But I bet it won't. It'll be that old burial ground or something.'

Josie felt as if she'd been trapped under a lorry, and Senara had just lifted it off her. Senara was right. She'd got completely carried away.

'Amazing. Thank you. I love you.'

'And,' said Senara, 'you look amazing, and this is probably the first and last time we're going to be invited to a party at Cliff House, so why don't you stop making up murder stories and have the most fun ever?'

Josie was looking around for Meg. 'Yes! Thank you. You're the best. You look gorgeous. What's going on with you and Rik? Meg and I have been desperate to know.'

Senara batted that away. 'Nothing. Less than nothing. More interesting – what's going on with you and Meg?'

Josie felt herself lighting up from the inside. 'Everything!' she said. 'It's been the most –'

She stopped because something hit her on the head. At first she thought it was hail, but the rain was still holding off. She touched her head with her hand. There was nothing there.

'Up here!'

It was Gareth, in a tree. He had climbed up and was sitting in its low branches. Josie saw that there were rungs nailed to the trunk. Senara was up there in an instant, but

Josie decided not to follow. She wanted to spend this precious time with Meg, not with her ex-boyfriend who she was certain would be having an existential crisis about the fact that he was a shit.

'What is it, Gaz?' she called.

'Why aren't you with Clem?' said Senara.

'Maya's crying. Why am I such a shit?'

'I'm out,' said Josie, holding up both hands as a barrier. She walked away, swinging her hips, back to the party, to the music, to Martha reigning at the poolside, to the girl she had only just met, but who had turned her world on its head.

Meg saw her coming, broke off from the conversation she was having and walked, then ran towards her. Josie sped up too. She opened her arms, and Meg ran into them. She kissed her. Kissing a girl was different. It was better. Kissing Meg felt right in every single way.

1988

Felicity couldn't sleep. The things Rachel had said about her parents went round and round her head. She didn't want to think of her in danger at home, and she definitely didn't want to think of her looking to creepy Andy Teague for an escape. Everything felt wrong.

Rachel had gone to bed in the attic room that had the bolt on the inside of the door. Felicity hoped she was sleeping.

She didn't know Lucy well, but she hated the thought of her trying to be the perfect daughter to keep herself safe. Their parents were church people: they were meant to be good! They were supposed to be about kindness and compassion. Everything felt wrong.

Alex was caught up with Jenna, and Mum and Dad were in Paris. She wasn't going to disturb Rachel. She didn't know who to talk to so, after midnight, she found the number of Grandma's hotel in Exeter and called it. They put her through to Grandma's room, but she didn't answer, and the call went back to the reception desk.

'Can I take a message?' said the woman, who sounded as if she was doing a lot of other things at the same time.

Felicity couldn't imagine what there was to do in the reception of an Exeter hotel at midnight. She bet the woman had glossy hair in a bun, a scratchy blue uniform, a white blouse with a bow at the neck.

Stop! She pulled her mind back to now. To here.

'Could I leave a message for Martha Roberts?' The woman agreed that she could. Felicity pictured her reaching for a pen.

'Could you tell her . . .' She paused, imagined Grandma getting an alarming message in the morning. She would rush back, and that wasn't fair. She loved her trips with Betty. 'Oh, just tell her everything's fine in Cornwall, and we hope she has a lovely time there.'

'Sure thing,' said the woman. 'That's it?'

Felicity hung up and went to bed. Jenna and Alex were watching a video of *Psycho*, and she didn't fancy that one bit. She wanted to check that the gates were locked so, even though it was the scariest thing she could possibly have done, she slipped out of the side door with a torch and ran down the drive. The gates were locked with the chain and padlock, and everything was silent.

The vicar wouldn't come in. Andy Teague wouldn't come in.

They both *could*, though, if they wanted to. The locked gates wouldn't keep anyone out – Rachel had climbed over them easily enough earlier – but at least it was a 'Do not disturb' sign. Anyone passing this point wouldn't be able to say they'd stumbled in by accident.

Somehow her trip down the drive made her feel better.

She'd done something. She'd gone out into the night, and everything had been all right, and so she went to bed and fell asleep.

In the middle of the night, Felicity thought she heard someone downstairs. She lay rigid with fear, waiting. Nothing happened, and in the morning Alex said it had just been him and Jenna, that they'd stayed up until two and that Jenna had slept in the green room. He was elated, grinning from ear to ear, shining brightly.

Grandma would be back on Sunday. Grandma would know what Rachel should do. Felicity told herself that everything was going to be all right. It was almost over.

24

'Gareth and Senara sitting in a tree!' The voice was below us, and, when I leaned over to look down, it was Clem looking up, laughing. I jumped out of the tree at once, hoping again that the dress was surviving this adventure.

'We were certainly not K-I-S-S-I-N-G,' I told her with as much dignity as I could manage, brushing the back of my dress. I noticed that I wasn't in thrall to Clem any more. Since Rik knocked me back, I didn't really care.

Gareth's voice was guarded. 'We were T-A-L-K-I-N-G, actually.'

'I know someone who'll be pleased to hear that,' she said, giving me a knowing look. 'Not the talking. The not-kissing.'

I walked away from the tree and straight into Rik. I stepped back and turned away as I heard Clem say, 'So, is there room in that tree for one more?'

I'd been getting through the evening by avoiding him. Now I'd walked into him, and I could smell him, and he made my stomach lurch, and I had to get away. I started walking off, but he touched my shoulder. I shook him off and walked faster. He walked quickly next to me.

'How are you doing?' he said.

'Fine.'

I didn't look at him. I set my course towards Martha. The bastard had told me that he didn't fancy me, and I felt it, a slap in the face. A jellyfish sting. I was done with being a sidekick. I wasn't going to be his Robin. Just for once, I'd thought I had a chance of being the main character.

I walked faster. He kept up easily. I slowed down. He slowed down.

I sighed. 'What?'

He stopped. 'I don't know, Senara. It's a party. I wanted to hang out with you. Look, have I done something else to offend you? I'm really sorry if I did. I don't know what it was, but I can see you think I'm a dick, so maybe it's the obvious thing again, or maybe it's something else, but please: all I'm asking is for you to tell me.'

I didn't look at him. I couldn't bear to. How could I possibly have thought that there could have been anything between us? A girl like me would never get together with a boy like him. Tonight I was the most stylish I'd been in my entire life, and that was because I'd borrowed a dress from a ninety-two-year-old lady. Go figure.

And I didn't even know if he liked girls. I'd built all my hopes on a thing that didn't exist.

'It's nothing,' I said.

We were near the house now, and I looked around. I thought there were maybe seventy people here, and I recognized almost all of them. They were people I'd known for years, people I vaguely recognized from school, people I'd just seen around. The music was light and poppy. I listened to some words – 'the river keeps on flowing and the party keeps on going' – and thought how meaningless everything was.

I saw Treve in the pool with Daniel, finally actually together after a year of flirting. Amina was lying on her back on the grass, her arms stretched out on either side. There was shouting, laughing, singing. I'd been worried that it would get out of hand, that with the gates open more and more people would come, that the house would be trashed, but so far it seemed all right. This place was pretty remote. We were hardly going to attract random passers-by, and there were no neighbours to complain.

Martha was still at the poolside, presiding over it all in her ballgown. She didn't see us walking past because she was talking to two people who'd been in the year above us at school. I checked the time. It was twenty to ten. I would take her home at ten, as she'd asked, and then I'd spend the rest of this evening avoiding Rik, spending time with my actual friends.

Megan and Josie were up against a tree, kissing. I pushed down the stab of jealousy.

'Tell me if you want me to go,' said Rik.

'I want you to go.' I still couldn't look at his face. I couldn't deal with the fact that it was so perfect.

'OK. Sure.' He started to walk away, and I wanted to call him back. He stopped. 'But please, Senara? Just tell me what I did.'

I looked at him because I had to. I melted a bit in spite of myself. My defences came down, and I put them back up.

'It's nothing,' I said. I had nothing left to lose, and I'd had a couple of drinks, so I added: 'I mean, you must know really. When we were on the beach? In Penzance. I was kind of gearing up to make a fool of myself, and you nipped it in the bud, and I just feel a bit stupid. That's all. There you go.'

I thought it would be good to have another drink, and so I walked as fast as I could towards the kitchen door.

Rik ran after me. 'What are you talking about?' His voice was urgent.

I shook my head. My eyes were burning, and I wasn't going to let him see me cry. I wasn't, wasn't, wasn't.

'No, Senara! Stop!' He put a hand on my arm. I shook it off. 'No – you've got it wrong! I know exactly what you mean, but I thought *you* shut *me* down. I'm shit at this, but I was trying to say, *I never fancy anyone, which is why it's so amazing, the way I feel about you*. It was there straight away for me. Feelings that I don't normally get, and I was wondering if you felt any trace of it. I was trying to be smooth.' He laughed, but in a not-amused way. 'I'm a twat. I mean, I know we established that already, but please file Penzance beach in that category.'

I stopped. I didn't want to meet his eyes. 'Seriously?'

His words were burned on my brain, and I jumped straight back into the moment. He'd said: '*I never fancy anyone*.' He'd said: '*I call it being super-selective . . . If you can imagine someone the exact opposite of Clem and*

Gareth? . . . Well, that's me. I just hardly ever meet anyone who I find even remotely interesting.'

I tried to press play, to see what might have come next.

I supposed it could have been turned round with a '*but*'.

'I really did feel as if *you* shut *me* down. Because I was about to go there, and you said you too never fancied anyone.'

'I was . . .' I searched for the word. 'Hurt. I was jumping in to say that I hated romantic things too, so that you didn't see that I was absolutely gutted.'

'I definitely didn't see that.'

Something in me, wound tight, was starting to relax. My breaths were deeper. I could look at him now. I could look into his eyes. He could look into mine. Was this real?

'I've always felt like a sidekick,' I said. 'Always. I've always been the one in the background, while other people have their dramas. I never have my own storyline. I've always thought I was too boring for the exciting things. I mean, look at me. I'm short. Not glamorous. I don't have any sense of style. I'm an extra.'

No one had ever looked at me in the way Rik was looking at me now.

'You're not an extra.'

He took my hand, and our footsteps crunched on the gravel as we walked away from the rest of the party and round the corner of the house. We sat on the steps in front of the big door.

It was quiet here, and the air was thick with rain that wasn't quite falling. There were no stars; the sky was a duvet of dark cloud.

We looked at each other, and everything changed. I felt the bones and the missing woman and all the rest of it slip away, just for a moment.

'You're not a sidekick. You're not in the background. You're right in the centre of everything.'

We looked at each other for a few seconds and both burst out laughing.

'Sorry,' he said. 'Possibly the cheesiest thing anyone's ever said. Please, stop me talking before I fuck it up again. Anyway, you look stunning. Breathtaking.'

I felt my cheeks going red and looked up at the black sky. We were lit only by the party lights, of which there were many.

'Amazing what a vintage dress can do,' I said. 'And low lighting.'

'It's not the dress. It's not the lighting.'

I wanted to be in this moment, right now, nowhere else.

I looked across at Rik and noticed that he was heart-stoppingly handsome. He was wearing a blue-and-white-striped T-shirt and denim shorts. The whole ensemble made him seem like a movie star. I took a deep breath and told him so.

He put a hand on my shoulder. 'Can I go back to what I was saying before?' he said. 'On the beach?'

'I promise not to jump in and shut you down.' My stomach was fluttering in anticipation.

'I never fancy anyone. I call it being super-selective, but Meg despairs of me. If you can imagine someone the exact opposite of Clem and Gareth? Well, that's me. I just hardly ever meet anyone who I find even remotely interesting – and I guess that's why I paused for too long, because the last thing I was expecting when I came to Cornwall was to meet somebody I liked straight away. But I did. I met you. I can't stop thinking about you. And believe me when I say that never happens.'

He was stroking the back of my neck. It made every hair on my arms stand up on end.

I looked into his eyes.

'Super-selective just means you wait for the right person. It means you know them when you see them. Right?'

We didn't need to say anything else. I felt like the most beautiful, luckiest girl in the world. I leaned up to him. He leaned towards me. Our lips met, and everything else melted away.

We had no future, and I had to accept that. He was going back to London in a couple of days. He lived in Chelsea and had staff. This was a holiday romance. It was going to end as fast as it had begun.

So I needed to enjoy it. Right now it was real. I wanted this, and nothing else, right now. Here I was, sitting on the steps of a huge house, kissing the boy I really, really liked on a hot, charged evening.

We sat there, not talking. I didn't want it to end.

I sighed, leaned my head on his shoulder and said, 'I think we need to get Martha home. Sorry.'

I felt him nod.

'That's why you're amazing,' said Rik. 'Seriously. You make sure everyone's OK. Let's face it, Clem's never going to think to do that. I can't believe Martha's been holding court here for hours, and she's, like, ninety or something. Yes, let's take her back. Then . . . maybe we could get away from here for a bit? Would you like to go down to the beach?'

I nodded. I very much did want to go down to the beach, away from the party, the camellias, the high fence.

We were walking towards the pool when someone screamed. It wasn't the kind of drunk shouting that everyone had been doing all evening. This was the kind of scream that makes you drop everything and run. Rik and I sprinted across the grass to where a small crowd was already gathering by the pool. The pool lights, which had been on, were switched off.

It happened in slow motion. First I noticed that Martha's chair was empty. There was a half-full champagne glass on the little table next to it, but Martha had gone.

I knew. But I kept my eyes away from the water and decided, quickly, that Clem must have taken her home after all. I looked at the others. Maya was the one who was screaming. She wouldn't stop. It was a sound that went right through your body, that sliced you in half.

'Maya!' I shouted, and I ran through the group of people, and Maya was pointing and yelling.

Someone switched the underwater lights back on. They lit the pool up, bright blue.

Maya had flowers in her hair and was wearing shorts and a plunging top, and she was still holding a glass of punch with flowers floating on top of it.

I followed the direction of her finger.

There was someone floating in the water. Someone wearing a deep red dress, a dress she had called her lucky charm.

The lights were on, and Martha was face down in the swimming pool.

25

Rik leaped in and started wrestling to get her out, but her dress seemed to be everywhere, and it was too much for him. I saw that no one else knew what to do. I couldn't help him in the water wearing this dress, so I started unzipping it at the side. While I was doing that, someone else took a running jump and swam over to help.

Josie and Rik pulled her out of the pool, and I looked for a phone. Mine was in the kitchen because this dress had no pockets. Maya's phone was sticking out of the back pocket of her shorts.

'Maya,' I said. 'Phone?'

She didn't answer. She was crying now, hiccuping, ugly sobs, wailing, 'I was talking to her just now!'

I grabbed her phone. It was a facial-recognition one, so I held it in front of her face to unlock it, then dialled 999.

It took me a long time to give the right details, and to explain the situation coherently, but eventually the operator told me an ambulance was on its way, and then I put her on speaker and she talked Josie through chest compressions.

I was here to look after Martha. That had been my job.

I'd been sitting round the corner instead, kissing a boy, full of wine and wonder, while Martha had fallen into the pool.

Josie had done a first-aid course because she was worried about her mum. If anyone could bring Martha back, it would be Josie: the most capable, responsible person I knew. And she had the 999 woman helping, and Meg was crouching beside her, ready to take over. I clung on to the hope that Martha would wake up, that she might, somehow, cough and splutter and be OK. I held on to the idea that you might be able to come back to life, even when you were ninety-two and had drowned.

I tried to speak. I had to try a few times, but in the end I managed: 'Where's Clem?'

She wasn't in the crowd. When I glanced around, I realized that, out of all the people who were here, only Rik, Josie, Meg and I seemed to be in any way sober. Everyone else was far more drunk than they should have been, considering that it was only ten o'clock.

I looked at the drinks some of them were holding, the 'punch'. It wasn't rocket science.

'Clem!' Everyone was shouting for her. 'Clemmie!'

I couldn't see Gareth, then remembered that I'd left them both in the tree.

Rik was kneeling next to Josie and Meg, also ready to help. I forced myself to look at Martha's face.

All the first aid in the world was pointless. Nothing was going to bring her back. She wasn't there. Her face was blank: peaceful, but not Martha. She was gone.

Twenty minutes earlier she had been talking to anyone and everyone. How had she ended up face down in the water without anyone noticing?

'She told us to go away and give her a moment to appreciate everything before she went home,' said a girl next to me, the one from the year above. It was as if she'd read my mind. She gave a big gasp. 'She asked us to switch the pool lights off so she could try to see the stars, and we did, even though it was cloudy. If we'd known . . .'

Everyone was a mess. They were shrieking and sobbing and getting in the way. I wanted to take control, but I didn't have enough presence. The music was still pumping out: now it was Taylor Swift's 'Shake It Off'.

I could do that, at least. I could turn off the music.

I walked round the pool, past Martha's empty seat.

I thought of Felicity's words. She'd asked me to keep an eye on Clemmie and Martha. She'd said she needed '*someone sensible and grounded*'.

She hadn't trusted Clem not to have a party, and here it was, the party. *Absolutely no parties* had been one of the rules. *Don't kill Grandma.* That was another. No one was allowed to stay at the house apart from me. My job had been to enforce those three big rules. I had brought an unsteady old lady to the side of a pool of water, given her alcohol and left her there.

We were all, I realized, *so* busted.

Rule number one? '*Don't kill Grandma.*' I could hear Felicity's crisp voice saying it on repeat in my mind. We had done it. We had killed her.

I wondered whether the police would turn up with the ambulance. Did they come out when someone died? Even if that person was in her nineties? Yes, of course they would, because I'd told them that she'd drowned in a pool. There were drunk people everywhere, and a contested will.

I stepped round Martha's chair. That was when I saw that, next to the half-full champagne glass, there were three envelopes piled neatly on the table. I stopped and picked them up.

One said: *For the Police*. The writing was wavering but beautiful.

The second said: *Felicity and family*.

And the third, the final one, was, weirdly, addressed to: *Senara*.

I looked back at Martha again. I remembered her listing the people she'd outlived, saying: '*It's like a fairy-tale curse*.'

I was staring at my envelope when Clem appeared. Gareth was semi-carrying her.

'Oh my FUCK!' Clem was hysterical. 'Gran! Wake up, Gran! Oh my God! No! The one thing I had to do was keep her alive. The one thing! Gran, stop it! Don't do this! Senni, you have to wake her. Wake her!'

I replaced the envelopes and headed back into the house. The stereo was in the living room, the speakers outside plugged into extension leads. There was a phone on a dock, and I took it out. The world went silent, apart from Clem's screams.

Back outside I could still hear sobs and screams and shouts. A few night birds. A drop of rain landed on me, and then another and another. Rik had taken over the chest compressions. I went to crouch beside him, and the rain poured down on us, soaking him, me, Martha. It made concentric rings all over the surface of the pool. I was vaguely aware of people melting away, leaving before the authorities arrived.

'Well done,' I said, though those weren't really the right words.

Josie nodded. Meg was holding her.

'It's not going to work, but we have to try,' she said. 'It's really hard.'

'I'm sure the ambulance will be here soon.' I looked around. 'I can't believe everyone's leaving.'

We all looked at Clem, who was wailing in Gareth's arms. When I went over, Gareth opened his arm and pulled me into their hug.

'Stop yelling, Clemmie,' I said quietly into her ear. 'It won't change anything. It makes it worse.' She clung on to me too; I had to wriggle around to loosen her grip so I could breathe. The three of us stood like that for a while, and then Clem spoke directly into my ear, her voice low and controlled. 'This is your fault, Senara. You did this. You were paid to keep her alive. I trusted you and so did my mum.'

I jumped back, my heart pounding. I heard sirens approaching.

'What did you say?'

She pulled away from me. Rainwater was pouring down her face. I heard distant thunder.

'I didn't say anything,' she said, using her panicky voice again, and then two paramedics and two police officers arrived, and we weren't in charge any more. I replayed Clem's words in my head.

She was right, but had she said it? I needed to ask Gareth, but this wasn't the moment. I looked for Rik and found him with the paramedics.

The police attempted to herd everyone into the house, though I noticed more people skulking round the edges of the garden, looping back to the corner in the drive so they could go home.

A woman was in the courtyard, yelling: 'Get into the house! All of you, in the house. Through this door! Right now. You! Yes, you. Come back!'

By the time everyone was in the kitchen, though, there were only eleven of us left.

I looked at Rik. I couldn't believe I'd kissed him. I'd been kissing him while Martha was dying. The best thing, and the worst.

'Maybe we should make some tea?' I said because I needed to do something. He nodded.

'Coffee might be better,' he said, surveying the remaining guests.

Most of them seemed out of it, soaked with rain, making no sense. Clem was back to fake hysteria, and Gareth was comforting her in a corner of the room. Meg walked in and went over to Josie, and they spoke in low voices, hands resting lightly on each other's waists. Maya was watching Gareth and Clem across the table, but her eyes were unfocused, and she kept fanning herself with her hand and making random sobbing sounds. Treve and Dan were sitting on the floor, gasping and laughing at nothing. Amina was talking very fast to a boy who had his head down on the table and was dribbling. Everyone's clothes were sticking to them, and there were puddles on the floor. I could hear the rain, heavier and heavier, outside.

'I don't know what they've taken,' Rik said, very quietly, as we got out all the mugs from the cupboard and lined them up along the worktop. 'No one offered me anything. Did they you?' I shook my head. 'I hope the police don't find it. That could be pretty bad.'

'Oh shit!' I felt so innocent, so sheltered. I'd never even thought that there might be drugs here. Of course no one had offered anything to me. 'What do you think it is?'

'Coke? Speed? Whatever it is, I hope they've got rid of it.'

'Clem said this is all my fault.'

He didn't look surprised. 'She would. Clem's projecting. I'd say she feels it's her fault, and she's lashing out. Try to stay away from her. And, Senara?' I looked at him. He smiled. For a second it warmed me.

'Yes,' I said.

Rik turned and surveyed the room, leaning back on the worktop. The kitchen was usually homely and comforting. Now it was a shitshow. There were empty bottles and cans everywhere. The plastic bowl of 'punch' was in front of the coffee machine, and I could smell it from here. There were flowers floating across the top of it, including, I noticed, foxgloves. If they were in the punch, no wonder everyone was feeling weird.

'Just – thank you. You know.'

I looked into his eyes. He looked back. We said everything we needed to say without speaking. *Yes. We'll do it again. Not now, but yes.*

I pulled myself back to the kitchen. 'Should we tip that away?' I said, nodding at the punch. 'Those are foxgloves on top, and they're poisonous for a start. I'm not sure they'd make people this weird, but I guess it wouldn't help.'

'Sure,' said Rik. 'Let's tip it all down the sink. Just in case.'

We didn't get a chance, though, because the two police officers came in and made us sit down. I walked away to the opposite end of the table from Clem.

My thoughts were spinning all over the place.

'We were going to make hot drinks,' said Rik to the woman. 'Would that be OK?'

She had short red hair and a smiley face, but I'd just heard her yelling at us to get into the kitchen, and I knew she was scary.

'Sure. I'll have a tea if you're offering. Who are you?'

'Rik Anderson,' he said. 'That's R-I-K.'

The man wrote it down, and I detected a little eyeroll. He was short and squat and had a face like a potato.

'Richard?'

'No. Just Rik.' There was a pause. 'I swear. It says Rik on my birth certificate. I'm named after Rik Mayall.'

'You're not local.'

'No,' he said. 'No, I'm not. I'm visiting Clem. Meg over there? She's my sister.'

'DFL, is it?' said the man. When Rik looked blank, he said, 'Down from London?' Rik nodded.

'Right,' said the woman. 'Thanks for that.' She looked round the room. 'Yes, your friends could do with something to sober them up. Thanks, Rik. Right, you're Senara Jenkin. I know your mother.' She pointed at Gareth. 'Not as well as I know yours, though. Does Jayne know where you are tonight?'

He winced. 'Kind of.'

She turned to me. 'Does Jenna?'

'She does actually,' I said, feeling quite scared now. 'I'm staying here while Clem's family are away. I mean, she knows I'm here, but she doesn't know . . .' I gestured around.

She didn't reply. She didn't need to.

Clem was right: this *was* my fault. I'd gone along with everything, caught up in her excitement, following her lead, even when I knew I should have stopped her. I couldn't have stopped Rik and Meg coming to stay (and I was glad they had), but I could have done more to keep the party from getting out of hand. I could have stopped Martha coming up here. I could have taken her a glass of champagne at her cottage and sat there with her. She could still have worn her dress.

I could have kept an unsteady, very old woman away from the edge of a fucking swimming pool.

The man, who said he was DS Spargo, put clingfilm over the punchbowl and took it out of the room, and Rik started firing up the coffee machine while I put the kettle on and got out things for tea.

'Who wants coffee and who wants tea?' I tried to shout it to the room, but everyone ignored me as usual. I felt like a crap supply teacher.

The woman, PC Williams, clapped her hands. 'Hands up for coffee!' she shouted. Six hands went up, including Rik's. 'Tea?' The rest put their hands up, and she did too. 'There we go. Thanks, guys.'

The police took everyone's names, and asked questions that were mainly directed at Clem. It didn't last long because they soon discovered that everyone in the room apart from them was under eighteen.

PC Williams, pulled out a chair.

'Senara?' she said. 'We need another adult. I mean, ideally we need everyone's parents, but I'm going to start by calling Jayne, and I need you to phone your mother for me too. OK?'

I sighed. Fully busted.

'OK,' I said. 'She'll be asleep, but I'll try.'

26

In 1944, the other evacuees returned home. Violet and Martha went to Penzance to wave them off. It was the very end of the line, and the tracks stopped here. You could only go in one direction from Penzance: east. The station was next to the ocean and near the harbour. The cold wind blew straight off the water, and they stamped their feet to keep warm.

'Write to me,' Martha said to Betty. 'Please, Betty.'

Over the past year they had become the closest of friends again, and Martha was going to miss her so much. She had never slept in a room on her own before.

'I promise. You write to me too.'

Martha nodded. Roy, who was fifteen and huge now, gave her a hug. Michael held her tightly. Even Miss Ward hugged her, and everyone promised to come back and visit. It was hustly and bustly, and then they were on the train, and all the doors slammed, and everyone was waving, and the train was loud, and then it was quieter and gone.

Violet tucked her arm through Martha's.

'We're going to go into town and have a cup of tea and a bun,' she said, and they did.

Penzance was down at heel, but full of colour and energy. Martha started to see what her new life was going to be like.

She was fourteen now, and she was a different person from the ten-year-old who had arrived that freezing November evening. She was going to finish growing up here. She went to school with the local children. She became the daughter the family had never had, and Violet and Aubrey became her new parents. They glued a family together, she thought, from the remnants of two broken ones.

She never called Violet Mother – she called her Vi, and Vi called her Marth. When she tried speaking with her London voice, it didn't feel right any more. She sounded fully like Violet now.

Aubrey started trying harder to be normal, but it didn't work. He was always kind to Martha, but she hated to see him change from one moment to the next. He would get angry and shout and throw things, and only Violet knew how to calm him down. The way he yelled, the terrible words he used, sent Martha running away outside, into the garden, down to the beach, as far from him as she could go. She had to get away from him because she had those feelings herself. She knew that, if she let herself, she could do that too. She knew that Aubrey had seen things that had broken him forever, had stopped him being the person he would have been if he'd been able to grow up with no war.

She had to work hard to live like a normal person. She copied Violet in everything. When she heard Aubrey out on the cliffs at night, screaming at the sky, she felt her own pain trying to get out, urging her to do the same.

She didn't let herself. She shut it all away inside. She put it into a box, locked it, and threw the key into the ocean, and she never, ever opened it.

27

The police didn't even let us go to the beach, so we sat on bin bags at the edge of the wet garden as the sun rose, drinking coffee and cups of tea and water and looking at the ocean. The rain had stopped, and everything was wet and new. I leaned on Rik. Megan and Josie were on my other side, their heads close together. We hadn't known these people a couple of days ago, and now Josie and I had both found people who'd changed our lives. Everything was different. I had met Rik.

The others had fallen asleep at various points around the house and garden. A few parents got the messages in the night, or answered their landlines, and turned up, talked to the police and took their children home. We didn't have a landline, and I thought of Mum sleeping through all this. I knew she'd wake at six for her run, and then there'd be trouble.

Clem wasn't with us. Neither was Gareth.

'Do you think Martha . . . you know,' said Rik. 'Planned that? It's a dramatic way to go.'

'Yeah.' I'd been thinking about this non-stop. 'She put on her best dress. She said the dress was her lucky charm. She hated being old. I reckon she hated the "Don't kill Grandma" stuff so much that she decided to be, like, "In your face!" And – did you see the letters? She left three letters on the table.'

'Josie said the police took them,' said Rik.

Josie looked round. 'I said what?'

'The notes. The ones Martha left. You said the police took them.'

'Yeah. After you'd gone inside, the guy put some gloves on and slipped them into a plastic folder, like they do on TV. One had your name on, Senni.'

'I saw it.'

I stretched my legs out in front of me. I really needed to get changed into normal clothes. It felt weird to be wearing a party dress right now, and particularly one of Martha's, even though I had a jumper on top.

'They'll have my fingerprints on. I reckon her letter will just tell me to keep this dress. She picked it out for me yesterday. She has the most amazing collection of vintage stuff.' I corrected myself: 'Had. It's weird she's gone. I mean, she was ninety-two, so it shouldn't be a surprise, but . . .'

'Just classic Gran.' I hadn't heard Clem coming up behind us. She sank to the ground, and I froze. 'She obviously had to throw herself into a swimming pool at a party full of people a million years younger than she was, wearing a vintage ballgown. That's so on-brand.'

Josie and Meg laughed at that, then stopped suddenly. I didn't and neither did Rik. I didn't trust Clem an iota.

'Martha's so cool,' Josie said. 'Was so cool. But she still is. Always. You know, the other day she ordered me and Mum a Domino's, for no reason.' She wiped under her eye with a finger. 'Just because she thought we'd appreciate it, which we did.'

I'd had no idea about that, but it was exactly what Martha would have done. I wanted to ask Josie how it had come about, but Clem spoke over me.

'My mum's going absolutely mental,' said Clem. 'It's tomorrow in Hong Kong. Today I mean, but a normal time. She's getting a flight back. Just her. We're going to be in so, so, so much shit, Senara.'

'Well, *I* am,' I said. 'Like you said: this is all on me.'

'It's not!' Everyone but Clem jumped in to reassure me.

Clem was trying to be bolshy, but she was shocked and subdued. This could have been the first time in her life that something hadn't gone her way. Our eyes met, and there was something hard in her blue stare. I felt pretty sure that our brief friendship had ended.

It would never have lasted. She'd wanted me as a temporary sidekick, and I was over that. I knew we would probably never speak again after she went home. I'd see her across the street in Penzance and hide from her, as Mum did with Felicity.

PC Williams was crossing the grass, and we turned to watch her approach.

'Clem,' said Josie, her voice low. 'The police are all over the place. Do you think we need to tell them about the skull?'

I looked at Clem, who shrugged and frowned.

'I don't give a shit, Josie. Tell them if you want. They won't care. My actual great-gran literally just died? Who's bothered about some old graveyard? Whatever.'

'Senara?' said PC Williams. 'Can you come with me? I need a word.' Rik and Clem both started to get up too. 'Just Senara, thanks,' she said, and they sat down. I felt self-conscious as I followed her across the dewy dawn grass, back into the house. *Why me? Why not Clem?*

She led me into a sitting room where Mum was perched on a big sofa in her running gear. She held out her arms, and I walked over and sat next to her, trying to judge how furious she was.

Mum was white and tense. I watched emotions flicker across her face like electricity, but when she looked at me it was mainly with sympathy. Her hair (which she dyed at home, always the same blonde) was scraped into a ponytail, and she wasn't wearing make-up.

'Mum!' I said.

'Oh, Senara. What the hell's going on? What's happened? I knew I shouldn't have let you stay. I knew it! I just knew it!'

'Martha died.' My voice came out as a whisper. Mum nodded. She obviously knew that already.

'So, Senara,' said DS Spargo, 'you may have seen that

Martha left some letters. We feel confident, now that we've read them, that her death was suicide, but of course there'll need to be an inquest. One of the notes was addressed to you, which we'll come to in a minute. First of all, though, she addressed a letter to us, in which she wrote about a body buried in the garden. She gave us the impression that you and the others might know about it.' He fixed me with a look.

Fuck. Why me? Why did I have to be the one ambushed by this? I felt Mum flinch next to me, and, from the corner of my eye, saw her other hand grabbing the arm of the sofa, her knuckles turning white.

I felt so tired, so sick. It wasn't fair.

'What did her letter say?' I asked.

My heart pounded so hard it was making my whole body twitch. I didn't dare breathe. I thought of Martha's bedroom window, imagined her sitting up in bed, watching Josie and me pulling up that skull.

'We weren't expecting this, I have to admit, when we came out last night,' said DS Spargo. 'I need you to tell me what she's referring to, in your own words. Do you know anything about a body in the garden?'

The silence was so loud. It smothered everything.

I felt Mum next to me. The tension was coming off her in waves.

I looked at the rug and started to speak. I edited out the first time I'd found a bone, back in January, because I didn't think we needed to go there.

'The other day there was a dog here, a dog I was

walking, and she dug up a bone, from under the camellias. It was just a normal kind of bone, and we didn't think anything of it. Clem said it might be a pet graveyard. Then we found a watch in there, and some other things. But then on Friday –'

I stopped abruptly. I couldn't say it, not after Martha.

The other officer stepped in. Everyone's names had gone out of my head.

'On Friday?' she said, her voice gentler.

I waited a long time. I felt myself being pulled down, underground. In the end, I had to whisper it.

'On Friday we found a skull. A human one. In the hole the dog made.'

There was a silence that filled the room like foam. It seemed to stay for ages.

'A human one,' said the woman, through the bubbles.

'Yes.'

'You dug up a human skull,' said the man, 'and you didn't think to report it?'

'We were going to!' My voice was louder now. I needed to defend us. 'We were going to, after the party. It didn't feel urgent.'

The man half stood up. 'Human remains are always urgent. Where is this skull? I'll need someone to show me exactly where it came from.'

'Back in the ground,' I whispered.

Mum sat there, pale-faced and catatonic.

'I can take you there,' I said. Then, because I didn't often have a captive audience of police officers, I thought I should do what Josie would have wanted. I said, 'Can you check it's not Rachel Thomas?'

There was a beat of silence. Another. Then he said, 'We'll check against known missing persons, of course.'

I'd done it. Now we were going to find out.

And then Mum threw up.

1988

Felicity went outside and stood by the fence, looking out over the ocean. The sun was pale in the grey-blue sky, and Grandma was coming back tomorrow. She felt the breeze on her face, smelled salt in the air. She loved summer.

'Hey.'

She looked round and saw Jenna next to her, wearing one of Alex's baggy jumpers and her shorts from yesterday. Her hair was tangled, and her cheeks were flushed.

'OK,' said Felicity. 'This is a bit weird. You and my brother.' She forced a laugh. 'He's had a crush on you forever.'

'Yes, he said. Sorry if it's weird for you! I slept in the spare room. It's not like we . . . Oh God, I really like him, Flick! Is that going to be too strange? I know he's going to Oxford so we have no . . .'

Felicity put an arm round her friend. 'It's fine. I'm happy for you both. It's lovely.' She felt strange about it: the two people closest to her in the whole world had pushed her out of the inner circle. But she didn't say that. Of course she didn't. She couldn't.

'Is Rachel up?' she said instead, and Jenna shook her head, so Felicity outlined what Rachel had said, about both their parents hitting her and her sister, even now when they were almost adults. About the bruise on her forehead, behind her hair. About how she was plotting an escape to Thailand with Andy Teague.

Jenna shuddered at the idea.

'That guy attacked a girl from my class. Like, properly attacked her. He got away with it because he denied it. Rachel can't go away with him.'

'I know! I told her to move in with us, but she said her dad would storm up here and push her off the cliff.' Felicity sighed. 'She said she might let me tell Grandma. I hope she does. Grandma will know what to do.'

'Yes. Tell Martha. Rachel can't go home. She can't go away with Andy Teague. I bet he can't believe his luck that Rachel wants to run away with him. Angie hates him. She hates being his sister.'

'Oh God!' Felicity tried to imagine what it would be like to live with someone like that. She loved her brother: imagine if Andy Teague was her brother instead!

'He waited for me at the bus stop,' Felicity said, 'but he never tried to speak to me. And then he came here yesterday.'

'He's set his sights on you.' As soon as she saw Felicity's face, Jenna backtracked. 'I mean, he was probably just looking for Rachel. I bet that was it. If they're planning something together, he was probably trying to find her. It'll be that.'

Felicity felt her heartbeat calming. 'Yes,' she said. 'Yes, it probably was.' She knew it wasn't, but she tried very hard to believe Jenna's explanation.

'I know it's still a bit cold, but I'm going for a swim,' said Jenna. 'Do you fancy it?'

Felicity wasn't going to swim. What if Andy Teague really had set his sights on her? He couldn't have come here looking for Rachel because she'd come over later, on impulse. What if he came back, and she was wearing a swimsuit? Her vision was filled with danger signs.

Alex appeared in his running clothes. He blushed when he saw Jenna. She stood on tiptoe to kiss him, and Alex put a hand on her waist. Felicity looked away. There were five seagulls swooping out there, over the water, shrieking.

'I'm going for a run.' He pointed to himself, then did a running motion with two fingers. Felicity laughed because he was still so awkward and trying so hard.

Jenna laughed too, but in a nice way. She stepped back and patted his arm. 'Have fun.'

'Thanks. I won't!'

'Don't go,' said Felicity.

He stopped. They looked at each other. He understood.

'OK,' said Alex. 'Yeah. All right. How about this? I'll run round the garden. Five times round the garden. Like a teddy bear.'

'On the inside?'

'Yep.'

Felicity relaxed. 'Fine.'

When he left, the girls looked at each other.

'Oh my God!' said Felicity. 'He loves you so much. He

can hardly speak in front of you. You make him say *really* stupid things.' She changed her voice. '"*Like a teddy bear*"!'

Jenna shook her head. 'He's perfect,' she said.

Jenna changed into her bikini and dived into the pool. Felicity realized it was Sunday morning, and Rachel's family would be at church, so she supposed that gave Rachel a reprieve. She made a cup of tea and took it up to the attic and knocked on her door.

When there was no answer, she tried the handle, not expecting it to open, because of the bolt. It did swing open, though, and for a moment she thought Rachel had left in the night. Then the heap of duvet moved, and her head emerged.

The attic room was dusty and little used, but it had a single bed in it and a few boxes of junk. It would be easy to make this Rachel's bedroom for as long as she needed it.

'Morning!' Felicity said. 'Sorry to wake you. I brought you a cup of tea. I was just going to leave it for you.'

Rachel yawned and sat up. 'I wasn't really asleep. I slept better than I have for ages, though. You're an angel.'

'I'm making brownies.'

'I'll be right there.'

Felicity put Radio 1 on in the kitchen and sang along to Kylie Minogue. She propped the courtyard door open with the metal doorstop, so the breeze would come in and she could keep popping out to talk to Jenna, who was swimming lengths of the pool. Up and down, up and down, with flip turns at the end because Jenna was brilliant at swimming. Alex passed by every now and then, waving. The sun was shining in a pale and cool way.

The brownie tray was in the oven, and Felicity had just put some milk on to warm up for hot chocolate when she heard Jenna's voice outside, with an unusual tone to it.

She walked across the courtyard and looked round the corner.

Felicity's vision lit up with slimy green. Slime green filled with black triangles.

He was back.

She stepped away. He was crouching down, talking to Jenna, who was in the pool. Felicity needed Alex to appear right now, but she knew he'd be a while because he'd just been past.

She was wondering what to do when Andy Teague heard her and turned round. The gates had been locked, but here he was.

He looked so normal it was hard to describe him. His hair was a bit longer than suited him, but he was unremarkable in every way. He seemed like a regular person, but he had climbed over their gate and was deliberately intimidating two teenage girls.

'Aha,' he said. 'Felicity, yes? I was wondering if Rachel might happen to be in residence?'

She wanted to tell him to go away, that he wasn't welcome, that he had to stay away from Rachel. Her voice didn't work.

'There's no need to look so scared,' he said. 'I'm only being friendly. I'm Andy. Rachel's boyfriend.'

He walked towards her. She stepped backwards. Every alarm bell she had was going off. It was so noisy inside her head that she had to shut her brain down. She backed into the kitchen, and he followed her inside. She heard the water splashing as Jenna got out of the pool, heard her shouting, 'Alex!'

'Rachel's not here,' Felicity said. Her voice was croaky, too quiet. She tried to send Rachel telepathic messages. *Don't come downstairs don't don't don't.*

Alex would be here in a second.

'Hey,' said Andy. She suddenly felt more sorry for this creepy man's sister than for anyone in the world. 'I don't bite. Well . . . not until we get to know each other better.' Felicity's stomach turned. 'Don't panic. I've seen you in the village. We spoke yesterday, remember?' His voice was strangely gentle. Felicity hated it. 'I know Rachel's your friend, and I know she said she'd come here if she ever needed a safe haven. Well, she's not at home, so I guess she's here. When she told me about her posh friend, I thought I'd like to be your friend too. And so here I am.'

He paused and his face changed, though his voice stayed soft. 'You think you're so much better than everyone else, don't you? You and your brother. Your little friend out there, living it up in the swimming pool.' His voice changed for the last two words, a grotesque impression of someone posh.

From the corner of her eye she saw Jenna appear behind Andy, in the doorway.

Felicity kept walking backwards, and he kept walking forwards. Everything was triangles.

'You can't go away with Rachel,' she whispered. She heard footsteps on the stairs.

'Oh, is that right?' He laughed. 'Pardon us for not running it by you first. She told you?'

Felicity nodded. She glanced over his shoulder. Jenna was looking round the room, trying to decide what to do. *Where was Alex?*

'Like a little bird,' he said. 'So scared.' It was the creepiest thing Felicity had ever heard. 'How old are you?'

She shook her head.

He said, 'How old?' in a much louder voice, and she was so terrified that she whispered, 'Sixteen.'

'Sixteen!' He liked that. 'Legal. Rachel's seventeen. Which is also nice.'

He was disgusting. She could knee him in the balls. She pulled one leg back ready.

'Hey, Felicity. Don't be scared.' He reached out to touch her face. His other hand went straight to her breast, and that broke her paralysis.

Felicity bit down on his finger hard, instinctively, and at the same time Jenna swung the doorstop at his head, and Rachel screamed, 'No!'

Andy Teague looked surprised, and then fell down.

Rachel was standing behind Felicity. They all waited. He didn't move.

Time seemed to stand still. Rachel and Felicity stood there, frozen. Felicity had no feelings at all. Then suddenly the spell was broken: Jenna began screaming and there was burnt milk all over the hob, burnt brownies in the oven, and a dead man on the kitchen floor.

'I didn't mean to do it!' Jenna was hysterical. 'I couldn't find Alex, and I didn't want him to hurt you! Oh shit! *Oh shit oh shit oh shit!* Is he dead?' She screamed and wailed, her voice a ribbon of shock and horror.

Rachel looked at him. She looked at them. Her face was green.

'What have you done?' she said to Jenna. Her voice was quiet and tight, stones dropping to the ground.

Felicity couldn't speak. Jenna carried on screaming. It was lucky there were no neighbours. Andy Teague didn't move, was never going to move. Rachel was kneeling next to him, shaking him, yelling into his face. Felicity knew she had to do something, but time had stopped.

She made her feet walk over to Jenna. She made her mouth open. She waited to see what words came out because she had no idea what they were going to be.

She heard herself saying: 'I'm glad you did it.'

That was a surprise. She hadn't expected those to be the words that came out. Andy Teague's aura had gone, switched off like a bathroom light. No more triangles.

Rachel was still shaking him. She tried some mouth-to-mouth. Felicity couldn't watch.

Jenna's wails were getting quieter. Felicity's mind started to focus.

'He's dead,' she said. 'So we have to get rid of him.'

Now that he wasn't going to threaten her ever again,

now that he wasn't going to ruin Rachel's life, Felicity found she could think clearly. In fact, she was pretty sure she was thinking too clearly. She had to take care of everything while she felt like this. Jenna was just standing there, in her bikini, still holding the doorstop, with the man she hadn't meant to kill at her feet.

'I wanted to stop him hassling you,' she whispered. She whispered it over and over again. Then she said, 'Rachel?'

Rachel didn't look up. She was muttering, 'Andy, Andy, Andy. Come on, Andy.' But it was easy to see that Andy was gone.

Felicity was the only one with any presence of mind. 'We can't call the police,' she said. She went out into the hall and took the phone off the hook so no one could disturb them. 'No one will know he was here. We could drop him off the cliff. So it looks like he's fallen.'

Alex stood in the kitchen doorway. 'What's –?' He looked at the scene.

'Oh,' he said. 'Oh fuck.'

There was no way they could let Jenna go to prison for this. When Rachel calmed down, after she'd thrown up five times in a row, she agreed.

'I did hear what he said,' she told Felicity. 'I'm sorry. He was being . . .' She broke off and took some deep breaths. 'I know Jenna didn't mean to do it. She was just trying to stop him. She can't go to jail for it. All the same, though – Jenna! What the fuck? You killed him!'

Jenna ran out of the room. They heard her footsteps on the stairs.

'We can't drop him off the cliff,' said Alex. 'The head injury would be all wrong. The police would come here because our house is the only place at the top of the cliff. Could you two handle lying to the police? Right now? Could Jenna?'

Felicity looked at Rachel, who stood up. Her face was set, her expression closed.

'I can't do this,' she said. 'No. I'm not lying to the police.' She took a deep breath. 'But I won't tell them, either. I don't want to ruin your lives.' Rachel paused, her eyes flicking to Andy's body. 'I actually liked Andy, but he was being horrible to you, Lissy . . . But he didn't deserve to die . . . I can't believe that happened. Look – I'm going to leave, and I promise you'll never hear from me again. No one will. Can you lend me a bag and a few things? I'll walk to Penzance and get a train.'

'I'll drive you to Penzance,' said Alex. 'It'll take too long to walk. Too many people will see you.'

'Where will you go?' said Felicity.

Rachel shrugged. 'London? Bristol maybe? I'll work until I've got the money to disappear properly. Work out how to change my name. All that. I won't come back. This is it for me. I'm leaving here for good. I promise I won't tell anyone, Lissy. I never will.'

Felicity knew she meant it. She knew she would never see Rachel again.

'Take whatever you need,' she said. She looked at Alex. 'We can give you some money, right?'

'Take my bank card,' said Alex. 'There's a few hundred pounds in there. Take it all out and throw the card in the sea. I'll say I lost it.'

Rachel went upstairs to gather her stuff. Felicity knew she had to go after her, and that Alex would go and find Jenna. For a few seconds, though, it was just the two of them.

'I feel like I can do this,' said Felicity. 'I don't know about Jenna, but she has to keep it together. We need to look after her. What about dumping him in the sea?'

'We'd have to do it when it's dark,' he said. 'Grandma's not back until tomorrow lunchtime. We can do it tonight. In darkness. For the moment I guess we have to hide the . . . hide the . . .'

Alex couldn't say the word. Even Alex crumbled.

28

I went to my bedroom. Mum followed, and we sat side by side on my bed. Mum put her arm round my shoulder, but she didn't speak. She was trembling.

I could rely on Mum for everything: she was fierce. She had defended me my whole life. So why, now, was she shaking violently and then tensing to try to stop it? Why had she thrown up? She gripped me so hard that it hurt, and I tried to pull away.

'You have no idea,' she said, 'what you've done.'

'No, I don't! What are you on about? How could I have any idea?' I paused. 'Is this to do with Rachel Thomas?'

'No! Why on earth do you think you know anything about Rachel?' She took a jerky breath. 'Have they got hold of Felicity?'

'Clem says she's going mad. And flying back.'

'Good,' she said. 'Good. Yes. We need Felicity. And Alex too. Is Alex coming?'

This was the first time I'd ever heard her mention Clem's uncle.

We sat in silence. Mum was rocking back and forth, and

her breathing was ragged. I didn't know what to say. I walked over to the window and looked towards the camellia bushes. I couldn't see them from here, but I could see police tape strung up between two trees, shutting off the whole of that side of the garden. It was early on Sunday morning, and I guessed they were waiting for reinforcements.

'Why, though? Why did you have to say that about Rachel?' said Mum in a tight voice. 'Now they're going to dig it all up and do forensic testing, aren't they?'

'Isn't that good?' I didn't understand.

'We could go away,' she said, standing up. 'But we couldn't, could we? You can't just disappear these days. They find you. You could live with your dad.'

'Mum?'

'Oh, don't worry. Just . . .' Her voice trailed off.

'Mum.' I said it louder this time. I heard an authority in my voice that I'd never had before. 'Mum, what's happening? Why are you being like this? Why are you saying mad things? You're really, really scaring me.'

She didn't react. I had no idea why she was being so scary. After a while, I wanted to talk because I hated this spiky silence.

'Did you know Martha came here as an evacuee?' Mum nodded, but she didn't look at me.

I'd only known Martha as an old lady. She had been seventy-six when I was born. I knew she'd lived an unimaginably difficult life, but at the same time I had no idea about the details of it; I just remembered all the things she had shared with me. Chicory coffee, the first sight of a cow, Aubrey and his 'shell shock'. Her little coat and gas mask.

It was light outside, the sky pale blue, everything new and beautiful, washed clean by the rain, but the room was stuffy. There wasn't enough air. I still felt drunk. It was morning, and I hadn't slept. I sat on the bed. I was scared Mum was going to run away, but she sat down too.

'I guess they'll be able to check how old they are,' said Mum. 'Don't you think? The bones.'

'I guess.'

'Would they even have Rachel's DNA?'

'They'd have Lucy's.'

Mum nodded. 'You're right. Of course.'

'Mum? Were you friends with Rachel too? I mean, I know she was friends with Felicity.'

Mum gave a tiny nod. She looked grey. 'Do you have a number for Alex?'

'Of course I don't. Get his number from Clem maybe? Mum, were you friends with Felicity and Alex and Rachel? What happened?'

She stood up. 'I used to be,' she said. 'Darling, sorry. You need to get some sleep. I'm going to go and find Clem, to get that phone number. You have a rest.'

I didn't want to let her go, but all the same I felt sleep pulling me down. She sat next to me and stroked my hair. I had meant to change out of this dress, but I hadn't done it. Her hand was comforting on my head. I felt myself sinking. The skull. Rachel. Martha. The police. It swirled round my head.

1946

Martha never thought about the first ten years of her life because she knew she would unravel if she let it in. Even when she longed for comfort and felt the ghosts of her family calling to her, she didn't let her mind go there.

As time went by, she found she could tell people her story in a controlled way: '*I came here as an evacuee and never went home.*' But she didn't go deeply into it. She never, ever described her parents and sister or her East End life. She asked Violet whether she could take her surname, and Violet cried and hugged her and said of course, so she stopped being Martha Driscoll and became Martha Roberts, because Martha Roberts had a life and a home and a family, and Martha Driscoll had lost everything.

Violet treated her as a daughter, and she came to believe that she was, indeed, Martha Roberts of Cliff House. A Cornish girl from the big house on the cliffs. A girl who lived in a huge, faded house that had the last remnants of a staff. She stayed in the yellow room with the two windows, even though Violet offered her a bigger room if she wanted it. She kept the drawings she had done of her parents and

Daphne in a drawer beside her bed because she couldn't bear to see them every day, but she felt that this was what they had looked like and was glad to have them. Sometimes, at night, she would take them out and talk to them.

She missed Betty, and she liked having her bed right there, as if she might come back one day. Both of them kept their promises and wrote to each other.

Everything, apart from Aubrey, got better after the war. They carried on growing vegetables in the garden, but they put flowers in some of the vegetable beds and grass seeds in some of the others, and it started to look more like a garden and less like a farm.

Aubrey, though, got worse. He watched Martha slowly learning to live with her loss, and he became angry at her because he couldn't do it. They couldn't talk and draw any more. Martha tried hard to stay out of his way because sometimes just looking at her made him spit with rage. They only had May now to help them, having run out of money for the other staff years ago, so with only four of them in the house it was harder for Martha to avoid Aubrey. He walked round and round, stamping and muttering.

Even when she was sixteen, Martha followed Violet wherever she went. If Violet was going out, Martha asked if she could accompany her. Violet was patient and always said yes. Martha copied Violet's way of talking. 'Gracious heavens,' she would say. 'Praise the Lord.'

Aubrey carried on dressing in his old clothes, even when Violet bought him new ones. He didn't eat much. He never stopped shouting in the night, and Martha would put her fingers in her ears and try not to think about her daddy, about how he had been sent to fight and had never come home. Aubrey was the one who stopped her being able to forget. She and Aubrey were bad for each other.

It was the middle of summer, but that night the rain was crashing on her bedroom windows. Martha was sixteen, and she was in her nightdress getting ready for bed. She pulled the curtain aside, as she always did, to look out at the sea, but the warm rain was too heavy, and she couldn't see it. She opened the window and leaned out, wanting to feel the rain on her face, to get her hair wet, to be in the elements, to anchor herself. She did this all the time, tethering herself to this place at every opportunity. *I am here*, she told herself. *I am at home. I am in Cornwall. I'm lucky. Violet loves me, and I love her.*

The downpour soaked her long hair. She stayed where she was, letting the sky fling water at her. The wind was wild, and she turned her face into it, exhilarated.

That was why she didn't hear Aubrey coming into the room behind her.

When she felt his hands on her shoulders, giving her a sharp shove, she screamed. Her scream was picked up by the wind and carried out to sea. She fought back, and at first she thought she had no chance because he was stronger.

'You!' he kept saying. 'You!'

His eyes were burning. She didn't know what she had done, except having tried to find a way to live her life in spite of everything.

Then she saw that he wasn't strong at all. He had been fighting his demons for decades, and he hadn't left the grounds in years. Martha, on the other hand, helped in the garden and on the farmland. She walked for miles every day. She ran up and down stairs and swam in the sea.

She spun round and pushed him away.

He fell on to Betty's bed. She looked at his face. His skin was blotchy, red in places and white in others. He was over fifty now. Old.

Time stood still. She had lived with this man for six years, and for a while he had helped her more than anyone. Those hours when he had just listened – that was what had helped Martha start to cope with it all. She loved Aubrey, and she felt sorry for him too, but nobody had ever scared her as much as he did. He hated her now; it felt as if he had hated her from the moment she'd started to heal.

He pulled himself up and walked back towards her.

She screamed: 'Vi!'

She screamed: 'May!'

She remembered that May had gone home. She screamed, 'Violet!' at the top of her voice.

His eyes were glazed, and she wasn't sure what he was seeing.

'Help! Vi! Help me!'

By the time Violet arrived, however, running in her nightdress, Aubrey had shouted something incoherent and left the room. They heard his footsteps going up the stairs, to the top floor.

They heard his footsteps running across the attic floor, above their heads.

They didn't hear anything.

And then they saw him falling past the window.

They knew he was dead before they got to his body. He had jumped head first from the attic window and had made sure he landed on the stone paving slabs. It was clear that he couldn't have survived. He had left Violet a long and incoherent letter that was, all the same, easy to understand.

He just couldn't do it any more. He didn't want to live. He said he wasn't strong enough. He'd never been able to get his head out of the Great War. He asked her to say sorry to Martha because he'd so wanted to heal like her but couldn't. He was sorry it had made him angry.

Violet was devastated, even though a part of her had been expecting this for years, even though she knew he hadn't been able to live a full life since 1916.

They stood by his body, broken on the paving slabs, in their nightdresses. It was a hot and stormy night, and the rain crashed all around them.

'Don't,' Violet said when Martha said she'd better call someone. She put a hand on Martha's arm. 'Please, darling. Don't. I've lived this in my head so many times over the years. I know what we have to do. We can't tell anyone.'

They stood and stared at Aubrey's shattered body. Martha edged closer to Violet for comfort. Her hair was wet, and she was sweating and trembling.

'Why?'

Her teeth were chattering in spite of the heat. She was working so hard not to think of her parents and her sister that she had no space for anything else. She knew she would do whatever Violet wanted.

'It's *felo de se*,' said Violet.

Martha had never heard those words before. She made Violet say them again, spell them out. *Felo de se*. A felony against yourself. A crime, said Violet. Illegal.

'But they can't do anything.' The wind was getting up, and it was raining harder, but they could hardly go inside and leave him here. 'I mean . . .'

They both looked at him. Nothing was going to hurt him now.

'This is what he's wanted for years,' said Violet. 'Oh God, Marth. I wish I'd made him go to that place in Scotland, but he just wouldn't. He came home from the war, and he was all right. I thought it was over. I was so happy that he'd survived. And then it started. I always thought it would stop one day, but it never did. He couldn't get that war out of his head. I mean, you know all that. I know you do. Sorry. I'm just talking.'

Martha didn't know what to say, so she put an arm round Violet and tried to comfort her, the way Violet had always comforted everyone else.

'So.' Violet was trying to be brisk, raising her voice so Martha would hear her over the wind. '*Felo de se*. It's a crime, Marth. It wasn't so long ago that the Crown would confiscate the estate of anyone who did this. I don't think they do that any more, but they might. It's possible.

And I'm not going to take that risk, darling. I'm not going to risk our house, and I absolutely cannot bear everyone knowing. The inquest. The talk. The scandal at the big house. I decided a long time ago that if this happened, no one else could know.'

The rain had stopped. Mist surrounded them.

'What do you mean?'

'I mean,' said Violet, 'that we give Aubrey his own burial. Here, in the garden, where he'll be at peace. We tell people he's gone away. No one but May has seen him for years anyway. We'll need to tell her that he's gone to visit a friend in the north. After that, we'll say he's stayed in Scotland. Will you do this for me, Marth? Would you? I just couldn't bear it. Couldn't bear to have them convicting him in his absence. Knowing that everyone was judging my poor brother. Knowing they could take our house. The law still exists, even if it's not applied any more. We'd have nothing.'

Martha's teeth were chattering. Sweat was dripping down her forehead.

'I'll do whatever you need.'

They dug up the flower bed in the corner of the garden, out of the way. It took much longer than Martha would have expected, even though the soil was wet and the earth was soft. They buried him in the suit he'd been wearing at the time, and Martha fetched his watch, which he had left in the library, because Violet said it had been a long-ago birthday gift from their parents, and he would want to keep it with him. Violet lost her mind for a while and started throwing Aubrey's things in with him, burying them; she was putting in the old cutlery when Martha stopped her.

They went in and cleaned the mud off themselves, and put their clothes in a bag under Betty's bed ready to launder on May's day off.

'If she finds them and asks,' said Violet, 'we'll have to think of something.'

'We'll just say we were caught out in the rainstorm. We fell over. She won't ask more than that.'

When May arrived in the morning, everything looked normal, though the energy in the house was different, and Martha was sure May would notice.

'Aubrey went away,' Violet said, her voice casual. 'He's visiting friends in the north. Army friends. For a break, you know.'

Martha saw the relief on May's face. 'Right you are,' she said. 'I hope it helps him.'

'It will,' said Violet. 'I'm sure of it.'

Violet planted a camellia in that flower bed and told the gardeners that they were never to touch it. They called it *the memory garden*, and sometimes Martha went there to talk to her London family as well as Aubrey, when she felt strong enough. Violet would spend hours at a time just sitting and talking quietly.

It came to be a magical place, a healing space.

29

Josie was looking out to sea, with Meg leaning on her, half asleep, when Clem grabbed her by the wrist and tried to pull her up. She resisted, and fought Clem off, but everything felt so confusing without sleep that she wasn't sure what was happening.

Clem's face was strange. She was blocking out the sun, filling Josie's field of vision. She didn't look like normal Clem. She wasn't happy Clem, don't-care Clem, hedonistic, sunny Clem. Her face was twisted so she was almost snarling.

Josie wrenched her arm away and fell back down. She saw Meg waking up.

'What?'

'What's going on?' said Meg.

'You have to come with me. I need to show you something. You too, Meg.'

They looked at each other, but Clem was on a mission. Martha had drowned; the police were digging up bones – no wonder Clem's façade had shattered. No wonder she needed them.

‘You OK, Clemmie?’ said Meg as the two of them stood up and followed.

The end corner of the garden where they’d found everything was shut off with tape, and the birds were singing. It was weird and other-worldly, like the Garden of Eden just after the apple or something. They walked over the wet grass towards the house, and Josie had the strangest feeling that she was out of all time and space, the way she’d felt when she’d snuck in on her own, except that now she had Meg. She reached for Meg’s hand. She loved the way it was smaller than hers; she held it tightly to warm Meg up. Meg squeezed back.

Clem led them into a room Josie hadn’t seen before. A sitting room, big and comfortable, with rugs on a wooden floor, three sofas and a huge television. There were people here: Gareth (looking as confused as they were), Treve and Dan, the policewoman, a couple of parents. No Rik and no Senara.

‘I didn’t know this room was here,’ said Meg.

‘We didn’t need it,’ said Clem. ‘Now we do. Sit down. Right, everyone! Thanks for coming. I just wanted to show you all something. We can talk about it afterwards, but it speaks for itself.’

Josie and Meg squeezed on to a sofa next to Gareth.

Josie saw the look Clem flashed to the two of them and realized what she was doing just before it started playing.

Her stomach flipped over, and she felt as if someone had dropped a sheet of bubble wrap over her. She could see the world through it, but distorted, insulated. She couldn’t breathe. *No no no no no.*

They all looked at the huge TV. Josie saw herself on the screen, with her long hair. Meg, who had no idea what this was, put her hand on Josie's head.

'Cute,' she said.

'This is awful,' Josie whispered. She half stood up.

'Turn it off!' shouted Gareth. He was on his feet now. 'Clem, you stole this from my house! I can't believe you did that! Give it back. This is private.'

Clem had clicked pause.

'Let everyone see it, and then I'll give it back.' She waited a few seconds. 'I've made copies, so sure – you can have it back.' She pressed play again.

Josie wanted to go and grab whatever it was that was playing it. Clem was probably screen mirroring from her phone, though, and her phone was in her hand, so Josie would have to tackle her and wrestle it away. She knew she couldn't do it, and anyway everyone was going to end up seeing it. Clem had probably emailed it out by now.

She stared at herself on the screen.

'*Above us stands Cornwall's most haunted house.*' Her voice sounded stupid. '*It is poised, empty and cursed, on the cliff . . . Should I say on the* edge *of the cliff? It is poised, empty and cursed, on the cliff edge. No – the first one.*'

She watched herself tying back hair that she no longer had and found that she didn't miss it. Life was much easier like this, and she liked the attitude that it gave her. She liked not looking *feminine*. Not conforming.

'*No one knows what lurks in its grounds . . . No one living, that is.*'

There was a flash of January beach, and Gareth started speaking. '*Even the people who own it – and remember these are people who –*'

Real Gareth jumped up again. Clem paused her video. He stood in front of the screen. 'We were messing around! It wasn't –'

'Sit down, Gaz,' ordered Clem. 'I just want everyone to see how you three repay the enormous amounts of hospitality you've accepted from me over the past week. That's all.'

'It's not repaying,' said Meg, 'if it happens first.'

'Shut up, Meg.'

'Clementine,' said the policewoman, 'I didn't realize we were here for some kind of personal vendetta. Stop this. It isn't necessary. Sort it out between yourselves. Believe me, we've got enough to be dealing with here without this kind of nonsense.'

'It's only another minute.'

The policewoman stood up to leave the room, but actually waited in the doorway. Clem pressed play and turned the volume right up.

'. . . *literally call locals "peasanty scum" – stay away. Such is their fear of the evil that lurks within* . . .' said past-Gareth.

This was terrible.

'Peasanty scum' and 'evil' in the same sentence. Clem was right: their acceptance of her enormous hospitality, their consumption of her food and drink, their swimming in the pool – it was terrible in the light of this.

They had been so easily bought.

'*. . . no one has set foot in the grounds of this house for over three hundred years. And today, my friends, we are going to find out why.*'

'*Gareth! Why did you say three hundred? It's* three *years. And that's only a guess. It's probably less. Plus, you can't include any of this.*'

Josie watched old-Gareth kissing her past self. She cringed and looked away, making sure to keep her eyes away from now-Gareth. Meg gave her a little smile and squeezed her hand.

'*Sorry, babe. I got carried away,*' said then-Gareth. '*Three hundred sounds better.*'

It played on. The damage was done. Now everyone knew they had flown a drone to look into the Cliff House gardens, and no one cared about the cover story, that it was for Gareth's coursework. The only thing left was the bit where they made their predictions, and that was, Josie knew, the worst bit of all.

Senara came into shot, because Gareth had taken the camera. She shouted: '*Zombies!*'

In a way, she hadn't been wrong.

'*I think it's ghosts,*' called past-Josie. '*But hopefully ghosts that are visible to the camera.*'

If only she'd stopped there, with something stupid and meaningless.

Gareth turned the camera on himself and said, '*Senara says zombies. Josie says ghosts. I say bodies. The family who live there murdered each other, and that lawn will be strewn with old corpses. The old lady did it. Last one standing.*'

There was a gasp in the room, a sharp intake of breath, but no one spoke.

'*The girl who hates us was the first to die*,' said then-Josie.

Now-Josie felt Clem doing something in her peripheral vision. She was probably pointing to herself.

'*The vultures have taken all the flesh*,' said Senara's voice, '*and all that remains is bones. The lawn is littered with the bones of the Roberts family. And that girl who went missing. Lucy's sister. You're not putting this bit in, are you?*'

Gareth had his head in his hands. Josie wanted to go home, to take Meg with her, never to come anywhere near Cliff House ever again. Why had Senara mentioned Rachel? When they were pulling bones right out of the ground, right now?

'*Course not.*' The footage was playing on. The drone rose up to the top of the cliffs and set off across the garden, while no one watched.

Clem was grimly triumphant. 'So this is what I've got to say to the three of you. First, I never called anyone "peasanty scum", and neither did anyone in my family. That's a fact.'

'You called us "peasants" actually,' said Gareth. 'A few years ago.' She ignored him.

'Josie – Senara's shut herself away somewhere, so you'll have to pass on a message from me. Please leave my house.

Get out and never speak to me again. That's why I didn't go and find her for this: because I can't bear to look at her weaselly face. I can't believe you wormed your way in and said that about my gran, who's actually dead, and about the rest of us, who are paying for your lifestyles. So it turns out Gran is not the last one standing. Fuck off. All of you, leave.'

The policewoman took two steps back into the room. She sounded exhausted. 'Clementine, I had no idea you were doing this to pull us all into your own drama. I couldn't care less what your friends said about your family before they were your friends. Or who said what to whom. You implied this had something to do with the excavation in the garden. In spite of your wishes, Gareth, Josie and Senara can't leave at the moment, though I'm sure they'd like to.'

She looked at Josie, who gave a little nod. 'Stay for the moment. Plenty of space for everyone to keep away from each other.'

Meg took Josie's hand with one of hers and reached for Gareth with the other.

'Come on, guys,' she said.

'Not you, Meggy!' said Clem. 'You're on my team.'

Meg didn't even look back.

30

When I woke up, I saw that there were people in forensic suits outside. Everything seemed to have gone up a million notches. My phone was out of charge, so I plugged it in and waited. I didn't want to leave the room. I wanted Mum to come back and tell me why she'd lost the plot.

This wasn't Clem's garden any more. It was a crime scene. It wasn't a luxurious second home. It was surrounded by dead bodies, and I was trapped here.

I turned away and picked up the phone, which had charged enough to use as long as it was still plugged in.

There were far too many messages for me to take them in. I had a barrage of missed calls and texts. They were from Mum, Clem, Rik, various friends and a couple of unknown numbers. The most recent were from Josie, Gareth and Meg.

I turned to the twenty-three texts that had arrived, but I couldn't focus on them, either. A while ago Clem had added me to a group chat called 'The fcking police are in my garden!!! 😱' and it already had over two hundred messages on it. My head was spinning.

I yawned and finally took off Martha's dress, wondering whether I should just leave it here when I left, or if I ought to wash it first. It was stained with grass, earth, probably more. I pulled on a big T-shirt and decided to go for a shower.

When I came out, wet-haired, wrapped in my towel, Rik was sitting on my bed. In spite of everything, my stomach flipped over at the sight of him, and I found that I was kissing him before I'd had time to decide what to do. For a few moments I didn't care about anything else, and didn't even have the awareness to hope that my towel stayed up, which it did.

'Senara!' He pulled away. 'Oh my God. I wish we could just . . . Look, I'll let you get dressed. We massively need to talk. Don't speak to anyone else and don't look at your phone.'

'What?'

He was going to say our kiss had been a mistake. I knew he was.

Was he, though? He'd just done it again.

'It's Clem stuff. I'll wait outside the door.'

'OK.' I looked into his eyes. He looked back at me. At least we still had this. It hadn't evaporated in all the drama.

He went outside, and I dressed quickly. Despite all this, I wanted to be near him. I put on my own clothes for once. My red T-shirt, my shorts. This was a time to be myself. When I checked the mirror, though, I found that I looked like an eleven-year-old. I rolled up the legs of my shorts and changed my top for a tighter one. That was better.

Then I went and dried my hair because there was a hairdryer in the en suite.

I let him back in.

'You look beautiful,' he said. Was it heartless of me to be grinning in spite of everything?

I heard Martha's voice in my head. *Go for it, Senara. Life is short.*

I would always miss her. I'd think of her forever, but she had lived a long life, and she'd chosen her manner of leaving. As the shock wore off, I was starting to feel more admiration for her than anything else. And I knew that she would have approved of me and Rik.

I remembered kissing him, how perfect the hot night had been, how it had felt. My stomach flipping around. The pressure of his hand on my waist. The clouds waiting to rain. I looked at the contours of his face. I'd waited so long to meet someone who made me feel something, and now here he was, and it was over before it had even started.

I mean, it had to be. Because he would be going back to London. We had no chance.

Did we?

I kissed him again. Everything faded out around us, and then it was just Rik and me in our own universe. He encircled me in his arms, and I felt safe. We pressed up against each other.

'Never go back to London,' I muttered.

'I'll stick around,' he said. 'For as long as I can.'

I swallowed. 'How long do you think that might be?'

Seconds ticked by.

'If you wanted me to,' he said, 'I could stay another week or so. But Meg and I have to go away with our parents after that. Maybe I could come back down?'

Another week or so. Maybe coming back down. I'd cling on to that for now.

'What's the Clem stuff?'

I felt him inhaling. He was preparing for something.

'You're not going to like it.'

'Tell me.'

He spoke into my hair. 'Right. While you were asleep, and I was dozing upstairs, she apparently gathered together everyone she could find and played a video of you and Josie and Gareth on the beach, back in the winter. Flying a drone? It seems that was why she invited herself to Gareth's house. She found it and stole it, and when she'd watched it she wanted to make sure everyone saw it in as dramatic a way as possible.'

This couldn't happen.

'How did she find it?' My voice came out as a whisper.

'According to Gareth, she asked him where he kept his most precious things. He said in his bedside drawer. When they were leaving, she doubled back to use the loo, found it and pocketed it.'

I half laughed, even though it wasn't funny. 'It's not necessarily difficult to outwit Gareth.'

'Not for Clem on a mission.'

'Everyone watched it? Oh my God. That's the worst thing.'

My whole body was tense as it sank in. We'd said terrible

things about Martha, and everyone had watched it the morning after she'd died.

'Then the policewoman told her off for wasting everyone's time. Clem said you all have to fuck off and not come back. The policewoman said you have to stay here for the moment. As far as I can piece it together, that's what happened.'

'Shit.'

I longed to go home.

'I know. I mean, it was from before you met Clem.'

'We got in her way once, and she called us "peasants".'

'Yeah. Josie said. Apparently Clem denied it.'

'She wouldn't remember.'

'So Josie, Meg and Gareth are all holed up in the attic bedroom. My room. Your mum's with Clem's uncle, who just got here.' He looked at my face. 'Neither of them saw the footage, by the way.'

'They will. Clem's probably got it online by now.'

He swallowed and nodded. 'Yeah.'

I went back to the window and looked out. The police tape was blowing in the wind. A couple of people were walking across the garden, heads close, talking. One of them was Mum. I frowned.

'Is that Clem's uncle?'

Rik looked over my shoulder.

'Yeah. He got here just before I came up to see you. Drove up in a shiny car and went straight in to talk to the cops. He lives in Devon, and he just bombed down the motorway apparently.'

I shook my head. 'Not a motorway. The A30. Also – "cops"? Are we in a TV drama now?'

He winced. We both smiled. It was nice to tease him.

'Thought I'd trial it. Sorry. The fuzz. The – the rozzers?'

'My mum's being so weird. I have no idea what's going on with her.'

We watched them talking intently, but then they walked out of our line of sight. All I could see of Clem's uncle was a broad back clad in a striped T-shirt, and a head of thick greyish hair.

I packed all my stuff and tried to work out how this had happened. Clem had gone to Gareth's house yesterday morning. At what point in the day had she watched his drone footage? Probably as soon as she'd found something to watch it on. After that, she would have been plotting how to expose us.

He was supposed to destroy it. That was his one job.

She'd kept her distance from me during the party, and then she'd told me very clearly that it was my fault Martha had died. She'd watched it before the party then, but not long before. She would, I realized, have been planning something. She would have wanted to show it to Martha, for sure, to prove to her that 'the community' didn't like her and that she shouldn't leave her house to anyone but family.

Martha had taken her big moment away from her.

Though, when I read her group chat, I wondered whether, in fact, she might not have watched it until early this morning, that she might have just said that thing to me out of shock. At first her chat was mainly memes and emojis. I extracted what information I could from it.

> No one was taking drugs.
> it was the foxgloves.
>
> What twat put poisonous
> flowers in the punch?
>
> Actually there was speed/
> coke etc around too but
> 👮 know 🤔 i think
> we took care of it.
>
> Are foxgloves seriously
> poison?
>
> Oh shit that mightve been
> me i was picking flowers
> that were pretty.

I looked to see who had written that last one. Maya. It was good of her to admit it, but all the same this needed to be deleted. I read on. Amina had posted a link to a page about foxglove poisoning. I skimmed the symptoms (blurred vision, confusion, disorientation or hallucinations, headache, lethargy and so on) and thanked my sensible side for stopping me being even slightly tempted by the punch. All of that, mixed alcohol and 'speed/coke etc' too.

I was struggling to function as it was, after drinking wine and champagne. God knows how they must be feeling.

My overwhelming emotion, hot on the heels of the panic, was shame. I'd taken most of that footage. I'd laughed at Gareth calling Martha a serial killer. I'd said the garden was full of zombies, and I'd said that the bones of the Roberts family were all over the lawn. Although I thought that Martha would probably have laughed at it too, I knew that Clem would say she'd have been devastated, and when someone was dead you could project anything you wanted on to them.

Rik and Meg braved the kitchen to get us all coffees. Josie, Gareth and I were now hiding in Rik's attic bedroom, another part of the house I hadn't seen before. His things were still in a wheely suitcase.

'I guess she was just hurt to hear us saying that,' said Josie.

'She can fuck off,' said Gareth. 'I hate her. I mean, we were a lot nicer there than she was when she called us peasants. And she stole from me and lied to me.'

'Other than that,' said Josie, 'how would you say things are going between you?'

We all managed a little laugh, but nothing felt funny.

We waited for something to happen. Rik and Meg came up with a tray of drinks and said they hadn't seen Clem, but that Gareth's mum was there and was coordinating people going home if they were collected.

'Here's an odd thing,' said Meg. 'The rumour downstairs is that Martha's letter told the police that her uncle was buried there. That it's his bones we found.'

I sat up. 'Aubrey?'

Josie was alert like a meerkat. 'Seriously?'

'I don't know,' said Meg. 'That's just what they're saying. Not the police, but everyone else.'

'I'll see if I can get Mum to tell me,' said Gareth.

Aubrey was supposed to have gone to Scotland. What was he doing buried here? Was it really him? The watch would have fitted, I supposed. If it was Aubrey, then it wasn't Rachel Thomas. If it was Aubrey, then there was no mystery apart from the fact that there was no way he should have been buried secretly under a flower bed. I shivered. I wanted to get out of here.

'Do you want to come to mine?' I said. 'My mum will take us all. The police will let us go if we're with an adult, right?' I didn't care any more about what they'd make of my house. They agreed at once.

I dreaded Felicity arriving home: she, like Clem, would take our video personally. I wanted them all to go to London, to leave the house empty forever if they wanted. I knew for certain that, when I walked out through those gates now, I would never come back.

I flashed forward to Martha's funeral: I wanted to go, so I'd have to sit at the back and stay away from the family. Josie and Gareth would come with me. Rik and maybe Meg, if he really was going to come back down after his holiday, if she might too.

I found myself fighting back tears. It was all too much.

There were footsteps on the stairs, and we looked at

each other, alarmed. I shrank into Rik, and he put an arm round my shoulders.

'Senara? Are you up here?'

'In here!' I called, and then Mum and the man who had to be Clem's uncle Alex were standing in the doorway. He was much taller than she was. I could see traces of Martha in his face. He looked a bit awkward, and he also, surprisingly, looked as if he really, *really* liked Mum. She glanced at him and then away again. Was it mutual? I tried to fire thoughts at her by telepathy.

Don't do it, Mum. Do not under any circumstances do anything to connect us to this family.

We must all have been looking at them with the same expression because Mum smiled, and Alex said, 'Don't look so scared, guys. Yes, Clem sent us her little movie, but I don't care. A few kids messing around on camera is so far down my list of worries that it doesn't register. I'm Alex, by the way.'

He advanced on us with his hand outstretched. We leaned forward and shook it, each saying our names as we did so. It was strangely formal.

'Don't worry about Clemmie,' he said, sitting on the floor and leaning against the wall.

Mum came over and sat on the bed next to me, put an arm round me. She seemed stronger.

'Honestly. She'll get over it,' added Alex. 'I'm more worried about what the hell Grandma was doing at your party, and . . .' He paused. 'Well. The rest of it.'

Mum cleared her throat, and when she spoke it seemed as if she was following a script.

'The word is, Martha told the police in her letter to them that there are two bodies in the garden. One is Aubrey's.'

'We heard that. Is it really him?'

'No one will know for sure,' said Alex, 'until they've done tests, but Martha explains it all. She actually told us, years ago, and we kept her secret as she asked us to. There's no reason to think it's not him: she said he committed suicide, which was a huge stigma then, and Violet wanted to cover it up, so she and Martha buried him here and said he'd gone away.'

'Two bodies?' said Josie.

'Yes.' Alex took a deep breath. Mum, next to me, stiffened. 'The other, according to her, is an intruder. She said Barney interrupted him burgling them years ago, and the man ended up dead. They panicked and buried him with Aubrey and waited to see if anything ever happened. It never did.'

Mum was shaking violently. I had no idea why she was so upset by this long-ago tragedy that didn't involve her at all. What was I missing?

'Oh my God!' said Meg.

'It's really not Rachel?' That was Josie. Her eyes were shining with tears. 'It's not Rachel Thomas buried there? It wasn't my . . .'

'It's not Rachel, Josie,' said Mum. She hesitated. 'I knew Rachel. We all did. I haven't seen her for a long time, and I have no idea what happened to her. But it's not her in the garden.' She took a deep, shuddering breath. 'I promise it's not. I was there when she ran away. Yes, her parents tried very hard to find her and put up lots of missing posters and made all those appeals. But she left of her own free will, for very good reasons. I've thought of her often.'

She stopped talking, and Alex actually got up off the floor and came over to comfort her. She squashed up next to me, and I ended up on Rik's lap while Clem's uncle put his arms round my mother, and she cried silently into his chest.

What. The. Fuck?

I saw Josie's face change, saw the weight lift from her and fly away as she realized her dead uncle hadn't murdered Rachel Thomas. 'Oh, thank God for that. I totally thought . . . This is . . . amazing. Not about the intruder, obviously. But that it's not Rachel. That it wasn't my uncle who did it. That all this has nothing to do with him after all.'

Mum shivered. I leaned over and touched the only part of her I could reach: her hand. She was freezing. I rubbed her fingers between mine to warm them.

After a while, I realized with a jolt that whatever was in Martha's mysterious will was, now, the thing that would happen. Had Martha left the house to (I tried to remember what Clem had said) '*drug addicts or whatever*'? Something like that. She'd died before they had a chance to find out for sure. She had pretty much told me that she only told them she'd done that to make them come down early. Whatever happened, Clem and her family had more than one other home to live in. Would Cliff House come back into Pentrellis village?

Of course it wouldn't. I'd spend my life avoiding it in the summer because I never wanted to see Clem.

Someone else was coming up the stairs. Again, I braced for Clem, but this time a very hesitant voice said: 'Josie?'

And Josie was on her feet, running to open the door, because it was Angie. Angie who, as far as we knew, hadn't left her house for years. But she was here to collect her daughter.

Alex and Mum stood up.

'Angie,' said Alex, and he did his walking-over-to-shake-her-hand thing.

She looked startled, but did it.

Mum hugged her.

Josie took her by the hand and looked into her face for a long time.

1988

That afternoon was the worst time of any of their lives. Nothing else was ever going to come close. They tried to come up with a plan. They stared at the body. The whole house seemed to smell of burnt brownies. They were paralysed. Alex drove Rachel to the outskirts of Penzance, dropped her off, and came home. Jenna was catatonic. Felicity tried to make plans, but they were stupid plans, and she felt herself spiralling, a whirlwind inside her.

Too much time had passed; if they called the police now, they'd have to explain why they hadn't done it straight away.

They swung between the two paths: confess and lose everything, be arrested and let Jenna go to prison; or they could clean the floor, find some way of getting rid of the body and, for cover, use the fact that no one except them – and Rachel – had known he was here.

They wrapped the body in the rug from Alex's bedroom, basing their actions on things they'd seen in movies. Touching him had made Felicity run to the sink to vomit. He was lying there, his lower legs and feet sticking out of the rug, and they were all trying to find the strength to do the next part, which was to move the body while they worked on a longer-term plan.

They opened the cellar door and got ready to carry him down, but he fell down the steps, out of the rug, over and over, thudding as he went, and they closed the door and left him there.

Late at night the three of them put the body in a wheelbarrow, took it to the edge of the cliff and tipped it over. It landed with a thud. They stared down.

'We'd better check,' said Felicity. They went down to the beach with a torch and looked at him.

This was no good at all. He was lying on his back, and, as Alex had predicted, there was no way the sharp dent on his head could have been made by a rock.

Jenna's voice was quiet. 'Put him in the sea?'

They all got soaked, and they couldn't get the body far enough out. Some days there was a rip current, but not tonight. They didn't have a boat, and there wasn't one they could borrow. The nearest harbour was miles away.

They fetched the wheelbarrow again and hauled him back up to the garden, using a gap in the hedge to stay away from the road.

It was one in the morning, and they were standing there, hopeless, when car headlights appeared.

Grandma was home twelve hours early.

There was no chance they'd get away with this. Even if they could get him back into the cellar before Grandma arrived, she'd see in an instant that something enormous had happened.

'Park it here,' said Alex.

They pushed the wheelbarrow behind a tree and ran to the house. Felicity looked at Jenna. She looked at Alex. Their auras were the same. Panicky, electric. They tried to appear normal. They ran into the sitting room, threw themselves on the sofa, put the TV on.

Grandma walked in through the front door. She stood in the sitting-room doorway and stared at them.

'Children,' she said, 'what's going on?'

They all looked over at her, and whatever she saw on their faces made her rush over to them. 'I knew there was something wrong from your message, Felicity. I know you, my darling, and I know that you wouldn't call at midnight to say that everything's fine. It was playing on my mind all day, and in the end I came back early. What's happened?'

They tried not to tell her, but the fact was there was a corpse in a wheelbarrow in the garden. And the moment it got light Grandma would find it. Alex and Felicity told her, while Jenna became hysterical. Grandma shifted over to put an arm round her. Grandma's aura sparked with electricity. There was an adult here, someone who was going to sort things out.

'Right,' she said. 'I'm sorry, but we're going to have to call the authorities. We have to. You'll be OK, Jenna, because you didn't mean to kill him.'

The last two words sent Jenna into uncontrollable screaming.

'No one knows he's here,' said Alex.

'We can't let Jenna go through this,' said Felicity.

Grandma listened. They talked. Her face changed. She looked at Jenna. She looked out of the window. Felicity could see her thinking.

'Do you trust Rachel Thomas?'

'Yes!' They all said it at once, even Jenna.

'She's never coming back,' said Alex. 'She told me her plans in the car. We won't hear from her again. She hates her dad. He hits her. She's gone.'

In the end, Grandma said, 'I may regret this in the morning, but perhaps we can take care of this without it ruining your lives. The man was no angel, by the sound of it. This doesn't have to destroy you too. Never, ever tell anyone, but there's already a burial place in this garden. Over there, in the corner, where the camellia grows.' She checked the time. 'Alex, you go and start digging. Right beside the plant. We can add another camellia before your parents get back and say we were doing some gardening.'

So that was what they did.

The flower bed was sheltered, tucked away in a corner. People rarely bothered to come this far down the garden. Grandma had stopped Dad putting a shed here, Felicity remembered, a few years ago. '*Let some of it stay wild, Leon*,' she'd said. '*Violet loved this corner. Just let it be. Let it be Violet and Aubrey's place. The memory garden*.'

Now this made sense. Was there really someone else buried there? Felicity found she didn't even care right now: she had no headspace for it. This was the best place to bury a body. And they confirmed, when they'd dug down far enough, that they weren't the only people to think so.

Grandma was right. There were already bones in there.

Grandma bowed her head. 'Good evening, Aubrey,' she said. 'We've brought you some company. Apologies for the fact that he's a scumbag.'

'We can tell people it's an old burial ground,' said Alex. 'I mean, it is, isn't it?'

'It's not, but I've been saying it is for years,' said Grandma.

Felicity knew she would never look at her grandmother in the same light again. She knew who Aubrey was, but she'd always been told he went to that hospital in Scotland. She decided not to ask, but Grandma felt the question in the air and said, 'He jumped out of the window, darling. Never recovered after the war. They were different times. There was a stigma about suicide, and a legal implication too. Violet wanted it kept quiet, so that's what we did.'

They calmed down separately, without looking at each other, without touching. Grandma was in charge now. She had made them take the clothes off the body, almost all of them. Then they put the new corpse on top of the old bones and shovelled the earth back on top. They didn't stop until it was done, and as soon as they'd finished Felicity was sick again. All three of them were sobbing, and they were trying not to make eye contact.

'There we are,' said Grandma. 'It's done now. You're going to be all right. We'll get rid of his clothes. I'll put them in the bin in the village, and they'll be gone tomorrow. And, kids, we need a drink.'

Jenna spoke up suddenly. 'We have to tell the police. I'm going to go to them and confess what I did. I am.' Her voice rose. 'I am. I'm going to do it now.'

'You're not.' Alex put a hand on her shoulder, took it off, and put it on again. 'It's over, Jen. Yeah, we should have called the police. But we'd be in so much trouble if we did that now. Honestly, we would. We can't call them and tell them we buried the body in the garden. And Grandma would get in the most trouble of all. Remember, no one knows he was here.'

'No!' Jenna's voice was higher. 'No! No, I'm going. I'm going to call 999. We can dig him up again and put him on the floor. I'll say it only just happened. We can't do this! What about Angie? She needs to know!'

Jenna turned and started walking, then running towards the house. Grandma and Alex went after her. They grabbed her, and all three of them ended up on the ground. The fight went out of Jenna.

'Stop it, Jenna,' said Grandma. 'We're going to protect you. I'm always going to look out for you. Always. Understand?'

Felicity walked over to them and spoke through her tears. 'He was going to go to Thailand with Rachel. Maybe he won't be missed. Can we just make it look as if he's gone away, so no one looks for him?'

‘I took everything out of his pockets,’ said Alex. ‘I’ve got a piece of his handwriting. Maybe we could, like, write a note from him saying he’s going to Thailand. Or something.’ His voice shook. ‘Isn’t that better? For his family to think he’s gone away . . .’

‘Yes,’ said Grandma. ‘We can send him to Thailand. Stop this in its tracks. Bring it all down to me first thing tomorrow.’ She paused. ‘I think this is what Violet would have done, and she’s always my compass. This would ruin your lives, and I can’t allow it. I just couldn’t bear it. The trial, the scandal at the big house. It’s going to be difficult, but this way is better than that.’

She looked at them. ‘And you need to keep an eye out for Rachel Thomas. Is she running away from that fucking vicar? I never trusted him an inch. If you hear one word from her, come straight to me. Now: brandy.’

In the morning, Alex drove to the garden centre and bought the most expensive camellia bush he could find. They planted it in that flower bed and tended both plants carefully. Felicity took control of them and banned anyone else from doing anything else with the flower bed ever. Her parents indulged her. The bushes grew well. Very well indeed.

Grandma concocted a trip to Thailand for Andy Teague. They had his handwriting and a little bit of information from the things Alex had taken from his pockets. Grandma found, in the classified ads at the back of her *Private Eye*, a company that, for a fee, would post things to get a postmark from anywhere in the world. Felicity practised his writing and found that, if she filled her head with the way the man had made her feel, she could do it. An envelope stuffed with postcards of Bangkok arrived at Grandma's cottage. They weren't sure it would work, but they assumed it did, and kept up an annual card from Andy Teague in Bangkok to his sister in Pentrellis. It was an awful thing to be doing, and it weighed heavily on all of them.

Rachel was reported missing. Posters were put up, and her parents went on television and to the papers to plead with her to come home. They did a great job of pretending to be doting parents worried about their little girl, but the fact was she had been seventeen, and she'd run away for a good reason, and she never came back.

When Rachel had been gone for a year, Felicity received a Christmas card, postmarked from London, that said: *Merry Christmas, Lissy. All fine xx*

And that was all she ever heard.

1948

'When I die,' Martha said to Violet, two years after Aubrey had gone, as they ate bread and jam for breakfast, 'I don't want anyone to wear black.'

'Oh, gracious,' said Violet, reaching for the teapot. 'Me too, darling. Me too. When I die, promise me you'll wear red, pink, yellow – whatever you want. Have a rainbow dress made. Every colour but black.'

'Well, yes,' said Martha. 'Except that you're not going to die, Vi. You can't. Ever. You mustn't.' She was irritated to discover that her eyes were prickling with tears. 'Please don't. Promise me.'

Violet's voice was gentle. 'Of course. I promise. I promise I'll never die, as long as you live forever too, because I'm going to need some company.'

'Yes,' said Martha. 'Fine. I won't die either.'

They shook on it.

Martha realized, at that moment, that she was sick of being sad. The war was over and she was eighteen.

'The next nice man I meet, I think I'm going to marry,' she told Violet, putting plum jam on her bread.

'*Excuse* me?' Violet looked up with a half-frown, half-smile.

'I'm eighteen! I need something nice to happen.'

Violet's voice was careful. 'If you want a marriage to be *something nice*,' she said, 'you'll have to be a bit more discerning than that, darling.' She thought about it. 'But you're right: we do need something to perk us up. Why don't we go out dancing?'

The following week they went to a dance in Truro. Violet had bought bright material and made them both new dresses, even though there wasn't as much money as there used to be. Martha's was bright blue, Violet's dark green ('because I'm too old for anything showy,' she said, and wouldn't move from this viewpoint, however much Martha argued). They'd used brand-new patterns, and the dresses were far more stylish than anything they could have bought.

Martha had never worn a dress like this before. It was silky and nipped in at the waist, and it clung to her. She felt like a star. She felt herself shining under the harsh overhead lights. Her shoes were Violet's and a size too small, and they weren't fashionable, but she didn't care because they made her even taller. She walked into the room feeling like a lady, like the woman who lived at Cliff House who could honestly say she had grown up there. She felt like Martha Roberts.

Barnaby Campion was on the other side of the room. She noticed him straight away. He noticed her right back. He lived in London and was in Truro visiting a friend. Barney came from money. He was gentle and kind: he too had been bruised by the war, but it had left him not wanting to harm anything or anyone ever again. He was, it turned out, the saviour not just of Martha but also of Cliff House itself.

When he proposed, she was standing on the beach, wearing Violet's lucky-charm dress, even though she knew it looked strange and old-fashioned. She had put it on because she knew he was going to ask her to marry him. He went down on one knee on the sand and stained his trousers, and she leaned down to kiss him and said yes. '*Yes, please. Yes, I will marry you because I love you, and because I need you. I want to look forward, forward, forward, and never back.*'

Later she added her conditions. They would live at Cliff House with Violet, and Martha would become Martha Campion-Roberts, rather than Martha Campion. Everyone thought that was funny, but Barney didn't mind one bit. He understood. Most people in the village never even bothered with the *Campion*, and she was generally known locally as Mrs Roberts.

She had lost Martha Driscoll. Martha Roberts was her own creation, her salvation, and she wasn't losing her too. And she never did. She lived at Cliff House with Barney and Violet, and then with Barney, Violet and Leon. And then with Barney and Leon. And then with Leon. Leon and Elizabeth. Leon, Elizabeth, Alex and Felicity. And then in the gardener's cottage alone.

31

Josie's mum was here.

Most people didn't realize what a massive thing this was: she hadn't left the house for months and months, and here she was, searching Cliff House until she found Josie in the attic.

She was wearing jeans and a T-shirt, just like a regular person. Josie reminded herself again that she was pulling all her energy together, doing this because Josie needed her, that it had happened before and didn't last.

'You came!' Josie put a hand on her shoulder and steered her to the chair Gareth had swiftly vacated.

'What's happened, Jose?' Her voice was just above a whisper. 'Jayne called. She said the party went wrong and was there anyone who could come for you. I thought the best person would be me.'

'You *are* the best person,' said Josie. 'Is this OK?'

She nodded. 'What's happened, though? Tell me. Are you all right? She said you were, and I can see you are, but are you?' She looked around and laughed, self-conscious. 'Sorry. I need to get better at making sense. Hi, Jenna.'

Josie crouched beside her. It broke her heart how hard Mum was trying. She didn't know what would happen in the future. No one did. For now, it didn't matter. That mortifying footage had taken her back to January, to a time when she'd been obsessed with the uncle who, although she didn't know it at the time, had just died in Thailand. A man she never needed to think about again.

She had concocted a story about him killing Rachel Thomas, but it had been her own invention, an outlet for her obsession and grief. It had been a way of distracting herself from a bleak future that, perhaps, might not be as bleak as she'd thought.

She had Meg right now. She had Mum right now. She had her friends. They had pulled bones out of the ground, but they were old bones, and their stories were not her story after all.

She would never have imagined, when they didn't dare go near the house, that she'd be here six months later, hiding in the attic with her mum and her girlfriend (could she call Meg that? Why not?) while the zombies and ghosts were, indeed, coming out of the earth; that the police would be here because Martha had died, and that was only the start of it.

Everyone began talking among themselves, and she started to tell Mum about everything. She saw the relief on her face when she realized nothing bad had actually happened to Josie, and then saw the guilt at the fact that she was relieved that it had been Martha, whom everyone loved, that had died.

She saw Mum looking at Megan.

'Hello, Angie,' said Meg.

'Nice to see you again, Megan,' said Mum. 'How are you doing?'

Meg took Josie's hand. 'All right, considering,' she said. 'Why don't I go down and get you a tea? Or coffee?'

It all felt so ordinary that Josie could hardly bear it.

32

We got out of Cliff House without running into Clem and headed back home. I rode my bike because I wasn't going to leave it there, and Rik and Gareth went in Mum's car with all my stuff. Josie and Meg walked with Angie.

It was strange going through those gates for the last time. They were open, just as Martha liked it. As I passed her cottage, I found myself looking across to see if she was at her window, but she would never be there again. The heatwave had broken now, and the day was normal. It wasn't hot or cold, and it wasn't raining.

Rik and Megan had packed their bags and left too, their allegiance transferred away from Clem, who I knew would blame me. I held on to the fact that they were staying around for another week or so, and then perhaps coming back later in the summer. For now, that was enough.

As I approached our house, I concentrated on not being embarrassed. I reminded myself that these things were accidents of birth. I locked my bike up outside, and, when I walked through the front door, I saw Rik and Gareth sitting at the table, looking perfectly at home.

'Senara!' said Rik. 'Look at me, in your house! I love it.'

Because of Mum, our house was always clean. It smelled nice. It was nothing like Cliff House, and right now that was the best thing about it.

'Alex is coming over when Felicity gets here,' said Mum. 'I'm afraid I can't rustle up bacon rolls or whatever it is that Flick does, but I can make a pile of toast, and you're welcome to help yourselves to cereal.'

'Flick?' I said. She gave a defensive shrug.

'She was Flick when we were your age.'

She turned away. I wanted to press her about what had happened, what had made her so weird, but for now I was just happy that she was functioning again.

We ate all the cereal and finished all the milk, and then I found I wanted to stretch my legs. I wanted to talk to Rik. I wanted to see Josie. And all those things led me to one idea.

'I should probably walk Molly again,' I said. 'It's been a few days.'

'And what a few days,' said Mum.

'Right?' I looked at Rik and Gareth. 'Coming? I want to stretch my legs.'

'Yep,' said Rik. 'Is it right that she lives next door to Josie? So I could check in with Meg?'

Gareth said he was going home to sleep, and face his mother. Mum was waiting for Alex and Felicity, so Rik and I set off together.

'Stay with us?' I said as soon as we were out of the door.

Rik smiled. He put an arm round my waist, and we

walked together. I'd never thought I'd be a part of a thing like this.

'Wouldn't that be a bit weird?' He paused. 'I wasn't going to ask, but maybe I could sleep on the sofa for a few nights? I went to book a hotel for me and Meg, and it turns out there isn't one available. Like, not in the whole of Cornwall. And no Airbnb. There were a few campsites, but we don't have a tent. I could get one! I don't want to impose.'

'You're not getting a tent,' I told him.

Mum had moved her boyfriends in often enough. It was my turn now. If Rik was based on the sofa, we would be able to take things at our own pace. I felt warm inside.

'Thanks,' he said. 'I really didn't want to have to go home. I want to be with you, Senni. All day, every day. And, as you know, this never happens to me.'

'Nor me.'

'So let's go with it? See where it takes us.'

I didn't think about the autumn. I just said, 'Yes. Yes, yes, yes.'

I'd forgotten it was Sunday: Lucy was at home and had no need for anyone to walk her dog. She opened the door with messy hair and wearing pyjamas, and blinked at us.

'Oh God, sorry!' I checked the time. It was half past eight. 'Sorry, Lucy. I just didn't think. It's been a hell of a night.'

'What's going on?' she said. 'It's fine, but don't take Molly. I'm meeting a friend later for a walk at Lamorna. Thanks, though. It's sweet of you to think of us.' She squinted at me. 'Are you OK, Senara?'

'Kind of.' I wanted to say something about her sister, but of course I didn't. I couldn't.

Molly came running at me because she knew what normally happened when I turned up. Lucy beckoned us in with her head so she could close the door.

'Sorry,' I said. 'We'll leave you in peace.'

'No, don't worry. Actually I owe you some money, don't I?' Lucy and I had long since cut the dog-walking agency out of our arrangement, and she paid me in cash.

'Don't worry about that now,' I said. 'Honestly. It's been a wild night and –'

'No, it's fine. I got the money out at the cashpoint the other day. Come through.'

I introduced her to Rik, and we stood in her sitting room while she rummaged through her handbag. It smelled of scented candles and fresh air. There was an old photograph on the wall showing Lucy and her sister, in school uniform, smiling fixed grins at the camera. I'd seen the picture lots of times before, but I tried to draw Rik's attention to it. Lucy noticed.

'Me and Rach,' she said. 'It's OK. You can talk about her.'

I wanted to fall down through the ground to the centre of the earth and melt there.

'Sorry!' I said. 'I'm really sorry. All the gossip – must be awful.'

Should I tell her about the bones at Cliff House? No. No, I shouldn't.

'I can't imagine what it's like,' said Rik. 'I have a sister and if anything happened to her . . .'

'Oh no,' said Lucy. 'Honestly. It's fine. Really.' She looked me in the eye and nodded. 'Really, Senara. Sometimes – well, no. It's just, it's fine. Trust me.'

That was bizarre.

She gave me the money, and we went next door to check on Josie and Meg.

The living room smelled bleachy, and the carpet was clean: I knew this was Angie's work. It was what she did when she was trying to feel better. She had gone back to bed, so Josie and I and the Anderson twins sat around, talking in low voices.

'I think Lucy knows that Rachel's OK,' I said straight away.

'Me too,' said Rik, and we explained what had just happened. I saw the relief on Josie's face and realized we would never know quite what had happened to Rachel Thomas.

'I guess it's all over,' I said. 'But, honestly, my mum isn't herself at all. She totally freaked out about the bones. Completely. I never even knew that Mum had been friends with Felicity and Alex. Or Martha.'

'Does it matter, though?' said Josie.

I thought about it. 'Yeah. Probably not. I'm just curious. I'm sure they know more about what's going on than they're saying.'

'So let them,' said Meg. 'Really. Leave them to it. Whatever it is, us nosing into it isn't going to help.'

'I'd say,' said Rik, 'that your mum and Alex are kinda smitten with each other.'

I winced. I was used to Mum going out on dates, fairly used to meeting her boyfriends. Alex Campion-Roberts, though? Not him. Please.

'She can't,' I said. 'She can't go and marry into the Roberts dynasty now. No way.'

Meg was laughing. 'I'm not sure they're talking *marriage*, Senni. It's only a bit of eye contact.'

'Stop catastrophizing,' said Josie.

Rik and Meg started talking about their plans. Rik told everyone that he was going to stay on my sofa, and Josie immediately invited Meg to do the same.

'Not the sofa, though,' she said, and they gave each other wicked grins. Josie was so much better at this than I was.

Still, I was doing OK. Rik's hand appeared on my leg, under the table, and I shuddered all over.

Mum would be at work tomorrow.

We would have the house to ourselves.

We were heading home to sleep when Rik picked up a postcard from the table.

'Oh shit!' said Josie. 'Don't look at that. It's one of my creepy uncle's cards. I thought I'd put them all away. I wanted to burn them, but I guess he was still her brother.'

'Bangkok,' Rik said. 'Nice.'

He turned it over, then held it out to Josie. I took it before she could and looked at it. It was weird to think that those words had been written by her unknown uncle, in Thailand, before he died.

I read the back of the card, even though Josie hadn't wanted us to.

I looked at it.

I looked again.

I thought about my mum and Clem's uncle, and their secret. I did some sums in my head.

Josie put a hand on my shoulder. 'What?' she said. 'What is it?'

The words on the back of the postcard said:

Dear Angie. A sunny Merry Christmas from Thailand. Hope all is ok. It's truely wierd to think of you still there in Cornwall. Have a lovely day, sis. Andy x

'Do you have more of these?'

Josie winced. 'Yeah. Like I said, we can't throw them out. We will one day.'

She went into the kitchen and came back with a stash of postcards. I looked through them and saw that they all had strange spellings.

That didn't mean anything.

I remembered the card with ***Felicity's Fancies*** on it. The way she had written *truely*.

No.

No.

I was massively stretching things.

I saw it unfurling in my head, what this could mean.

Martha's letter, her uncheckable story about Barney killing an intruder, with no details.

Mum's weirdness.

Her desperation to talk to Alex and Felicity.

Andy, the creepy man who visited Cliff House.

Rachel leaving Cornwall forever.

I shook myself. I was being ridiculous. None of this meant anything. I was making things up. As Josie had just said, I was catastrophizing.

Of course it wasn't that. Mum was on edge about Cliff House because she'd fallen out with Felicity. Andy Teague had died; there'd been an email to tell them.

This was stupid.

'What is it?' said Rik.

I pushed everything back into its box.

'Nothing,' I said.

I didn't know what I was thinking. I was making things up, and they were things that I could never say out loud.

After 1988

Felicity, Alex and Jenna took it one step at a time, always expecting to be found out, to be arrested, questioned, put on trial. They drew all their strength from Grandma.

Felicity barely made it through her cookery course. She couldn't sleep, and her dreams were filled with Andy Teague. She saw him every night, coming towards her with his hands outstretched. In her dreams, she bit down on his finger, and her mouth filled with blood. She saw his body pulling itself out of the ground, coming for her, his arms always reaching for her.

She told her parents she was terrified of intruders, and when she was twenty, and still living with them, they capitulated and got a high fence, electric gates, proper security, because they were worried about how anxious she was and wanted her to be happy again.

Grandma understood, but refused it for her own cottage; they only spoke about it once, when Grandma said quietly, 'He's not coming back, darling. You don't need this. You're safe.'

She wasn't safe, though. Felicity knew the fences shouldn't have made sense to her: apart from anything else, Andy Teague was enclosed by them. Yet they did.

In 1997, when Felicity was living in London and working as a pastry chef, her mother called with some long-overdue news.

'I'm afraid your father and I have decided to go our separate ways,' she said. 'I'm sorry, darling. We tried to hide it from you, but it's been on the cards for ages.'

'Don't be stupid,' said Felicity. 'We know! We want you to be happy. I'm glad.'

She almost meant it: she did want her parents to be happy, but she wished they could have been happy together.

Then Leon had called. 'We're going to put Cliff House on the market,' he said. 'Your mother and I both need our share of the money.'

That prompted a crisis meeting between Felicity, Alex and Grandma. They converged on Exeter and sat in a hotel room, door double-locked, to work out what to do.

'We can't let them sell it.' Alex was pale and strained. 'New owners could do anything. They could dig up the end of the garden to put a garage there.'

Grandma sipped her tea and winced at the long-life milk. 'Absolutely. I won't let Leon sell, darlings. I technically own it, so I can block it. I'll sort them some money from Barney's trusts instead.'

'Can you do that?' Felicity hardly dared believe it. Her mind had raced miles ahead to the day when the new owners of Cliff House dug up the camellia bed and called the police.

'I can, and I will. We'll keep the house in the family for as long as the three of us plus Jenna are alive. After that, it doesn't matter what happens.'

'Grandma,' said Alex, 'you're the best. Does it matter if I stay away from the house forever? I just can't –'

Alex and Jenna had split up before they'd even begun. Felicity was still friends with her, but it was difficult between them. The thing was too huge.

By 2008, Felicity had married a banker she didn't love enough, because she hated living alone, and she'd had that little girl, Clementine Rachel. She remembered herself describing Clem to Rachel, and hoped her friend was alive, happy, thriving away from her family. Clem turned out to be exactly the child she'd imagined: an energetic girl with an orange aura, who had the world at her feet. Jenna had also married for companionship, and she'd had her own daughter, Senara, who was small and cautious.

When Felicity was in Cornwall, they tried to be friends, and mainly talked about motherhood and the babies, but it ended with a bang when the girls were toddlers. Felicity had found Senara with a little trowel, digging under the camellias. She had screamed at her. Senara cried. Jenna took her away and never came back.

Felicity remembered that Grandma had promised Jenna she'd always look after her, but actually, even though they both lived in the village, they never saw each other. Everything had fractured.

*

In 2014, Felicity was married again, happily this time, and her sparkly baby Jackson was born, to Clementine's horror (Clem felt that forty-two was *way* too old to have a baby; she found the whole thing 'gross'). Felicity was still writing postcards to Angie from Bangkok every year. She locked herself away and wrote them, then posted them off to the same address. She never knew whether or not they actually arrived because she kept as far from Angie Teague as she could.

She told Dylan everything, apart from this. She left it all where it was, until the day in summer 2022 when she answered the intercom and found that her Clementine had invited Jenna's daughter over for lunch.

That day she stood at the side of the house and watched her cycling up the drive, a girl who looked so much like the young Jenna that it made her gasp, made the world spin out of control. Senara's aura was blue and yellow, like Jenna's. Felicity felt that everything was happening all over again.

She knew it was time to make it stop.

When Jenna didn't respond to her approach, she waited until Senara was at Cliff House and went to her office in Penzance at the end of the working day to ambush her. Jenna had hardly changed at all. They talked in a strained way, and Jenna agreed that they needed to make it end. Felicity said she'd get Alex to do it because he was the best with technology. He would send a message on Facebook to Angie, letting her know, thirty-four years too late, that her brother was dead.

By the time they sent the message, Felicity was on her way to Hong Kong for her father-in-law's funeral, leaving her daughter at home. Felicity would never have invited Senara to stay, but Clementine had taken to her, and it was Martha who insisted.

And, when she got back, she discovered that Grandma had chosen to die, and had left a confession in which she said that she and Violet had buried Aubrey Roberts there because he'd committed suicide, just as she'd told them all those years ago.

We knew he was beyond consequences, of course, but Violet had been so strong, and she couldn't take the stigma of it, plus the risk that the estate would be confiscated. I was devoted to Violet so I was always going to do whatever she wanted.

It has been on my conscience ever since. Poor Aubrey. He deserved a funeral, a gravestone, a send-off. Please give him one. He was buried with his watch; it was seeing the kids pulling it out of the ground that brought it all back.

The last bit of her letter was their lifeline.

And there's another body in there too. Barney killed an intruder one night. I was away at the time. I'm sorry I kept it secret. It was a long time ago . . .

Felicity hoped that, wherever Grandma was now, she could hear their thanks. She hoped this was going to be enough.

33

Rik and I got a taxi into Penzance. I'd never done that before – had never begun to imagine it as an option – but it was nothing to him. We sat side by side on the back seat, our fingers interlinked.

'I'm glad you're here,' I said.

'Me too.' He paused, then spoke fast.

I looked at his cheekbones, at his shiny hair, and I pushed down the word *love*. You couldn't love someone this fast. I did, though.

'Come to London,' he said. 'Will you come? Not now, but maybe at half-term? Come and stay with us. I'll show you everything. We can have so much fun.'

I didn't know what to say. I couldn't even afford the train fare. Me, staying at his Chelsea townhouse.

'I don't want to –' I tried to work out what I meant. 'I mean, I don't want to feel like some kind of clueless country girl. I don't want people to laugh at me.'

'They won't laugh.'

'Promise?'

He held my hand tightly. 'I promise,' he said. 'I absolutely do. And also, are you kidding? A girlfriend in Cornwall – you make me look good. You really do.'

I held my breath, and waited for him to retract the word, but he didn't.

'Girlfriend?'

'If you want?'

The taxi stopped outside the Jubilee Pool, and Rik paid the fare without appearing to notice how much it cost, which was over five hours' work for me. I took his hand and led him along the wide pavement in front of the outdoor pool, to the rocks behind it. The tide was out so there was plenty of room to climb from the path down on to the rocks, which were huge and warm. There we'd be screened from view, and in front of the ocean.

The water was so still that it looked like a lake rather than an ocean. I stared at the surface, the shape of a jellyfish below it, a clump of seaweed drifting by.

'Different,' Rik said, 'from the last time we sat on the beach together in Penzance.'

'This isn't the beach,' I said. 'This is Battery Rocks.'

I looked over to our left, at St Michael's Mount. I'd never been there. You could walk over at low tide; maybe we should do it. I wanted to do everything with Rik. I wanted to see everything. I felt that with him at my side I could do anything.

'I keep thinking,' I said. 'About those bones.'

Why? Why had I said that when we'd come to Penzance on a date? When I'd wanted to sit on the rocks and kiss. And talk about our plans.

Rik didn't look surprised or pissed off.

'Me too,' he said. 'It's a hard image to shake, isn't it? Josie holding that skull. Aubrey, and an intruder, right?'

I wondered whether to say it. To tell Rik the way I was imagining it all tying up. It was too flimsy. I was imagining it, like Josie had. It was no more real than the story she'd constructed.

'I wonder if Martha's story is true,' I said. 'About that intruder.'

I wanted to say, *You know my mum and the others have a huge secret*. I wanted to say, *I think it's* . . . But I knew I couldn't continue. I couldn't follow the hypothesis through to its end, even in my head.

'We can't ever know,' he said. 'You know that. It's something that happened years before we were born. It's nothing to do with us.'

I inhaled. I breathed in the salty air, the smell of a barbecue somewhere down the beach. I listened to the birds shrieking overhead, a child behind us doing that sudden crying they do when they fall over. I reached for Rik's hand, and I told myself to forget about it. I was spinning away from logic, freaking out. I needed to ground myself.

I made an effort and pulled myself together.

'Yes,' I said. 'Your other question. The girlfriend one. Yes.'

He put a hand on the back of my neck, and I shifted up so I was almost on his lap.

He whispered into my ear, and it made all the hairs on my arms stand up.

'Do I get to be your boyfriend?'

I nodded. 'Yes, you do.'

I turned my face and kissed him. He kissed me back. Fireworks went off inside me. It was everything I'd ever wanted. I wanted to do everything with Rik. Everything.

34

A week later

I was ready to go, but Mum wasn't. I paced round the living room, which wasn't easy as it was so small. I didn't want to do this at all, but it had been overshadowed, for me, by Rik leaving this morning. He and Meg were on the train back to London, to go to Antigua with their parents tomorrow. Between me and Rik and Josie and Meg, it had quite possibly been the most emotional farewell Penzance Station had ever seen.

I felt bereft. And now I had to go to Cliff House and see Clem. I was desperate to get it over with.

'Mum!' I shouted up the stairs. 'Mum – we need to leave!'

'Sorry, darling! One second!'

Mum was always ready first. I mean, I didn't want to go, either, but apparently we had to because of the letter Martha had written to me, which I still hadn't seen. Because of that, I would be forced to sit in the same room as Clem while the lawyer talked to us all together.

My phone pinged with the special tone I'd set up for Rik.

Just crossed the bridge.
Not in Cornwall any more
😭 Miss you 🖤

Miss you too! 🖤🖤 Waiting for Mum to get ready. She wants to go even less than I do 😬 🖤 Come back soon!!!!

He had booked a train ticket to come back in August, and I was already counting the days. I was tired. I missed Martha with every atom of my body and soul, and now I had to miss my boyfriend too.

'*Mum!*' I shouted.

She came down the stairs. 'Sorry.'

She was wearing her bright pink jumpsuit and pink lipstick. That meant she was nervous. Did it also mean she wanted to look nice for someone? Of course. I'd spent the week with Rik, and Mum had spent it with Alex. Who was nice, but nonetheless a direct connection to Clem and Felicity. 'OK. Let's put our brave faces on. Where are the car keys? Time to go.'

We didn't need to drive, but Mum wanted to. I thought she felt stronger turning up in a machine, as if it was a tank rather than a Renault Clio.

For the first time the gates were wide open as we approached, and I felt that every muscle in my body was tense. Felicity had tried to call me a couple of times, but I hadn't answered because I had no idea what to say. I knew Clem must have shown her that footage, probably multiple times, and I hadn't been able to face the conversation. Today I was going to have to.

We parked outside the house, next to Felicity and Dylan's massive white car, their tiny green one, a blue one that must have been Alex's, and a red one that I'd seen outside Martha's cottage a few weeks ago.

Mr Mitchell.

The carved front door was wide open. Mum shouted, 'Hello?' into the house, and Felicity was there in an instant. The two of them looked at each other for a long time and then hugged. Their hug went on for ages. They rocked from side to side.

Felicity extended an arm to me and pulled me in too.

'Thanks for coming, Senara,' she said. 'We're all in here.'

'Felicity,' I said in a quiet voice. I held the sleeve of her cardigan to keep her back. 'Can I just say I'm just – I'm really sorry. For the drone thing. Which I know you must have seen. We were just being stupid, and I really, really regret it. You must hate me.'

'Oh, that!' she said. 'God, Senara. Of course I don't! Don't give it a moment's thought. Water under the bridge. There are so many other things to think about. I know Clem was bothered by it, but she's being ridiculous.'

I didn't completely believe her, but I felt fractionally better.

She ushered us into the big living room, which had extra chairs in it. Its windows looked over towards the camellias, and I knew I wasn't the only one avoiding the view.

Mr Mitchell, who was younger than I'd thought now I saw him up close, was sitting on the highest chair. Alex was next to him. They both stood up when we came in, and I cringed inside as I watched Alex smelling Mum's hair as he hugged her hello.

'Jenna,' he said. 'Good to see you.'

Clem was on one end of the middle sofa with her feet up on a stool. I looked at her quickly, then away. I felt her staring at me. With my peripheral vision, I sensed her turning away, and when I glanced back she was ostentatiously looking in the other direction, her chin raised, pretending to laugh at something her stepdad had said.

I exhaled. That could have been a lot worse, and it probably would be.

Because this was a serious occasion, Clem had dressed in a white shirt and a pair of cotton trousers, and she looked as if she was doing work experience at a solicitor's office. I glanced down at myself. I was in a blue-and-yellow dress I'd found in a charity shop, to echo the dress Martha had lent me. I actually thought I looked quite stylish, but when I saw Clem I felt scruffy again.

Mum and I sat on a two-person sofa, as far from Clem as possible.

Alex cleared his throat. I looked round the room. There were seven of us in here: Felicity and Dylan, me and Mum, Clem, Alex and Mr Mitchell.

'Right,' said Alex. 'I'm Grandma's executor, and I'm a lawyer too, and Nick here is, as we all know, her solicitor. As you're well aware, this has been complicated, so we're going to start by looking at the letters she left just before she died, and then move on to the will. Senara, I'm sorry that you haven't been given your letter yet. I have it here for you today, and I'll give it to you shortly.'

Clem let out an elaborate sigh. She was fully committed to hating me. 'Tell us the *family* stuff, Uncle Alex,' she said. 'And get on with it.'

'Believe me, Clemmie – this is the short version. As you may know, Grandma explained the bones that had been found in the garden. It's all in the hands of the police, so we won't go there. But they've confirmed what she said: there are the remains of two bodies, one of whom has been identified as Aubrey Roberts, while the other is currently unidentified. They're testing the DNA against known missing people, but so far it's thrown up nothing.'

The atmosphere was so tense that I felt I could pluck the air and make a musical note.

I saw Mum look quickly at Felicity, who was hanging on to Dylan's hand. Felicity didn't look back at Mum. Alex was strained.

The three of them definitely knew something we didn't.

They knew who the mystery person was.

I pushed it out of my mind again. Of course they didn't.

'The police aren't looking for anyone else.' Alex's voice was just holding out. 'So . . .' It tailed off.

'Moving on,' said Felicity.

'Moving on. Grandma's letters to Felicity and to Senara concern the will, and it's only Felicity, Nick here and me who currently know their contents, so I'm going to go there next as they contain, well . . .' He stopped and drew breath. 'We'll have probate soon, but for now I can tell all of you, as her family and beneficiaries, broadly what it says.'

I tried to work out what I would do if she'd left me loads of dresses that I'd never be able to wear. Maybe I could sell some. The money might get me through university, if I went. How did you go about selling old dresses, though? Vinted? Or eBay?

'Senara?' I looked up. Everyone was looking at me. 'Sorry. I'm going to need your full attention for this.' He picked up some papers.

'I'm reading directly from Grandma's will now, and I'm starting with the big one. "*To Senara Jenkin, I leave all my old frocks. I also leave her Cliff House and cottage, all its land and such of the contents that belong to me at the time of my death, as well as an endowment for its upkeep.*"'

I blinked and frowned.

That couldn't be right. It had started right, but then . . .

All the air left the room. I felt myself floating to the ceiling, imagined myself looking down on the scene. Was it my ceiling? My windows? My walls and floorboards and door?

She must have been joking. They would read the real will next.

I sensed Clem's eyes on me, imagined her willing herself up to the ceiling next to me, to take me down.

She stood up.

Felicity pulled her back. 'I know, darling,' she said. 'This is why you had to sit with me, away from Senara. This is all true, but it's OK. Hear it out.'

Mum held my hand. Alex carried on reading.

'"*I want it to go to Senara because she shares my vision of the house as part of the village. She is free to live in the house, or the cottage, to rent it out to people who need a home, to do whatever she wishes, as long as there's life in the place all year round. That is a non-negotiable term.*" She goes on to talk about her other bequests which are, of course, going to the family, but this, as I said, is the big one.'

He put down his piece of paper and looked at me.

Clem stood up and stormed out of the room, slamming the door behind her, opening it, and slamming it again, louder. Alex ignored her.

'There's much more here,' he said, 'but that's the gist. Sorry to spring it on you, Senara and Jen. Be aware that we all support you.' He passed me an envelope, one I'd last seen by the pool that night. 'This is her letter to you, which goes into more detail. Digest it at your leisure. And, Senara? I know I speak for Felicity as well as for myself when I say that we are, in fact, happy that the house is going to you. We've talked it through and come to terms with it. In fact, I agree with Grandma. It needs to be lived in. This is a relief as far as I'm concerned, and I hope it's not overwhelming for you. It'll all be kept in trust until you're eighteen, and I know that Jenna will be with you to help at every stage.'

'What?' said Mum. 'Alex, this can't be right? Flick? Seriously? She's left it to *Senara*? But . . .' Her voice trailed off.

Felicity gave me a tentative smile.

'I second what Alex says,' she said. 'Coming down every summer has been quite a commitment and when Covid hit, and we could use it as an excuse not to visit – even though everyone else in the country was heading to Cornwall – that showed me how desperate I was to escape its clutches. Those last few years I neglected Grandma terribly. I mean, it is a wrench as it's the house where we grew up, but overwhelmingly I can see why she's done it. Honestly, Senara, do whatever you like with it. Let this news sink in, and then we can talk about logistics. But of course you already have a bedroom here, so let that be a start.'

I looked at Mum. Her eyes were wide, and she was gripping the arm of her chair.

'Really, Flick?' she said. 'But –'

The door flew open, and Clem was back.

'Excuse me?' We all turned to look at her. 'Is this for real? Are you all just sitting here in our house, and being nice to Senara as she steals it out from under us?' She looked at me. 'You played it well, I'll give you that. You were way more devious than I thought. *Oh, I'll just go and check on Maaaarrrrrtha!*'

Felicity stood up. 'Clem, I did suggest it might be better for you not to be present.'

'Fuck that! Fuck you, Senara. You knew exactly what you were doing. From the moment Gran caught you trying to get that drone out of her garden, so she wouldn't see you calling her a murdering zombie, you realized that you'd got your hands on a rich and confused old woman. I knew as soon as I heard you talking about the footage that I had to –'

'Clemmie!' shouted Alex. 'Please ju–'

'No! You guys might be all "yeah, whatever, have our actual home" but I'd like to point out that *I'm* not fine with Senara getting my inheritance. Jackson won't be either. Didn't we drive down three weeks early because Gran said she was giving it to a community group, and you were upset? Senara's not a community group – she's worse. She's a schemer and a liar. This house has been in our family since it was built. Our family worked hard for it. Not hers! It's not Senara's house. That's the most ridiculous thing I've ever heard. It's ours.'

I couldn't meet her eye. I kind of agreed with her.

'It hasn't been in your family for generations,' said Dylan.

He hardly ever said anything, but now he stood up.

'As I understand it, Clem, Martha came here when she was ten, as an evacuee. She was taken in by Violet Roberts when her birth family died. The house ended up coming to her because they didn't have an heir, and now she's doing the same thing. Passing it to Senara. To be honest, Clem, I don't like it either, but it's Martha's decision and we have to accept it.

'We have a house in London,' said Felicity. 'And the apartment in Paris.'

'We're still the Roberts family,' said Clem. 'It's ours.'

'We are the Roberts family,' said Felicity, 'by unofficial adoption. By deed poll. Not by blood. We're the Campions and the Driscolls, and that's perfectly fine.'

'You're saying we already have a house so we don't need this one? So does Senara. She lives in some shithole in the village. Why not give our house in London to a homeless person while we're at it, hey? It's bullshit. She can't just give my house to some random local. Jesus – I was only pretending to be friends with her because she sucked up to Gran all the time. I thought she could help me keep my inheritance. Not that she was planning to steal it.' She stood up, without looking at any of us, and left again. Felicity went after her.

Some shithole in the village. That was what Clem had thought of me all along. Living in a shithole. I looked at Mum.

'We'll leave,' she said.

'Sorry, Jenna,' said Alex. 'I thought this would be a good idea, to show Senara that we're all OK with it. I did tell Flick that Clem shouldn't be here, but there we go.'

Later, at home, I sat with Mum and read my letter. It was printed out, and I imagined Martha dictating it on to her computer. I wondered how long it had taken her to fold the three letters and get them in the envelopes, to write the names on the front.

Dear Senara,

This is going to be a surprise and I hope it's a happy one. I have been on the brink of discussing it with you so many times, but I always pulled back and eventually decided to leave it because I didn't want it to create any kind of awkwardness between you and Clementine. Although, gosh, I imagine it will now: selfishly, I suppose, I've just shunted the awkwardness forward to a time when I wouldn't be around to experience it.

I started to tell the family too, but I couldn't do it. They thought I was mad already, and I couldn't face the interrogation it would have brought, so, as I write, no one knows my plan but Mr Mitchell.

When Leon, Elizabeth, Felicity and Alex moved away, I wanted to sell the whole place and move to a manageable home, but I couldn't because of the unfortunate incidents involving the flower bed. For my lifetime, I couldn't risk any excavation happening. As I write, I have just looked out of my bedroom window and seen you kids pulling up Aubrey's watch, and so I know the truth will eventually come out, and I'll write a full explanation to the police before I go. What a relief to be unburdened. I feel Violet and Aubrey can rest easy now too.

It feels every sort of wrong to see a house dark and blank through the autumn, the winter, the spring, and then coming wonderfully to life in the summer, though even that hasn't happened lately. Although you've been so careful about what you've said in front of me, I know you feel it too because you see it when it's empty. You were interested enough to fly a thingy over the garden and then climb the fence to retrieve it, and I'm glad you did, because that was when you and I started to become – I hope – friends. I imagine you know now why I've always been so careful about gardeners and the like. I used to have nightmares about Aubrey rising up from the camellia bed.

Felicity and Alex and the children know they'll want for nothing, and they will all do well financially from my will. They lead lives of unimaginable luxury, and, rather than allow this house to continue to be a spare house for people who live elsewhere, I want it to be a real home. Senara, my dear, you don't realize how important you have been to me this year, the last year of my life. Since we met, you have checked in with me in some way every day. You make me tea the way I like it and indulge me by looking at my dresses and listening to my ramblings.

That has meant a lot to a bored, housebound lady who may have been ninety-plus (trust me, you lose count) but who is still, at heart, the confused evacuee, heartbroken about losing her family, but filled with wonder at the fact that she was living in a big house on the edge of the ocean, that she was going to school and learning new things, that she had friends, and grew vegetables, and breathed fresh air. I could write a book about it, my dear, though it seems I never did. I have lived the life of a well-to-do lady with a big house by the sea, but I've never stopped being an East Ender, and if my parents and Daphne have been waiting for me somewhere for all these years then I will be happy for all eternity.

You understand what it is to struggle day by day. I share that with you. I, too, was born into a life in which owning a house like this one was unthinkable. I like the symmetry of the house making its way to you, as it made its way to me. I feel Cliff House knows what it wants.

You love this place and, Senara, by the time you read this, the house will be yours, held in trust until your eighteenth birthday. I don't want it to tie you down: you mustn't let anything stop you going to university if that's what you want to do, and I hope it is. You can sell it (though Mr M is inserting a provision that it can't be a second home), or live in it, run it as a hotel or a business of some sort. You can lend it out or rent it out: all I insist is that it's alive. Jenna, live in the house or the cottage or your own house, whatever you want, but help Senara come up with a plan.

I hope this won't affect relations between you and Clementine too badly, Senara, because it's been a joy to me to see you two running around, thick as thieves.

Jenna, I hope you can regain that kind of relationship with Felicity and, especially, with Alex.

I told you once that I would look after you, Jenna. You will remember that day. So here you are. This is it.

Take care, my dears, and heartfelt thanks.

Martha

35

Josie was getting ready for her first day at college. She had her bag of books, her bus pass, her keys. She said goodbye to Mum and walked down the road to wait for the bus. She messaged Meg as she went: Setting off! Love you xxxxx

Meg replied at once: Let me know what it's like! I love you too. FaceTime this eve? xxxxx

Everything felt lighter now. People who said money couldn't buy happiness had absolutely no idea what they were talking about.

Senara was at the bus stop already. They smiled at each other as Josie put her phone away.

'My mum was desperate to drive me in,' Senara said. 'I felt like I was four, starting school all over again. She was all, like, "What are you going to have for lunch and have you got your pencil case?"'

'And have you?'

Senara looked good. She was wearing green, which suited her. A crossover green top, tight jeans and flip-flops.

'I like your top, by the way,' Josie said.

Senara froze. She smiled.

'No one's ever said that to me before,' she said. 'Not when I've been wearing my own clothes. Thank you.' She paused. 'Actually Rik likes it too, but he doesn't count.'

Senara was carrying a tote bag. She peered into it.

'I have to check every time anyone asks. Yes, I've still got a pencil case, even though probably by the time you're doing A levels you could just take a pen. It's not like I'm going to be needing a protractor and a set square any time soon.'

'I've just got some pens,' Josie said. 'They're in the front pocket of my bag.'

'Now I feel stupid!'

They both watched Gareth approaching. He was still dressed as a surfer, to the point of wearing a rash vest, even though he didn't actually surf, and a pair of beach shorts. His legs were tanned and hairy, and he too was in flip-flops. Josie was pleased to see him, but she had no idea why she'd ever imagined she was in love with him. He was hardly Meg.

Meg. Josie had known, from their first kiss, that she and Meg were real. They were serious. They had bypassed all the early stages and gone straight into a committed relationship. Everything between them just worked, and the sex was incredible. They had become excellent at doing it over FaceTime.

'Look at us,' said Gareth. 'Trespassers reunited.'

There was a moment's silence. Josie wanted to laugh, but that was because she was less bruised by Clem than Senara and Gareth had been. He turned to Senara. 'How's life at the big house?'

'We don't live in the big house!'

'OK, how's life in the cottage.'

She smiled. 'Yeah. It's lovely ac and the sale of our old place is happened fast, right? The legal we're OK to live in the cottage in the big house anyway. All right, I do.

'So, what are you doing with it?'

Senara sighed. 'You know what? It's one thing to say that second homes are a blight on the community, which they are. It's another to figure out what to do with them. But we're working on it. We might see if we can make it into a cafe downstairs, maybe staffed by people who need a leg-up, with a little display of Martha's dresses. And something about her life, and the evacuees who came to Cornwall. I don't know.'

'Sounds awesome,' said Josie. She shifted from one foot to the other. She could see Maya and Treve approaching. 'Well, let me know if I can do anything. I hardly even knew Martha, and she transformed my life.'

She still wasn't used to it. Martha had made Josie and Angie a bequest from what turned out to be the huge amount of money she had in the bank: it was Barnaby Campion's fortune, rather than the remnants of the Roberts money. Compared to everything else, her bequest to Josie and Mum wasn't even much, but it made all the difference in the world. Mum was doing well currently, but Martha's money allowed them to access more help for her, from therapy to having a cleaner, to take the pressure off Josie.

ld take the pressure off. She didn't have to play r badly for enough money for a loaf of bread. She have to stand on a chair to scrape the mould off the ing when she should have been studying. She still had er job at the bookshop (she loved it), and she could see a way through.

And she had Meg. Meg had come down again in August, and she was going to come again at half-term, and, in the meantime, they spoke all the time.

And every Friday night a delivery of pizzas arrived. Martha had set it up as a weekly event, and they had no idea when it would stop.

Every Friday night, they thanked her, wherever she was.

1990

At the age of sixty, Martha finally went back to Ridley Street.

She would never have recognized it. All the houses had been pulled down long ago (and numbers one, three and five, of course, had been flattened by that bomb decades earlier). Now the street was home to two restaurants, a greasy-spoon cafe, a warehouse and a block of flats. Martha stood and looked around, confused. There wasn't a landmark to hold on to. There was nothing at all. If it wasn't for the sign, she'd have been certain they were in the wrong place.

She looked at Betty.

'I know,' she said. 'It's all different. There was too much damage. It all got rebuilt. The curry house isn't bad. Fancy it?'

'Why not?'

They sat in the window and ate biryani, which wasn't something Martha ever did in Cornwall, and she liked it. They cracked poppadoms and spooned mango and yogurt on to them. Betty ordered two bottles of lager. Martha watched the life on the street outside and thought how different it was, and yet how much the same. She remembered how she had missed this bustle when she first went to Cornwall.

'In some ways,' she said, 'I've never stopped missing this. I just forgot that I missed it, for about forty years.'

'I bet,' said Betty.

Betty had worked for years as a florist. She'd started on a flower stall, and had been so good at it that she'd worked her way up: for the past twenty years she'd had her own business, culminating with a flower shop in Kensington. She had done well out of it, and it was all her own work. Now that they were sixty, Betty still looked the same. Her hair was white, shorter but still curly, her smile just as wicked.

'I couldn't have stayed there all that time, down in Pentrellis. It would have driven me crazy. I mean, it's a magical memory, but I couldn't do it forever. I know you didn't have the choice, Marth.'

'No, I didn't. And I love it there. It became my home, and my family are there. Leon and Elizabeth and the children. Alex is at Oxford, you know.'

Betty smiled. 'Yes. You said.'

'Did I say it too many times?'

'Exactly the right number.'

Martha tried not to think about that night, two years ago, when she'd come back from Exeter and found the kids trying to dispose of a body. It had been one of the worst moments of her life, but she'd swung into action and coordinated the plan. Had she just fallen back on the same course of action as before? Without a doubt, she had, and it had been madness. Her mind had closed in, and the only thing she could see was Violet's plan.

The consequences of calling the police had been much greater than they would have been for Aubrey, as Jenna had actually killed this man because he was attacking Felicity. Martha had thought she was doing the right thing to protect them, but in fact it was one of the biggest regrets of her life. Of course they should have called the police. Jenna had been acting in self-defence. She would have gone through a difficult trial, but she'd have been all right, and it would have been over long ago.

There was nothing to be done now. Martha had already written a letter making up a story about an intruder and taking responsibility, and stored it with her will. Then, when she died, the children would be free.

'Is our school still there?' she said.

'It certainly is,' said Betty. 'Let's have another drink, then go and take a look.'

Martha sat back. She felt Martha Driscoll waking up.

'I'd love to,' she said.

36

Felicity and Jenna were sitting at a table at the back of the village pub, talking in low voices. It was one of those sunny September evenings so everyone else was outside: they had chosen the darkest indoor corner, a spot in which they wouldn't be overheard.

'Cheers,' said Jenna. Felicity clinked her glass of wine against Jenna's beer and thought again that Jenna had hardly changed at all.

'Cheers,' said Felicity.

'What was Martha thinking of, though!' Jenna was talking quietly, but her voice was impassioned. 'I *did it*, Flick. Why does she leave me and Senara the house when she knows what happened, and she knows it was me? I caused all this. I don't deserve her house.'

Felicity reached out and put her hand over Jenna's.

'She didn't leave it to you. She left it to Senara. I don't know why, because you never really could know with Grandma, but it's probably just for the reason she said. That Senara reminded her of her own young self. Not being born into it, but coming to Cliff House by chance.'

'I don't blame Clem for being furious. Honestly, I don't. I wish none of it had happened. I wish the house was staying with you. I'm so sorry.'

Felicity took a sip of wine. 'Don't be,' she said. 'I don't want it. I'm glad you and Senni are in the cottage. I'm so pleased it's gone. And mostly that I don't have to write those fucking awful cards any more. Thirty-four of them, I did. I'd feel it hanging over me all year.'

Even though she'd grown up in Cliff House, Felicity hadn't realized what a burden it had been. She was delighted to be rid of it, hadn't enjoyed any part of being a second-home owner with all the baggage that brought, quite apart from the fact that they'd conspired to bury a man in the flower bed, and they could never move out because, if they did, the body would be out of their control.

'Maybe it's a curse,' said Jenna. She fixed Felicity with her sharp gaze. 'That's what I've been thinking. She's given it to us to take the curse off her own family. And now Senara's earnestly trying to work out what we can do with it. She's talking about making some kind of a museum of Martha, but can you imagine? Everyone knows there were bodies in the garden. Everyone would come for that. It's a terrible idea, but she won't listen.'

Felicity nodded. She was only down from London for a few days, and it was such a relief to stay at Chapel House in Penzance, a gorgeous B & B where her room had a huge bath, a shower, perfect furnishings and a view across the bay. And someone made her breakfast. It was all so much easier than turning up at Cliff House and having to start cleaning.

She'd been wondering the same thing as Jenna: Martha had done Felicity and Alex a huge favour, and Martha didn't do things by accident. Maybe this was some kind of payback for Jenna, in a weird, twisted moneyed sort of way.

'You didn't mean to kill him,' she said, dropping her voice to a whisper. 'And any one of us would have fought him off if we could have.'

Jenna was making a strange face, trying not to cry. Felicity knew they wouldn't stay friends, unless Jenna and Alex's relationship really did become 'a thing', in which case they'd have to. The guilt they shared was too big, too destructive. It smashed everything it touched: it had destroyed Clem and Senara's friendship in the same way it had destroyed theirs.

'It was madness,' said Jenna. 'The whole thing. All of it.'

'But it's over.'

They finished their drinks. Felicity didn't think she'd come to Pentrellis again, and she never did.

37

My train was cancelled, as were the rest of them.

'Go home,' said the woman in the hi-vis jacket at Penzance Station.

Everyone complained a lot, but when she confirmed for the third time that, no, there weren't going to be any rail-replacement buses, we all drifted out of the station and started making new plans.

I called Rik.

'Oh, no way!' he said. 'Bastards. Even the sleeper?'

I remembered him and Meg coming down on it in the summer. It felt like a million years ago, but it was only three and a half months.

'Even the sleeper. I'm going to have to go home and come in the morning instead.'

'Let me know when you have a time, and I'll be there at Paddington. Waiting for you. I can't wait.'

There was a teeny-tiny part of me that was relieved. I was beyond excited about seeing Rik, but I was petrified about going to stay with him. Even though, technically, I now had a big house too, I would never feel like someone who could fit into his life. He was my boyfriend, and Meg was now one of my best friends, and it was only because of them that I could even contemplate it. And Meg wasn't even going to be there; she was coming to Cornwall to visit Josie.

Mainly, though, I was frustrated. I couldn't wait to see him – I had been counting down the days since August – and now I'd have to take my bag and go home. I saw the Pentrellis bus revving its engine at the bus station and ran for it. They were rare beasts. I didn't bother to tell Mum I was coming back. Alex was down for the weekend so she'd be out anyway. They were definitely a thing now.

The gates were unlocked because they were always unlocked now, and before I went into the cottage I stepped into the garden to look around. I had loved it here that first time we'd come over the fence, and I loved it still. It was the most autumnal day today: there was mist over the grass, and brown leaves swirling through the air, and it was half dark already. Summer was over, but its secrets were still swirling round us. I walked a little way up the drive. I liked the way my feet made the stones crunch.

When I got to the curve in the road, I stopped. There it was: Cliff House. I loved everything about it. The bad things that had happened here were in the past, and I was in control of its future. It was going to be amazing: I was going to channel Martha and do only positive things here.

I walked right up to the front door. The heating wasn't on, and it would be freezing inside, but all the same I wanted to be in my house. I pushed the carved door and stepped in.

The hallway was cold; the tiles underfoot felt as if they were radiating ice. I walked, hardly breathing, my trainers making no noise.

Just as I was approaching the kitchen, I realized there were people in there. I could hear voices. I froze. Everything paused, suspended.

Then Mum's voice said, 'Well, yes, and I'm glad,' and I realized it was just her and Alex, and I was about to walk in when I heard his voice and stopped again. It was something in his tone.

'And there's no point. What earthly good would it do, going to the police now and confessing? They'd think you were mad. Turning up out of the blue to say you killed a guy when you were a teenager, but it was self-defence? Jenna – you can't.'

'Not self-defence,' said Mum. 'Flick-defence.'

'Yes. You saved my sister. I've always blamed myself because Flick asked me to stay, and I went for my stupid little run anyway. I haven't been for a run since – as you can see from my fine physique.'

'Hey,' said Mum. 'There's nothing wrong with your physique.'

'But don't, Jen,' he said, his voice low and urgent. 'It wouldn't just affect you. Felicity and I covered it up. Martha's out of it, thank goodness, but what about Senara? What about the scandal? It's a terrible idea. The tabloids would love it. We'd all end up in prison, everyone would hate us, and nothing would change.'

Mum's breathing was ragged. 'I know. You're right,' she

said. 'Sorry. I do know. And I know that if I *was* going to do it, I'd have done it years ago, so clearly I'm not anyway.'

What came next sounded like kissing noises. I turned and crept away, out of the front door, down the drive. As soon as I was a little way from the house, I started running. I ran as fast as I could. I got to the cottage out of breath, stepped indoors and sent Mum a text.

Train cancelled. I'm at the cottage. Are you around?

Five minutes later she replied:

Yes, with Alex. We're just looking at the view from the cliffs. Back soon xxx

I thought of all the other things I could write.

I went upstairs. My legs were shaking.

What should I do?

I had a boyfriend I loved, the best friends ever, a house and money. Three of those things would have been unthinkable back in January when we had trespassed at Cliff House (or as I was trying to call it: home). I was lucky beyond my wildest dreams.

My house had secrets. It had given up some of them, but clearly not others. I'd known that Mum had a secret and now, finally, I understood what it was. Everything made sense, and I had to decide what to do about it. I took my phone out again and looked at it. Should I tell Rik? Josie and Gareth?

The police?

I sat on my bed, in the room that had previously housed Martha's clothes. *What should I do?*

Had I heard her right?

I played it forward in my head. They had got away with it for decades. The broken friendships, the postcards, Josie's missing uncle. Martha had helped them cover it up.

Martha.

What should I do, Martha?

I beamed the question at her, wherever she was. I waited, and then her voice spoke in my head, as clearly as if she was there.

Nothing, darling. Look forward, not back.

Look forward.

I messaged Rik.

I love you.

He replied.

Me too. See you tomorrow.

Some secrets needed to stay in the ground.

Acknowledgements

It turns out that writing a book with three time strands and four point-of-view characters is quite complicated, and I'd like to say thank you first of all to my wonderful editor, Ruth Knowles, who helped me straighten out a lot of tangles through multiple drafts, with her trademark brilliant suggestions and insights.

Thank you to everyone at Penguin involved in the production of this book, and particularly to the lovely Wendy Shakespeare, copy-editor Jane Tait, and proof-readers Sarah Hall and Niamh O'Carroll-Staton. Thank you to Bella Jones for designing this gorgeous cover.

To my super-agents Steph Thwaites and Isobel Gahan at Curtis Brown: you are brilliant!

Heather Williams: you generously donated to the Books for Vaccines auction back in 2021, and as a result you've named Megan Anderson and inspired her lovely character. Thank you!

Thanks to the people on Twitter who helped with the technicalities of the police involvement at the end of the book, including Matthew Mehen, Graham Bartlett, Naomi

Jones and Tracy Ann B. Thanks to Nick Latimir for advice on the liberties I could take with will-reading technicalities.

Thank you to Becky Quick for reading the manuscript with a Cornish teenager's eye and for your suggestions, which are much appreciated.

In the summer of 2021 I worked for the National Trust at Lanhydrock House in Cornwall, and was fascinated by the story of the Agar-Robartes family, who owned it until they gave it to the Trust in 1953. Although Cliff House is not remotely like Lanhydrock, that job started me thinking about life in a big house in Cornwall, and I was particularly inspired by the fact that the family at Lanhydrock took in seventeen evacuees during the Second World War. Thank you to all my old colleagues there, and everyone I met through the job. Violet is named as a tribute to Violet Agar-Robartes (1888–1965), as I loved her portrait on the wall, though the character and all the events are entirely fictional.

Finally, thank you to everyone who both supported and distracted me in the writing of this book: Gabe, Seb, Lottie, Charlie and Alfie, as well as Adam Barr, Tansy Evans, Bess Fox, Silvia Salib and Clare Wells. Above all, thank you, Craig, for the constant support and love, as always.

READ MORE BY EMILY BARR

What do you do when – with every day that passes – you're literally growing apart from the best person you've ever known . . . ?

Flora has amnesia.
She can't remember
anything day-to-day.
But then she kisses
someone she shouldn't –
and the next day she
remembers it.
It's the first time she's
remembered anything
since she was ten.

But the boy is gone.

I call her Bella because
she is the dark side of me.
It's Ella but not.
It's bad Ella.
Bella.

About the Author

Emily Barr worked as a journalist in London, but always hankered after a quiet room and a book to write. She went travelling for a year, which gave her an idea for a novel set in the world of backpackers in Asia. This became *Backpack*, a thriller that won the WHSmith New Talent Award. Her first YA thriller, *The One Memory of Flora Banks*, has been published in twenty-seven countries and was shortlisted for the YA Book Prize. Emily's third YA thriller, *The Girl Who Came Out of the Woods*, was published in 2019 and nominated for the Carnegie Award. *This Summer's Secrets* is her sixth YA novel. Emily lives in Cornwall with her husband and their children.

Follow Emily Barr
on Twitter @emily_barr
and Instagram @emilybarrauthor
#ThisSummersSecrets